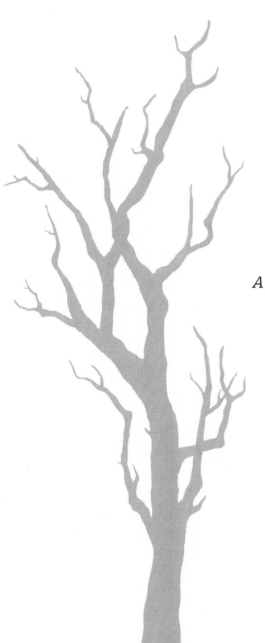

Winter's Dead

A Strand Murder Mystery

WINTER'S DEAD

A STRAND MURDER MYSTERY

Philip Warren

ISBN: 978-1-7367794-5-3 (Amazon EBook)
ISBN: 978-1-7367794-6-0 (Amazon Paperback)
ISBN: 978-1-7367794-7-7 (D2D Ebook)

Cover and Interior Design by Stewart A. Williams
Copyedit by Brooks Becker

Printed in the United States of America

First Printing edition 2022
The PineLands Company, Publisher
New Wilmington, Pennsylvania

www.philipwarrenwriter.com

*"Winter's Dead" is about children
raised without parents
who love them, and what may
happen when society fails to notice.*

Also by Philip Warren is the historical fiction novel, *Irina,* published in 2021. Writing as John P. Warren, the political thriller novels, *Turnover* and *TurnAround,* were published in 2013 and 2014, respectively.

AUTHOR'S NOTE

Winter's Dead is a work of fiction, and while most novelists have a disclaimer stating any resemblance to persons, places, or events is entirely coincidental, there are a few exceptions in this instance.

Foreston is my fictional representation of Grove City, Pennsylvania, where my family and I lived for nearly twenty-five years in the white brick home on Pine Street. Likewise, the Penn Grove Hotel and its proprietor, the late Earl Shannon, are real, and I have portrayed them in a deferential way. In passing, I mention Bill Keely, a respected Pennsylvania State Police Trooper, a friend I do not see often enough. Of course, there's Bo, our family beagle, and great friend to me until his very last breath.

Other names appearing in this novel may be familiar to some readers inasmuch as they are used as a nod to some of the good Grove City area people I've run across. I've taken some geographical liberties with several scenes in an around Grove City, but that should be expected. It's a novel, after all. Thanks should go to the Grove City Area Historical Society, from whose archives the opening scene in Winter's Dead is borrowed, albeit with a fictional touch.

Some local readers might think parts of this story are an autobiography of sorts. They are not. I have no Scots-Irish heritage, have never been a criminal investigator with any law enforcement group, have never lived at the Penn Grove Hotel, and my family life is not in the least bit similar to that portrayed in *Winter's Dead.*

A central theme of this novel has to do with society's ambivalence toward unwanted children. The fictional Dr. Harkansen at the Corinth Institution has much to say on the topic and as of 1990, the statistics he cites were accurate. How terrifying those numbers—and the real people represented by them—must be at this writing.

I have always thought Grove City was where Beaver Cleaver grew up, and if you're of a certain age, you know what I mean—it's a great place to raise a family. Having said that, there is no such person as Georgie Hallon, Foreston's Chief of Police, and while I suspect there may be many like him, I've met none in Grove City over the years.

The religious and racial biases I've described were true in Pennsylvania in 1990, and were true every place I've lived—simply because the human condition doesn't always line up with our better angels. If it did, Moses would have been wasting his time on Mt. Sinai. In this author's view, raising children with love is never a waste of time.

Special thanks go to Kathy Dillaman and Dan Kirwin, advance readers who found the story's many flaws and helped me to right them. Their help was of immense value. Thanks, too, to Brooks Becker and Stewart Williams, whose technical and design expertise helped make this novel come to life. What grammatical, typographical, or plot errors remain are solely my own.

I

May 1924

I T WAS JUST after noon on Saturday, and with the sun still high, the two men marched away from Mine #5, happy a long weekend was in front of them. Decoration Day was to be a paid holiday away from the coal seam deep underneath southeastern Mercer County, and the clear skies portended pleasant days ahead. Today, however, proved to be a perfect day for murder.

Best friends since their families emigrated from Napoli, Giovanni Tomaselli and Angelo Sanderi had been mining coal together since the Great War. As had often occurred, they were the last to leave the yard after the whistle blew, and they laughed and talked as they plodded along the dusty road toward Foreston, the small Pennsylvania town they called home.

"Tomorrow, we go to Mass," Tomaselli said in Italian, "and afterward, we'll stop at the cemetery to see Francesco. I miss him so."

"It's too bad the Spanish Flu took him," Sanderi replied in the same tongue, "like so many others. He's been gone how many years now, Giovanni?"

"He went to God October 1918, but you know, Angelo, we still see his face in the picture on his gravestone. His smile is still there."

"Ah, it is sad, my friend," Sanderi said as they were halfway home with only two miles to go, "but you still have Maria and three more Tomaselli's." He paused. "You should think about them."

For a few moments, silence walked with them, but Sanderi broke the spell when he reached in his rucksack for his battered squeezebox. "Let's have a song, then," he offered, and began to play the still popular "Funiculi, Funicula!" After a few tentative taps on the keys, he began to sing the catchy words. In moments, the two harmonized, their notes filling the air with fun.

Before the song ended, a short, thickset man in rumpled clothing ran up behind the pair, reached around to clamp his hand on Tomaselli's mouth, and slit his throat with a barber's safety razor. Blood spurted from the stunned, struggling miner, his eyes finding Sanderi's to silently demand, "Why?" Attempting to stanch the river of blood, Tomaselli took two steps and fell to his knees, then forward, face to the ground. A puddle surrounded his head like a halo, bright red until it seeped into the waiting earth.

"Remember, Sanderi, you saw nothing!" the killer said in the language they both knew, and ran back into the woods.

Shaking, Sanderi closed his squeezebox before turning in every direction to make sure no one had seen him, then gave his friend a last look and walked home.

JANUARY 1990

Fletcher Strand found himself sitting in front of the blank, blue computer screen waiting for words to come. They didn't.

It was Monday, the eighth day of the new decade, and he hoped the year would end better than it had begun. As a well-experienced detective with the Pennsylvania State Police, he'd amassed plenty of material to hook a reader of crime-thrillers, but little inspiration came, even after downing a pot of strong coffee. What resolution he thought he'd found on the 31st had evaporated like puddled water on a steaming August day. Now, it was a week later, and still, words failed him. Something stood in his way, he knew. Something he could not seem to fix.

Outside, the temperature remained at thirty above, and as the January sun appeared between fast-moving iron-gray clouds, it filled the windows in front of him, forcing a squint and further carving the lines under his deep-set blue eyes. The sun's flash also caught the grayed edges of his chestnut hair, highlighting the auburn traces still left there.

Rumpled and unshaven, he slid the 190 pounds of his sixfoot, oneinch frame into the most comfortable position the Penn Grove Hotel's old chair could offer. He leaned back and with his hands, shuttered his eyes. In his own darkness, he faced the real reason he could not concentrate on his book.

He'd moved out of the family home—at his wife's request the day after Thanksgiving—but still with him were the questions, the persistent ones which forced out all other thought. *Will I see Aurora again? Can we have a future together?* Could she bury her resentment toward his family for their constant comments about her being Italian and Catholic? Her people had been coal miners, and his people, at least on his father's side, their Scottish, Protestant overseers.

Long topping the social heap, such as Foreston's was, people like his family kept prejudice their frequent companion, and the others like them spat their favorite slurs. Immigrants spoke little English, had too many children, were superstitious papists, and were not real Americans, they said. That he had never harbored or expressed such views mattered little. For Aurora, he was the visible representative of their intolerance, and it seemed an unbridgeable divide.

"The past is always with us, Fletch," Aurora said, "and you can't escape it." These were words he'd heard often. *Was that about his past or hers?*

What about Aarie and Anna? What will happen if Aurora takes this further? He had spent the last weeks trying not to think about it, and some of the time, he managed to avoid the heavy hurt within his chest.

Now, in a small apartment in the Penn Grove Hotel—Foreston's only—and only a block from the Pine Street home in which he'd raised his family, he had all the time in the world, but it didn't matter. Even worse, Aurora had taken the kids to her parents' home in Columbus, and except for a miserable encounter on Christmas Day, he hadn't seen them at all. What he knew for certain was that there was no home, no hearth without Aurora, Aarie, and Anna, the Triple A of his life.

That he was already in a race for time and life he could not have known, but had he been invited to conspire in the events to come, he undoubtedly would have preferred to be any other father in any other place but Foreston, Pennsylvania.

I I

Jamie Hilton knew it was going to be a bad day—just how bad, he had yet to learn. He'd overslept, and his mother's voice had none of its Christmas cheer.

"Jamie, if you don't get down here right now, you are not going to like what your father has to say when he gets home." Peg Hilton hurried to put a hot breakfast on the table for her son to inhale before running off to school, the first day back after the holidays.

"Here I am, Mom!" The eleven-year-old sat down, surveyed the two pancakes swimming in butter and syrup, and picked up his fork.

"Eat up," Peg Hilton warned. "It's a long time to lunch."

"Aw, Mom!" her son whined. "Lunch is at eleven, and besides, I'd better go."

"No son of mine is going to school on an empty stomach. It's cold out, and these'll warm you up. Eat!" she commanded with a mother's love.

Another skirmish lost, he savaged the buttery delights on his plate. "How cold is it out?"

"Around freezing, I think. Watch out for the icy patches, especially when you cross the footbridge."

"I know, Mom," he said in exasperation. "This is not my first winter, ya know," he said, smiling up at her through the syrup glistening on his lips.

"Yes, well, if you're late the first day back, I'll be getting a call from the school, and that won't be good, will it?"

"No, ma'am." He swallowed, jumped up, wriggled into his new coat—the bright-blue one he had asked for—tied the muffler around his neck, and pulled on the knit cap his godfather had given him. "I'm ready," he said, "and I still have time."

"Off you go, young man, and come right home after school, you hear? No messing around with those other boys. Just a minute, my big man!" she added. "No kiss for Mom?"

"Sure," Jamie said, sheepishly, and kissed his mother goodbye.

~

"Awful cold out here. Waitin' for somebody?" asked Harold Carney, the portly, toothless crossing guard who commanded the foot of Center Street. There he stood with his white belt over a yellow and white safety jacket, steadfast in his dedication to the protection of Foreston's school children. He knew everyone, but hadn't seen this woman before—or anyone in a long bright-green coat like that—and *if she's a mom, then I'm the King of England.*

The object of his question was startled. "I didn't notice you standing there," she whispered, turning toward him but remaining several feet away. Ignoring his question, she studied her watch for a moment.

"What time ya got?"

"Seven-forty," came her reply, and she shifted her gaze up the street.

Just then, a gaggle of kids rounded the corner and headed toward them. Carney waved his flag and walked to the middle of the street while the kids made their way across. Within a minute, the street's life ebbed, and Carney looked around him.

The woman was gone.

~

As an eighteen-year PSP trooper, the last six as a senior detective in the West Central District, Fletcher Strand supposed he should have plenty to write about on his brand-new XT PC, complete with floppy disk drives. The ideas came without difficulty, but he couldn't seem to make the leap from interesting anecdote to compelling story to written word. Strand sipped the stale, cold coffee, mentally savoring the Magursky case.

Francis Magursky had been a model husband and parent, much beloved in his community for the unending kindnesses and works of charity he performed for so many. His fondness for young girls, on the other hand, was not known except by the few who chanced to fall victim to his clumsy advances. First, there had been Karen Wilhelmsen, a fifteen-year-old last seen hitching a ride from someone outside a convenience store in Butler—that had been in 1963. Another victim was, by horrific coincidence, a friend of Karen's, Melanie Bishop, who disappeared six months later.

Neither girl had ever been seen again—until 1987, that is, when Strand's partner, Joe Bentsen, answered an incoming call they'd long remember. As it happened, the call was from an old farmer who had purchased neighboring property on which sat the crumbling remains of a long-abandoned house.

The sobbing man barely controlled himself. "I didn't know there was anyone in there—they didn't say a word. Why didn't they shout out?" They hadn't uttered a sound, Strand and Bentsen later determined, because Karen Wilhelmsen and Melanie Bishop, friends in life, had been together in death for almost twenty-five years.

Farmer Jacob Millerson had purchased the property intending to convert it to arable ground, he said afterward. No time-waster he, Millerson promptly burned out the remains of the old house. Two days later, his grandchildren ran home screaming they could see two blackened skeletons in the basement. Millerson assumed he had burned the house with two runaways hiding inside. Instead, he had unwittingly helped to uncover what the locals later called the

Magursky Murders.

It took a week of painstaking detective and forensic work to conclusively identify the bodies, and it took a little while longer to connect the engraved belt buckle found with them to Francis Magursky.

Community servant, father, and killer, Magursky was sitting quietly at his kitchen table when Strand and Bentsen came to arrest him. He said not a word and neither did his wife and grown children. Magursky, sometime seeker of the common good, hung himself before the trial could begin.

The case had a lot of appeal, he felt, especially if he brought out the stark contrasts in the murderer's life over the two decades. Strand often wondered how many nights of hellish torment the man might have spent waiting for his generation-old crimes to be uncovered—because, as Aurora liked to say, "the past is always with us."

There was, however, no sorrow for so very flawed a human being. The emotionally twisted man regained public approval with his final act, as it appeased most people's sense of what the judicial system ought to have done if Magursky hadn't. As Strand drained the last few drops of coffee, he told himself to save Magursky for yet another time.

He simply did not want to write, or perhaps, was not ready to do so. A walk downtown with Bo, the family beagle—Aurora's only allowance to him for all their years of marriage—would allow him to secure the morning Pittsburgh paper and another cup of coffee. Just how cold it would be on that little trip was another matter entirely, but it didn't make much difference. He and Bo had to get out.

III

EDDY SNYDER STAYED out too long, and he knew it. Snow coated him on the way back to the haven cornered by Pine and Princeton Streets. In the entry hall of the old brick residence, he waited, listening for sounds from other tenants. Quiet surrounded him.

Slowly and with labored breath, he climbed the creaky stairs leading to his two rooms, one of four furnished apartments in Mrs. McKittrick's converted single-family house. The simple sanctuary had cost him three months' rent in advance—half of the $2,000 in his possession—but it was home to him, one of the few he had ever known.

Locking the door behind him, Eddy took a step or two and stumbled in the half-light of the overcast morning, as he ripped off the wig, threw it on the bed, and sank himself into the apartment's one soft chair. He hugged himself, thinking it would make his chest stop its heaving, but the ache in his feet and ankles did not disappear as readily. *The ache will never go away.* He remembered, as he often did, when it began.

It was winter then, too, and not the worst part of it, but that made little difference, because Eddy was never warm—then, or since. His foster parents, the Nicholsons, did not heat his attic room, and what passed for bedcovers resembled more the ragged, soiled sail of a washed-up dinghy than anything of use in a house. The bed on which it lay was a plywood board balanced on cinder blocks. It didn't matter. The mice found their way to him in the night, exactly the right company for his nightmares.

A few days after yet another mirthless Christmas, he was foolish enough to complain of the cold, to hope for a mother's comfort, but his State-ordained custodian, Jody Nicholson, decided to teach him a lesson, one she said he would never forget.

Like an oft-played tape, Eddy dwelled upon the remembered images of wind-whipped, frozen fields while he was made to sit, in shirt-sleeves, hunkered down on the lowest of the back porch steps, his feet in a bucket of water. The air whistled around him, quick-chilling his upper body, and within minutes, the water itself.

Soon, the soles of his feet grew leaden in agony at the bottom of the galvanized glacier. Eddy lifted his feet out of the water, saw the bluing skin, and wanted to run away into any warm place, but he knew Mom Jody was watching from the window. There was no place to go, no one to help him, no one who wanted him; and any act of disobedience, he believed, would make it that much harder on him.

For what seemed endless minutes, Eddy was made to learn life's chill. When she hollered him back into the house, he crawled in, unable to stand without help. He received none. Streaming tears were the only source of warmth left to him.

"Cold enough for yuh?" she demanded, glaring down at him, his face a few inches from her stockinged, warm feet. The woman laughed at her joke, her tongue wagging between broken, picket-fence teeth. Eddy's feet were never warm again. Neither was his heart.

～

Strand was glad of the dog's companionship. An old dog now, Bo was afflicted with cataracts and poor hearing, and had become less and less certain of his master's whereabouts. When his feeder rose, donned his winter gear, and moved away, Bo hurried to escort Strand down the one flight of stairs to the hotel lobby, where Earl Shannon dozed at the ancient switchboard in a niche behind the reception desk.

Bo sat back on his haunches and waited for what had become standard instructions. Strand scratched under the dog's collar, wagged his finger at the whitened whiskers, and, as he had done so many times before, reminded his dog to behave himself on their walk. Bo yawned.

Strand's highly irregular schedule meant Bo's needs were not well met. "That's probably what she had in mind," Strand muttered to himself as he leashed the old dog and coaxed him out the Penn Grove's rickety front doors, the air slapping sharply at Strand's face, making him wince in surprise. Down the steps and onto the cracked pavement they went. It was early and almost no one was out.

The two or three inches of fresh snow crunched under his feet as the pair began their new ritual. A right turn took them across the bridge, past the Post Office, and past all their favorite stores on Broad Street, the town's main drag.

In a feeble attempt to keep warm, Strand and his pal tarried little. Leafless trees bent themselves in the pressuring blows out of the north and west. The branches outlined in the sky were like so many bony-fingered hands raised up in warning for Strand to turn back before choices were no longer his, but their insistent signals were lost amidst the other forces at work that morning.

Subconsciously, he felt cued by what he had sensed but not seen. The happy times of courtship and honeymoon with the girl of his dreams had vanished, replaced by creeping disappointment and bitterness. The early years of sharing and giving and raising children had ebbed to the point of routine indifference, neither love nor hate, but an abiding tolerance of a longstanding relationship. *And then, there's whatever ghost is haunting Aurora.*

～

In just over twenty minutes, Strand and his little buddy completed their circuit—interrupted a few times for Bo to take care of his most urgent needs—and they headed back to the hotel, but on the other side of the street.

As was his habit, Strand glanced around him. On the opposite walk was a young couple, obviously warmed by each other's presence, and right behind them was a woman in a long, green coat, hesitant when she saw he had noticed her. Strand assumed she was sizing him up as just another unkempt man with an impolite stare. She continued, clutching a small package in her arm.

Past Grace Methodist church he and Bo marched. Back onto the bridge again. The welltravelled span's seventyfifth anniversary was not a glorious one as its oncegleaming silver paint now sported creeping rust.

The hard winters would hasten the end of the Wolf Creek Bridge, but not before it became a focus of attention in a different, altogether unpleasant way. Nearly across the span, Strand paused, caught in a chilly reverie about the warm-weather walks he used to take with his children and Bo when Aurora worked weekends at the store in town. He rested his elbows on the rickety steel railing, and the scene's tranquility changed abruptly when he chanced to look straight down at the coursing water below.

It wasn't the frigid air that shook him loose of old memories. It was a color, the wrong color registering with the winter water, the skims of forming ice, the browns and blacks and dark crystals. It was the white pallor of cold, dead flesh that nearly stopped his heart. *Aarie? Oh, my God, is it Aarie?* It couldn't be.

Staring up at him were sightless eyes belonging to a boy his own son's age. He appeared to be dressed for school, arms outstretched, his body pointing south, a small arrow into eternity. Then other instincts took over, startling him into action, the unloved reflex of a homicide detective steeled by year after year of experience with death, and the kind of people who made sure his job was not a temporary one.

Later, he would not remember what he did with his dog, but in a flash, he ran the few feet to the bridge's far end, scrambled down the embankment, picking his way amongst the stacked shale and tree limbs lest he fall headlong into the creek himself. Although he knew death when he saw it, he knew strange things happened with a body thrown in freezing water. *Is he alive?*

At the water's edge, he stepped into the creek's flow where the body had snagged itself on a dead branch. In a few seconds, Strand could see the boy was not more than ten or eleven, and the remains of a bloody stain discolored what had once been a bright blue, winter coat. His eyes were fixed, and there was no pulse. "My God!" he muttered.

Securing the body as best he could, Strand made his way up the bank, his chest heaving as his head rose above ground level. Adrenalin had begun its work as he absorbed what he had just seen.

IV

E ARL SHANNON WAS out front of his hotel, customary white apron still tied around his waist, tossing sand and cinders on his walkways.

A voice was calling to him. It was a familiar sound, but when he looked up, he couldn't find its owner.

"Earl!"

Shannon looked in all directions before noticing a head and arm beckoning frantically, as if the man had risen from the earth. "Who? Who's there?" Shannon bellowed back.

"It's me—Fletcher Strand!"

Shannon at a gallop was not an impressive sight, but he dashed across the street, braking himself at the top of the bank's edge and opening his mouth to form the words for, "What's up?" His brain simultaneously registered the sight below: A young face, eyes open and lips parted, staring into the gray heavens, and on it, tiny rivulets of creek water trickled down his lifeless cheek like sharp tears over all the things he would never get to do.

Strand could only watch as Shannon could not force his teeth to catch the vomit roaring up in his throat when the contents of his stomach splattered onto the snow.

"My God! He's dead, isn't he?" he half-sputtered, vomit bubbling on his lips.

"Take it easy, Earl...you've seen this before in your business," said Strand, alluding to the Penn Grove's principal source of income: modest retirement suites for the ambulatory elderly—and stragglers like Strand and his dog. He exhaled when he saw Bo sitting, watching, waiting. *Thanks for that!*

Shannon nodded, forcing back a tear in reaction to his body's convulsion. "Oh, God, Fletch," he gasped. "You know I've been the one to find lotsa old ones who died in their sleep—they look," he paused, "—kinda like you'd expect after a long life. But never like this. And never so young—not in my place." His voice thickened. Shuddering and coughing the last of the acid from his system, Shannon worked to control himself. Finally, he asked, in hope of escape, "What do you need me to do?"

"Now, listen," Strand commanded. "Take Bo and get to your switchboard. Tell whoever you get at the police department there's a dead boy here—probably no accident—they need to have all the usual stuff happen. Tell 'em to get an ambulance, and I'll wait here for the Chief. Got all that?" Seeing Shannon's nod—and hesitation—he added, "Then, go!"

Turning away, Shannon propelled himself into the labored, disjointed jog reserved for older, tireder people, with Bo trailing at his leisurely pace.

Already Strand could see faces filling the old hotel's Palladian windows, their breakfasts pushed aside in favor of any excitement. He could well imagine the hotel's more ambulatory residents, having survived the excitement of *Geraldo!* for the day, hearing of the commotion and making their way to the lobby to find out if all was well with their dear landlord.

∾

The hotelier and residential manager for the aged had not anticipated the small crowd there to block him from reaching the safety of the switchboard.

"What's going on, Mr. Shannon? Can you tell us?" Mr. Dunkel was the first to demand as Shannon advanced toward his goal.

Mrs. McConnell, never in a mood for pleasantries or tactful approaches, did not wait for an answer to Dunkel's polite inquiry. She got right to the point, several times. "Mr. Shannon," she insisted, "we saw you arguing with that man, and it just didn't look right. What did he do to you? What did he say? Just exactly what is going on?" And she showed no signs of stopping to let him answer her interrogatories.

Addressing all of them, he said, "He's a State policeman—he lives here, for cryin' out loud. There's a body! A boy! Probably not an accident." He wasn't sure why he said the last, but it was the comment which not only silenced them all, but turned them on their heels and sent them scurrying to their telephones. What might have begun as an unexplained death handled discreetly was forever preempted by Shannon's instant decision to shut the woman up, to stun her into at least one second of precious silence.

Turning to his task, he did as Strand had instructed him, knowing full well a murder in Foreston, the first since the 1960s, would knock the town on its ear.

V

F OR STRAND, THE wait at creek's edge seemed unending. Within a minute or two, the sub-freezing temperature stiffened his lower pantlegs, numbing his flesh. A satiny finish polished his loafers while they held the frigid creek water close to his aching feet.

He tried not to think of Aarie and the dead boy down below. He was a veteran homicide detective, to be certain, but he had never become inured to murdered children, and certainly not boys who resembled his own. In a moment, however, the professionalism within him shoved aside his maudlin drift, and he began to appraise the body and the scene from a totally objective standpoint.

He did not want to move the corpse more than he had already done, but doing nothing went against all training and instinct, which urged him to scan along the creek for whatever there was to find there. Somewhere, within a half mile, he suspected, the killer had done his work and placed the body in the water. He made a mistake, Strand surmised, in thinking the body would seek the creek bottom, and in fact, it would have except for the air pockets in the boy's jacket—it didn't take much to keep the body afloat.

The killer was close by, Strand felt certain, and all of his instincts drove him to begin an investigation to find the boy's killer. Yet he knew that as much as he wanted to, looking for evidence in another cop's backyard without being invited to do so was a serious mistake. He might live in Chief Hallon's jurisdiction, but that small fact gave Fletcher Strand, the State Trooper, no poaching rights.

All he could do was keep silent vigil, acting as a bodyguard for someone who needed no protection now, no companionship and no love, only grieving. As he crouched beside the lifeless form, he observed that he had been dressed comfortably for the weather. There was no cap on his head and maybe there had never been one; he had on some pretty worn sneakers—Strand couldn't make out the brand, but they seemed—he shuddered—like what he'd seen Aarie wear around the house—and there was thick mud and small bits of gravel still stuck on the sole under his right instep. In between, the boy had on the rest of the typical uniform worn by most boys his age, and from what he could see poking out from under the jacket collar, the knitted crewneck of a light-colored jersey top. The jacket itself, he had already noticed, was blue nylon, nicely insulated, and its collar, fake fur. It looked new.

Not yet lined by worry or marked by puberty, the boy's face seemed almost angelic. Blue eyes looked no more for a mirror in which to straighten the light hair matted to his head. The more personal the details became, the harder it became to hold back the anger as he thought of Aarie—separated as they were—and this boy, this boy who would never grow up.

Drawn back to a more clinical detail, he speculated there would have been a fair amount of blood initially, but the boy's mercifully quick death in the frigid water left little, and in the cold air, it was beginning to gel. His hands were ungloved and unclenched—no sign of any resistance, and Strand noted that even if the boy had fought and scratched, those fingernails, bitten to the quick, would likely hold little evidence.

Rising to his full height, he squinted in the direction from which the body had drifted to see if any activity or object caught his eye, but he could see only a few dozen yards or so before his view was obscured by the bend in the creek.

With the police station less than a half mile away, Strand was surprised at Chief Hallon's slow response, but then the official music of a police cruiser pierced the air, and back up at street level, Strand waved him down. To his further surprise, it wasn't Chief Hallon's pudgy face over the steering wheel, but that of a kid, probably a newly sworn officer.

"Yessir. I'm Officer Rettig," said the young man in his best police academy fashion.

"Say who?"

"It's Rettig...R-e-t-t-i-g... and just who might you be? Sir?"

"Strand." He added, "Fletcher Strand," hoping that his tone was a bit warmer, but realizing Rettig probably did not know him, he tacked on, "State Police."

"Any identification?" Rettig asked, tension in his voice.

"Sure," Strand said, pulling his credential case from his jacket pocket. "But are you here to check me out or to check this out?" the detective added as he pointed to the body with his proffered credentials.

Rettig's eyes followed the gesture and Strand could see the rookie policeman's breath freeze in his throat. Apparently forgetting his officious veneer, he declared, "Oh, God!" Still looking at the body, he asked slowly, his voice reedy in shock, "Did you find him?"

Strand looked at Rettig appraisingly; because the young policeman did not look back at him when asking his question, but continued to stare at the body, Strand surmised he'd never encountered a corpse before.

"Yes. About ten minutes ago." He paused and asked quietly, as if to suggest they might keep the obvious answer a secret, "How long have you been with Foreston?"

"Oh, quite a while," he said, glancing at Strand, but returning his gaze to the dead boy. Rettig caught himself. "Well, about six months, anyway," he almost whispered. Then, in a stronger voice, "I graduated from community college—criminal justice—last June. I've been with Foreston ever since the academy in July."

The ambulance still hadn't arrived, so small talk didn't get in the way of anything. Rettig did not ask any other questions and Strand was pretty sure that Hallon would take over, showing his novice how a real cop did it, so he saved his recitation for the one runthrough he intended to make. Anyway, Rettig didn't seem in a hurry to begin the routine, if he could remember it from the classroom. In the quiet, he muttered to himself, thickly, "The Chief said I'd probably never see anything like this."

Strand nodded. "Can't say for sure, but it looks like the kid was stabbed by a sharp, thin blade—an ice pick, maybe? There's a half-inch gash in his jacket. Just under the heart. Quick, anyway." Strand checked himself. He might be just a guy on vacation, yet the notion of a murdered boy the age of his own son, a block away from the family home, in the town where people liked to say Beaver Cleaver grew up, jarred his emotions more than he wanted to show.

Rettig began to lower himself for a closer look. "Don't touch anything," Strand said needlessly. "I think it's still pretty fresh."

The police officer looked up, the expression on his face saying, "I might be new, but I know." Strand decided that the rookie, probably in his early twenties and still honest enough not to try hiding his ignorance, was somebody he could deal with.

Sirens suggested two more vehicles a block away and getting closer. Strand wondered why all the noise; there was no need to hurry and no traffic to block. He simply preferred the quiet approach when officious, hurried hoopla made no difference—to the boy or anyone else. Indeed, the noise unnecessarily punctuated the respectful stillness surrounding the body.

Chief Hallon arrived first, and the law enforcement executive bounded from his vehicle, or at least as fast as his girth allowed. Embarrassingly short and rotund, the Chief marched toward them. "Hallon Wheels," as he was known in the trade, had been Chief in Foreston for over fifteen years, and before that, one of the only three officers the town had for at least ten years. He took himself very seriously, indeed.

Cordiality was not a trait Hallon carried with him, Strand knew from experience. It was as if he thought it was a commodity in limited supply, and it had to be used sparingly. Unless Hallon was dealing with a person or group he perceived to have control over his destiny in some way, he kept what little charm he possessed well hidden. Over the years, he narrowed the focus of his smile to elected and appointed officials above him and citizens who could cause him trouble. State Police officers and subordinates, on the other hand, did not seem to merit any special effort on his part.

"What're you doin' here, Strand?"

"Found the body."

"You always screw around on somebody else's property on cold mornings, or you just lucky?" Mister Personality persisted.

"Look, Chief," Strand retorted, with heavy emphasis on the title, "I was on the bridge, spotted the body in the water, and ran to pull it out. Knowing how you feel about things, maybe I should have let it float out of your jurisdiction into ours, but shame on me for doing the right thing."

"Awright, awright, I don't need your lip, Strand!" the Chief said, backing off a little. "What happened here, Rettig?"

"I don't know, sir. We were waiting for you; this is my first..."

"Never mind," Hallon said, cutting his man short. "But next time, use the time a little better and take the witness's statement." Hallon seemed to notice that the two guys who had come with the Bowers Ambulance Service were waiting patiently while the trio of professionals exchanged their peculiar set of courtesies. "Okay, Strand, let's start again, and give me everything."

"There's not much to tell," Strand began before he rattled through what he knew. Hallon listened, blinking his eyes in acknowledgement, nothing more, before he made his way down to the creek's edge to examine the scene for himself.

The boy had to be pronounced dead, but there was no doubt of the fact, Strand thought but did not say. There was no reason to summon the medical examiner because the formality could be accomplished elsewhere, and in any event, the boy had not been killed where he was found.

After a few minutes, Hallon stood up, motioned to the Bowers boys to pick up the body, and, apparently considering their probable inexperience, added, "Be careful with the clothing." To one and all, he said, "Probably a family thing or drugs."

"Hmm! No pictures, Chief?" Strand asked. The ambulance attendants paused.

"Just what did you think you were gonna get with a picture of this?" he countered, his temper rising a little.

"I guess you never know; just SOP, I thought."

"When it's in your backyard, you can do it your way," the Chief maintained. "Listen, Strand. You know how I feel about you guys in my territory when it's not your case—you can stay the hell out—and by the way, I don't need your suggestions on procedure. Now take off—you're done here, and if I catch you nosin' around this case, I'll be givin' Montgomery a call. Maybe I'll call him anyway—just so you don't get any ideas."

Unused to Hallon's brand of uncivil service, particularly in front of a new cop like Rettig, Strand couldn't help himself. "Chief, I don't know how you intend to solve this one, but from what I've seen of you so far this morning, you better hope this town has to wait another twenty years for the next murder!" He nodded to Rettig and walked off, but just then, in the single moment's satisfaction, he didn't feel very good about his confrontational coup de grace. Montgomery would hear about it and then, he would hear about it. It wouldn't be the first time Strand had ruffled local feathers.

As he moved away, he heard Hallon chew on Rettig for being too friendly with the likes of a Statie, and surprisingly, told the ambulance guys to wait for photos, giving precise instructions to his newbie for processing the crime scene. Strand chuckled to himself as he crossed Pine and walked toward the hotel.

VI

"FIRST OF ALL, Tony, don't be giving that guy the time of day," Chief Hallon said, gesturing to the departing figure. "The State has no business here in Foreston unless and until we ask 'em, and I ain't planning on asking. Got it?"

"Yessir."

"Now," Hallon ordered, "I want you to roust Morelli and Jasowitz from the station or wherever they're drinkin' coffee, and you can help them check out the creekbanks. Pay attention, Rettig, because I'm only going to explain it once. When they get here, you stay with Morelli and walk this side of the creek. Jasowitz can do the other—and he's senior man on this. Walk slowly and stay close to the water. We might get lucky because of the new crust of snow—nobody would have been along here this morning except maybe the kid and his killer, so watch for footprints, any sign of a struggle, blood spatter, anything like that. Got it?"

"Yessir."

"If by chance you find anything that looks like it might be of interest, or if you find any tread marks, take some mud and snow samples. The kid's shoes weren't new—did you notice that?—so you might not get much, but you never know about the killer's. Oh, two more things."

"Yessir?"

"Make that three, Tony. Get the stars outta your eyes—murders ain't fun. Now, keep people from tramping all over the scene until Jasowitz says you're done, and most important, don't say nothing to nobody. Got it?"

"Yessir."

"That means nothing, and I mean nothing to the *Herald,* an' nothing to nobody else—in particular, I mean that Statie you were just talking to. Got it?" Hallon didn't wait for the last "Yessir" from his rookie. He had already taken a few steps, when he heard the young officer clear his throat, and in a chastened voice, make the expected sound one more time.

"Oh, and Rettig—don't forget photos." Hallon smiled to himself and looked up at the ambulance men, patiently waiting. "What're you two looking at?"

Without waiting for a response, Hallon admonished them to take the body directly to the hospital—after Rettig took his pics, of course—making sure Doc McCreary, the Mercer County Coroner, knew it was there. His tone was not lost on them, and they did not want to give the Foreston Chief a reason to call their supervisor. After a few minutes, the Bowers men proceeded to do what they did best, and in a twinkling, were gone.

The Chief had not had to investigate a murder for many years, in actuality not since he had been a Foreston patrolman, but he knew standard police practice and intended to follow it, chapter and verse. Strand might be a hotshot State homicide detective, but so what. *Besides,* he swore silently, *the boy's murder will be solved within the week.* He weighed the probabilities of a local bad actor, or perhaps a family member being the guilty party. Did the kid see a drug deal he wasn't supposed to? Had someone abused him? The point was to get it taken care of soon. That's what the Borough of Foreston solons kept him on to do—make sure everything was smooth and quiet.

Guys like Strand were a pain in the ass—they always wanted to do things the "right" way, without consideration for local necessities.

Hallon knew, for example, that if one of the old timers in the borough were to have a little accident behind the wheel, the idea was not to make a big deal out of it. If possible, the policeman's first duty was to make sure the victim was dusted off and alright, and then, see that the ancient, halfblind driver made it home safely.

State and Federal types, on the other hand, were more than likely to want to pursue such matters—they just didn't understand how things worked in small jurisdictions, where the Police Chief was always subject to the whims of the Borough council, one of whose members might be the son or nephew of Aunt Minnie, the errant driver.

A murder was a little more serious, of course, but the general idea was still the same. Take care of it quickly, pay attention to the players, and do everything as quietly as possible. *If people like that asshole, Strand, were under the same pressures he was, they would do the same.*

As the Chief surveyed the creekbank, he wondered what kind of trouble the boy had been in to wind up dead. It wasn't fair, he knew, but he held strongly to the very private belief that murder victims were, in some way responsible for their fate.

$\sim$

The siren's shrill jangled his nerves, but it went past and away. The door was locked, yet again. Eddy's heart began its racing, its pounding with fear whenever policemen were anywhere nearby. *Are they looking for me? How long's it gonna take 'em?*

He never thought what he'd done would be so easy, and it felt so good. The makeup, the wig, the clothes—made him feel invulnerable. It didn't take away his own pain, it didn't give him the happiness he craved, yet the rage within him competed for the thrill of satisfaction.

After a few minutes, he calmed a bit, and when his head ceased its pounding with the surge of energy the possibility of discovery gave him, he took pleasure in reliving the oh, so satisfying events.

That he had been so clever about it was just another mark of his brilliance. *They'll never figure it out. They'll never find me, not in a million years!* Eddy smiled, and slipped into a long nap.

~

As Strand mounted the seven front steps from the sidewalk to the esplanade fronting the Penn Grove's 1924 façade, he could see a few old faces still populating the mullioned panes. He guessed they'd been curious about him since he and Bo had moved in, the only ones in the building not collecting social security.

Earl Shannon was among the guardians, Strand saw, but Shannon averted his eyes, and guessed he was embarrassed by his lack of control at the scene. Strand had seen it so many times before in grown men who had trained themselves never to show emotion. They were the macho, so-called tough guys, who acted as if they could handle anything, but almost all blew lunch the first time coming upon an unnaturally dead body.

Strand himself had been no exception, and dealing with the results of nature's darkest urges had never gotten easier for him. This boy, whose name he didn't know, was already imprinted with him, an image of vivid reality which would accompany him every waking minute until he was satisfied the killer was caught—or dead. Inside the lobby, he ignored the stares and headed for the stairs, all the while thinking about the ache the boy's parents would feel, an ache that he felt thankful was not to be his.

Altogether, he had been gone less than fortyfive minutes, yet he felt it had been a near lifetime. The weather was no worse, the temperature no colder than when he left, but in his inner self, there was a rod of ice stiffening his steps upward, and only then did he realize how numb his legs had become.

Somehow, Earl had managed to situate Bo in #204, and although the old dog hardly had time to get comfortable in the chair by the window, his eyes were already closed. Even so, Bo's tail wagged with affection, as if he'd never left the spot, as if he knew his owner would return in need of welcome. Strand perched on the chair arm and stroked the dog for the longest time, thinking about the killing, his children, his whole family not being together.

Impulsively, he reached for the phone to call his wife, but knew he would wind up saying too much about the morning's event—and that would be a mistake. Aurora, who could easily have wordprocessed a bestseller titled "Hysteria as a Way of Life," would worry herself silly and everyone around her for a week. He left the receiver where it lay.

There was no way to stay in his rooms. Though he had not formed a plan to insert himself into Hallon's investigation, he knew he couldn't operate on the edge of jurisdictional courtesy. Somewhere in his subconscious already stood the conviction that the task of finding this particular murderer belonged not just to the Foreston PD, that he could not hold himself in reserve with all the other uninvolved of the modern world.

In moments, he left the hotel, jolted the Ford Explorer into life, and pushed the limit on SR58 on his way to what Aurora always called his real home, the PSP's Mercer Barracks.

VII

I N THE DISTANT glint of the January sun, the gilded dome of the county courthouse caught the light and Strand's eye. His destination lay just beyond. After crossing the courthouse square, the PSP Barracks was just a glide down the hill.

As he walked into his other home, he heard the voice he'd hoped to avoid.

"Strand! Hey, Strand! Just the young man I wanna see!" By itself, the voice made the dust balls loitering on the tile floor skitter along the long hallway. In mid-step, heading in the opposite direction, Strand tensed, not when he heard the familiar rasp, but when the words "young man" slapped at his reddening ears. He turned slowly, tightened his lips, and wordlessly walked toward the irritant's source, Lieutenant Walter Montgomery.

At five foot eight and 165 pounds, with closecropped hair and a graying, thin moustache to match, Montgomery was someone to be reckoned with. In public, he was all business and reacted negatively to anything other than totally appropriate behavior; in private, he could be human—sometimes. But he was something else: he was black.

In the early 1970s, when the PSP was under pressure from the then powerful Equal Employment Opportunity forces to change the face of the all-white department, there was a concerted effort to recruit and train a small but suitable cadre of African-American men. To be sure, they were not well-received in the ranks, the usual slur being they hadn't earned their place and they took good jobs away from troopers' brothers and cousins.

Montgomery fooled them all. Not only was he a crisp former Marine who knew about proper bearing and comportment, he was also a quick study of police procedure. It was no surprise that Montgomery, winner of many commendations over the years, moved up in the ranks because he'd earned every stripe.

He'd been the man overseeing the PSP's West Central District as long as Strand could remember, and early on they'd formed a bond, especially when Strand broke another barrier—marrying a Catholic and later converting to her faith. In one particularly revealing conversation, Montgomery had said, "We outsiders understand what it's all about, don't we, Strand." It wasn't a question, and he never referenced it again. Despite Strand's respect for him, he nonetheless gave his boss a wide berth.

"Yessir," said Strand with a weak attempt at respectful civility. "What can I do for you," he paused, looking straight into Montgomery's eyes, "on my day off?"

"Day off, my skinny ass!" retorted Montgomery, accurate in at least one respect. There were no fat rolls under his well-pressed uniform, and underlings envied his recruiting poster appearance. "Sounds like you've been working already this morning, pissing off the local constabulary, to boot. Now come this way, my young friend, and don't tell me it's your day off because I've already been working too hard on your behalf, just so old Georgie Hallon don't throw you outta his town."

"Jesus, Walt, all I did was find his goddam body for him! What'd he want me to do—just walk on by and go have my morning coffee like on any other vacation Monday? Huh? Yeah, that's right—that's what I could have done and should have done—what the hell, I see bodies of floating kids every damn day in Foreston—what's another one?" Strand had gotten on his wagon, too, and knew that otherwise, Montgomery would make him sit in his office for a solid hour while peddling political crap about keeping the locals happy. And that, Strand didn't need, Lieutenant or no Lieutenant, Georgie or no Georgie. Shove back just a little harder, and tea kettles without much steam will just whistle down, Strand promised himself. The tactic worked. And Montgomery did.

"Alright, I hear ya. But you know how Georgie Hallon can be—he thought you were gonna horn in on his case because it looked to him as if you had his new guy, Retchy or something..."

"Rettig."

"Yeah. Whatever. Georgie told me when he arrived at the scene, he thought his guy thought he was working for you. So he got pissed."

"You mean you couldn't have just mentioned that? Instead of giving me all that other? Who you working for anyway? Is Georgie your cousin?"

"Hey! Watch your mouth! I'll take that detective's shield away from you and you'll be sitting on I-80 crossovers the rest of the winter."

"Okay. Sorry," Strand said, calmer now.

"So, what happened?" Montgomery asked, with a professional, not political interest. Strand laid it out for his chief, with all details. Both knew the percentages being what they were, the investigation might soon be taken right out of Georgie's hands—and into those of the PSP. "You back on the job, or what?" Montgomery asked after Strand had concluded his recitation.

"Not today. I just came in because I knew Georgie would call you and I thought you'd want an opportunity to get it off your chest."

Montgomery actually laughed, an acknowledgement by one professional to another that the pressures accompanying certain situations required certain kinds of behavioral reactions, and the Lieutenant's whole act this morning was a Montgomery trademark of necessary, but false bluster. "Okay, wise guy, but I've got something for you—not too big, because I know you've been laying around and you ain't in great shape," he said, arching his eyebrows in mock concern, but halfsmiling at the same time.

"Something you can't handle yourself?" Strand suggested, carefully continuing the banter.

"Read this morning's paper?" the lieutenant asked, more seriously, and pointed to the lead story in the *Herald*.

"No. Been busy...with your cousin Georgie," Strand rebounded sarcastically.

"He's not my cousin! So, knock off the cute stuff long enough to read the story, and then I'll give you the file for your afternoon off—this needs to be done tomorrow. If Piper were here, I'd give it to him, but he's not, so you and Bentsen are it."

At the sound of Piper's name, Strand recoiled, not sure whether Montgomery had made a mistake or had lost a stitch somewhere. Piper was Sergeant Jake Piper, a helluva good officer who got it in the line of duty one night in late November 1984, six years earlier. Strand remembered it clearly; he had just gotten his detective's shield. His first murder case as a homicide detective was Jake Piper's. Shot by a panicked coke dealer stopped on I80, probably for doing over 85 in the 55mph zone, Piper never had a chance. The PSP had no trouble getting the killer—while stopped by Piper, his car had stalled, and foot tracks in the day-old snow quickly provided a trail.

"Chief," Strand spoke slowly, "Jake Piper?"

"Piper made the collar in that case," he said, pointing to the file in Strand's lap. "The Knotting case, a big one back in '68," continued Montgomery, not having lost any marbles at all, "and if he was here, this job'd give him a good deal of pleasure. Sit down! I have a few minutes—I'll tell you the story."

VIII

OR MORE THAN a few minutes, Montgomery gave the account in such vivid detail, his listener had to wonder if the lieutenant himself had been there. As if to signal the blessed end of it, the phone rang, and Montgomery spoke into it briefly. Hanging up, he turned to Strand and said, "Anyway, just read the file, and tomorrow morning, you'n Bentsen show up at Morganville prison, and take that idiot over to the courthouse to let him have his day."

Strand didn't ask any questions, figuring that the case file would make clear the hazy parts in the newspaper story and Montgomery's chronology. He smiled. It was actually light work if he guessed right.

As Strand walked into the nest of detective's offices down the hall, he ran into Joe Bentsen, his partner in crime, as it were. He didn't want to answer the inevitable questions about Aurora and the kids, his activities over the New Year weekend, and, mostly, about the book that was not being written.

Attempting to cover his surprise, he said, "Why, I would've sworn Montgomery just told me you weren't around, and Jesus, I shouldn't be seeing you—you look like the flu hit you like a ton of bricks."

"So nice of you to say so," Bentsen responded in a nasal voice so pronounced that it was barely recognizable, "but I just stopped in—read about the Knotting case and wanted to get out of the house. Sylvie won't even let me be sick in peace."

For Bentsen, both sentences came out in slow speed, every word a struggle, and it was clear that whether it was the flu or a bad cold, Bentsen had captured it in his head and chest.

"You know, Joe, we're supposed to transport Knotting tomorrow. If you're not feeling well, I sure as hell don't want to be in the car with you."

"Yeah, I know. Don't worry. I gotta go down the hall," Bentsen added, this time with the sound and look of urgency, his eyes glancing sideways at Strand, then longingly in the direction of the men's room.

Strand always thought that big guys like Bentsen laid low by any illness—even if just the flu—were a pitiable sight. Strand himself fell into the broad category of "normal," but Bentsen, at almost six foot four and weighing about 240, even slouched over, was huge. It was dispiriting to see him sick because he tended to think of him as rock-hard and reliable, adjectives that placed his partner in the category of "immovable object." In his present state of the punies, however, Bentsen was a threat only to Strand's good health.

Real work would follow the Knotting assignment, and he wanted Bentsen by his side. Not only was he imposing just by his physical presence, he was quick on the uptake, and a godsend in any tight situation.

Neither one was the senior partner, and it worked out well. When questioning a witness or a suspect, their modus operandi was for Strand to face the person directly and do most of the talking. Bentsen, on the other hand, stood over Strand's shoulder—literally—and eyeballed the witness. If the subject of the interview was cooperative, Bentsen smiled approvingly and let his eyes wander, but when the situation called for it, his eyes narrowed, drilling holes in the story pouring forth, and that, coupled with an aggressive thrust of the jaw coming from a behemoth less than three feet away, often worked miracles on the cooperation index of otherwise clam-like sources.

Glad the bigfoot had a reason to go down the hall, Strand took advantage of the opportunity to gather up the Knotting file and make good his escape.

The drive to Mercer, his interludes with Montgomery and Bentsen, and the further distraction of the Knotting case, had allowed enough time for the morning's murder to simmer in his own intellectual kettle. As a result, he drove home at a slower pace than he had left it, and wasn't in a hurry to return to a town where, he sensed, a killer would strike again.

His frightening conclusion was based on a few simple observations. Foreston was a conservative, dry Borough of about 8,000 people, largely Protestant, where crimes of violence and passion rarely escaped the confines of tight public discipline. Of course, it was possible the boy was murdered by a family member, but such killings were usually not done with a knife and not away from the home setting.

Drug-related? Anything was possible, naturally. Foreston had a drug problem—no town or borough was exempt. But this kid? Nah! This kid with a regular haircut, straight, working class clothes right out of Walmart? Possible, but not likely.

This was not the work of someone passing through, he surmised, but by someone who had a sense of the town's rhythms and geography, judging by the where the body was found. This was the work of a male killer, Strand supposed, his conclusion was based on the answer to the question: would a woman stab a kid and throw his body into a creek? No way. Again, anything was possible, but solutions to most homicides came as a result of focusing on the probables, not the possibles, and probabilities came from experience.

He also supposed Hallon's boys would check out the parents and talk to a lot of people in the neighborhood and in school, and thereby eliminate or point to certain working scenarios. Strand guessed that when all the legwork was done, Hallon would be left but one conclusion: it was a male killer, still loose in Foreston, who would strike again. But when?

IX

ETURNING HOME FOR the second time that day, Strand gave Bo a good scratch, then made himself a bowl of Lipton Noodle Soup, dumping in a half dozen saltines—low sodium, of course—in the little kitchen Earl Shannon had set up for him.

When he pulled the Knotting file from the manilla envelope, its several inches gave the air around it the dank, musty smell which attaches itself to anything archived in an airless basement for years on end. Opening the file jacket itself was like revisiting the mind's secrets from a forgotten past and being reminded how much they are always part of the present. Immediately, his attention was drawn to the yellowing pages before him where dates and facts took him back to the height of the Vietnam war years—the spring of 1968—when he was getting out of college.

It was usually in mid-May when the college kids, local and from the surrounding area, began celebrating the end of another year, but 1968 was not just any other year in America. There was the Tet Offensive, President Johnson's decision to leave the political field of battle, the unending demonstrations on the major campuses and big cities, and the hope by not a few that marijuana would replace beer as young America's drug of choice.

A strong thread of resentment wove itself through the nation's social and political fabric, and the upheaval which came with it had not been seen in the United States since the 1930s. While most of the citizenry was not prepared for challenges to the status quo, it was being forced to become more tolerant of those who represented change. Those historical snippets, like film clips, flashed through his memory bank, and he could feel his own tension as he began to read.

Strand began what became a two and a half hour sitting to capture for himself a working summary of events he wanted to have on the case. Though plowing through the entire jacket was unnecessary to his assigned task, it had piqued his interest for one reason: when Forestonians spoke about the local crime rate, they warmly related with full chamber-of-commerce fervor that the last murder in the Borough of Foreston happened twenty-some years earlier, and this was the case to which they all referred—the Knotting case. It was so named because Marty Knotting was the only one who actually came to trial for the crime, thus treating the *Herald's* more pruriently interested readers to a seemingly endless recitation of the crime facts. It was an amusement to which they otherwise would have been denied.

The ancient witness statements found their rhythm, and in seconds, Strand let himself be pulled to a scene of grisly mayhem. With the Montgomery version as his guide, he easily pieced together an orderly reconstruction of the entire story. It laid itself out this way:

"Yeah! Let's do it tonight!" Marty Knotting declared. "We can pick up a few of those college kids and do it right," this according to Larry Vincent and Notchie Falerno—the two who later pleaded guilty for a deal.

"Right on, man!" his listeners agreed.

"They ougtha get what's comin' to 'em," Knotting urged.

It was May 22, 1968, and after two days of heavy beer intake, the three men, chambered in the closed gas station where Falerno worked, boozily convened the impromptu, kangaroo court which was to undo them all. They were unlikely triers of fact. Vincent and Falerno were high school dropouts while Knotting, their erstwhile representative of the intelligentsia, had one failed year of junior college to his credit.

Knotting, at least, looked and acted as if a productive thought or two had crossed his mind, witnesses later reported. At nineteen years of age, he was five foot five, weighed in at about 135 pounds, had clear, light-blue eyes, unmarked but slightly freckled skin, and dark rust-colored hair. He had always been the wise guy in the Foreston Soda Shop and to that job he returned when a college degree proved not to be in the cards for him. There, he waited on high school compatriots, most of whom had bettered themselves. They had found education or a job or a family, and they were building upon the fruits of stability.

Knotting's choices had not been quite the same, old *Herald* articles maintained. With a girl barely of legal age, he had had one child, a daughter, never married the mother or took responsibility for the baby, and unsurprisingly, got her pregnant again the year before the crime. None of that had mattered to Marty. That someone was raising his two children was of little interest to him, and he never acknowledged them. His girlfriend committed suicide, and both his daughter and the infant were shuffled off into the system.

Afterward, Knotting's view of a relationship extended to one-night stands in somebody's third-rate boarding house. Otherwise, his life revolved around his dead-end job and the few of society's castoffs who would pay attention to him. It was in his world of the Foreston Soda Shop that Knotting had the opportunity to serve Vincent and Falerno, classmates in fulfillment of their destiny as ne'er do wells. Although not friends in their teen years—Knotting never thought he'd be hanging around with the likes of them—they became inseparable.

Vincent jockeyed a gas pump part-time and otherwise, laid around the house, drove his mother crazy, and got drunk on weekends. For extra money, he and Falerno broke into pop machines, payphones, and church poor boxes, financing their unexceptional ignorance day by day.

Falerno did nothing most of the time except hang around the

station where Vincent attempted to imitate honest labor. They could have been brothers, not quite twins. Both were nearly six feet tall and weighed about 210 pounds, little of it in muscle. They met in freshman football where they occasionally played defensive tackle, but more regularly, held the bench to the ground—they went out for the team hoping only to get away from class and reproving teachers. One season of them was all the coach could take.

"C'mon, let's have one more beer, and then do it!" Knotting enjoined.

"Who do those disloyal, Commie punks think they are?" Vincent demanded of his friendly audience. "This is Foreston, not someplace in California. We don't need no anti-war stuff goin' on here!"

"And they're all alike," Falerno muttered. "They ain't so smart, just because they're in college."

As judge, prosecutor, and jury, they unanimously conferred the ultimate degree of guilt upon any and all college students for everything that was wrong in their America. Just at dusk, they realized they hadn't eaten, and needed a satisfied stomach to savor their sense of justice, whatever it happened to be at the moment.

They climbed into Falerno's Chevy Malibu, and weaved their way through downtown, Friday night Foreston. Amazingly, their night's quest did not begin with a vehicular homicide. Managing artificial sobriety, they slowly cruised through the intersection of Broad and Elm Streets, where Officer Morelli normally parked the scarecrow cruiser, a warning to would-be miscreants, but Morelli wasn't there. The Justices of Nothing At All merely moved up Broad Street, passed the railroad tracks, made a sharp left, and landed at Burger Chef. Having fueled their furnaces, and having regained some semblance of clear-headedness, they resolved to finish what they had begun.

The trio left the foodery, sped down Center Street, and found State Route 58, the main road between Foreston and Shining Hollow, a village about eight miles to the east. Just outside of Foreston, a target appeared at which they might cast their forged fury of indignation.

"Stop here. This is the place—it's right. I've heard a lot of them hang out here," Vincent maintained.

"Yeah. This has been the right place for a lotta years. Why didn't I think of it before?" asked Knotting of no one in particular.

Sampson's Roadhouse had been the hangout of choice for Mercer County's drinking youth for at least a generation, and many warm and memorable moments created themselves there, from the night of V-J Day in 1945 onward. This May night's activities did not, however, fall into the same category. Calvinistic Foreston barely tolerated Sampson's, yet recognized, hypocritically, it was a social safety valve to be winked at but never discussed openly.

The firm of Knotting, Vincent, and Falerno ambled into the tavern and attempted to blend themselves into the small crowd of perhaps three dozen patrons. The tactic was largely unsuccessful as most people were reasonably clean, sober, and appropriately dressed for a Friday night out. The contrast could not have been greater. It was clean sport shirts and college sweatshirts to Vincent's sweat-stained, formerly white T-shirt, and a pack of Luckies rolled up in his left sleeve. It was washed, stylishly long hair, male and female, to Vincent's and Falerno's long, over slicked, unwashed duck tails. It was white Levi's and loafers to oil-stained dungarees and work boots. Knotting, somewhat kempt and cleaner, also stood out in his wrinkled white shirt, black pants, and pointed black shoes.

"Lookit 'em and their cool clothes. I bet they all do drugs, too! And the girls—ain't they into free love, man?" Falerno was just warming up.

"We're not goin' to let them get away with it, guys. This is the night they're goin' to pay." Knotting pressed his point home. "They think they're better 'n us, don't they?"

His listeners just stared, the incendiary words having their effect. "Yeah, they do," Falerno agreed.

"Yeah, man. Tonight's the night, ain't it?" Vincent seconded.

Most people in Sampson's were in their early twenties, and with dates. Such a crowd would dominate the place until about 10 p.m., and be replaced with couples in their thirties and forties, some of them marrieds needing a break from the kids, while others were couples unabashedly on the cheat. For the younger ones, however, their partying would climax at Sampson's, after which they would double date to a favorite lover's lane, or to a friend's apartment where furtive smiles would pass over a dessert of spiked brownies.

For their part, Ronnie Lassiter and his roommate, Frank Duffy, had managed to wangle dates with the prettiest girls who had ever spoken to them, a pair not as well known for partying as many of their friends. Louise Martin and Carolyn Novak wanted a change of pace from the usual round of sorority parties and the devotions of pesty linebackers, they said later. Besides, they had that kind of action lined up for Saturday night. The girls had been to Sampson's before—many times—but for Ronnie and Frank, it was their first experience at public, underage drinking—and with dates. Not all of Sampson's patrons would live through the night.

X

HIS BONES ACHING from sitting in the same position, Strand rose and stretched, his unfinished soup cold and pushed aside. He turned the water on to boil for a cup of instant coffee.

While waiting, he riffled through the news clippings and miscellaneous notes at the back of the file. Had Piper collected them? He couldn't tell. On one stapled item, he saw that Frank Duffy had died outside Saigon in November 1973, serving in the war Knotting, Vincent, and Falerno thought people like Duffy would manage to avoid. The young women, Louise Martin and Carolyn Novak, hurried from the area in June 1968, and except for Knotting's trial, never returned. As for Knotting's accomplices, both were sentenced to life without parole for having raped the young women, and for the slaying of Ronnie Lassiter.

Later, another kind of disposition was reported. In 1977, Vincent almost made good an attempt at freedom: he jumped, completely unnoticed, into a garbage truck departing from the State Penitentiary at Williamsport. Unfortunately for him, he picked the type of truck that mashed and masticated the garbage as it rode along, shredding the trash into small pieces, then compacting it. It took the authorities a while to find all of him.

At his trial, Knotting attempted to portray himself as a skinny soda jerk physically intimidated by Vincent and Falerno, claiming he had gone along with them unwittingly and unwillingly. Indeed, there had been sentiment perversely sympathetic to Knotting. Yet, Strand noticed, midway through the proceeding, the defendant changed his plea to guilty. He had been turned down for parole after twenty years and now, in 1990, was contesting the original trial on the ground that he had been wrongly advised by his attorney, that were it not for his advice, he would never have entered a guilty plea.

In surprising support for the defendant were the testimonies of the young women themselves, who swore, several months after the immediate horror of the night of crime and cruelty, that Knotting's inner goodness kept them from the same fate as Lassiter, and that was a fact worthy of judicial consideration.

Mercer County prosecutor Foster Stevens convinced the jury that Knotting was the mastermind of the evening's activities, actually participated in the crimes that occurred—certainly did nothing to prevent any one of them—and though he may have let the women walk away, he was as guilty as his compatriots. At the time of the trial, in October of 1968, the betting was about even, according to the *Herald* clippings, that Knotting would wind up a free man in fifteen years—but that was before he changed his plea. And now, in 1990, Knotting was re-storying events, there being no witnesses able or willing to contradict him, with the claim he was misled by his attorney so as to minimize the agony of his last cancerous months on earth.

Current *Herald* clippings revealed more than one op-ed wondering why a modern-day judge would hear the appeal. And how Judge Hanscomb would uncloak his earthen mantle and utter some other-worldly words at such news! Feelings in Mercer County, and in Foreston in particular, ran high about the Knotting case—the whole episode had been a low point in the history of the area and no one wanted the story to come up again, or worse, see a free Knotting walking their streets.

Strand saw what his assignment would be: escort Knotting to

court, reassemble the evidence, and search for missing witnesses. His line of thought returned to the chronological crime facts in the file when he took the cup of dubious brew back to the table and sat down again to the place where he'd laid his bookmark.

There, in that other dimension, Sampson's Roadhouse reappeared in his mind's eye. Many patrons departed early from the clammy, stale, not yet air-conditioned air laden with cigarette smoke and the tang of cheap beer. The double daters, Lassiter-Novak and Duffy-Martin, poured out of the Roadhouse, followed by Knotting, Vincent, and Falerno into the steamy spring night. They attacked from behind. With knives drawn, the latter two avengers warned everyone not to scream for help or one of them would die.

Knotting led them: "Hey, Vince! Notchie! Jump in the car with them and head to town. Hah! We're gonna have fun!"

Too naive to look far down the chain of circumstances likely to follow, Lassiter and Duffy made little attempt to overpower their kidnappers, and soon, they traversed the one-mile distance, where, blanketed by night, all were in parody's court, the station where Vincent worked. It had closed at 8 p.m.

At that point, the pages of the case file took a sickening turn, riveting Strand to his chair as the facts revealed themselves. Next, the collected statements indicated, Vincent kept Martin with him in one room while the others, stepping over debris, moved into the part of the building once a garage.

"C'mon, honey," Vincent said to Louise Martin, "come for papa," and then laughed at his own crude humor. One by one, Vincent, Falerno, and Knotting raped Martin and after her clothes were ripped, her face bloodied, and her virginity stolen, it was Novak's turn for a nasty slice of life. In about fortyfive minutes, they repeated the process, much as mechanics delightedly taking their turn at tuning a balky engine, amid the sounds of screaming and slapping and punching.

Falerno was not interested in the usual kind of sex. Carolyn Novak had prepared herself while listening to Louise Martin's pitiable cries, but she was not prepared for Falerno. He surprised the nineteenyear-old when he turned her around, bent her over the desk, and with one hand on the back of her neck, violently pushed her skirt up, tore off her slip, and pulled down her panties before thrusting his penis forcefully into her anus. The girl's muscles contracted involuntarily as the breath was strangled from her body, and she thought she would breathe no more, but Falerno would not accommodate her unspoken wish to die.

"Now, for dessert," he said as he finished with one act, then pulled her off the desk, forced her downward, and holding her head by her hair, rubbed her face with his flaccid, wet, bloodied instrument, making her lick him and revive him.

Martin made no sound except for a few grunting, choking noises of revulsion. Finally, she pushed Falerno away, and fell to the floor, staring empty-eyed at the old tires still hanging on the wall.

Each of the three self-appointed jurists brought the young women to the lowest level they thought possible, to the point where the educated, privileged coeds were beneath them; thus, they drunkenly carried out their sentence, one designed by them to even the social score, so they felt.

While Knotting busied himself with the evening's entertainment, Vincent and Falerno guarded the remaining members of the ill-fated foursome. Intermittently, they exercised their punching arms on Lassiter and Duffy. Soon, Duffy fell back, unconscious.

"You shitheads!" Vincent screamed, as Falerno handled the physical side of the conversation. "What makes you think you run our country?" he demanded.

"What's wrong with you two?" Falerno chimed in. "Can't serve your country like real men? Buncha pussies, you are!" Heady with an adrenalin rush, he focused his greatest rage on the nerdy, helpless, whimpering Lassiter, first smashing his glasses into his right temple, and then proceeding to withdraw bits of his life with each succeeding blow to every part of his physical being.

Lassiter raised his arms. "We're just on a date!" he cried. "We're not against the war. Please leave us alone!"

"You're guilty as hell!" Knotting shouted from the next room.

"You're getting just what you deserve."

Vincent, not to be left out, added, "You're gonna wish you'd gone in the Army, turkey!" Then he continued the bombardment, most of his blows landing on the already fallen Lassiter.

The young man's ribs, left arm, pelvis, and finally, his skull gave way to the pounding fists and kicking boots, according to the coroner, and as Ronnie Lassiter's few remaining thoughts became more fragmented, more unreal, he must have begun to give up the idea of walking away from a nightmare no one ever prepared him to expect. Did he see the coming of life's end? A stairway of light? Strand paused, difficult as it was to fully imagine what had happened.

Only when Vincent and Falerno saw blood gushing from Lassiter's mouth, and the body no longer raised arm or leg in futile defense, did they end their rage. "How you guys doin'?" Knotting yelled when he detected the sudden change of pitch, the sullen quiet in the next room. Receiving no answer, he withdrew from the young woman, looked around the corner, and became sickened by the effects of too much alcohol and the sight of his minions' handiwork.

"Holy shit!" Knotting whistled as he took one, long look at the body on the dirty, scarlet-pooled concrete floor, and felt sure the boy was dead. Had he been calloused to his criminal acts, Knotting said later, he would have readily seen that multiplying the murder by four was their only real opportunity for complete escape. He didn't see that then. In fact, he told all who would listen, none of it had been planned—roughing up a few college brats was all they had intended.

Yet, it was clear from all statements, Knotting compounded the long string of horrible misjudgments in his assumption of Lassiter's death, the medical examiner later testified. Without checking to see if Lassiter was breathing, Knotting directed Vincent and Falerno to bury the bloody pile of a human being just outside the back door of the station. For several minutes, the pair busied themselves with their grisly chore, the metal against dirt and pebble sounds clanging away in the humid stillness of the night. In fact, the coroner testified, Lassiter was still alive.

The noise was enough to rouse Frank Duffy to a fully conscious awareness of transpiring events. As Vincent and Falerno dizzyingly shoveled the last spadefuls of dirt on the inert Lassiter, Duffy burst through the open doorway, slamming into Falerno hard enough to knock him to the ground.

Caught unawares, Falerno fell onto Vincent, and as they fought to steady themselves, Duffy pushed past and into the night. The murderous pair gave chase, and though not as smart as their leader, they quickly determined the only safe alternative lay in killing Martin and Novak.

As the facts and later testimony suggested, Knotting must have seen the hopeless situation in which he found himself, particularly if Duffy made good his run. Just on the edge of town, it wouldn't be long before help came. It was likely Knotting realized their night of fun was over, and his only salvation lay in doing whatever was in his power to assist his young victims to safety.

"Run. Run!" he screamed. "Get out of here." He signaled them to exit the one other door in the makeshift, but very real hell. At first disbelieving, Novak and Martin quickly realized that the man's motives didn't really matter. All that mattered was the one chance he was giving them. They ran.

In a few minutes, the dumbstruck Vincent and Falerno returned without Duffy, and looked in surprise and rising anger at Knotting when they realized the girls weren't there. "You son of a bitch!" Falerno shouted at Knotting. "You let them go!"

"No, I didn't," Knotting flung back his lie. "You dumb bastards let them all get away—if you had been guarding the door, none of 'em could have run, so don't look at me."

Vincent said little; he was beginning to understand what had happened, he swore later.

Finally, when all was quiet, they agreed their one and final choice was to run themselves; Sampson's bouncer could point to them being at the roadhouse, however, and each could be easily identified by the surviving victims.

While Duffy, Novak, and Martin ran with the tearful exultation of probable survival, Knotting, Vincent, and Falerno ran, too, but they with the fear of jackals on the wrong end of the hunt. Within a few days, all three were caught. Knotting had gotten as far as Akron, but Vincent and Falerno were still together in a bus station in Meadville when finally apprehended. With the testimony of the survivors, there was little point in trusting a decision to a jury, Vincent and Falerno were quietly but quickly advised by their separate attorneys.

Knotting had held out, though, hoping to receive credit for his heroism, as he put it, in helping the women escape. The prosecutor saw no merit in Knotting's novel approach to the murder statutes and went for all he could get. Knotting's attorney, a courtappointed pro bono defender by the name of James Milcher, was a well-practiced and respected professional in the legal community. That he improperly convinced Knotting to change his plea midway through the trial was a charge unanswered by the file lying on the table before an eye-weary Fletcher Strand.

The answer to that charge would he his—and Bentsen's to prove, if a judge allowed Knotting's appeal to go forward. This was not going to be an easy gig, after all.

XI

"Bo! Bo!" Strand called again to the aging beagle. The dog roused himself from his reveries in front of a heat vent, stretched, and ambled over to his master, who, standing next to the window fronting Pine Street, was likewise contracting and relaxing his own body muscles after a long sit with the Knotting file.

"Go for a walk, Bo?" Not often did Strand look for exercise and when he did, it was not with the dog. For Bo, the not altogether un-familiar question promised a rare treat: the smells of frozen lawns, old tree stumps, and dormant bushes growing along Pine Street's fabled Bradford Pear trees.

They sauntered down the hotel's front steps and turned left. The other direction had brought death too close that morning, and now in the fading light of day there they were across the street, a small gaggle of people, young and old, including a few hotel residents, standing and staring at the roped-off spot on the creekbank.

Strand and his tethered friend proceeded in their easterly direc-tion, determined to avoid the curiosity seekers. Moreover, the sud-den impulse for physical movement had another purpose altogether, to let the details of the Knotting file simmer for a while. There were so many questions left unanswered by the surprising guilty plea midway through the trial. Milcher, he remembered, had an excellent reputation as a criminal trial lawyer and Strand wanted to believe that Knotting's basis for appeal would wind up groundless. However, his strength as a homicide detective was his unflinching objectivity, and he knew there was always a possibility of error, of weakness in any man, no matter the reputation. Therefore, he wanted time to consider reasons why Milcher might have taken a short cut.

The off-duty detective could not escape death's drawstrings, however. A few blocks into their walk, Strand found himself less than fifty feet from the front door of Craig's (Remember...It's Forever!) Funeral Home. It was the time of a winter's day when the sun was almost down and no matter how brightly it had shone minutes before, the temperature dropped ten degrees in an instant. Despite a down-laden jacket, flesh, and muscle, the cold always scored deeply into bone. The fact that he was in sight of a funeral parlor did nothing to dispel the chill of the day's end.

In the near-evening gloom, he could see two cars at the curb, a 1987 Chevy Celebrity Wagon and a Foreston police cruiser. As he approached, the driver's side door of the cruiser opened and out stepped Anthony Rettig. Strand sensed a familiar, unwelcome feeling. Like a magnet dragging iron filings quickly to it, the detective seemed to draw near to him shards of broken lives, pieces of death.

"Can't stay away from it, huh!" cracked the young officer, cockier than he had been that morning, his nerve emboldened from the initiation rite of a stomach-wrenching, unnatural death few new cops witness. Hallon's disdainful treatment of the unimposing state trooper apparently lessened the respectful, professional distance Rettig should have maintained. "Snooping, Strand?" he challenged, mimicking Hallon's tone when the detective failed to respond the first time.

"You got a problem?" was Strand's rejoinder. The question's intensity let the young officer know Strand didn't appreciate the familiarity of unequals.

"No, s-sir," he said, his words a little more tentative now.

"You want one?" Strand continued, just to be sure.

"Look..." the other began, then stopped, uncertain of his response. "Sorry," he spoke, carefully, "I guess I spoke out of turn." When the detective returned a deadpan look, the officer said, "Hey, I said I was sorry and that's all you get from me," and he started to get back in the cruiser.

"You and your boss don't sing the same song then?" Strand finally interjected.

"Not necessarily. He's my Chief, not my master," Rettig asserted bravely.

Strand smiled. Rettig shut the car door and approached. It was dusk now. Strand motioned with a leftward jerk of his head toward the funeral home, "The kid's family?"

"Yeah. The Chief said I should drive over with them. A courtesy. Doc McCreary hasn't released the body yet, but you know, they need to get some things started."

Strand nodded, then asked, "Find anything along the bank this morning?"

Rettig didn't answer, not knowing whether he should discuss it with anyone—after all, Strand was only a witness but most of all, he didn't want Hallon finding out he had talked too much about Foreston business to a Statie. "Is this for yourself?"

"Don't worry about it—call it a cop's natural curiosity," Strand said, and looking right into the young officer's eye he added, "I don't talk too much."

Rettig hesitated no further. "Nothing much on the body. At least as far as we could see. Maybe we got lucky, though. Up the creekside, we found two sets of footsteps, only about three or four actual footprints, in the short patch of snow on the path leading from the parking lot down to the walkway under the bridge."

"How do you know they were the kid's prints?"

"Don't for sure yet and maybe we won't, but one of the footprints appears to match in size the boy's tennis shoe. With only that light crust of snow, there wasn't much under the shoe to emboss an image on the ground, but we think it's his."

"Why're you so sure?"

"Can't prove it, of course, but there was only one set of footprints coming off the grate on the other side—an adult's, looks like."

"The adult's—they match any on the approach to the bridge—next to the boy's?"

"Yeah. We think so, but now it gets iffy. There was only one larger footprint there."

"Only one?"

"Well, there may have been another one, but it looked like the party may have slipped in the mud under the snow. There's about a two-foot gash through the snow where someone's shoe may have slid, and what's probably a handprint near it."

"Was there enough of the smaller footprint for you to tell for sure if it was the boy's?"

"Maybe just enough. They tried to lift the tread fragment and were going to keep it frozen until they try a match at the lab, but the kid's shoes were pretty worn, you know."

Craig's front door opened. The policemen looked up at the same time, and saw Morty Craig solemnly shepherding a man and woman out the door. The couple was in their early forties, but had been shocked into a cold, alabaster pallor, emotions temporarily stilled by the duties before them. They came down the steps, closer into the electric lantern light between sidewalk and curb where Strand and Rettig stood.

Strand was surprised when he saw who they were: Jim and Peg Hilton. They operated Hilton's PharMart, a drugstore with sundry other goods. Jim Hilton was an active member of the local Kiwanis Club, which in fact met weekly in the restaurant of the Penn Grove Hotel. Strand remembered having bowled with him on Tuesday nights for one season a few years earlier, and thought well of him. He hadn't known Margaret except to see her in the store, yet he was surprised to connect them with the dead boy.

The man and his wife passed the two policemen wordlessly. Peg Hilton was not present emotionally, but in an in-between state where her brain refused to acknowledge the absolute certainty of the loss she was now trying to deny, a state in which she knew the hours of hurt, angry tears, and self-inflicted guilt were yet to come. Quietly, Hilton put his wife into the front seat of the station wagon, her face with its unblinking eyes just discernible in the glare of the lantern on the windshield.

Hilton did not walk around and get in the car himself as the two policemen expected. Instead, he walked over to them, looked at Strand, and said, "I hear you found him."

Strand could not maintain eye contact. "Yes. I did. I didn't know he was your son. Sorry, Jim," he said, wishing he had somehow known it was the Hilton boy, though what good that would have done, Strand did not know.

Hilton did not acknowledge the condolence. He grieved, to neither of them in particular, "Jamie was such a happy kid—you could've told that just by talking to him. Why would anybody want to take that away?" His anguish was palpable.

It was the kind of question no one could answer. It was the kind of non-conversation no one could carry on. After a short silence, Strand looked at the hurting man and mustered, in a throaty voice, "Anything I can do, Jim?"

The question brought the father back. "Yeah," he said quietly, evenly, and without venom, "Just get the son of a bitch!"

XII

I N HIS SECOND-FLOOR apartment, a choice residence with a bow window on the street, Eddy tried not to think about what had happened. On his second walk into town to buy an evening paper, talk of the little boy's death at the newsstand provided the grist for conversation. There was no mention of the weather. Only a dead little boy—murdered right there in their little town.

Facts about the Hiltons were widely catalogued with everyone contributing. They'd run Broad Street's PharMart for years together, and were perfect partners. They had two children, but of course, had only the teenage daughter left now. And how could such a horrible crime occur in daylight with nobody seeing a thing?

There was an edge to their talk, he noticed. *Is it fear?*

Eddy was pitiless. *Had the Hiltons been more concerned about their children, they would have been more careful. They still have another child, don't they?*

~

The telephone's insistent ring pierced the shroud of Strand's deep sleep. His dreams about the dead, one from twenty years earlier and one from just that morning, troubled him as the landline's jangle forced him into a welcome consciousness. On the end table behind his head, the ringing phone persisted, oblivious to the hour, sometime after 11 p.m.

Grimacing when his anatomy would not conform to his wishes, he swore as he sat up halfway, turned, and with not a little irritation, grabbed the receiver. Impromptu aerobics aside, he answered the instrument's call, none too warmly, "Yeah?"

"Hey, you awake?"

"Who...?" He recognized Aurora's voice in time to prevent the vulgarity about to escape his lips.

"Aurora—everything OK?" They had spoken but twice since her departure, once to make sure he had her parents' phone number, and later, when she called on Christmas Eve to see if he was coming the next day.

On that Christmas Day, a mirthless Strand had driven to her parents' Columbus home for what amounted to a strained two-hour visit. Her parents had met him at the door, and were civil, but barely so. Given their oft-expressed feeling their daughter should have married someone with "a big job," there was no reason to have expected a change to Leo and Gina Tomaselli's years of disappointment. Not even the seasonal spirit of forgiveness and goodwill could have thawed those two, yet he had hoped whatever bond remained with Aurora would have served to warm her welcome. In that, he was keenly disappointed. Her appearance was brief and her demeanor, brisk.

"Hello," she had said without much feeling that day.

"What? No 'Merry Christmas!' or 'Happy Holidays!' from Mrs. Strand?" His attempt at lightheartedness could not dilute the acid lacing his tone of voice, however.

"That would be a very difficult greeting to make—don't you think?"

"Yes," he paused. "Yes, I suppose it would. How are Aarie and Anna?"

"They're fine. They've missed you, Fletch."

"Enough that you'd want to come back to Pennsylvania with me tonight?"

There was no pause. "That wouldn't be a good idea. You know that. I'll get the kids." With that, she turned and left the room, and he saw her no more that day.

In a few minutes, Anna and Aarie were with him and Strand was forced to spend time with his children in the living room of a home unwelcoming and uncomfortable to him. The kids, on the other hand, were resilient and smart, and they had many questions they obviously wanted to ask. Realizing there was but a short time, everyone shied away from unpleasantness, until it was time for him to go, that is.

"We want to come home, Dad, but Mom won't let us," Anna had blurted, when he was at the front door about to leave.

In recalling those moments, Strand felt like he had been just another convict's relative at the prison on visiting day—no way to talk about the things that meant the most. In the few weeks that followed, seeds of bitterness found a fertile place in his heart. Although the time spent with Aarie and Anna had made the drive worthwhile, putting aside that holiday memory would be hard. Aurora's was not a welcome voice.

"The kids alright?" he finally managed.

"They're fine," she answered with a certainty suggesting that was not why she called. "Fletch, how are you? No, I guess I have no right to ask. I know you're not great—you must miss the kids terribly, and I...Fletch!...Fletch, are you there?"

"Yeah...what do you mean?" he responded, distantly.

"Fletch, are you paying attention to me?"

"Aurora, did you have a reason for your call, or did you just miss giving me a punch in the gut?"

"I called to say that I missed you—but you didn't give me a chance to say it."

"You have a funny way of expressing a feeling—you always did."

"Hey, look, I called to see how you were doing, to see how things were with you, and right away you start in!"

"No, Aurora, you 'look.' You walk out on me, take my kids away, give me the chill on Christmas Day, and then call here two weeks later expecting sweetness and love? Do you have any idea what it's like to walk by my own empty house? Your perspective is a bit off."

"Fletch, I want things to work out—I guess I'm not good at saying it very well—but you sure don't make it easy! Either you don't pay attention to me for other reasons, or maybe it's the same old reason—your job." She stopped, and hearing no acknowledgement, went on, as if she had expected to. "Isn't it?" she demanded.

Strand made no answer, and after a few moments, heard the electronic click ending the call.

~

Afterward, Aurora cried for the first time in many years. Theirs had been a good match from the time they met on a blind date in November 1977, through the courtship and marriage in the summer of 1978, and through the births of both children, Aaron James in June 1979, and Anna Aurora in April 1982.

Shortly after the last birth, though, there began a chilling, a distancing in the relationship. Aurora realized a major part of the problem lay in her continuing issues with Strand's "people," as she called them, especially given the ongoing comments about how "Italian-looking" the kids were, and whether they really had to be raised Catholic just because Fletch had promised on their wedding day. It was a wedge, and the elder Strands drove it hard.

When Fletch became Catholic himself, that ought to have shut down the verbal assaults, but his conversion seemed to have made it worse. Aurora knew Fletch had done it for her and the kids, and indeed, it was a loud statement to his people, but to no avail.

Some of Foreston's residents saw themselves as superior to all others, and there was no getting around it. Aurora's parents decided to decamp when they had the chance, but there was no way out of the state for a PSP detective. For Aurora and Fletch, the gulf widened.

Their last fight was about that. Fletch had mentioned to her more than once he'd heard things about the goings on amongst the Italian clans many decades before, and he wanted to know how the Tomasellis might have been involved. Aurora's family baggage was heavy, and there was a lot about her background and the Italians that she had never told him, and refused to talk about. The secrets weighed on her, but *they were in the past, weren't they?* That's what she told herself, in contradiction to what she'd often said to Fletch, "The past is always with us, isn't it?" Yet she could not bear to tell him about those years, even if in truth, she didn't know all that much.

Fletch's mistake was drawing a line on the floor, but she remained as stubborn about it as her ancestors. It was then that she said he could leave anytime he chose.

That night, he packed a bag, and left. Within a day or so, she discovered he'd just gone down the street to the hotel where he knew Earl Shannon would take him in. When he hadn't returned in a few days, Aurora left Bo and his leash with Earl, packed suitcases for herself and the kids, and drove to Columbus.

∾

Strand should have been bruised awake by the call, but he wasn't. He slid the receiver back in its cradle, and without ever having turned on a light, let himself slip into a round of lighter slumber. Aurora and the kids seemed too far away. His mind floated just below the surface of consciousness, as if underwater, seeing and hearing but not clearly, and wanting to reach up into air, to wakefulness, yet unable to do so.

Then a cold, clammy dampness made its way to the back of his neck when Jamie Hilton's end came to mind. In the utter quiet, as he became Jamie Hilton's corpse floating down Wolf Creek, he could hear the air as it brushed the moving, eddying waters just above his skyward staring eyes. Mimicking his dream, Strand's eyes opened, and then he saw it.

For a few seconds, he wanted to convince himself it was the street lamp playing light tricks on the ceiling, that somehow, moving dust and dim light had magically combined to produce the image of a sparrow flying back and forth across his room.

Then he accepted what he knew it to be. A bat! In January, for God's sake! He moved, and the bat altered its zoned divebombing to zero in on him. Strand's white shirt the attraction, the bat made two deep passes, instantly awakening the drowsy detective like no telephoned ego-bashing from Aurora could ever have done. He danced around, waving his arms like a banshee, and emitted guttural sounds he didn't know he had.

First, he opened the window so the bat might find an escape, and then he turned on all the lights in the room. With any luck, the little critter—carrying rabies?—might find the window and leave him in peace. Otherwise, he'd have to find Earl, borrow a suitable weapon, and send it to eternity.

Fortunately, the bat sensed air and streaked through the open window. Once he'd secured the room, he lay back on the couch and let his chest stop its heaving. Slowly, his thoughts returned to the first unsettled awakening he had experienced that night. The nap on the couch probably had ruined any opportunity for a steady six hours, but if the nap hadn't, the call from Aurora had. His gaze went to the telephone, and he wished he could roll back the life tape to the instant of its ring and the content of the conversation which followed.

Strand had to admit that after the Christmas Day fiasco, no satisfying words could have reached his throat when she called. That he still loved his wife and would never stop loving his children was beyond doubt, but his love was becoming tempered with the depressing reality that his relationship with Aurora might never be what he had hoped.

He rose and paced the room for fortyfive minutes thinking about the call and his choices. Not least, he thought about a cigarette. Three years without the coffin nails might come to an end if he could not regain control over his life's pressures. Were the bonds of marriage as strong as he thought? Could he ever walk away? There was a time when he was certain of his answers, but not anymore.

XIII

WHEN HE AWOKE at 6 a.m. the next day, light was just beginning to form shapes in the winter darkness. Strand showered, shaved, and dressed for the drive in to work, his first official day on the job in more than a week. Earl was kind enough to look after the dog during the day, in part because his older residents enjoyed Bo's company.

The trip to Mercer Barracks took the usual quarter hour, and he arrived just a few minutes after seven. Walter Montgomery was already there, no doubt since 5:30 a.m., at the front end of another twelve-hour day. Nobody seemed to know if Walt had a life outside, or ever had one.

Strand knew he did not have time to joust with Montgomery, or for that matter, neither did he have time to shoot the breeze with the other coffee-sippers that morning. He barely had time to pull Bentsen away from his second donut and get him moving in the direction of the coat rack.

Morganville prison was over thirty miles away, and counting drive-time both ways, the administrative bullshit at the prison, and the need to get Marty Knotting to the courthouse for a session with his lawyer before the 10 a.m. hearing, there would be no buffer for them.

Bentsen understood, reluctantly. With a grunt, he pulled his big frame out of the old oak swivel chair, and moving one size fourteen foot in front of the other, slowly propelled himself toward the door, grabbing what once may have been a decent raincoat on the way.

The ride to Morganville in Columbiana County proved a quick one. The state road was clear and dry for the time of year, and Strand remained quiet while Bentsen launched off on his wife, Sylvia.

Amazingly, Bentsen showed fewer signs of the bug bothering him the day before, but without anyone to talk to for six days, Bentsen had saved up his commentary. In the forty-minute ride, he related at least three anecdotes involving what he referred to as the summa cum laude graduate of "wife school," some mystical institution run by every young girl's married aunts. It was Bentsen's oft-repeated premise that girls attended this imaginary academy where they learned early on to control, manipulate, and otherwise corral the man of their choice. Just as often, Strand would ask his friend and partner, "Joe, why do you complain about her as much as you do?" Previously, his interest in Joe's ongoing commentary about his marriage to Sylvia had been merely polite, but now, he became curious about the apparent success of the Bentsens' marriage. *What secret do they know?*

"Oh hell, Fletch," he snuffled, "you know I just gotta get the gripes off my chest. It wouldn't be any good if I didn't have anything to complain about. Don't take me so seriously." He glanced sideways at his partner.

"Don't give me that look, Joe. I'm okay. Aurora's okay, and the kids are okay. Things just have to sort themselves out, you know?"

"I know, but you and I both know marriage breakups and suicide are as much a part of a career cop's life as a good collar and a cold beer."

"Good Christ, Joe—don't worry about me."

"Actually, I probably owe you a debt of gratitude," he said, coughing into the windshield. "Ever since you and Aurora split up, Sylvia's been extra nice to me. Low-level nagging, good meals, a little kissy face."

"Stop! Just tell Syl we're never getting back together and your life will be heaven."

They arrived at Morganville's forbidding gates shortly after 8:45 a.m. Warden Johnston had Knotting ready and waiting. After a quick cup of coffee and some chitchat with the warden, ending with signatures on custody forms, the trio departed for Mercer's courthouse.

Ordinarily, Knotting would have been transported in a van reserved for the exclusive use of ferrying prisoners back and forth from surrounding county courthouses. Knotting's case posed different problems, however. Despite the age of the crime, the sentiment around Mercer and Foreston toward Knotting was unkindly, to say the least, and enough media attention had already been drawn to the convict's unusually belated appeal. The prosecutor's office thought the wiser course was to bring the man into the courthouse with more discretion than the prison van would offer; moreover, a ride with a couple of professional detectives might prove to be of value for the State's case—should Knotting prove talkative on the way.

Strand and Bentsen had never seen Knotting before, but even after having read the case file, Strand was surprised, nonetheless. What he had retained was the mental picture of a runty, wiry, red-haired punk, 1968 vintage. What they had before them, on the other hand, was not someone about their own age, as chronologically he was supposed to be, but a bespectacled, slightly overweight man, thinly thatched on top, who appeared to be in his mid-fifties, and more likely to be guilty of small bookkeeping errors than rape and murder.

Knotting looked at the unmarked car, and apparently noticing the car's interior was not divided by heavy pig wire and plexiglass, and thus not used for the purpose of transporting prisoners, he barked, "Hey, whathehellsziss!" His eyes darted, rat-like, as a streak of paranoia overtook him.

"It's a goddam police car, Marty. Bright boy like you should figure that out pretty quick, I'd say," Bentsen muttered with just enough finality to signal the handcuffed prisoner the mode of transportation was not open to negotiation. "Besides, you get to ride in the back with little 'ol me."

Knotting surveyed "little 'ol" Joe Bentsen with the expected irony, and nodded, as if in surrender of any inclination to verbal abuse or a plan of escape. Without another word, he allowed himself to be put in the back seat, passenger side, while Bentsen went around and sat behind the driver.

On their way, Bentsen played his card. "Say, I ain't been to Morganville for at least six months, so what's happenin' in 'ol 'Johnston's Jungle'?"

Knotting's response was a smirk. "That Johnston's a crazy asshole—he's doing Hurry Searches every other damn day, seems like," Knotting claimed, alluding to the spot-checks prison guards made with lightning speed to prevent last-second hiding.

"Every other day, huh?"

"Damn straight. Johnston's on an anti-drug kick and thinks his raids are going to stop it. They should make him a high school principal where Hurry Searches would do some good while there's still time. Can't believe it!"

"Can't believe what?" Bentsen continued as the brittle countryside passed anonymously outside the car windows.

Knotting didn't answer right away. Outside his prison's walls for only the second time in twenty-one and a half years, he said, "You can't believe how changed it is. And to think," he muttered at the end, "free air is just one thickness of windowglass away."

"You've had a lot of time to think about things, haven't you?" Bentsen prodded.

"No shit!"

"I guess what puzzles me is why didn't I take this ride with you eighteen or nineteen years ago? What took you so long to come up with an appeal?"

Instantly, the prisoner tensed.

Strand noticed the fraction of a second delay and threw in his diversion, "You know why we're driving you?"

"You read my mind. Just why the hell are ya?"

"To keep you from getting run over by people and reporters."

"What's wrong with reporters?" Knotting asked. "They're just the people I wanna see—I wanna talk to 'em all."

"Well, maybe the DA's office didn't want you to have to put up with that—kinda did you a favor, they thought."

Knotting became apprehensive. "Yeah, well, news people might tell a good story about me, an' help me get a break." He paused. "I better git to talk to somebody!"

"You will. Your attorney. Matter of fact, we'll be there in ten minutes or so—then you can talk to him."

"That's not what I had in mind."

"Well, shit, Marty, tell us," Bentsen swore, sympathetically. "We'll have to go check it out sooner or later, anyway."

As if weighing the best of a bad bargain, he said, finally, "Well, I'm gonna win this, anyway, so you might as well know." With a big grin on his face, he added, "I got a witness—best proof there is that Milcher turned me for personal reasons alone."

Strand, taking the bad guy role, egged him on, "Kee-righst, Knotting, you're lucky you didn't get the chair—you were guilty as hell and you know it!"

"Guilt has nothin' to do with it," declared the inmate. "I got screwed 'cause my attorney wasn't there for me, and I finally got the proof."

"Geez, Marty, you sure?" aided Bentsen conspiratorially.

"You bet I'm sure," he said with a brag on his face, "and you two assholes'll be chauffeurin' him around before it's all done."

What he'd implied was not lost on Strand. No one spoke the last two miles before the shimmering dome of the Mercer County Courthouse rose up before them.

XIV

Eddy did not go out much, and when he did, always it was for a brief, necessary purpose. He'd put on the wig, and the rest of his disguise because he didn't want to be recognized by anyone. Yet, in his rooms, he often sat at his vantage point, gaze outward, focus inward.

As he slid back into his past, he slouched down in the easy chair, buttocks on the front edge of the seat and shoulders at the level of the overstuffed arms. The chair was the kind which, in the old days, had doilies on the arms and at the top of the back support so that hair, washed weekly, would not ruin the mohair. It would take more than a doily to improve its present appearance.

What was important to him was comfort and reaching the radiator with his stockinged feet. His toes having frozen too many times in his life, he curled and uncurled them to bring back the circulation. Within a few minutes, the icy pins no longer pricked his feet, and he felt only the soothing warmth of the steam heat. The exercise further kindled memories of a childhood he could never share with people who didn't care to understand.

It was 1976 again. His birthday, January 10, was not bitterly cold, but it may as well have been. He had come home from school with the expectancy of a child who never gives up on hope. That morning his parents, his foster parents, had not mouthed a single word to him as he left for school, and he smiled secretly to himself thinking they meant to surprise him that evening. Sure, they didn't have much money, at least as far as he understood what that meant, but the County gave them money for taking care of him, so she would make him a cake, wouldn't she? They would buy him something, wouldn't they?

When he came home, however, he had forgotten to take off his boots. The wet snow and mud were all over the linoleum when Jody Nicholson walked into the room without shoes or slippers, her hose layered around her ankles.

As soon as she felt the cold mud on the soles of her feet, she looked at him, and spat the greeting he'd never forget: "You little bastard—no wonder nobuddy will take ya, yure too dam stupud! Geddoutta here—go on, geddout!" And with that, she pushed him out the back door, tore off his boots, threw them out in the snow, and marched back in the house, leaving him out there in the twilight to shiver and stamp to no avail.

He fell asleep in the chair remembering they had no cake for him that year, the three years before, or the one year afterward that he and his sister remained with them. It was worse than that. They didn't remember his birthday and neither did they mention it to him. *Why did I ever think Mom Jody would care about me?*

≈

The two detectives presented their prisoner to the bailiff who, in turn, walked Knotting to the room in the courthouse where he met with his attorney, Reinhard Koenig, at precisely 9:55 a.m.

As Strand and Bentsen left the bailiff's office, the ancient pneumatic door closer slammed, rattling its opaque glass panel as it did so. Their heavy brown wing-tipped shoes, actually relics of a bygone era, clapped the marble floors on the main level under the rotunda as they approached what frequent courthouse visitors knew as "the blind stand." Ubiquitous in every public building across Pennsylvania, the coffee and snack bars staffed by the legally blind served as a quenching oasis amongst the dry, fine sands of justice dispensed in the paneled rooms nearby.

A step or two away from the coffee urn, Bentsen's stomach made its own thunderous crack. The two exchanged glances, Strand's martyred look beseeching heaven about the term of his suffering. Bentsen said, "I still ain't over it, I guess," and headed down the hall to a familiar place. Strand reached for a welcome cup of coffee when something caught his attention. Looking up to the second-floor balustrade, he saw the plume of blue-gray smoke emanating from a cigar being fondled by Jack McCreary, County Coroner.

McCreary crooked his finger at Strand, signaling him to come up. Strand pointed to his brimming cup of coffee. The medico gingerly saluted with one hand and proceeded to clap his way down the limestone stairs toward his friend and frequent official associate.

The PSP's West Central District, composed of six counties, seemed to experience about two dozen unnatural deaths each year from Mercer County alone. On at least half of that total, McCreary and Strand worked together—sometimes briefly, when the crimes were resolved and legally disposed of quickly; and sometimes closely and at length, when a disposition required detailed and specific forensic evidence.

When McCreary appeared at the bottom of the marble steps, Strand could not mistake him, a fortyfive-year-old man going on sixty. The graying and receding hairline, masking what once had been the red hair gifted from his Scottish ancestry, topped a cherubic face nicely accommodating the paunchy physique below it. Dressed in his usual ash-burnt clothes, another era's double-breasted style, the coroner had a sense of drama that seemed to be a few steps ahead of him. Strand smiled with the relish of a friend meeting a friend, and as if by unspoken agreement, he and McCreary walked to a small, vacant office down a side hall a few yards from the blind stand.

"What's up?"

"You tell me, Fletch," McCreary said, chortling. "Sounds like Foreston's going to have to change its whole pitch from the Chamber of Commerce."

"Not funny, Jack. You been at it too long," returned Strand. Seeing McCreary's surprise, Strand added, "Sorry. I guess you see a lot more than I do—and a lot worse."

"You got that right, my friend. I only wanted to talk to you because I figured you had a question or two for me."

"About?"

"Fletch, I know you found the Hilton boy. I know what this kind of killing does to you. Are you telling me you're not interested?"

"I've been told to stay out," observed Strand flatly. He paused, scratched his chin, and threw out his line, "Well...what?"

McCreary smiled, then began his grisly recitation. "It's hard to tell, of course, when a body comes out of near-freezing water like that, but Fletch, I think you must have been close."

"What d'you mean? Close to what?"

"Close, Fletch. Close. What I mean is that boy couldn't have been in the water more than a few minutes, ten, fifteen minutes at the outside, but probably less."

"Are you kidding?" Strand asked incredulously, and at the same time thought back to the morning before. *What did I see? What did I miss?*

"Like I said, I can't be sure, given the conditions, but didn't you notice? There was still some color in him when they pulled him out, I gather. He didn't look too bad when I saw him at 11 a.m., anyway."

"You're right. I can't believe I missed that. I guess I saw it, but didn't see it."

"Easy to miss when you pull somebody out of a cold creek. He was dead, though, no doubt about that. Whoever got him made sure of it."

"Meaning?"

The coroner puffed on his cigar, and looked Strand square in the eye, to make sure the point was not lost. "The murderer used an extremely sharp, thin blade. When he rammed it home, he pierced the boy's heart." McCreary stopped, for effect. "His death would not have been instantaneous, but nearly so, and my guess is, exquisitely painful for the few seconds he waited to die."

Strand made no response; he gulped his coffee hard, and for a moment, did not breathe.

McCreary went on. "What that means, my friend, is that this guy—I'm assuming male—is going to be a problem for you. And don't give me that crap about staying out of it just because that fart, Hallon, growled at you a bit. I'm mentioning all of this because my second assumption is that you are going to get quietly interested in a case you won't be able to let go."

His turn to smile, Strand responded, "What do you mean, 'a problem'?"

"This guy," Jack McCreary said slowly, "just walked up to the Hilton boy and cut his heart in two. There was no fight, no signs of struggle, no nothin'. I didn't find a thing under his fingernails, so either he trusted whoever he was with, or it was a complete surprise. No, in my opinion, he trusted his killer. Fletch, the kid was not molested in any way and there were no drugs in his system. Nothing except the remains of a pancake breakfast.

"So...? What're you trying to tell me?"

"This was no transient killer who parked his car, stabbed a kid for no reason, and drove away. The report indicated footprints—walking, not running. Fletch, you got a local killer, I think, a coldhearted son of a bitch who will do it again. The sad part is, if he doesn't, so you can see a pattern or he drops a clue, you're done, 'cause unless you get some crazy to come in and confess—and I wouldn't bet the ranch on that—this'll be another in Hallon's unsolved column."

"Jesus, Jack, you're a real optimistic guy to be around." Strand's ears perked up at the sound of heavy-treading footsteps in the hallway. He would know the walk anywhere and was cocky enough about his certainty that he yelled out, "Joe, in here!" Two or three more steps, and Bentsen's frame crowded itself through the doorway and dropped itself in the only other chair in the room.

"Thanks for leavin' a trail," the bathroom-weary partner muttered sarcastically. Bentsen sat down heavily on the honeyed oak side chair just on the left, inside the door. Strand enjoyed watching his partner settle himself, like a dog circling for a nap.

"Don't blame it on me, Joe. Doc Life-of-the-Party here led me down the path."

Bentsen and McCreary exchanged greetings, but had never developed the close professional friendship Strand and McCreary had. Although there were now three in the room, the conversation would likely continue between the first two. Strand knew Bentsen didn't resent that fact. It was just the way things were.

Strand picked it up again. "Hey, Doc, a minute ago you said something about the 'unsolved column.' Want to elaborate a bit? The only other murder around Foreston was the one in 1968, and the guilty party is down the hall from us right now!"

McCreary didn't answer. He looked at the stump of a cigar, now no more than two inches long, rolled it half a turn as he held it between his thumb, index and middle fingers, and rounded the ash in the chipped, red metal bowl on the table. His studied motion served only to heighten the suspense.

Enjoying his friend's theatrics, Strand could not resist at least one shot: "Waiting for just the right moment, Jack?"

"Maybe. I have your attention, then. My only comment is one that cannot go beyond this room." Looking at both Bentsen and Strand and waiting for assent before he went on, he trumped, "The last murder in Foreston may not have been twenty-two years ago. It may have been less than twenty-two days ago." McCreary looked up from his cigar, looked again at his companions and took a puff. The listeners waited, refusing to take the bait. "Ever hear of the Russells? The fire in Foreston on the 23rd?"

"Yeah," said Strand, remembering it being in the Christmas Eve *Herald.*

McCreary brought them up to date. "The newspaper articles mentioned a nighttime fire which had apparently ignited in the living room—a Christmas tree fire, someone speculated. What was not in the paper was that after the usual arson inspection by the fire chief, no one could be certain of the fire's origin. The bodies were badly burned."

Bentsen jerked his head toward the coroner. "So, why, Doc, is there any reason to think it happened other than accidentally?"

"Just because. I know that's not a very good answer and it would never be the official one. Yet I couldn't find much smoke damage to the interior of the lungs of either of the Russells—do you see what I'm getting at? The bodies were found in a reclining position, so the assumption would be they fell asleep in the living room in front of the tree. Combustion occurs, they're overcome by smoke, and quickly die by asphyxiation. Nice and neat, but it just won't wash. For that to have been true, they would have inhaled great gobs of smoke—excuse the medical jargon—and tried to cover their mouths in their last moments. Natural physical reactions. But there was very little to suggest that. Some would call it a tossup, but me? I put it in the suspicious column."

"If you feel that way," Strand interjected, "what're you going to rule?"

"Nothing—right now. I mentioned the possibility to Hallon and, of course, he thought I was chasing goblins. Now I'm mentioning it to you. If you're interested, you might want to talk to the daughter, Wendy Russell. She wasn't home that night—she's an RN at Foreston Medical Center—she was on duty."

"Thanks for saving me the questions, Jack. Now I can really get in tight with Hallon. We'll be so close, he'll want to make me part of his family. Joe and I don't have enough to do?"

XV

BY ANY STANDARD, Reinhard Koenig was an imposing figure.
Towering over his client, Koenig moved his frame around the
room in the same way four gallons of water swirled in a five-gal-
lon bucket—when agitated, there wasn't much room for anything
else to attract attention. He used his size to deal with less than cooperative clients and other courtroom operatives, including bailiffs,
prosecutors, judges, and juries. His Teutonic good looks masked the
power and cunning present there, and few were the women, and
men, too, who were not influenced by what passed for charm and
charisma. The lawyerly skills were thorough and well-practiced, the
learning several layers deep, but morality and decency were largely
absent from his kitbag.

Credentialed from the best schools, he seemed to have derived
nothing more than the mechanics of the social contract, never anything about its substance and his role in maintaining it. Of course,
the glib and guileful rationale he used to butter over the deeply pitted
surface of the small monument that was his life's work simply stated
that people like Marty Knotting were entitled to the very best defense they could get. For the Koenigs of the world—crass, classless
eels suckered to the underbelly of social justice—not merely working

every angle, but squeezing from it every degree of social discomfort on behalf of scumbags like Knotting, was a labor elevated to the otherwise unassailable heights of mother and apple pie.

Koenig's detractors would say that the only difference between people like him and his clients was about two feet of prison wall. His fans, on the other hand, might admit their champion was up to his knees in his own bullshit, but what difference did it make that his motives were not pristine? What mattered was that someone competent listened to the wails of anyone at the business end of the disciplinary system, and then did something about it.

Koenig built his reputation upon taking sides with the unpopular and impossible, thus making him the begrudged hero to many whose aims were not shared by the general public. Much like the ACLU's defense of Rockwell's swastika thugs marching through Skokie, Illinois, home to many Jews, Koenig enjoyed, more for the sake of his ego than anything else, taking on the difficult defense of criminals for whom the public wanted nothing more than a room with a no exit sign above the door.

Knotting's was just such a case. His client's ultimate goals being pecuniary in nature would prove suitable to him as well. His motives for taking the Knotting case had little to do with a possible money suit down the road, however.

For what he had done, Knotting probably did not deserve a good deal, but if his appeal had any merit whatsoever, then he deserved a better deal than he'd received. The entire issue boiled down to one and only one question: Did Knotting's attorney, James Milcher, responsibly represent the interests of his client or not?

When they had gone over Knotting's story two months earlier, preparatory to filing for the appeal itself, Koenig knew there seemed to be a probability of success. However, he had not been entirely satisfied with that conversation, particularly since Knotting failed to be completely candid about all available evidence. On the drive from Pittsburgh, Koenig had replayed the earlier conversation for himself, the repetition of it was less comforting to him than the original had been.

Careful though he usually was, he had committed himself to a far more tenuous position than he ordinarily would have considered acceptable. Basically, Knotting's approach had so interested the attorney that he had agreed to pursue the appeal without having first been absolutely clear about all the facts. Though he had verified certain of the inmate's claims, more questions arose in the process. Had he allowed himself to be conned by Knotting? He wasn't sure, but it would be difficult to gracefully disengage himself from the case after the preliminary hearing not very many minutes hence. This was his last chance to decide if he had a winner.

"Can we go over it again, Marty?" the attorney requested with a smile, but with power behind it that made it more an immediate expectation than a polite request. Koenig was well aware that the room in which they were sitting contributed to the intimidating force of his height and personality. Ten feet on each side, it had no window to relieve the hard right angles created by twelve-foot ceilings. The heavy Victorian oak woodwork had been badly refinished, and instead of stripping the wood, staining it, and revarnishing it, the workers had applied a sponged overcoat of imitation oak. "Cheap veneer. Like life," Koenig mumbled to himself.

"What?" Knotting's tone suggested he'd just been insulted.

The lawyer was quick to observe further that the illusion created by the pseudo-woodworkers of twenty years earlier was not much different than the Hollywood false fronts society had conjured for itself in many other ways. The contrast between the woodwork and the none-too-careful white paint job made Koenig perfectly in proportion to the small, high room, whereas the runty Knotting, sitting and staring at his counsel, was once again the board piece in someone else's game. "Nothing. Your story?"

"I was railroaded, and don't roll your eyes!"

The attorney did, indeed, lift his eyes to heaven and the cracked courthouse ceiling in search of gifted patience. "Marty," he mocked in reproach, "I am not a nun and this is not St. Violet's Nursery School. Save it for the reporters who haven't interviewed you before. For me, let's get right to the meat of our case—your conversations with Milcher and the facts we're going to present. Now," Koenig finished soothingly, "tell me again how it came about that you changed your plea."

"Like I told you before, all along I wanted that son of a bitch Milcher to take it all the way to the jury. Which we were doin' seein' as how there didn't seem to be no deal from the DA's office...."

"Marty," he cut in, "why are you so absolutely certain that the State did not offer Milcher a deal?"

"'Cause they wanted the death penalty for me—they were tryin' to prove I was the ringleader and that I was behind the whole thing. They told Milcher the best they could do was life with the possibility of parole if I plead guilty and told 'em everything."

"So why didn't you? They had you good, according to the record, and your attorney had little negotiating room. When you testify today, Marty, you're going to have to be a lot more convincing than you've been so far."

"I keep tellin' you and everybody else. They wasn't goin' to give me any credit at all for lettin' those girls go—those two crazies, Vincent and Falerno, woulda killed 'em for sure. All I wanted was twenty years and parole—I woulda been out after eighteen."

"Marty, we've gone over that ground already. The question is, how well is your version of the facts going to hold up against a county establishment whose interest in protecting the memory of one of their brighter legal lights has got to be greater than believing in... you." The oily sarcasm was beginning to get to Knotting, Koenig could tell, but he had to bring out more of the substance of his client's position, rather than jailhouse cliches.

"Look, counselor," Marty hissed, returning some sarcasm of his own, "one day in the middle of the trial, this Milcher—hey! that's funny, ain't it—like m-i-l-k-e-r—that should be your name, counselor..." Knotting laughed the inane prison laugh often heard by those who've been close to it—the kind of laugh reaching out for almost any comedy to relieve the all too unfunny boredom in a place without free sunlight. "You know, we've never talked about payment, have we? I dunno what you want outta this, but what I want is my freedom—and money, lots of it."

Koenig waited, no warmth in his expression.

"Anyway, Milcher came to me and began to tell me everything I was up against: Vincent and Falerno pleading guilty, their testimony against me, the testimony of that little shit, Duffy, the bad feeling in the community, and all that crap. I reminded him that those dumb girls admitted I let 'em go—and I thought that balanced it out, but Milcher just went on and on about how I didn't stand a chance, that I might even be executed after all, and even if I didn't get the death penalty, they might hold it against me if I made 'em go all the way through a trial. The way he explained it, I thought I'd better go along—an' look what happened: a thirty-year sentence."

Of course, Knotting's version was only that, a convict's lie unless the other information could be brought to bear in the right way. "Go on..."

"Then I met Frederick Cathcart," Knotting minced as he uttered the name, "and after what he told me, I thought maybe I might actually get somewhere. Like I told you before, it was like a col' beer to a man dyin' a thirst, when he tol' me what he tol' me. This Cathcart is an accountant and the dumbshit gets himself sent up four years ago for State income tax fraud and cheatin' his clients. I see this asshole every fuckin' day in the library—we play chess together, eat together, and—become friends, you know—and three months ago, out of the blue, the sweet thing mentions Milcher. An' I come to fine out Milcher and Cathcart were buddies—in the country club and everything!"

"I hate to interrupt your story, Marty, but why don't you pretend you're under oath right now, so I can visualize how you'll come across without all the 'dumbshits' and 'fuckins.' Okay?"

As if cleaning up the story would somehow diminish its effect, Knotting gave his attorney a reproving look and continued, "Anyway, one day he tells me how Milcher died. Milcher was only forty-one and died of colon cancer, Cathcart claimed, and the odd thing was that even though Milcher knew it was coming, everybody else was surprised to learn he had a totally clean calendar. I mean: no appointments, no clients, no nothing. The guy had a family and everything. When Cathcart first mentioned all that, I didn't think anything of it—I mean, who cares—the guy dies and he's organized about it. Cathcart was his accountant and became aware that Milcher, that shithead—sorry—didn't have any new client income for about six months before he died. Then one day, I guess it just sorta hit me, I asked my little sweetheart with the green eyeshade just when did Milcher die anyway. When he mentioned it was about April or May 1969, I thought I would go nuts!"

Knotting clearly relished reliving his moment of discovery, the second it occurred to him that maybe he could tunnel out of prison in a different way, that he might be free in a matter of weeks or months. He was almost giddy as he continued his recitation. "What Cathcart was saying, though he didn't know it, was that if Milcher was dying of cancer and knew it, and was not taking on any new work, then it just might be that he wasn't giving my defense all of his attention. And if that's true, then I didn't get a fair trial, and the motherfuckers gotta let me out. Ha!"

"And I keep telling you, my friend, not to count your chickens before they're hatched. If your story hadn't had a certain appeal when you first wrote, of course, I wouldn't be here now. But I must remind you," and Koenig pointedly looked at his genuine Rolex, which signaled to him and Knotting that it was less than five minutes to showtime, "that though you have a good story, it's a long way to party time. Cathcart is not exactly an untarnished witness, and your apparent personal relationship with him—and don't think the State won't bring that out—will be seen as biasing any testimony he might give. Circumstantially, your case has merit, it has the challenge I enjoy most particularly, but proving it to a reasonable degree after all these years may not be a simple matter. Think about that."

Rest easy, Marty, because with me, you're halfway there.

XVI

"**H**OW DID IT go?" Montgomery leaned back in his chair, a maneuver which threatened the aged venetian blinds between him and the window pane a few inches beyond. Though Lieutenant Montgomery commanded a squad of detectives for the entire West Central District, his official quarters clearly did not reflect his position or the power he wielded amongst his men and in the PSP. The frame which housed the physical presence of Walter Stockton Montgomery belied the awe in which he was held by those around him.

Some men, like Reinhard Koenig, stirred electricity in a crowd with their physical size and charm. People like Montgomery, on the other hand, compelled the attention of a roomful of people through their natural leadership skills and the sheer power of their presence. And so the simple query, "how did it go?" was uttered not to fill the space of conversation with the expectation of an idle answer, but with knowledge that one professional will get nothing less in return than a responsible reply. That knowledge, particularly amongst those who cared deeply about their work, sometimes had a petrifying effect on the addressee, and competent though he was, Fletcher Strand was no exception.

"You want the long answer or the short one," Strand replied with just the slightest hint of a stammer.

"Just a good answer'll do, my young friend. Just a good one."

"Well, chief, it's like this. In my opinion..."

"I can wait for the editorial page, Strand. Jus' let's start with the front-page stuff, the who, what, when, where, why stuff. Okay?"

Strand raised a hand, palm facing his superior, in a gesture of surrender and acknowledgement. "Got it. Here it is. This slick Pittsburgh lawyer, guy name of Reinhard Koenig, has somehow leeched onto this case. If you noticed on the paperwork, the hearing was in Judge Morrison's courtroom, and you could tell Morrison wanted to throw it out. It seems Koenig's brief was either a bit half-baked, or the evidence presently available may not be fully convincing."

"I knew all that, Strand. Quit dancing around it."

"This is how I understand it," Strand noted carefully. "Koenig is stating that Knotting was denied a fair trial back in '68 because his pro bono attorney, James Milcher, influenced Knotting's decision in the guilty plea, and may in fact have misled him, due to purely personal reasons unrelated to the case."

"You mean his cancer."

"Right. Koenig's brief indicates that Frederick Cathcart, Milcher's former accountant and personal business manager, and now, by the way, a guest of the State at Morganville, is willing to swear that Milcher may well have been informed he was terminal during the Knotting trial, and was so depressed by it, that he simply wanted the trial done with, irrespective of the outcome for his client."

"May have?" Montgomery prompted. "That's a long way from a positive statement."

"That's where Morrison had a problem. There was considerable discussion at the bench—loud at times—about the probative weight of a convict who 'thinks' Milcher 'may have' done anything."

"Well? Why didn't Morrison toss it?"

"'Cause there's a hook," Strand said, reeling in the line. "There's one piece of circumstantial evidence that lends credibility to Knotting's story. Cathcart maintains that for the last six months of

Milcher's life, he had no new client income. In other words, his legal practice came to a sudden and complete halt."

"So? The poor bastard was sick."

"Milcher died of colon cancer in April 1969; subtracting back six months puts it right in the middle of the whole Knotting thing."

"Oh, bullshit! I knew Jim Milcher. He was as honorable as they come—matter of fact, he was one of the few decent and responsible attorneys ever to stand up in that courthouse," Montgomery spat out and gestured in the direction of the court. "I can't believe a guy like that would ever have thrown a case—for any reason. You probably don't remember him, but I'm tellin' you, Strand, those bastards better not muddy up his name."

"Hyper down, Chief. Look, it's a no-win situation for Morrison. He's got this flashy attorney standing in front of him taking a shot at a local hero of the bar, and if it comes close to real, Morrison can't appear to be shoving it behind the furniture. So, he gave Koenig a 'go.'"

"Wait a minute. A 'go' on what? What exactly was the motion?"

"Oh. Didn't I tell you? A full hearing on the issue."

"For the love of God!" Montgomery fairly exploded. "Everybody's dead, damn near! How they gonna have a hearing on this, for Chrissake?"

"Chief, how do you know everybody's dead? You the one who's been keeping notes in the jacket?"

Montgomery was stunned that Strand had caught him by his own admission. Not that what he had done was a crime, but it was not the usual practice for the head of the homicide unit to clip and paste newspaper articles and notes in old files. He recovered himself with, "Yeah, what of it?"

"Nothing. Just wanted to know. You going fill me in on that?"

"Some other time," the Chief responded. "For now, just answer my questions. Did we have an attorney present? I mean, did the State bother to protect its interests in this case, or did we sleep through it?"

Strand knew that when Montgomery began italicizing his words and loading his questions with sarcasm, a nerve had been struck and that he had better be careful in his response. "First of all, Chief, Alice Wagner was there representing the State and I don't need to tell you she's first class. From what I've told you so far, you've got to figure Alice has to carry a big bucket of rocks in this case. This Koenig's a sharpie—and he doesn't take on losers. This is a highly sensitive case and everybody will be walking on tacks.

"By the way, when I said that Morrison gave Koenig a 'go,' I didn't mean to imply that his motion for a new trial was granted. When Morrison called them up to the bench—from what Alice told me later—he told them he saw Koenig's whole game plan and there would be a new trial over his dead body. They set a new date for a hearing, at which time Morrison will take arguments and testimony on the whole shebang. Then, presumably, he'll take it under advisement while he figures which way'll go down best. But," Strand emphasized, "it may never get that far. Morrison looked at Alice—she told me—and dropped her a big hint that if Koenig had anything substantive, they'd better come up with a deal."

"Did that old gasbag also give them the terms of the deal?" Montgomery rasped, still with more than a trace of sarcasm.

"Chief, you know Morrison isn't that bad. And no, he didn't deal them any cards, but Alice indicated the options might be workable. Knotting got thirty years. He's claiming that in return for a plea in 1968, he was supposed to have gotten twenty with parole. He's already served twenty-two years, so the earliest he could have gotten out was four years ago with luck. So, what it means is that Koenig has to do a lot of work and in effect, his client may get off with time served."

"What a crock! I can't believe this sleazeball Knotting can make a farfetched allegation like that, against somebody like Milcher, and walk. Pretty shitty, if you ask me! People around here are gonna have a lotta confidence in the judicial system, aren't they?"

"Look, Chief, what do you want me to do? Go blow away Koenig, Morrison, and Wagner just because a shitbird like Knotting might wind up lucky? Won't be the first time!"

Montgomery looked up at his subordinate with a measured bit of respect. "Not that long ago, you would have been railing about 'the system.' Now it's me who finds the system wanting and you, the sage counselor. Hah!"

Joe Bentsen poked his head in the door, and Montgomery motioned him in with a raised, wrinkled right hand.

"Chief," Bentsen asked, "do my eyes deceive me? You're smiling at each other? No yellin'?"

Montgomery chuckled in acknowledgement of Bentsen's mock surprise. He addressed Strand. "Okay, Fletch, you're right." Then, to both men: "From what you saw this morning, what do you think we need to do? When does Morrison want to hear something?" Montgomery's gaze landed on Bentsen.

"We've got two weeks or so—January 22nd, I think."

"Fine. I'll only mention that Milcher had a couple of children and I think the son still lives around here—at one time, there was some talk about the boy writing a book about his father for the County Historical Society. You could start there, I think, but on second thought, boys, you probably ought to dig around a bit—just to see what kind of deal might go down. Let's get the book on Cathcart, too. And anyway, we owe it to Wagner to give her something to work with."

Bentsen nodded, and left the room. Strand was right behind him. "Thanks, Chief. See ya in a day or two."

"Hey! Hold on there, young fella. Let's talk a bit about the Hilton killing."

"Now?" asked Strand, surprised.

"Yeah. Now. If it isn't an inconvenience," Montgomery parried with more supervisory sarcasm. "Matter of fact," he observed, looking at his watch, "I could use a bowl of chili and some coffee. Why don't you grab Bentsen before he gets too far and we can go to the diner—there we can talk unofficially, so to speak, about your activities on Hallon's ground." He smiled.

"Gimme a few minutes, first. I've got to make sure those two troopers took Knotting back to Morganville. Otherwise, Morrison's bailiff, wizard that he is, might think Knotting was released on his own recognizance, and there he goes." Over his shoulder, as he went out, he added, "Wouldn't be the first time for that, either! Be right back." Strand walked quickly out of Montgomery's dusty cupboard of an office and went down the hall to check with the dispatcher.

Their walk to the diner was punctuated by greetings to Mercer regulars, but none of the three looked up at the courthouse—either in admiration or in dismay—when they went past. Heads down and shoulders hunched up against the cold, they skirted the building as though it was one more barrier in the judicial system, not the pinnacle of it. They had long ago lost their innocence in the naive belief that wrongs would be righted, that all men would be equal in the law. They each had known too many Knottings, too many Koenigs, and unfortunately, had seen too many Jamie Hiltons. The mills of justice might indeed grind exceedingly fine, but not necessarily in single lifetimes.

The diner itself, on West Pitt Avenue, had been there for over thirty years, and only recently had undergone a re-sheathing of stainless steel. The long, 1930s-style railroad car effect had been carefully preserved, right down to the blowzy waitresses in black uniforms and small white hats and aprons. The place was in a class by itself, Montgomery always proclaimed publicly, but under his breath, added that nothing else would want to be in the same class with the Mercer Diner. They occupied the booth furthest from the door, Montgomery asserting seniority in taking the seat which would keep his back away from the door, thus precluding the once in a lifetime surprise lawmen and criminals always fear.

As Montgomery ordered the chili, Strand felt glad he'd not be spending time in Montgomery's office that afternoon, at which point its pungent atmosphere might be confused with that of a farmer's outhouse. Bentsen wanted a club sandwich, and Strand's order mirrored what he always ordered at Wendy's, which he was famous for: a Single Cheeseburger, Onion and Tomato only with a medium fry. $2.27.

Bentsen always wanted to know, "If you like Wendy's so damned much, why do you order the same thing every other place you go?"

"Why, just checkin' the competition, naturally," Strand always answered.

While waiting for the traditional mid-day serving of grease and unmitigated cholesterol, Montgomery opened with, "Anything new in the Hilton killing?"

Responding with serious innocence, Strand asked, "Why would you think I would have some pipeline to Hallon's crack detective force?" Then he added without impertinence, "Besides, I seem to recall your telling me just yesterday to stay out of it so you don't have to put up with Georgie's bullshit."

"That was in my office where I have to say things officially. You know that. Now we're in a public place, 'an don't be reminding me what I said yesterday. This is today."

"What's changed?"

"Nothing's changed. That's the whole point. Not that I would have expected Hallon to make a positive ident or arrest in twenty-four hours or anything like that, but that bureaucratic birdbrain knows this killing is beyond him and he should have asked for help. He won't. That would be breaking fifteen years of tradition. Get the drift, men?"

"You got a phone call or two," Bentsen stated, there being no question in his tone.

With the spoonful of chili halfway to his mouth, and his head bent slightly forward to receive it, Montgomery only stopped to raise his eyes in Bentsen's direction. The look, caught by both Strand and Bentsen, signaled a direct hit.

"You going to give us any more clues?" prodded Strand. He was not hoping for any and neither was he disappointed by his chief's response.

"I have to draw you guys a diagram or what?"

"No," Strand rejoindered. "What you want is for us to go quietly snooping around so that Georgie doesn't miss anything before it's too late, but you don't want to come right out and say it, so that if Georgie calls and gives you a pile of crap, you can tsk, tsk, and pass it on to us with a clear conscience. Jesus, Walt, sometimes the politics of it all really gets in the way, doesn't!" It was not a question.

He received another unspoken answer when Montgomery paused again—with the same look of affirmation—as he raised another soupspoon full of ground beef, colored by beans and red peppers, all swimming in a small puddle of grease.

XVII

A T THEIR DESKS, Strand and Bentsen digested lunch while completing the necessary Morganville paperwork for the Knotting trip. They exchanged incomplete sentences which, for them, served as a plan of action for the following days. Their conversation was neither meticulous nor deliberate, and all that mattered was to get the job done—and live to tell somebody about it. In the real world, their world, homicide people never planned more than a day or two in advance, and schedules always remained loose because one thing or another—usually a body—always changed them.

With the Knotting case to fool around with, Strand and Bentsen also put the Russell deaths on their itinerary, as well as a look here and there in the Hilton murder. But first, Milcher's son. That afternoon and the following day, Strand and Bentsen began what should have been the relatively easy task of locating Milcher's remaining family. The most obvious place to start was the telephone book, but no Milcher was listed.

Next, they sought the City Directory for each of the nearby communities. With up-to-date directories, people and places were cross-referenced by name, address, phone number, and sometimes occupation. In most well-developed areas, banks, loan companies, other commercial establishments, and law enforcement agencies maintained their own supply of City Directories. Libraries always had them as well for bounty hunters, repossessors, or bill collectors.

The detectives knew that occasionally, letting their fingers do the walking for a few minutes through the Directories saved days of footwork out in the elements. This time, however, there was no Milcher listed in the current editions. The detectives immediately went to a shelf where they had been before. They pored through the dust-laden old phone books and directories for further information, but gleaned only a little. In the well-thumbed 1968 volumes, Milcher & Swanson were listed as law partners, and both men knew that an Elroy Swanson was still practicing in Mercer. Bingo.

On the other hand, they weren't so lucky in finding anything on Milcher, Jr., except that James and Doris Milcher, attorney and housewife, and sons James, Jr., and Thomas, were listed in that fashion and living in Mercer until the 1969 update. Afterward, Doris Milcher showed up at the same address for one year and then disappeared from any of the local listings. Either she left the area, or more likely, remarried, they both surmised.

Donning their raincoats, Strand and Bentsen dutifully retraced their lunchtime route in the direction the courthouse, where they knew Elroy Swanson had an office on the south side of the square. They were disappointed to find that Swanson and his family were deep-sea fishing off the Florida Keys and would not be back until the first of the month. The receptionist, Marci, grudgingly provided a Florida telephone number for Swanson, but warned that he was not easy to catch. Bentsen was tempted to make a smart remark about the unintended play on words, but made no comment.

"Milcher?" she inquired, absently. "No, I don't know anybody like that. I've been with Swanson for ten years now and no one named Milcher ever came around here."

"I didn't ask you if anyone like that came around. Have you ever heard that name before?" Bentsen was more impatient than he should have allowed himself to become, but Strand hadn't done his good guy routine and Bentsen apparently didn't feel like polishing his manners on the likes of an uncooperative Marci.

The pair exchanged looks. The Swanson they'd heard about but never dealt with, handled mostly divorce and minor civil suits, and for some reason, they'd expected to enter a prosperous law office and be dealt with professionally and expeditiously. Instead, they found themselves standing in a tiny reception area, feet planted in a multi-colored shag carpeting, dirty and worn from years of use, and facing cheaply paneled brown walls, broken in their lines only occasionally by starving artist landscapes in gaudy yellows and greens.

It was almost as if time had passed through the office in the early 1970s, and never returned. Strand half expected the chunky, blonde incompetent sitting at the desk to be in a miniskirt with some sort of patterned hose underneath. That look would have complement-ed the bouffant hairdo and smeared, red lipstick nicely. She seemed to have little to occupy her time or her mind and she wanted it left that way.

"No, buddy, I ain't heard that name before neither. Zat clear enough for yuh?" The veneer had fallen away quickly, as much by the cracking gum as by the attitude. How many anxious new clients had left the reception area never to return over the ten-year period was anybody's guess.

Out on the street, Bentsen looked at Strand, raised his brow a bit, and inquired, "What're you supposin'?"

"I'm supposin' that Milcher was clearly the senior partner and the talent. When he died in mid-career, Swanson's luck died with him. Now he scavenges on the low end of the civil side and makes enough for fun in the sun once a year. But you'll never see his name heading the roster of the county bar association. Funny thing how luck can deal you a bad hand. If Milcher was as good and decent as Mont-gomery says he was—and that means he probably was—then had he lived, Milcher & Swanson would have dominated the country club set, Milcher probably carrying Swanson for thirty or more years, with Swanson sitting near the top of the heap." Strand inclined his head back over his shoulder to the office they had just departed. "Didn't turn out that way, did it?"

Strand walked into the Mueller insurance office next door to the Swanson establishment and asked to use the phone. "Guess I should have asked you the obvious question earlier, Chief—whatever became of Doris Milcher?"

There was a pause at the other end of the line, then the chuckle followed by a world-weary admission that: "Wouldn't have made a bit of difference. She remarried as you might have guessed—some government guy, I think, but for the life of me, I can't remember the name. Call me back in a while and I can check it out," offered Montgomery.

"Thanks, anyway. We'll get it." When he hung up, Strand and Bentsen exchanged the look that close partners knew well. This was one of those days—if you didn't have the bad luck, you wouldn't have any luck at all.

Bentsen said, "You know, Fletch, I wish people who watch all those cop shows on TV knew what our daily lives were really like. No fancy plots, no witnesses dyin' to talk to us, and of course, no damn luck. If a relative didn't do it, murder investigations are usually a walk through the mud."

"And when we catch the perp, it's only through hard work. Only once in a while does luck have anything to do with it."

"You got that right."

Strand dropped off his partner to an evening of Sylvia's company and headed home to Bo, no doubt tap-dancing to be let out for a necessary leg lift.

∾

Wednesday, January 10 was not a particularly special day to anyone except, perhaps, someone born on that day some twenty-three years before. There had been a birthday every year, but none were filled with toys, gifts, cake, or a little love. Love and caring in the earlier years might have made a difference, but Eddy's parents were the State of Pennsylvania and the child welfare system. There was no mom or dad, and neither had there ever been a real home for him except the local Children and Youth warehouses, or any number of foster homes.

The Nicholsons were the first foster family Eddy remembered well, but he knew nothing for sure except what Jody told him. He had been with the Dixons when he was a baby, his sister once told him, but he had no memories of them. The Nicholsons were harsh to his sister and their own children, but reserved a special meanness for him, and over the months and years, the hurt and rejection were replaced by hatred and revenge—for anyone who had what he had not.

Eddy was always on the outside looking in—and he was never sure where his sister stood, but she always seemed to be "in." Surely, she loved the bit of affection given her by the Nicholsons, and she always said she loved him, *but did she?*

His day and night dreams were colored by the same recurring image—a boy looking through a closed farmhouse window at a table heaped with food and pastries where adults and children—all people he knew—were laughing and enjoying themselves, all warmed by a glowing fire. That is, they relished their feast until they spied him peering in the window—then they stopped smiling, the dream went on, and one of the children, ordered by Virgil or Jody, no doubt, came over and pulled the curtain so that Eddy could not see. The same dream haunted him week after week until there came a time when the tears dried, and he learned to cry no more.

Lucky for the Nicholsons I couldn't find them!

Eddy decided to stay inside. It was too much trouble to go out, and to be something he wasn't, a person with a job, a place to go, or something to do. Besides, he reminded himself, he liked sitting in the warmth, thinking about the police who would never find him, and eating the cake from the Carter Farm Bakery. He had no need to go out for a few days, at least. He sipped his milk. *I didn't find the Nicholsons, but I found somebody else, didn't I?*

XVIII

THE MERCER COUNTY Courthouse was built of limestone quarried one county over, and on Wednesday, its dusty gray surface was trimmed in sleet and snow clinging to its mortar joints on the north and west sides. As the structure mantled itself, greeting-card like, the snow seemed to soften the edges of a system spiked with prickly points of law. Not an otherwise big day in the judicial week, it was more or less dominated by the quiet gossip about what was already becoming "the Milcher case."

The polished halls echoed with memory files creaking open again and again by the old timers still around who could speak knowledgeably, and there were many who were glad to offer a whispered opinion to friends and coffee companions at the blind stand, but not necessarily to private detectives hired by a fancy Pittsburgh lawyer. Strand and Bentsen knew that much of the recollection and opinion trading that day would be fondly inaccurate, a defense mechanism protective of one of Mercer's best and brightest lights, though twenty years extinguished.

The people who repeated the same phrases over and over did so in the mystical hope that endless repetition would weave a seamless garment concealing a truth they all knew was possible, but could not admit. The fact that two PSP detectives were asking about Milcher only tightened the yarn on the loom, but not before the right piece of information had reached their official ears.

Doris Milcher had remarried in the early 1970s, the pair finally heard, and now lived with her husband, Elbert Watkins, on a rural route just east of Foreston. It had not taken Strand and Bentsen long to glean the necessary bit of information, and "No," their sources stated, they had not shared their recollected treasure with anyone else. The two homicide men climbed in the unwashed Vic and headed for Foreston, where they hoped Georgie Hallon would not see them, but that Doris Milcher Watkins would.

~

The ride to the country road address a few miles beyond Foreston took less than half an hour in good weather, but today, the slush on the roads prompted the local radio station to warn of "greasy conditions," a phrase which always conjured for Fletcher Strand the image of little boys tobogining through runny mashed potatoes. The sleet hurried its way to the earth's surface as if drawn by a magnetic field, and the windshield wipers labored with the new weight upon them. Inside the car was a quiet mingling of sounds made by tires splattering their way along, the Mercer radio station muttering obituaries, and the wipers swishing their best against the weather.

The ride was barely long enough for the heater to dry and warm their feet, but it felt good anyway. The mesmeric effect was broken by Bentsen. "It just burns my ass to have to spend our time screwin' around with a twenty-two-year-old case. It isn't as if we're reopening the main issue—whether or not Knotting was guilty. It's crap like this—a goddam technicality—that gives us all a bad name. The real crime is that sleazeball Knotting might walk just because his attorney was dyin' on him. Him and those other two bastards shoulda been fried a long time ago."

"Tsk! Tsk! I can see now why the ACLU rejects your membership applications. There's just no hope for wild-eyed reactionaries like you." Strand glanced sidewards at his passenger and smiled, waiting for Bentsen's usual response to one of his sendups.

The Rockefeller salute was not long in coming. "Yure nothin' but a wise guy. Yuh know that, dontcha, Strand?"

Their interchange had at least broken the tension left in the air from the fruitless efforts of the afternoon before. Strand became serious. "Say, Joe, what's the book on Knotting while he was in prison and what is it that's pushing him right now?"

"You mean aside from the obvious? Twenty-two years in the slammer would put me in a sweat. Wouldn't it you?"

"Sure. But there was something else about him yesterday."

"Oh, yeah. Guess I forgot to fill you in." Bentsen received a "Gee, thanks!" look from his partner before he could go on. "Seems as how ol' Knotting got religion in Morganville"

"Don't they all 'get religion' when it suits their purpose?"

"That ain't all, pardner. There's a woman that goes along with the religion."

Once more, Strand gave his partner a look, this time expressing disbelief. "A woman? C'mon, Joe, he damn near told us he and that old fruitcake, Cathcart, were an item in the prison social swirl."

Bentsen was happy Strand walked into his trap. "Maybe they became an item only to keep Freddie's information flowing good. Ever think of that?" His arched eyebrows bespoke his little victory.

"Okay, Einstein. I'm not sure that's what happened, but with guys like Knotting, anything's possible. So, what's the story on the woman?"

"Name's Viki Mae something—seems she was a honey way back when an' now, she's got religion, too."

"Joe, you're just breaking my heart. You were right when you said it a few minutes ago."

"Which was?"

"They should have fried the bastards. For what those creeps did to those girls and the kid they were with, Knotting should be in the hereafter."

When they pulled up in front of the Watkins home a minute later, they looked at each other, their eyes expressing the hope fate would rule in their favor.

When Doris Watkins opened the front door, two things were immediately apparent. To Strand, it first seemed as if there had been some mistake, or the former Mrs. Milcher had a daughter no one had mentioned. The woman at the door did not seem to be the sixty-plus matron he had expected. She was—or at least seemed to be—a radiant woman of forty years, a person who kept her figure and wrinkle-free complexion by some natural or chemical sorcery. Apparently, she enjoyed the effect on others, particularly those who were the age she appeared to be and had no reason to hope they would look as good twenty years hence.

The other fact, just as apparent, was the woman's clear expectation of visitors who looked just like Strand and Bentsen. The certainty of that expectation told the two detectives there was no daughter and there was no mistake. This was Doris Milcher and maybe, just maybe, the fates had indeed placed a bit of luck just inside the door.

"What can I do for you, gentlemen?" asked Mrs. Watkins as she swung wide the door.

The PSP men properly identified themselves, but a glance at their feet by Mrs. Milcher was suggestion enough for the two to wipe them carefully before advancing too far. One look around further told Strand that the lady of the house was indeed that, and that life had not treated her unkindly since the loss of her first husband.

Bentsen opened the conversation quietly. "Mrs. Watkins? Doris Milcher Watkins? Perhaps you've been aware of events in the Knotting case?"

"Yes. My husband and I were in Florida for several weeks and just returned yesterday. Last evening's *Herald* did not have much else but this case on the front page, unfortunately."

Bentsen had struck just the right tone with the lady, and so continued in the same fashion. "Perhaps you wouldn't mind talking about that period of time."

"You must know that my husband died shortly after that trial and that this is not easy for me."

"Surely," Strand said softly, but was a bit put off by her demurral. After all, it was over twenty years ago, he thought, and she had remarried, so why the shy maiden routine?

"I've never really gotten over Jim's loss," she affirmed, not quite convincingly. "And until now, it has been my private tragedy. In all honesty, I am very uncomfortable with the publicity."

"We understand," Strand said. He'd entered the match with a slightly firmer tack than his partner had taken earlier. It was not to undercut Bentsen, but to further the direction of the inquiry. He and Bentsen had played the game many times, and generally, they scored well together. This time, he was the bad guy. He continued, "But you must understand that in all probability, we will only be the first to ask you about that time. There will be others. Private detectives hired by the other side. Reporters."

He let that sink in, then pushed on. "You can make it as easy as possible on yourself and your family by talking with us completely and candidly right now. Your interests and ours would be similar, I would think," he concluded, the hook baited. Strand waited and, in the moments spent awaiting her response, he began to tally for himself the mixed reactions he was having with this witness. He could indeed understand why she didn't wish to resurrect the past unnecessarily, but her hesitancy was beginning to bother him.

"You're right, of course, Detective..."

"Strand."

"Yes. Thank you, Detective. And your name was Bentsen, wasn't it?"

Bentsen nodded absently. Strand looked at him, too, and felt certain Bentsen was having the same reaction he had. Now that Mrs. Watkins was delaying any substantive communication with polite reintroductions, he assumed Bentsen was becoming as convinced as he was that when the end of the story came, not everyone would live happily ever after.

"I can see that you gentlemen are wondering why I appear reluctant to discuss this whole issue. I'll tell you as best I can." She had their attention. "When Jim found out he had colon cancer, our whole world ended. We were very close, in the prime of our marriage and family life. We had young boys of whom we were very proud. We wanted nothing more than to finish raising them together—did you know that our oldest, Jim Jr., was only eleven years old?"

"No, ma'am, we were not aware," Bentsen responded, eyes cast downward.

"Picture if you will, then, our lives back then. Jim had a wonderful career starting with service in the Korean war and law school—Case Western Reserve. He did extremely well in his practice and my goodness, there was talk of him for political office—maybe even to the Congress. Financially, we were just beginning to do well, and Jim's reputation for excellence and integrity could not have been at a higher point.

"Our two boys, eleven and eight, were old enough to understand and cry themselves to sleep at night. And believe me, Mr. Strand and Mr. Bentsen, I wasn't too old to do that either—it took three years and Elbert Watkins to stop my tears and self-pity. Jim died less than a year after Robert Kennedy was assassinated and the phrase 'cut down in the prime of life' was used often—in our own little world, it could have been said about Jim, too. Please remember that back in those days, colon cancer was a veritable death sentence—like some lung cancers still are. Oh, they attempted to treat Jim's tumors, alright, but the chance for success was tenuous at best. Jim knew that. We all knew that." For a few seconds, Doris Milcher looked her sixty-some years as she lowered her head. "Jim's chance proved to be zero—his last six weeks were agony for him, utterly helpless, just waiting for the sentence to be carried out."

"Mrs. Watkins, do you understand that should Knotting's attorney wish it, you could be called to testify?"

"Of course, I understand that, but what good would that do anyone?"

"Mrs. Watkins, everything you just said to us would be extremely valuable to Reinhard Koenig."

"To whom? Oh...him." Her eyes were red and full. "Why would he want to ruin a dead man?"

"Reinhard Koenig does not strike us as the kind of fellow who would give your position much consideration, ma'am. To put it as bluntly as he would put it, your husband is dead. His client is not."

"I can't believe anyone would put a creature like Knotting above what my husband stood for."

"Believe it, Mrs. Watkins, believe it. It's his job, like it or not, and he will want to show that your husband was so devastated by the diagnosis of his illness that he threw aside everything else for you and the children. A lot of people, including Judge Morrison, would find that a very human position to be in."

"That's absurd, gentlemen. I know full well what I just said and I would say it in court, but one thing is certain. My husband would never, never, have given up on a client."

"Even though life had given up on him?" It was a harsh remark for Strand to have made, but he knew that harsher things would be said about Jim Milcher before this case was over with.

Mrs. Watkins stood up. "Mr. Strand, that was cheap." She looked toward the door. "I don't see how I can be of any further help to you."

Strand began moving toward the door, but in a slight panic. They hadn't gotten the two pieces of information they really came for. He tried again. "Mrs. Watkins, I'm terribly sorry if anything we've said might have offended you—I can assure you we intended no harm, but it is our job, too, to determine the facts as best we can."

"I'm sorry, too, Detective. I had a wonderful first marriage that was taken from me and I've been lucky enough to have been given a very pleasant second life. The ending to the first was painful, and I seldom think about or discuss it. Obviously, I'm very sensitive about it—this has not been easy."

"We understand," Bentsen soothed. He knew as soon as the words were out of his mouth, Strand would give him a raft of grief about his bedside manner—later. "Certainly, we cannot appreciate what you've been through."

"What remains, Mr. Bentsen, is for me to protect Jim's memory for myself and my sons—I would hate for the last public mention of his name to be in the context that he deliberately failed to do his best for a client."

"Yes, ma'am."

"That simply was not the case. I don't pretend to know much about the legal profession, of course, but there were other options, weren't there? I mean, if he thought he was too ill to proceed, he could have asked to be relieved, or Mr. Swanson could have taken over. Or maybe, what Knotting got was the best he was going to get—or deserved. I hope someone considers that before they go burying my husband's reputation with him." The fervor in her voice belied the fact that the husband she just referred to had been dead for two decades.

"Yes, ma'am," Bentsen agreed, "I'm sure a lot of people will be thinking all those things. For now, we need as many facts as possible, and we were hoping James Jr. might help us out."

"Why him? I told you he was too young to remember."

"You did, ma'am, but we've been given to understand he was writing a book about your husband at one time, and that he has all of Mr. Milcher's records?"

"Yes, of course. You're absolutely right," Doris Watkins spoke without enthusiasm. "He's now a professor of English at Green Mountain College. Of course, they're on break for another week, you know."

"Do you know how we can reach him?" Strand asked.

"No. You see, he's traveling somewhere out West, and since Elbert and I have been away ourselves, I really have no idea how to reach Jim." She lied. They knew it, but couldn't say it.

Strand did not blink an eyelash. "Then, Mrs. Watkins, could you tell us who your husband's physician was? I mean, who would have been treating him during his last illness?"

Whether she expected the question or not, Strand and Bentsen couldn't tell. A few seconds went by before she spoke.

"You mean Dr. Holcomb? He's retired now. I don't know where you'll find him."

Strand and Bentsen had run up against a woman whose instincts might be older than theirs, but were just as strong and protective as one might expect. Had Doris Watkins been just another perpetrator and under intense questioning, it would have made no difference. She had no obligation to provide assistance to either side in this case, and except for the minimum level of cooperation necessary to preserve her world as she wished it to be remembered, it was clear that she intended, with grace and tenacity both, to give them nothing of value. Strand and Bentsen thanked her for her time, and left quickly.

XIX

A S THEY SETTLED back against the cold vinyl of the Vic's front
seat, Strand and Bentsen each breathed silently, and in disgust,
said nothing at first. Strand kept his hands in his pockets while
Bentsen drove. Thankfully, the ride into town was a short one, as
the cold air blasting from the car's heater vents seemed to symbolize
the effectiveness of their investigation thus far. Yet, as the whine of
the blower motor continued to fill the silence, it also served as a reminder that like the heater, their work was just beginning.

"Maybe *Dragnet* could let us have Joe Friday for a few days and
our luck would improve!" Bentsen said, slapping the dash with the
flat of his hand. "Son of a bitch!" he added in frustration.

Strand was unstartled by the explosion of temper, feeling the
same sense of helplessness as his partner. Repeated dead ends, like
those of the last twenty-four hours, were not unusual in their business—they peppered the daily menu of all homicide investigators.
The depth of Bentsen's feeling was all the more understandable because their case—Knotting's—was different. Different, because it
should have been an easy one to work.

Strand added, evenly, "You're right, Joe. It smells bad, and we're
thinking the same thing: it's gonna go bad, but we'll have to play it

through." With a trace of a smile, Strand teased, "There's a bright side, you know..."

"There is?" Bentsen asked with the mask of disbelief he reserved for Strand's occasional pretense of unrealistic optimism.

"If we're having a bad time of it, do you really think that whatever two-bit keyhole peeper Koenig hired is doing any better? Just wait. If we all keep walking into walls, Koenig'll have to ask for a continuance, and that's okay by me—as long as they're in court and you and I are out looking..."

"Yeah," Bentsen smiled, "and Knotting's still in the slammer."

~

On the way to Wendy's for a burger lunch, Strand wondered aloud, "What do you think is going on with her?" He was referring to Mrs. Milcher.

"I was wondering the same. Everybody seems to have a secret, a past they don't want remembered, right?"

"For sure, but why did she lie about not having a contact number for her son? I don't know of anyone who would leave the home base without some way of getting in touch with someone dear who's also left town. What do you think is up with that?"

Bentsen sighed, "My guess is that she realized her testimony about the devastation of her hubby's illness would devastate his memory, as you suggested, so I'm guessin' she wants time to talk to her son first, to make sure there's nothin' in the old man's papers to make things worse."

"Yeah, that's probably it."

Without either of them having actually said it, Strand felt Knotting's might easily become a dead bang loser of a case in the 1990 judicial climate. Having no luck whatsoever on a case like Knotting's was hard to take, but add to that the half-bridle on the Hilton kid's killing, and a powerful frustration level would begin to build.

Bentsen changed the subject. "By the way, I never did ask you where your folks came up with 'Fletcher.' That's a real blueblood of a name for a cop. What's the story on that?"

"I know we've talked a little about this before, but here's some more. I guess I'm a crazy mix of Scottish and Polish."

"Now there's a soup!"

Strand chuckled. "And 'Fletcher' is an old family name, meaning a maker of arrows, but it's not helping us hit any targets today, that's for sure."

"And Aurora? She's as Italian as they come, isn't she? At least that's what her cooking tells me. How come you don't weigh as much as I do?

"Hah! In the genes, I guess. You know, my father was the first renegade when he married a girl who was neither Scottish nor Protestant, but back then, the pressure was so great, my Catholic mother went to church with him. Then I married the beautiful Aurora Tomaselli, and made it worse for myself, anyway, by returning to Rome, as it were. My mother was happy!"

"Jeez, Fletch, no wonder you had to put up with a lot of PSP crap when you converted. I remember that now, but I never really understood what that was all about."

"And didn't you tell me you were Lutheran? So you at least jumped the Protestant bar."

Bentsen laughed out loud. "Yeah, but I don't practice, and you know Sylvie's Jewish. She goes to temple in New Castle and drags me along sometimes, but it's not for me." After a moment, he asked, "Does Aurora ever talk about her family way back when?"

"Come to think of it, Joe, she's only rarely dropped a hint or two, so God only knows what's there in that closet." *There's something there—I know it, but will I ever get to ask her?*

Quiet enveloped the car. Strand liked his partner, and having worked with several over the years—the last nine with Bentsen—he knew that almost any combination of people worked—as long as they had a few common threads to hang onto. It was okay if both were quiet, if both were talkers, or if one talked and the other didn't. Those combos were all okay—if and only if they had something to respect in the other. If not, partners drove each other nuts in a few months, or they complained to everybody who would listen, but almost never would they request a change.

Strand also knew that the better two officers got along, whether they talked or not, the better the job they did whether together or apart, and the longer they lived when in a tough situation. Even so, partners knew the sore points to stay away from. They were well aware that, as in any other close relationship, there were tender spots just below the surface and, if scratched, life in the car could be as raw and miserable as any of the worst moments in a good marriage.

"I'm guessin' I know what's really bugging you," Bentsen said.

For a full thirty seconds, each one seeming daylong, Strand made no response. Finally, his voice filled the human silence in the car. "I guess I didn't realize how much that Hilton kid's murder hit close to home, how much he and Aarie might have had in common—age, school, a lot of things. Now I don't have Aarie, and the Hiltons don't have their Jamie."

"Fletch, are things that bad with you two?"

Strand shrugged his shoulders, but said nothing. They had not talked much about the separation. Bentsen understood the privacy of the matter—oftentimes partners kept their marriage out of their working relationship in a foolish attempt to convince themselves that one had nothing to do with the other. Nevertheless, it had been sitting with them in the car, between them in the office, around them on the job.

"Never mind. I shouldn't have asked—none of my business."

"That's OK, bud. I guess it gets down to the notion that we are who we were."

"Are we gettin' a bit dramatic here, Fletchy boy?"

"No. No drama. Aurora still holds it against me that people on my father's side have been complete assholes about her background—that's one of the reasons I became Catholic, by the way, to maybe shut them up—but it didn't make any difference. 'The past is always with us,' Aurora always says, and she says she has her reasons to feel that way."

"Well, I can see why the Hilton thing is getting to you, but you gotta get a grip, man, if we're gonna be any good with these cases."

"I know, Joe, you're right."

"So how 'bout letting me agree with you on one thing? Let's get some grub," he pleaded.

Bentsen's deliberate non-sequitur hung in the distance between them. Continuing his stare out the window, Strand said, "Sometimes you have to wonder what the Hilton kid would grow up to. Another war like Vietnam? Or worse? And Aarie with him?"

"Oh, Jesus! Couldn't you be morose on a bright summer day? That would be easier to take."

Strand turned his head back to Bentsen. Into the quiet, Strand measured his words, "Maybe, too, I'm just a worry-wart type, and we'll all live happily ever after. Some people see in the coming world a better blending of people and problems, more coming together to work out solutions. That would be the happy ending."

"But?"

"But I don't see it that way. No, what I see is that people are still people, and although we've had the Ten Commandments for three thousand years, we don't seem to be that much more civilized than when Moses was a boy. There'll always be greed and lust, and because of that, people like us will always have a job, right?"

"Godammit, Fletch, you don't give up, do you! Christ, stop talkin' right now, or otherwise the world'll end before we get to eat." He took a breath. "Here I thought I was ridin' with Strand the cop, but no, it's Philosophy 101 I get on a cold winter's day! Don't take yourself and your bad dreams so seriously. Lighten up, will ya?"

"Okay, Joe," Strand surrendered, half-smiling.

Bentsen sighed, deeply, as they pulled up to Wendy's. "Thank God! We're here."

XX

AFTER THEIR ROUND of hot grease with a Diet Pepsi chaser, Strand and Bentsen drove out to the address on Capitol Boulevard, where the Russells had lived. It was not heavily populated, and most houses were owned by upper middle-class people.

"We doing this to keep McCreary happy?"

"Yeah, that, and maybe a fresh deck of cards," Strand muttered.

While nearly all of the houses seemed to be on two- to threeacre lots, this was a street typical of small towns in Pennsylvania, maybe small towns everywhere. It was distressingly clear that homes which might value at one hundred thousand dollars were immediately adjacent to modest affairs topping out at thirty thousand.

"Could be worse," Bentsen said. "Could be trailer houses still on wheels right next to these mini-mansions. These people are lucky— no old refrigerators on the front porches." The mood was changing.

"Yeah. Or truck tire flower gardens in the front yards."

"What're you laughing it up about, Polack? If you lived here, there'd be a flock of pink flamingoes out front. You people just can't resist it."

"Better than a sauerkraut factory, you fat-assed old fart!" They were both laughing as they pulled into the deserted driveway at number 633.

Strand, in particular, appreciated the house immediately. He had lived in several homes in his life, had to do restoration work on all of them, especially the present old barn of a place, and consequently, had developed an uncommon insight to older construction patterns and architectural detail. Before the fire, he thought, the house must have been an impressive, red-brick colonial with white trim, dark-green shutters, and black asphalt roof to match the glossy black front door.

From the street to the house itself, it was almost two hundred feet, and the drive was the kind that circled around to the right so that you drove into the garage from the back. Strand supposed the house must have been one of the earliest to use the concept of an integrated garage not visible to passersby.

The fire had not confined itself to the back of the house, but neither had the fire consumed it. As Strand and Bentsen began to circle the home, the damage was partially masked by the frozen white blanket caressing it, as well as the blackened debris undoubtedly on the ground underneath. Built in the 1940s, Strand guessed, the house was still about 80 percent intact.

Standing directly on the walkway in the center of the main part of the house, Bentsen could see that the fire had taken most of what had been the living room, which occupied the space left of the front door and running from front to back. Through the hole in which a large bay window might have been mounted, they could see a fireplace centering the east, outside wall of the house, and a pair of French doors complementing the room on the back, or south, side of the building.

Recalling the description offered by McCreary, Strand guessed that the Russells' Christmas tree must have been centered in the now-missing front window. It took little imagination to picture the lit tree in that window two nights before Christmas and the elderly couple enjoying it in their favorite chairs close by. Harder was it to conjure the fire that took them away forever.

While Bentsen remained still, apparently reconstructing the scene for himself, Strand walked around to the left and was now behind the house, where from a new vantage point, the structure looked essentially undamaged. He surmised that the fire, though intense, must have been contained within fifteen or twenty minutes, but too late to save the Russells. They must have been close to its origin and deeply asleep, he decided.

"What're you looking at?" Bentsen asked as he came to stand alongside his partner.

"Just peeking through these French doors to the front to see what I can see. I'm a bit surprised that the daughter hasn't had more work done on the house by now—it's been three weeks and it looks like all they've done is to seal the fire-damaged spaces from the rest of the house. The damage we can see is fairly extensive, but the rest of the house may be habitable."

"Maybe to a young woman who just lost her parents here, it's not. Besides, not many contractors work around the holidays—not unless they can help it."

"Yeah. You've got a point, Joe. Definitely not what you'd want to come home to. Christmas or any time of the year. She works second shift, do we know?"

"Yeah. That's what McCreary was saying. So, what's so interesting about these doors?"

"Oh, I was just curious. See this pane?" he asked pointing to the bottom of the left-hand fifteen light door. "Looks like a piece shaped like a small pie wedge cracked in the frost of forty winters, I expect." Strand grabbed the door handle near the cracked pane and rattled both doors in an attempt to see how secure they were. As he did that, the pane of glass he'd just inspected fell out and, in the cold, broke into three or four smaller shards on the frozen wood surface of the deck. Strand was surprised, and looked closer at the place where the glass had been. "Hey, what do you make of this?" he asked, and pointed at the spot from which the wedge of glass had fallen.

They both bent close to the door, where it became apparent someone had used a glass cutter to cut it about three inches out from each corner of the pane—what must have been thin strips of glass were still visible in the mullion of the door. "Glass doesn't crack quite that way from the weather," Bentsen said.

"Whoever did it," Strand noted, "had simply arced the glass cutter from point to point. Either the piece had never been taken out once cut, or it had been carefully replaced so as to look like an ordinary crack in an old window of an old house." He looked down at the deck, at the pieces of glass lying there, and wished one of them had realized the piece's significance before it became plural.

Bentsen donned a pair of latex gloves, pulled an envelope from his pocket, and as best he could, slid the shards inside for analysis by the PSP labs in Harrisburg. "Probably an easy explanation for this," he remarked, "but I just don't know what that might be."

Next, they took the short steps toward the double-doored garage, each door having four, one-foot square glass panes at eye level. Peeking in the windows at the one car occupying the two-stalled garage, they saw a 1988 Chevrolet Caprice Classic—a vehicle one might expect an older couple to have, Strand said, and added, "I hope that the daughter starts it once in a while before the battery dies."

Otherwise, there was nothing remarkable about the garage or the rest of the house, for that matter, except that Wendy Russell was no longer in residence there.

Stamping their feet to shake off some of the wet and cold, they climbed in the state car and drove the hundred yards or so to what appeared to be the closest neighbor. She was waiting for them.

XXI

M RS. MILDRED MARAVITZ almost never had much to do, contrary to what she'd been telling her husband for the past twenty years. Generally camped in her front window with the sheers pulled back, she sat reading magazines and watching the goings-on along the parts of Capitol Boulevard she could see.

It had not caused her eyestrain to have spotted the muddied, dark car pull into the Russell drive about twenty minutes earlier. The two men who had gotten out were reasonably well-groomed and well-dressed, she had noticed, but they had on old raincoats, and didn't care about walking through the snow without boots. Of course, Mrs. Maravitz couldn't see much detail over that distance, but once she got out her binoculars and went to an upstairs window on the west side of the house, she could. Ultimately, she concluded that the strange men were police officers of some kind, but she was almost certain they were not Foreston men. She had just made up her mind to give Chief Hallon a call about the two when they got into their car and headed toward her house. The phone call could wait.

Hurrying down the stairs, straightening her dress as she did so, the squat, square woman forgot to wait for the bell. She pulled open her door just as the two men were reaching in their pockets for

ID—there was a moment when neither resident nor visitors knew what was going to happen next.

"What can I do for you men?" she asked in a shrill, excited voice.

Bentsen introduced himself and Strand, and indicated that they wanted to talk to her about the Russells.

"Well, I don't know," Mrs. Maravitz responded coyly. "Would Wendy want me to be talking to you?"

"Yes, she would, ma'am. Can you help us out?" Bentsen continued.

"I suppose so. Won't you come in, please?" Immediately casting her eyes downward, she pointed and ordered, "but wipe your feet." The last was not a polite request. She ushered them into her living room filled with winter's daylight, making the afternoon shadows surrealistically overbright.

"What can you tell us about them?" Strand prompted.

"What, precisely, did you wish to know?"

Bentsen moved toward the window, squinting as he did so, obviously to determine her angle of view. "It looks to me, Mrs. Maravitz, that you have a great view here."

"Indeed, I do," she smiled.

"The entire front of the Russells' house, along with the driveway, right?"

"Yes."

"So, Mrs. Maravitz, how did it all happen?" Bentsen asked with his sweetest voice. "Would you mind if we took a minute to go over that?"

"No. I don't mind at all. I was wondering if you people would ever get around to asking me about it, but then again, I told myself, it was all an accident, they said, so why would anyone want to talk to me?"

"So," Bentsen continued, "I take it you haven't had a chance to tell anyone your story yet."

"That's right, Detective, so I hope I can remember everything. Where do you want me to begin?"

Strand and Bentsen exchanged expressions of relief. *Maybe we have an actual witness here—somebody who remembers something and wants to tell us!* A second part of the exchange suggested disgust that no law enforcement officer had yet asked her any questions before writing the fire off as an accident. Bentsen helped her along. "Start with whatever you remember first."

"Certainly. Let's see." She sat down in the peach-colored club chair, evidently her perch for all occasions. "It was a night cold with a light snow, and I remember hoping that we'd have a white Christmas if it kept up. I think we wound up getting about an inch or so—the temperature stayed right at the freeze mark for three or four days after that, and oh, we did get that white Christmas after all, because it snowed about two inches the next day. It was wonderful," she observed, forgetting entirely the context of the conversation.

"Mrs. Maravitz," Bentsen interrupted politely, "was there much activity on the street the night of the fire?"

"Well, I think the Knudsens were having a party that night and there were quite a few cars near their home—you can just see it—about two doors down and across from the Russell house. Otherwise, there was just the usual sort of traffic now and again."

"Do you mind if I ask were you home alone that night, ma'am?" asked Bentsen.

"Why do you ask—does it make any difference?" she asked, not impolitely.

"It makes no difference, of course, ma'am, but I was wondering if you were busy around your home, watching TV, perhaps. I just wanted to get an idea whether you were able to steadily observe the activity on the street or whether you just casually noticed the goings-on as you walked past the window."

"Just why do you do all that wondering, young man?! Why don't you just ask?" Without a pause, she went on, "For your information, my husband had the flu that night and was laying on the couch in the family room—he was the one watching TV, but he was making such a fuss about his little aches and pains that I came here in the living room and sat without the lights on for the better part of two hours or so."

She stopped, obviously reaching back for the most exact fix on the time. "I think I came in here about nine-thirty. I just sat here watching the snow fall and listening for Rudy—my husband—in case he really needed me. I left the room two or three times for a few minutes, so I missed very little."

"Could you tell if there was any activity at the Russell house that night?"

"I'm almost sure there wasn't. I had talked with Kathleen Russell that very afternoon—she told me that she and Johnnie were going to take it easy that night. They and Wendy had been very busy getting ready for Christmas and they were all very tired, she said. I know she mentioned Wendy was going to be at the hospital, and that was a perfect time for her and Johnnie to sit in the living room and just enjoy the tree." Mrs. Maravitz's voice cracked slightly. "You know, I've hardly talked to anyone about this, except Rudy, and it's just so hard for me to think of them dying right there in front of their tree." She stopped briefly.

Bentsen spoke. "That's all right, Mrs. Maravitz. Take your time. We know it's hard for you. Were you very close to the Russells?"

"No. Not close," she said with a tissue to her eyes and nose. "We were very good neighbors—almost ten years—and we socialized on occasion, but we were not close friends, if you know what I mean."

"We understand," Strand said, not knowing exactly how close was close. "Did Mrs. Russell say anything else that day?"

"No. Just casual conversation. I remember laughing a little when she told me that Johnnie was getting antsy because of the weather forecast. The Russells were several years older than we are, and to them, an inch of snow predicted was something to be concerned about. Anyway, she said Johnnie was getting nervous because he had only a quarter-tank of gas in the Chevrolet and he wanted to get it topped off before the weather hit. Can you imagine?" she asked, laughing a little. "What am I laughing about? Rudy is like that now—I don't have to wait until he gets older."

"Do you know if they had any visitors that evening?"

"I'm almost certain they did not. As you can see, from where I was sitting, I can see past the front of their house, across their driveway very easily, and I saw no one drive up."

"Anyone walk up?" Strand asked carefully.

"Of course, that's possible, but I don't think so. Capitol Boulevard is not well-lighted, but everyone's home was lit up that night and with the snow falling, it was even a bit brighter than normal. Except for the few minutes I was out of the room, I'm sure I would have seen someone on foot near their house, or anywhere for that matter. Just why are you asking such a question?"

"Oh, no reason in particular, Mrs. Maravitz," Strand said, "but naturally, we have to check out all possibilities," he said easily, then went on, "Now, Mrs. Maravitz, about the fire itself. What happened, as best you can remember?"

"As I recall, it was about 11:15 p.m. I might have been dozing slightly. Anyway, I remember thinking I would go watch the weather on KDKA, when I looked down the street and noticed that a lot of the Knudsens' guests had already left, but the street seemed bright as day. It took me a minute or so, I'm terribly sorry to say, before I realized all that light was coming from the fire. I remember standing up, horrified, before running toward the telephone. Somebody—maybe at the Knudsens'—must have called already, because I heard the sirens before I could dial the number. I remember shouting out to my husband, who must have been sound asleep. Then I put on my coat and stood on the front walk where I could see the flames coming out of the bay window and climbing to the second floor. All I could think of was that Kathleen and Johnnie were supposed to be sitting in there. Oh, my gosh!" She held her head in her hands and shuddered.

The men waited.

"It didn't take them long to put the fire out—it seemed to be mostly in that one area of the house, but it was pretty clear that no one walked out of there. I went closer—with the other neighbors—and after a while, we saw them carry out two stretchers, all covered up." She paused while trying to compose herself, not totally successful. "What was especially terrible was that when they were bringing out Mr. and Mrs. Russell—sometime around midnight—was exactly the same time Wendy came home. From what I was told, she hadn't known about the fire until she drove up to the ashes of it—and the scene of them carrying out her mom and dad. It was awful!"

"Had she been very close to her parents?" Bentsen asked.

"Very much so. Have you met her? Wendy is an extremely attractive young woman—maybe in her late twenties—and she spends—spent—most of her free time taking care of her folks. There was very little social life for her, and she did everything for Johnnie and Kathleen. They were wonderful people, very loving, very community-minded. The Russells will be missed, I'll tell you. I just hope that Wendy decides what she wants to do with the property so that it can be fixed up for some nice family to move into. Not good for a nice home like that to stand empty, if you know what I mean."

"Yes, ma'am, we understand perfectly. Now if you'll be so kind as to tell us how we can reach Ms. Russell, we won't take any more of your time."

"Oh, it's no trouble. No trouble at all. Wait a moment, and I'll see if I wrote down the address. Of course, you can always catch her at the hospital after about 2:30 every afternoon, you know."

While she searched, she said, "I don't often enjoy the company of others, you know, and this has been a pleasant change from Mr. you-know-who." She fussed in her purse. "Here it is. I thought so. She's staying with a friend on Woodfield Drive. It's a two-family home at 212 Woodfield. She and her friend live upstairs, I believe."

"You said you haven't seen her much since the fire?" Strand asked, fishing for more.

"That's right. Once, I saw her in town with her roommate, Darla something, and another time or two, she came to the house, usually with somebody, to pick up some things."

The two detectives expressed their thanks for her very detailed memory and her willingness to help them out a bit. Before they left, they asked her if anyone else might have known or seen as much or more than she had. Mrs. Maravitz, expert witness that she believed herself to be, noted without irony that it was unlikely anyone on the street had noticed as much as she did, but of course, the men were free to check it out for themselves.

Once out on the driveway, Strand and Bentsen smiled at each other. "You know, Joe, that was a very satisfying interview, but for the life of me, I don't know why I think so. For almost two days now, every contact we've made on a criminal case has been a dead end, yet the one source we talk to about an accidental fire gives us everything we could ever want to know. If that don't beat all!"

XXII

DESPITE THEIR LUCK in finding Mrs. Maravitz so easily, the detectives checked out a few more homes—with the eyes of Maravitz upon them—finding no one at home except at the one house they had hoped: the Knudsens. After all, they were home that night, and either they or their guests might have noticed something of interest. Not so.

Mrs. Knudsen wanted to be very helpful—at the door. She saw no need to invite the two men inside, thus indicating her helpfulness would be brief. She was careful to note that she and her husband, and most of their guests, whom they had seen over the holidays, had all discussed the Russell fire and had compared notes. No one had noticed anything the least bit unusual—it might have been difficult to notice any person or vehicle out of the ordinary that evening— the Knudsens and their guests all assumed that others on the street might have had company that night, but no one knew for sure. And no, she did not know who called the Fire Department.

Strand and Bentsen knew that tracking down the guests and quizzing them about strangers in the neighborhood would be, likely, a waste of time—how would the guests know who belonged or did not belong on Capitol Boulevard that evening? They decided not to spend the time unless the Russell incident became a case actually assigned to them.

"Of course," Bentsen said, "we've satisfied Doc McCreary's curiosity, right?"

"Yes, but two facts rule against an easy disposal of this case—what the doc said about their lungs, and now a wedge of glass." He looked at his partner. "So, we have something to chew on while we deal with the likes of Marty Knotting and the Hilton boy's murder."

"Hmm! That piece of glass—we'll see what the lab says."

~

Bentsen looked at his watch. "You know, it's just about two o'clock. Think she's still there?"

"We'll find out," Strand said as they drove off to the Woodfield Drive address, less than a mile away. "Whether we get her there or at the hospital, we'll need to get as much information as we can before going to the fire chief. Otherwise, we run afoul of Hallon."

"Right."

In the company of mixed emotions, they soon found themselves in the Woodfield driveway. While no luck accompanied them on the Knotting affair, they were having luck on a case they were never assigned. "Fingers crossed," Strand said as they climbed out of the Vic.

At the door, they met Mrs. Simpson who, at that moment, spoke just the right words: "Come right in, gentlemen. You're in luck. Wendy is still here. Let me call upstairs to make sure she isn't in the shower yet; then you can go up." A pert woman with a commanding energy, Mrs. Simpson quickly left the room. She returned momentarily, but when the visitors began to rise, she gestured them down and suggested, "You may as well stay seated, gentlemen. She'll be down in a minute."

"Uh, Mrs. Simpson, have you known Wendy Russell long?"

"Why, Officer Strank, it's only been since Christmas that I've known her personally, but our daughter has talked about her a lot from their work at the hospital. You know these nurses. They have their routines. Shower before their shift and shower right after. It's all about germs, you know. And these days, with AIDS and whatever else is out there, they can't be too careful. They say you can catch these crazy diseases at the dentist, you know. Well, as I was saying, often, they've worked the same shift together, but today is different. Darla's working a double for someone who called in sick..."

"Strand."

"I beg your pardon," she said, as if wondering why on earth the policeman would be mentioning another name at this point.

"Nothing, ma'am. I was asking, has Wendy been staying with your daughter since Christmas, then?"

"Yes. That's correct. What a shock it was. We received this phone call around midnight—of course, Darla had just come home and was still up, but me and Frank, we were in bed already, and wondering who in the world would be calling here at midnight and all."

Strand concluded that the poor woman must have nobody to talk to during the day. He wanted to conclude the daughter invited Wendy Russell in, not in sympathy for her tragedy, but in self-defense from Mother Simpson—or possibly, someone else for Mother Simpson to talk to. He bet that Frank worked nights most of the time, slept days, and did it that way on purpose. Strand cast a quick, penetrating glance at his partner, who sat on a nearby side chair with a dreamlike expression on his face, probably trying not to laugh.

Finally, Bentsen coerced himself into participation. "It was awfully kind of you and your daughter to take her in at that hour. Can you remember, Mrs. Simpson, how it all came about?" Though his voice was gentle, Bentsen's compelling glare suggested she stay on the narrative track.

The woman with the densely curled hair, sixtyish, slack skin, and well-worked, thin lips, wasn't sure she liked addressing two men at once, and showed her preference in that regard by continuing to voice her remarks in Strand's direction.

"Like I said, we got the call at midnight. Darla had stayed downstairs watching *White Christmas* on TV. I wasn't completely asleep and heard her answer the phone—naturally, I listened—we never get calls that late. Why, it could have been an obscene call or something like that."

"And..." Bentsen prompted, sighing.

"I listened," she repeated, again avoiding eye contact with Bentsen at all and continuing to cast her lines to Strand, "and next thing you know, I hear Darla saying something like, 'Oh, my God, Wendy' or something like that. So, I got up—I let Frank sleep—and Darla told me what happened. Darla hadn't changed yet..."

Strand was tempted to ask about all those germs, but contained himself.

"...and she offered to go get Wendy, but the girl asked if she could come over and spend the night. Of course, we said she could—my, was she broken up! She was still in shock, almost numb-like, in a trance. I don't think she comprehended what happened yet. Poor girl. How would you like to go home to find your home burned and your parents in it...dead. That's not easy for anyone, I daresay."

Bentsen, again: "So, the Russell girl was going to spend only the one night?"

"That's right, but once we—Darla and I—heard all the details, and she and Darla were such good friends, why it was only natural that she stay on for a while. You know, we converted our third floor to an apartment for Darla—keeps expenses down for her. It's a big enough place—plenty of room for another girl."

"Makes sense," Strand said.

"Wendy has no relatives here, and after the funeral, she needed someone around her. When it finally hit her, she took it real hard—didn't eat for several days and just cried her eyes out. I didn't know the Russells myself, but I've heard around that they were just wonderful people and Wendy had remained very close to them. She's a pretty girl—you'll see—and she could've married and had kids and moved away a long time ago, but a good daughter she was, and stayed right there with them. Why..."

Wendy Russell walked into the room and everything stopped. The men stood up immediately. In front of them stood a beautiful young woman whose presence filled the room like the scent of lilac fills a yard in June. She was dressed for work. It wasn't simply that her beauty was striking or overpowering—it was everything about her which caused the effect. A soft brunette with radiant, unmarred skin and unflawed figure, she was a nurse who must have kept a few male hearts beating long after their time. Until she reached the middle of the room, she hadn't made a sound, but she must have heard at least part of the conversation. With just a slight emphasis on the personal pronoun, so as not to offend her benefactress, Russell said, "How can I help you, gentlemen?"

Standing, Strand introduced his partner and then himself, and indicated they'd like to talk to her privately, if possible.

"May I ask what about?"

There was nothing odd about the question, but the manner in which she asked it surprised him. He couldn't say why—not then, not ever—but at the time, he believed she had something she wanted to hide. Was there a tone of guilt in her voice, a point of concern, or merely, a legitimate question? What he could say for certain was that she was cold.

"Your parents. The fire. Do you mind?" He was deliberately terse, in fact, blunt, in his attempt to stir an emotion in her.

"No. I don't mind. You can come up, if you like," she said flatly. The three of them climbed the stairs to the comfortable, spacious third floor which consisted of a sitting room, two small bedrooms, and bath. It was decorated in rosy and light-green hues, probably the colors Darla Simpson put together for herself not long before, when she accepted her life with mom and dad for at least a few years longer.

Wendy showed them to a couch and they all sat down. She seemed careful to look down the stairs before closing the door to the studio apartment. "You should know I have to leave for work in a few minutes."

"I understand," Strand said.

"Also, I think you people owe me an explanation."

"How so?" It was Bentsen's turn.

"It's been almost three weeks since...since the fire, and no one—I mean no one from any police department—has uttered a word to me, and all of a sudden, two men show up...and from the State Police? What's going on, and why is the State involved?"

Strand watched the young woman intently. Doing so became more difficult as her scent loose in the closed room assaulted him with springtime fantasy. Russell stayed cool and self-possessed, and while she showed no outward antagonism, there was a tense defensiveness about her he found off-putting.

"The State is not involved, Ms. Russell. The fire at your parents' home occurred within the Borough of Foreston, and of course, that would be within Chief Hallon's jurisdiction."

"How helpful, Mr. Strand. The Borough hasn't done anything—if anything is to be done—but the State, which you say is not involved, is around asking questions. How can it be clearer? You might try a little harder."

Strand wondered on which side of the window glass clung the frost, but tried harder. "Sorry. I guess that wasn't very helpful, but in return for my candor, may we ask for your discretion?"

"You'll have to take a chance, Mr. Strand. Right now, I don't know what you two are up to, but of course, a call to the Foreston PD would settle that, wouldn't it?"

"Not exactly," Bentsen chipped in, grabbing her attention. "It would bring on something none of us would want. Go ahead, Fletch," he said, looking at his partner, "lay it out for her."

Strand did not speak right away. He clasped his hands, elbows on knees, and leaned forward, set his jaw, and appraised the young woman in front of him. The studied actions were for her benefit. He and Bentsen had known they'd have to explain their presence at some point—how and when they did it was to be largely up to the witness.

"Ms. Russell, it's this way. Do you know Dr. McCreary, the coroner?"

"Yes, of course. I see him at the hospital often enough, but I really don't know him personally. What does he have to do with this?"

"A lot, if you respect him as we do. But if you don't, he has no part in it at all."

"Mr. Strand, you're getting cryptic on me again, and with a shift ahead, I don't have much patience for it."

"Sorry—again. Joe and I don't seem to have this much of a problem interviewing our witnesses, yet I seem to be saying all of the wrong things to you. Can we start over?"

"Oh," she asked assertively, "am I a witness being 'interviewed'?"

"Yes, I guess you are—and you didn't answer my question. Do you have a high professional regard for Doc McCreary?"

"Yes."

"Then I'll put it simply. He is not satisfied with the conclusion Chief Hallon wants to draw about the fire and the deaths of your parents—that they died accidentally as the result of an ignited Christmas tree."

"What?! Why doesn't he simply talk to Hallon about it?"

"The Chief is looking for a comfortable solution to what may be the cause of death. It's just that Doc isn't willing to dispose of it that easily."

"I'm listening. How does he think it should be disposed of?" The unveiled sarcasm was heavy, challenging.

"Doc McCreary hasn't offered an official opinion as to what's happened, exactly. One fact seems to bother him: there was very little smoke residue in the lungs of either of your parents. That suggests to him that they may have been dead before the fire began." Strand stopped talking abruptly so he could concentrate his full faculties first on Wendy Russell's face, her eyes in particular, and secondly, on her hands. He did not have to wait.

The words had the same effect on her as an unexpected slap on the face. Wendy half inhaled and stopped, all without melodrama. A second or two later, when she recovered her natural rhythm, she spoke, the weight of Strand's last statement slowing down each word as it left her lips. "How can that be? I mean, what could have happened to them?"

Was she being too naive, too unsuspecting? Strand didn't know, but her innocent tone did not easily replace the measured sarcasm of her manner moments before.

"We don't have an answer—yet." At that point, he hesitated, then continued. "As your parents' bodies were badly burned, it is very difficult for the more common autopsy tests to make anything at all very conclusive. Anyway, no other than the obvious cause of death surfaced." He watched her face when describing the condition of their bodies—she didn't flinch. *Is it because she's a nurse and she's calloused to it, or is it because she arranged for it all to happen that way? Farfetched, maybe, but that kind of bloodlessness wouldn't be a first.*

"So, the coroner has been dawdling around for three weeks now, and he doesn't know. Well, I know. They're dead...d-e-a-d, and what else I know is that I have no mother and father and nothing to go home to anymore!" She didn't cry. There was only anger.

"Ms. Russell," Bentsen joined in, "can you tell us more about that night, the events leading up to it, the activities of your parents?"

Wendy didn't need to compose herself, just focus her attention. Her overall demeanor didn't change. "What do you think you'll find in my answer?" she asked coolly.

"Don't know, Miss, until you give me one." It was a classic Bentsen comeback, and it prompted the desired response.

A barrier gave way. In a monotone, she began the narrative she had evidently recounted for herself a hundred times before. "I've thought about it over and over again, that last day. Of course, I saw them last about two-thirty in the afternoon as I walked out the door to go to the hospital. Everything was normal—it always was with them. Dad was fussing about a storm warning and Mom was trying to ignore him. The usual.

"I called during my dinner hour—it was quiet at the hospital that night—right around seven o'clock. They had just finished with the supper dishes and were going in the living room to light a fire..." Her account came to a stop while she remembered, then suppressed the image. "...light a fire," she repeated, "and enjoy the tree. We talked briefly about a few things we needed from the store, but that was about it."

Bentsen continued while Strand intently observed her reactions. "You know, Wendy," he submitted, "the holidays are sometimes a stressful period for some people, despite what they're supposed to be about. You and your folks have anything to feel stressed about?"

"Talk about loaded questions. Look, detective, I think I already gave you my answer. Everything was normal—and I meant it," she said, irritation showing.

"Sorry, I didn't mean..."

"Yes, you did. If you have any more like that, let's get them out now."

Strand got back in the game, and 'game' it was. His tone was not aggressive, nor his voice loud or intense, but quietly direct so that he had her complete attention. "I have to say something very candidly, Ms. Russell. I think we've been honest with you—we're taking a chance with our jobs here just to check something out that does not look right—and your reactions tonight seem less than cooperative. You seem to resent what we're doing. Can you explain that?"

Her response was a bit warmer, but still not satisfying. She inhaled deeply. "Mr. Strand, I guess you don't understand how I feel. I'll put it this way. This past Christmas, I lost everything I had—you can imagine this so-called holiday will never be the same for me again. For the last three weeks, I've been trying to accept the burden I've been handed, and now come a couple of strangers who have no business in the case, they tell me, and inform me that maybe it wasn't an accident after all. Well, if somebody did that to you, just how thrilled would you be with the whole thing?"

"Not much, I guess. Okay, that's all we have for now. Can I ask you a favor?" he asked, not waiting for her answer. "And that is, would you mind not discussing this with anyone? As I said before..."

"Don't worry, Mr. Strand," she responded agreeably.

They all stood up and walked to the door. Just as they took their first downward steps, Strand turned and commented, off-handedly, "When we were at the house today, I noticed the car still in the garage, and it didn't look like it had been moved. If you don't mind a little bit of advice, you ought to turn that engine over a time or two before you won't be able to."

"Thanks, Mr. Strand. I went out there to do just that about a week after the fire, and you know, when I started it up, I let it run to warm up a bit, but it stalled out. I don't know what the matter was, but I think it was out of gas. Can you believe it? Out of gas! I just haven't gotten around to going back there much—it still bothers me—a lot." She paused, then said, "I've got to go," she said, and followed them downstairs.

After a few seconds of totally unnecessary pleasantries with the inquisitive Mrs. Simpson, the detectives made good their exit and the Vic carried them away into another of winter's gloomy days.

XXIII

N THE CAR, Bentsen said, "You know what I can't get over?"

"I can't imagine."

"Mrs. Simpson has to be Mrs. Maravitz's sister, don't you think?"

Strand chuckled. "You know what I can't get over?"

"Wendy Russell. A strange one, isn't she?"

"Yes, and I wonder why she seemed so nervous," Strand added.

"Don't know, but I don't see her as having any part in the deaths of the Russells."

"I'll give you that. Otherwise, we still do not have enough for Pat Curtiss to declare the fire an arson."

"Right, Fletcher, my boy. Tomorrow's another day and we'd better hit it hard on the Knotting thing."

At the hotel, Strand exited the car, and the frigid darkness grabbed at him as he walked up the steps toward the hotel's front doors. He half-expected Bo to be sitting near or on one of the lobby's worn mohair couches, and he hoped Earl had remembered to let the old dog out a few times. To see his tail wagging in welcome would have been a treat, but no such luck. He looked around for signs of a cleanup. "Bo, are you here?" he called out to the deserted lobby.

Strand knew the dog would not be at his side if there had been an accident. No, Bo would appear when the evidence was gone. That was his M.O. As if on cue, he stood at the head of the stairs, tail wagging so vigorously, his entire back end swayed in rhythm. The dog didn't care if he was going to get the world's longest lecture on his personal habits; he was glad just to hear his master's voice. Not any voice would do. Bo was old, and lonely for Aurora and the kids. Strand didn't want to think about that. He was glad to see his four-footed buddy, and for a few hours to sort out the day's gleanings.

After a supper of fried hamburgers, microwave French fries, a small salad, and a cold beer, coupled with the evening news, Strand sat in his room, feet up on the coffee table, and continued his musings about the day.

He was surprised, at first, at his attraction to Wendy Russell. In his line of work, he'd had many opportunities to go beyond casual conversation with any number of women. He had always been faithful to Aurora, however, and resisted considering other options.

Wendy Russell was different. Maybe it took a month of loneliness to make him think about the young woman in schoolboy terms, certainly in less than professional ones. Her youth scared him, her indifference teased him, her distance pulled him. He could not think about Knotting, the Russells, or the Hilton boy any more than he could lay new shingles on a roof in the middle of a cold January night. It was a perplexing young woman who occupied his waking thoughts, and soothed him to sleep with idle dreams of distraction.

He ached when he awakened at 2 a.m., slumped against the couch pillow and chilled to the bone. He rose to turn off the TV, then fell back on the couch, pulling over him a heavy afghan for the rest of a long night.

The hours of easy reverie left his mind's landscape in favor of other, more compelling pictorials. They were snippets of the week's footage, shots from a private, lifelong movie which he continually edited and improved, but never released for public viewing. There were the dead eyes of the Hilton boy staring up at him from their watery rest, Knotting and the criminal carnage at the abandoned gas station, the Russells' gasless car.

~

The next two days passed quickly, but without the progress Strand and Bentsen had hoped for. Finding Jim Milcher's doctor, Winston Holcomb, had not been difficult. At seventy-eight, he had been a resident at the Lee Manor nursing and retirement home in Mercer for a little over a year.

Facing him in the sunroom—gloomy with the subdued light of snow-laden clouds—Strand could see a man unduly victimized by age, and he wasn't sure exactly what they would hear. A few minutes into their interview, he hoped that the doctor's evident senility had not been a hallmark of his practice for his last years on the job, since Bentsen's wife, Sylvia, had had a hysterectomy at his hands.

"Dr. Holcomb," Strand was asking, after the pair had introduced themselves, "do you, by chance, remember an attorney from town named James Milcher?"

The old doctor immediately surprised them both when he said, "I certainly do!" He began talking about the longdead lawyer as if it were yesterday—indeed, in Holcomb's mind, it seemed to be. "Cut down in the prime of life," he said with the kind of reverence reserved for what had become an oft-uttered phrase. "I had warned him many times about diet and the need for more frequent physicals, particularly since his own father had died of stomach cancer. Like many people back then, he paid no attention." Holcomb's was the pleased voice of vindication when he recalled giving Milcher the news.

"It was on an early fall day—I'm not exactly sure of the date—but I think it was the day after the Columbus Day golf tournament—we both played that day. 'You've got six months!' I told him. I explained to him about chemotherapy, and radiation was another option, but I told him he'd better not plan on another season of golf."

Holcomb had the tone of one who had survived many seasons of dread and death—somehow triumphant that his current state was a testament to the celebration of life. Just as quickly, however, the light in Holcomb's eyes evaporated and he began muttering about his service with Eisenhower's staff just before D-Day and how quickly a rifle could rust in the English damp and fog.

Bentsen chanced a question, nonetheless. "Doctor, do you have any idea where your old records might be?"

Holcomb was blank and silent for what seemed a hundred-second minute, then laughed, when he cried, "Swanson knows! Ha! Swanson knows!" Strand and Bentsen exchanged glances and left the sunroom.

In the lobby, Bentsen spoke first. "That ties that!"

"Guess so," Strand replied. "Good thing they can't put that one under oath."

"Yeah, but if somebody caught him at a lucid moment, he would sound pretty convincing—and Knotting could walk. Even so, we'll give this to Wagner and she can decide what to do with Holcomb and Doris Milcher."

"You give up too easily," Strand counseled. "Even if there's tons of evidence that Milcher had terminal cancer and knew it, Koenig still has to show that Knotting didn't get the best deal he could get—and that Milcher let it happen."

"Maybe you're right, Fletch, but I can just hear Koenig now when he tells the judge, or a jury if it comes to that, that James Milcher, eminent man of the bar who had just received his own death sentence, devoted his last energies to see that a crumb like Knotting didn't get his best deal. They'll all believe that one. Sure, they will..." his voice trailed off.

"We live in an upside-down world, Joe. The good guy's the bad guy, and the bad guys get to walk among us."

They knew, of course, that the Swanson in Holcomb's meanderings was none other than the none too apt survivor in the partnership of Milcher and Swanson. With Swanson still fishing in Florida and his mindless flunky of no help, Strand and Bentsen judged it pointless to pursue the lead. "We'll circle back to Swanson when he returns to the land of snow and slush."

They stopped at the PSP barracks, scratched out some paperwork, and made a few phone calls before trying to unearth any more dead ends out "on the bricks." Milcher's son had not checked in at the college, but Bentsen obtained an address for James, Jr., and after lunch, they took a ride to Harrison, PA, in an attempt to find him at home, or at least, determine if he had returned to town. It was all to no avail. Milchers house was closed up tight, confirmed by the number of weekly throwaways near his front door. If Mother Doris had reached him by telephone, James, Jr., would not be coming home until his calendar required it.

~

Their evidence bag empty again, Strand dropped Bentsen at his house in Mercer that evening. He could see Sylvie waving at the door. As they parted, Bentsen pointed at the gas gauge and suggested that with the temperature expected to drop to near zero, Strand might want to fill it up on the way home. Bentsen also mentioned chatting with Pat Curtiss, the Fire Chief, the following day to see if they could nudge the Russell case—such as it was—a little further along.

At the KwikFill, Strand pumped in the Super Unleaded the car's engine required. Dark was coming, and he was glad to be getting that little job done now, even in the subfreezing air, rather than in the morning hours when it would be much colder and the tank, near empty. As he capped the filler tube, his mind raced through conversations which had not digested themselves well over recent days.

There it was! Mrs. Maravitz's telephone conversation with Mrs. Russell on the afternoon before the fatal fire played itself back and he compared it to what Wendy Russell had said. Could the two be accurate? Of course, if her father never went to town that day as Mrs. Russell indicated he would, then that would explain it. But if he had gassed up the Chevrolet as he expected to, how could it have been out of gas when Wendy tried to run it? Absently, he paid the clerk at the window, and began the ten-mile drive back to Foreston.

On automatic pilot the whole way, he could not have later recalled the brief journey if his life depended on it. His mind was filled with

Wendy and the apparent fact of her father's empty gas tank. He brought himself up short a few times during the ride, and later as well, for allowing himself to weigh a source's testimony in less than objective terms. She might be lying about a great many things, including her father's car, but for whatever reason, he did not know. *And why didn't she do something about the house?*

A couple of chipped ham sandwiches and kosher spears safely tucked away and eased down with a cold Yuengling, Strand searched his notes for the hospital number and poked the touchtone phone carefully. After going through the phone tree and waiting for the third-floor desk to summon her from a patient's room, he finally heard her voice.

"Ms. Russell, this is Strand, PSP, and I'm sorry to get you off the floor, but I need to know if you've done anything yet about your father's car."

"You called me here for that? Is that the only reason you called?"

"Because it's out of gas, and yes, that's the only reason for the call."

"Mr. Strand, I'm going to hang up if this is your idea of a joke."

"Sorry. I guess you don't see. Let me be sure of something before I say more." He proceeded to review her statement from the night before. She had started the car, he noted aloud, but ran it for a short while, and then, it stopped. Strand asked her to be sure she hadn't let it run very long while she was doing something else, forgetting about the time.

She insisted she hadn't. "In fact, I went into the house for only a few minutes to pick up a some personal items and to make sure the heat was still on in the parts of the house that had been sealed off from the fire. Ten minutes. Maybe fifteen. I went back out to the garage, and the engine was already dead. I tried to restart it, but it wouldn't turn over." She added that she was running late for an appointment, and so left the car as it was.

"Would you mind if I checked the car myself?"

"That would be fine, but what's this all about?" When Strand asked her about getting into the garage, she told him what most other people knew, that an extra key was under the decorative flower pot to the left of the garage door. Also, she noted there was a set of keys under the driver's mat, explaining that, "Since Mom and Dad rarely locked the house and didn't like to carry keys, they always left them around."

Strand finished the nighttime quiz by asking Wendy where her father got his gas. She told the detective that her father had been dealing with Phineas Geiser for over fifty years, that Geiser and his wife, in their eighties, still ran the small store and twin gas pump that formed the source of their livelihood, at a crossroads a quarter mile from the Russell house.

Strand said he knew the place, thanked her for providing answers to his unusual questions, and said goodnight. Later, when he replayed their conversation, he told himself she seemed more open, less defensive, and more willing to share what she knew. At least, that's what he wanted one part of himself to believe.

XXIV

F RIDAY WAS A miserable day in virtually every respect. The light
snow from the midnight hour spread a shiny glaze on all the
roads, making travel difficult, and to compound Strand's early morning ride, the mere act of checking in at the office invited
the assault of Walter Montgomery's dozens of questions about their
activities over the few days past. He expressed disappointment in
Strand's and Bentsen's progress, particularly in the apparent direction of the Knotting case, reluctantly acknowledging he could think
of no angle they hadn't tried.

The lack of any new or worthwhile information in the Hilton case
was next on Montgomery's impromptu agenda. Bentsen and Strand
reported to Montgomery, and he to them, from his own sources.
It looked to be a page ten *Herald* story in very short order, they all
agreed.

Last, Montgomery's subordinates detailed the interesting subtle-
ties of what was best described as the Russell inquiry. Helping them
to take their next step in the quasi-official effort, Montgomery mentioned seeing Foreston's Fire Chief climb the courthouse steps not
twenty minutes earlier. "Probably going to visit his girlfriend in the
county tax office," Montgomery winked broadly, and added, "she

might be the only one Curtiss's wife didn't know about."

Strand and Bentsen donned their coats and headed in the direction of a witness about to be coaxed into a talkative mood. The policemen had been avoiding a contact with someone like Curtiss because of their assumption that the man's first telephone call after a conversation with the PSP would be to none other than Chief Hallon. For the moment, chance offered a friendly hand.

Bentsen walked into Ginny Gervase's office and in a few minutes, walked out with the errant Curtiss. Over coffee, they reviewed Curtiss's knowledge of the Russell fire. "Of course, my file on the case is back in Foreston, so the details may be a little gray," he stalled.

"Never mind where the file is, Patrick me boy," Bentsen carried on, "just focus your mental abilities on the main points and we'll be alright."

Curtiss glanced at his inquisitors and said, "Look, there's no point in trying to hide anything. The circumstances of the fire raised a few questions in my mind, but every question has an acceptable explanation for it."

"Such as?" Strand asked.

"As I explained to Georgie Hallon the following morning, Christmas tree fires are tough. If the tree is dry and the fire ignites there, then it burns very hot very quickly, and that explains the burn path of the fire through the ceiling. The Russells lived in an older home filled with older furniture pieces, and being in the usually dry winter season, there were enough factors to explain the heat of the fire."

"Say more," suggested Bentsen.

"Look. Joe. Fletch." He looked at his questioners pleadingly. "What do you want me to say? It looked like an accidental fire to me. Short in the tree lights. Tinsel and tree decorations are ignited, and in less than two minutes, you have an inferno."

"Right," agreed Strand, "and Mr. and Mrs. Russell just sat there and enjoyed it. They didn't even move out of their chairs. Neither of them."

"You're saying they were already dead?" Curtiss's eye seemed to wander inward.

"Doc McCreary says there was no smoke in their lungs."

"Hmm!"

"I think you get it," Bentsen said, and added, "I'll also point out that most people's trees don't get that dry until after Christmas. The question is, did the tree burn hotter than it should have? Could it have been helped along by an accelerant? By kerosene or gasoline maybe?"

Curtiss answered quickly and carefully—he had apparently anticipated the question. "Of course, it's possible, but we found no traces. Your suggestion would explain the unusual heat and power the fire must have had at first ignition."

"Just to repeat. A flammable agent introduced to the scene would explain certain facts about the fire and its course. Is that what you said?"

As if he were answering an attorney's questions under oath, as indeed he knew he might be at some later time, Curtiss opined, "Yessir."

"By the way, Pat, who's the girl in there?"

"W-who do you mean?"

"Where I saw you leanin' over her desk? That one?"

"D-don't get the wrong idea, Joe."

"I already did."

"So, what of it?"

"This whole conversation should remain under the cone of silence, know what I mean?"

"S-sure thing, Joe. You can count on me."

~

At lunch, Strand knew Bentsen could see his thoughts might have been elsewhere, on his kids, missing from him and missed. As good friends do, Bentsen steered the conversation toward departmental gossip, the major question always centering on Montgomery's replacement should he ever retire. While reinforcing with repetition their never-changing opinions on that and a number of other equally low-tension topics, the partners inhaled their cream pie slices and a few more cups of coffee.

Finishing up, Strand asked Bentsen about something in the back of his mind. "Joe, you noticed, didn't you, all the news clippings in the Knotting file? I mean clippings about events long after the trial?"

"Yeah, now that you mention it, but I never gave them a thought."

"You know, I think Walt must have been collecting those. Any reason you can think of he'd want to do that?"

"Naw, unless it was just curiosity on his part."

After a relieving turn in the tiny restroom, they stepped outside into the twenty-degree temperature, well-warmed and whetted to the case at hand.

Strand pointed the car toward the Capitol Boulevard address that had seen years of the Russells alive and, suddenly, dead. In a few minutes, the car crunched through the snow in the driveway and came to a halt, their entrance, no doubt, witnessed by Mrs. Maravitz. In step together, they walked to the rear of the empty home and stood facing the right-hand garage door, the one closest to the main part of the house. Eyeing the foot-high stone pot, Strand gingerly tipped its weight away from him and reached under for the key—exactly where Wendy Russell told him it would be.

"Wait, Fletch! Gloves!"

Nodding, Strand gloved up and eased the once-shiny brass key into the garage door's gritty lock, then raised the paneled wood door it on its rails as the two of them ducked a bit and went inside before the door was all the way up.

Strand looked around. On the inside, right wall was a door leading to the house. Halfway back on the same side was a faucet and next to it, on the floor, a garden hose casually coiled near the wall bracket where it probably hung at other times. There was a small workbench against the rear wall, which was, in fact, the front the house, and on the left of the double bay, the left bay being were Wendy Russell parked her car, Strand concluded, there was a row of neatly mounted hooks for all manner of garden tools. "I wish my garage looked as neat."

"Yeah. Everything in its place."

Strand nodded, surveying the scene.

Bentsen reached for the driver side door of the Chevy and clambered in behind the wheel. With winter clothing on and a few too many pounds forming a large center of gravity, Bentsen groaned as he reached down and fished around under the floor mat. Finding the keys, still on the little metal ring provided by the dealer, Bentsen fumbled one into the ignition, and attempted to start the car. The engine wanted to turn over, and cranked itself with no result. He tried several times with the same outcome, but didn't continue for fear of running down an already weakened battery.

Strand unscrewed the gas cap and bending close, sniffed.

"Bet it smells of gas," Bentsen offered in his best wise guy fashion.

"No shit, Sherlock!" Strand retorted. "Yet it doesn't smell like a tank with gas in it. Look around. See anything we can stick down here to see if there is any?"

"Don't see anything of use. Wait a minute." Bentsen crouched down, careful not to soil his coat, and reaching under the rear of the car, he knocked on the bottom of the tank. Even with the heavy rustproofing, the sound rang hollow. "I don't think we have to bring in a mechanic to prove the point. Do you?"

"No. Guess not. Still, it doesn't make sense, does it? The guy has a quarter tank of gas—or more. He goes to his favorite pump, tops it off, and probably comes straight home. Okay, maybe he and the Missus go an extra mile or two running some errands in town. They come home and put the car in the garage. Less than eight hours later, they're dead. So where did it all go?"

Bentsen shrugged. "Maybe we're making too many assumptions," he added hopefully. "Maybe he had less than a quarter tank, a lot less, and maybe he never made it to the station, and maybe the Russell girl ran the car longer than she thought. So, it's out. Don't tell me we're standin' here freezin' our asses off while we figure out what happened to the gas! For cryin' out loud, Fletch, it's pretty damn cold out—you ready?"

"Yeah, I guess," Strand conceded reluctantly. One last time, he glanced around the garage before he went out and closed up after them. "Let's go see whatsisname, the guy Russell dealt with all those years."

"'Right. Guy's name is Phineas Geiser," Bentsen said, consulting his small, for him, palm-sized notebook as he walked back to the car. As he looked up, his partner had a vacant expression on his face once more.

Strand had stopped still a few feet from the car, still deep in thought, waiting for the pieces of the puzzle to right themselves and begin fitting together. Bentsen did not disturb him—he knew not to—but waited until he could wait no longer. "Fletch!" he bellowed.

"What's your hurry?" Strand asked, still in semi-trance.

"Gotta go again. Too much coffee and too damn cold. C'mon, let's get to this gas station. This is one of those times when personal and professional needs nicely coincide."

"Go on the side of the garage."

"And give Mrs. Maravitz a show? Hell, no. Let's go."

XXV

EISER'S GAS WAS something from another era. As they drove up, Strand could easily imagine their car as a 1946 black Ford Coupe, and out they would step, two plainclothes cops in gray cloth overcoats replete with shined black shoes and dark-gray fedora hats. The effect on him was heightened when he looked closely at the white frame building, green-trimmed, and shingled on top, one of hundreds of such small roadside stops with an attached single-stall garage and covered drive that punctuated the byways of America for thirty-five or more years—until super-highways made them extinct, or nearly so.

Two pumps were out front, and Strand guessed there had never been more. The old man kept his head above water by selling more than gas, motor oil, and cigarettes. As they saw when they entered, it must have been easy for him to add groceries at decent prices for people who just needed bread and milk, and the like.

Mrs. Geiser was behind the counter, itself not that much newer to the world than the rather elderly woman behind it. After identifying themselves, Mrs. Geiser cocked her head to one side and yelled out, "Finny!" in the clearest ear-splitting tone she could manage.

Bentsen took advantage of the wait for the male Geiser to ask for a certain room's location. He moved to his task, and during the minute or so he was inside, he heard another "Finny!" but this time with a note of forced patience. His return to the main room was timely.

From the back stepped none other than Phineas Geiser himself, gallussed trousers complementing the pale-striped collarless shirt tucking itself up under the stubbled white whiskers, all two days' growth of them. Over the rimless glasses, rheumy eyes focused keenly on the two men standing there, and finally, he said, "You the tax people? If 'n ye are, you kin jist git the hell outta here!"

"No, sir," Strand responded quietly and in the mildest, least threatening tone he could muster. Again, he identified himself and his partner, and explained they were just checking into a few details on a matter of interest to the coroner, and he was wondering just how good Mr. Geiser's memory was.

Geiser took the bait. "Memory! Bet mine's better 'n yours, buddy! Go ahead, ask me somethin'," he stated, issuing a challenge of his own.

Pausing for emphasis, Strand asked, "Do you remember how the day went on Saturday, December 23rd last?"

"The 23rd? Sure, I do," the non-plussed Geiser said when, then stalled a bit. "Let's see, it was a pretty cold day with a threat of snow for the next. Had quite a few people in picking up odds and ends they forgot in town."

"Sell much gas?" Bentsen prompted.

"Oh, about normal for the time of year. Whyda yuh ask?"

Strand took over. "Do you remember Johnnie Russell coming in that day?"

"Sure do! T'was the last time I ever saw him—I 'spect that 'cept fer Missus Russell, who was in the car withim, I wuz the last one to see 'im at all." The words were spoken with the conviction of one who had survived much.

"Tell us what you remember about Mr. Russell's stop here that day."

"Well, it was kinda funny, now that I think about it. Him and Missus Russell musta been a fussin' at each other for one reason or t'other. Anyways, he musta been a little flustered. Seems he left home with nothing but a few dollars in his pocket, and she had no money on her at all. He was mad as hell when he handed me the $3.48 he had on him and told me to give him what I could for that. He muttered something about wanting some peanuts, but decided he needed the gas more. Well, I enjoyed the hell outta that little scene. They both sat stone-faced in the front seat of thet car while I put in exactly $3.48 worth of gas—about three gallon. They both gimme season's greetings—none too merry-like—and drove off."

"Mr. Geiser, do you mind me asking how long the Russells have been customers of yours?"

"'Bout half a century, I 'spect," he said with certainty.

Bentsen scratched his chin. "You mean to tell me you wouldn't have trusted him for the remainder if he needed a full tank of gas on a cold night?"

Geiser spoke with all the patience he had, knowing that those who didn't know it always had to have it said to them, "Mister, he didn't ask and I didn't offer—that's why we did business with each other for fifty years. Can't say it any plainer."

With a joint "Thanks," they left the Geisers to what they liked best: their own business. Bentsen could not resist it. "Now, what do you think? That didn't get us any further than we were before."

Strand chuckled. "Old Finny wouldn't be my best friend!" His tone turned serious. "Actually, I don't think anything right now. Let's stop back at the office. We can call Harrisburg to make sure yesterday's courier got that piece of glass to them. Other than that, I'm not sure the rest of the day will be worth any more to us than any other part of the week has been."

"You got that right. Let's go." Bentsen said he couldn't allow himself to disagree with an idea taking him closer to home on a late Friday afternoon. Reasonable hours. Dinner at home. That was the kind of policework he liked—when he could get it.

Strand politely declined an invitation to supper at the Bentsens', Sylvia worrying aloud that Strand looked unrested and stressed; that, or he didn't like her cooking. Strand claimed the latter an impossibility, but indicated he didn't feel like company, no matter how good the friends or delicious the food.

XXVI

BACK IN FORESTON, he stopped by the hotel, made sure the dog was okay, and walked up to Anthony's, run by his barber's uncle, Anthony—not Tony—Thomas. Aurora had once told him she and Anthony were distant relatives. "A couple of things you should know about this town," Aurora had told him when they moved there after their marriage, "half the people around here are related, so you'd better watch what you say about someone—you're probably insulting a cousin."

He had laughed, he remembered, and asked, "What's the other?"

"Way back when, some of the Italian miners here did one or two things they're not always proud of. They made their last names sound like easy, 'English' names so they'd fit in better." She lowered her eyes. "Still others gave up on their religion. Few talk about it. They don't want to be reminded."

Why any of that came back to him on his walk, he had no idea. At Anthony's, he spent exactly ninety minutes, first savoring a fresh tossed green salad along with a half dozen garlic rolls swimming in their own oily lake at the bottom of the plastic bread basket lined with waxed paper. Mariana, his favorite waitress, had come to expect him every Friday night for a month or more, and she knew he was in no hurry to finish and leave. He always asked for a booth near the back with enough light to read by. An open book or newspaper kept people from inviting themselves to join him. As usual, Mariana waited before turning in his dinner order, and it was always the same: a large, deep bowl of thick, meaty tomato sauce and meat balls mounded over steaming spaghetti, all accompanied by Thomas's homemade bread slathered with a good grade of butter. Coffee, several cups of it, with the extra cream he requested, followed the meal.

At 8:25 p.m., Strand glanced at his watch, decided the weight of the food he'd consumed wouldn't throw off his balance, and eased himself out of the booth, leaving Mariana a good tip. Not only was she a good server, she never asked why he was always alone.

On the way back to the Penn Grove, the week's collection of misaligned facts began to break out of his subconscious, and vied for guidance from the owner of the intellect. The puzzle pieces were not ready to tumble into place, however.

As he entered his room, the telephone rang its first signal of brighter times to come. Strand knew it was Aurora and he was glad for the call. "Hello," he said into the receiver, his voice carrying all the expectation of a high school junior talking to the date of his dreams.

"Fletch, is that you?"

"Who else but," he answered, expectations realized. "I guess I knew it was you."

"Then you read my letter."

"What letter? Just a minute." Strand picked through the stack Earl had left him. Back at the phone, he said, "Yes. It's here. Should I read it now?"

"No, silly! Honestly, Fletcher. It's from me and the kids—it says we miss you."

"Does it say when you're coming home?"

"No. We're not ready for that yet."

Strand's patience was thin. "When do you think that might be?" His voice was a little cooler now.

"I thought we covered that earlier. I need more time."

"Time will be our undoing, Aurora. Time will tell us we can

live apart, not together. Time will make us consider alternatives we might have once thought unthinkable."

"Fletch, is that supposed to be some sort of dressed-up threat or something?"

"No threat. Not dressed up. It's just that our partnership will never get any better in separate cities, houses, rooms, or beds."

"Sounds like you ought to be writing your book instead of talking to me—plainly—about our marriage. "

"Not at all, and I am speaking plainly. I want my family together. Here. Now. That's not too literary, now is it?"

"No, I guess not. Honey, you know the kids and I love you—it's just that things aren't completely sorted out yet. I know this hurts and it's not easy for you—for us either—but I need more time. That's what the letter says. I've been getting some counseling, and it's doing me—us—some good. I want to finish that—then I'll be surer than I am right now."

Strand was at once relieved and stunned. That she would ever admit she needed professional help, much less actually seek and use it, was a giant step forward. He was momentarily speechless. He could only think to say, "All right, honey, whatever you think." They talked about the kids for a few minutes, and Strand promised to call them on Sunday. A tender goodbye ended the conversation.

Immediately, Strand sat down and tried to absorb what he had heard. Not only might the marriage continue emotionally, but rationally as well. He tore open the letter and read it over several times. Yes, it was all there. What she said. She meant it.

~

Eddy Snyder spent his Friday dressed in the clothes which had hidden him well. He walked all around Foreston pondering what to do next.

Careful to wear some makeup and have his wig on just right, he felt more comfortable that people he didn't know would have no reason to connect "her" to him, and the one person who could identify

Eddie Snyder would never notice him. At least, that's how he sorted it all out for himself.

With each step he took on the slick, unsalted sidewalks, Eddy reflected bitterly on the houses he had lived in, the people who had abused him and then used him for what monies the State might bestow upon them. They were all the same, the Nicholsons, the McGruders, and the others. When he was little, they would hold and love their own children, but not him. He would try harder for their affection, but they would push him away all the more. When he cried, they would laugh, and tell him what a big baby he was. When he would strike out in frustration, they would strike back—hard.

His foster siblings would make fun of him and tell stories on him at school. The only people he could feel superior to were other children, smaller children, and them he beat up as regularly as he could get away with it. When he slammed Natalie Hobson's head up against the bleachers in gym class one day, he hadn't expected to hurt her as badly as he did. On the other hand, she had hurt him by the things she said to him, and when they took him away over the incident, his sole conviction was that at least someone had finally taught her a lesson. She wouldn't hurt him anymore.

He might not have had to go away but for the one couple who had him. "We're sorry, Eddie, we just can't do it anymore." With a mocking mimic, he reproduced their voices in his head. They were the only ones he could find.

On the way back to his apartment, a grocery bag under each arm, he walked by the armory, apparently now a community center, and saw it was a place likely to be full of kids, especially on Saturday mornings.

~

Strand eased himself into bed after a few fruitless hours in front of the computer screen. Nothing came to him except thoughts of Aurora and the kids. His dinner lay heavy in his gut, and the beer he'd had only made him sleepy.

Closing his eyes signaled his drop on some mystical elevator to a murky bottom of indecision, of tortured misgivings, of desperate longings. He could see Aurora pulling into the driveway in their Olds, but getting out of the car were not his wife and kids, but Wendy Russell. He struggled. Why would he mess around with her? Aurora or Wendy? Guilt tossed him right and left as thoughts of the beautiful, teasing young Wendy proved difficult to wall out from his roaming subconscious.

After a while, he slept deeply, but was jarred by visions of children in cold, terrifying places he had never been. It came again, the dream of the bridge. He was there, standing by the railing, leaning against it when he saw Aarie in the water staring up at him, eyes unblinking, lips unmoving, but arms outstretched wanting him, waiting for him. He bent down looking for something, something to throw for Aarie to grab, to hold onto, for him to pull the boy out of the water. There was nothing there. Why could he see so clearly through the water's surface, but not as far down as the pocked cement just under his feet? He reached, grabbed in the foggy stillness on the bridge deck, and found something. A rope. No, it was thicker, heavier. It was rubbery—a hose, a garden hose. *Why is the hose from the Russell garage here?*

XXVII

THE ALARM HADN'T gone off because Strand hadn't set it. He awoke just as the furnace came on, and the warm air rushing into the room served its invitation to get out of bed. Then the light of the thirteenth January day joined in as it crept through the front window in silent reminder he had also forgotten to lower the shade before going to bed.

Aurora had always insisted that a pencil-thin beam of light anywhere in the universe would keep her awake, wide-eyed; shades had to be lowered completely, but after a few days of respecting the old habits, it was one of the very first to be abandoned. He rather enjoyed the bright greeting, he found, though warmth was not always its companion.

Strand sat up and reached for his notebook. Dialing the Simpson number, he promptly heard the Mister's voice. "I don't know who you are, but who calls at 7 a.m. on a Saturday morning?"

"Sorry, sir, it's Detective Strand, PSP, and it's important I speak to Ms. Russell."

"It's still early. She worked her usual shift yesterday, Strand, and I'm sure she's still asleep. Why don't you call later? After lunch would be better," he added, hanging up without waiting for Strand's answer.

Well, at least I have Saturday morning to myself and my best friend. What do you think, Bo?

Strand smiled and hummed to himself as he showered and dressed. Whether his disposition was due to a spark of midnight reasoning which might advance a conclusion in the Russell matter, he wasn't sure. All he knew was the hallmarks of a great day were there, and he planned to enjoy it.

~

Eddy Snyder, too, arose full of anticipation. He had slept well, and in fact, was sleeping better than he had in years. Escape from the institution, independence, and an installment of satiating vengeance were beginning to ease the pain that as a young boy had moved from his heart to his head.

How the Hilton boy death did not seem real to him. He was coming to understand that, like the prescription drug he had taken day after day to maintain his functional level, the deaths of others, people he didn't know, would not be as fulfilling, say, as sending Mom Jody and the others into a hell of their own. *If I could only find her next!* That would be a maintenance medication of a totally different sort, he laughed to himself, as he pictured Dr. Harkansen's reaction to his substitution of one drug—satisfying murder—for another.

Eddy considered himself fault-free in his need to make paybacks. If there was any hesitation, any pause in transition from the damaged to the damned, it was merely for the sake of the slight intellectual adjustment necessary to the long-term nature of his killing quest.

The more he thought about it, the easier it was to conclude the debt could not be settled by a one-for-one exchange of the dead for the living he could not find or reach. For what they had done to him, for what they had taken away, for what they had given to others instead, there was much more he needed to do in return. Moreover, he knew he enjoyed the instant of pleasure and danger in the taking of life, of seeming invisible to the police, and after all, in being invincible.

Carefully, Eddy arranged himself for the morning. He dressed in the one outfit available to him, the one he wore since his first day back in Foreston, pulling on the high, black leather boots last, after the padded bra, pantyhose, dark blouse, and dowdy wool skirt were in place. Finally, he applied a bit of makeup to hide the masculine bristles his otherwise fine, almost pretty, facial features allowed him.

Atop his head, he placed the wig of light hair which, along with the blue and green silk scarf around his neck, completed the transformation of a slightly built young man of medium height, to that of a tallish, light-complected, blonde woman in her twenties. Alone, on the street, "she" would give the appearance of a moderately dressed young mother out for a walk. A long wool coat completed the transformation.

Being out and about the late afternoon before gave him the courage to be in daylight again. *Who's going to catch me?*

∾

Strand finished his cup of coffee in the company of CNN, savoring what the otherwise dull Saturday offered. The heads were talking about David Dinkins having been sworn in as Mayor of New York, the NCAA approving random drug testing for college football players, and *Les Misérables* opening in Baltimore. He checked his watch several times waiting for the morning to end so that he could see Wendy Russell and perhaps move toward some conclusion in the house fire. He felt certain now what that conclusion might be, but that was only the half of it. Then, *who?*

Bo had already been outside for his morning routine and had quickly scampered inside. A house beagle through and through, it was as if the dog had carefully weighed the alternatives and decided that sleeping in a warm spot—preferably where the sun streamed through a window—was better than freezing his paws off any day.

Clearly, Bo was disappointed when he saw his master don his parka, hat, and gloves, but everything changed when he heard his master's whistle. The dog shot off as if from a starting line, and danced circles around the man who loved him enough to take him along—wherever he went. Strand and his dog climbed into the seven-year-old Explorer, and headed to McDonald's drive thru for a sausage and egg—scrambled—McMuffin.

Driving by the Community Center where Aarie and Anna had spent many a Saturday morning, everything seemed quiet except for what appeared to be a woman and her son having the kind of discussion mothers have with their children when something isn't going right. The only reason he noticed the exchange was the woman had on a long, green coat. *Is it the same woman I saw near the Post Office the morning Jamie Hilton was killed?*

...

The woman had done what she had come to do, but with such vicious force and hatred, it surprised even her. So absorbed was she in her task, she looked up and around, but incredibly, no one had come by. She leaned him up against the stonework surrounding the doorway, wiped the blade clean on his dark green corduroy trouser leg, and rose, sheathing the weapon.

Just as a florist arranges blooms in a vase, the woman bent down again to position the body so that the casual passerby would think the boy was simply sitting quietly, waiting for someone. Legs bent with arms straddled across the knees completed the picture. It felt good. It looked good. The murderer walked away just after 9 a.m.

~

After having breakfast in the car—Bo hoping against hope for another breakfast for himself—Strand drove around for a bit, killing time. Back at the Penn Grove, he stopped in the lobby to see what Earl was up to and passed the time with him, another cup of coffee in hand. Next, he and Bo sauntered around the parking lot, went through the alley to check on the family home. *I suppose I could have stayed at the house, after all, if Aurora was going to leave town anyway, but rattling around an empty barn of a place would be more painful than being at Earl's.*

Passing on the beet salad and cheese sandwich Earl had planned for his oldsters, Strand went up to his room and finished with the Saturday *Herald.* He heard sirens, but thought nothing of it.

After a catnap, he put on his coat and headed out, delighting the dog with another invitation for an outing. He'd decided to go in person to the Simpson house rather than call as the Mister had suggested. Though he found himself attracted to Wendy Russell, and was ashamed of himself for having such feelings for a woman two decades his junior, he was at the same time bothered by the edge he saw in her personality. That, he wanted to see again in person.

XXIX

RAN SENNETT HAD been director of the Foreston Community Center since the day it opened in 1987, and was justifiably proud of the impact the Center had on the town. As a place for craft and athletic skill-building, and as a haven from the streets for the active teens, it had become a mecca for young and old. In short, the facility had a reputation as a clean, drug-free, and healthy environment for all of Foreston's children. Except one.

When the telephone rang at 10:40 a.m., there was a quiet urgency in the caller's voice. "Fran, this is Nancy Paulson, Bradley's mom."

"Oh, yes, Mrs. Paulson, how can we help you this morning?"

"Is the nine o'clock basketball program over yet?"

"Why, yes. It ended at ten. Is there a problem?"

"Oh, probably not," Nancy Paulson laughed, but without conviction. "It's just that Braddie usually comes right home on Saturday mornings if we don't pick him up, or he calls to let us know what he's up to. You know boys, though; he probably got into something in the game room and forgot the time." Mrs. Paulson said she was embarrassed to bother the director as she probably had more than her share of worrying mothers.

"Oh, don't you worry, Mrs. Paulson. I have a few minutes, so let me take a tour around the place and I'll send him home to you." Though childless, she had developed a limitless reservoir of patience for mothers with children who forgot to go home. After jotting down some notes about what the boy was wearing, she said goodbye and began her hunt.

Looking first in the gym, she next went downstairs to the game room, where she was willing to bet Bradley Paulson was playing pool with the other would-be sharks of the same age group. Amidst the din, she carefully inventoried the fast-moving bodies for red hair and a bright green knit hat with yellow jacket. No luck. Well, okay, she thought, maybe some boys were fooling around outside, cold though it would be.

She grabbed a sweater from behind the service counter and walked out through the glass doors. No one was there. Pulling the cardigan close to herself, she stepped toward the sidewalk, glancing to the right in an inspection of the empty tennis courts as she did so. Unlikely though it was, Fran decided to check the other two sides of the building: she hoped it would reveal a group of boys, whom she suspected might be standing around, telling off-color jokes and giggling about what they thought they meant.

As she turned the corner, she relaxed. There, sitting in the seldom used side doorstep, was the object of her search. She called, tentatively, but with relief, "Bradley!" There was no answer, and no wonder. His posture suggested a terribly disappointed little boy, perhaps crying and too embarrassed to answer. She smiled to herself.

Fran walked up close to the silent figure and knelt down. She took a warm hand from under her arm and reached for his elbow. She stopped. He was too still. Neither were there the necessary sounds of air exchange or the small clouds of frozen breath. There was nothing. She swallowed hard and touched the boy. The arm moved, stiffly, but without will.

Bending herself further, Fran saw an open, lifeless eye, and following its sightless gaze, a dark-red stain on the yellow jacket. It was Bradley Paulson's yellow jacket. Instantly, she knew.

"NO!" she screamed, but only into the reaches of her own mind.

She stood up, backed away in two quick steps, turned, and ran.

In a few minutes, the police and an ambulance were on the way. The sirens were already piercing the frigid morning air when Fran reached her party on the telephone, and heard the fear in Nancy Paulson's voice. "You'd better come."

~

Strand eased the Vic into the Simpsons' driveway and brought it to a halt. He didn't know if Bo riding in the front seat was against the rules or what, but decided not to concern himself. Naturally, Bentsen would wrinkle his nose and wonder what creature had been seated there come Monday morning when Strand picked him up in Mercer.

"Bo, stay here." Obediently, the dog curled up in the most comfortable position he could manage.

When he answered the front door, Mr. Simpson was surprised and insisted he see some ID since they'd not met before. Ushering Strand into the living room, he said, "Wait here, and I'll see if she can come down." His attitude said it was about time for Wendy to move on, but it also signaled he would likely suffer in silence. Strand sat.

In a few minutes, Wendy Russell made her way down, fresh and ready for whatever the day brought. "Mr. Strand, I thought you were going to call."

Strand cleared his throat. "That's what Mr. Simpson suggested, I know, but I needed to be out anyway."

"Okay. So, what's so important? Can we make this quick—it was a long night and a busy morning."

Strand forced himself to keep his mind on the task at hand, distracting though the vision before him might be. *I must be crazy.* Aurora's physical and emotional absence was more overpowering than he had ever imagined it could be. The emotional gymnastics took little more than a second, yet he foolishly hoped she wouldn't misinterpret his hesitation and accompanying blank look as ineptitude.

"Y-yes, of course. Sorry. Let's use the time wisely, then. Please think carefully in response to my questions. Tell me as exactly as you possibly can how long you ran the engine of your father's car when you went back after the fire."

"I don't know why that's so important—you policemen do dwell on trivia, don't you?"

With a bit of irritation, Strand said, "Did you say our time was valuable?"

"Sorry. Alright. Let me walk through it again. I got to the house, went into the garage right away, and started the car—no trouble at all. Naturally, I entered the house through the door from the garage, went upstairs for a few personal things, and back down to Daddy's den for some papers. Everything was off in the house—appliances and water, I mean, but I remember glancing at the kitchen clock, which runs on battery.

"Let's see," she continued. "It was twenty past two that afternoon when I picked up my bag and walked back out to the garage—and I know it was just at two o'clock when I pulled in the driveway. I sat and listened to the weather on Youngstown radio—they give it right on the hour—and I also sat for a minute and tried to remember the wonderful home as it was, and now, so empty. So...you can figure maybe it was two or three minutes after two when I turned the key in the car. About seventeen minutes, altogether. How's that?" she asked, pleased with herself.

Strand nodded, smiling. To most witnesses, he and Bentsen had to address ten questions for half the information and half the accuracy. *This woman pays attention to detail.* He pursed his lips and nodded appreciatively, "Yeah, not bad. Next. When you went into the garage, do you remember where the garden hose was—you might have noticed it as you were going in the house—can you see it?"

Wendy, quick to get the drift of his suggestion, showed no surprise. Visibly concentrating on her answer, she began to speak, then paused, seeming not to agree with what she knew she was about to say.

"Problem?"

— 155 —

"Y-yes. My memory tells me that the hose was lying on the floor and not connected to the faucet..."

"Anything wrong with that picture?"

"Yes. My first response was going to be that the hose was hung on the wall bracket—where it always was—winter and summer, the only difference being that in the summer it was always hooked up to the faucet and in the winter, not so. Daddy was very particular about that hose because if left on the floor, you practically had to step right over it to get to the front passenger door of the car, and at their age, leaving it there presented one heck of a hazard to them..."

"Whoa...! Got it."

With mocked indignation, she responded with, "Look, Sherlock Strand, you asked the question—if you ask a nurse for details..."

"I know, I know, you get details. Okay. Just one last question. I can check with the fire department, but do you recall, is there any possibility that the fire department, or a neighbor, or anyone else might have used the hose to help fight the fire that night and just left it on the floor?"

Russell considered her answer. "I don't honestly know, but I don't believe a neighbor or anyone like that would have used it—I think I would have heard about it and thanked them. No, I don't think so, and I can't picture the fire department using it, but it's possible—they might've needed it in back of the house. And I'm thinking that if it was used by someone to fight the fire, it would still be attached to the faucet, right? Why, is that so important?"

"I think it might be—I'm not sure yet—I need to go out to the house and check something out. That'll tell me if it's worth pursuing."

"If what's worth pursuing?"

Strand did not answer right away. Then in a quiet, measured voice, he explained it. "How your parents died...before the fire."

XXX

A T THE COMMUNITY Center, onlookers had gathered quickly. Fran Sennett's most difficult task was keeping the children away from the terrifying sight of their little friend, still and quiet in the deepest sleep of all. Children and adults stood helpless and frightened.

The familiar Bowers Ambulance Service arrived within seconds, the police car right behind, both vehicles pulling up and over the sidewalk close to the scene. The Bowers men hurried to the body and performed what were perfunctory tests for vital signs while Chief Hallon and Officer Patterson carefully began to inspect the area for clues that would be useful in the courtroom. The chief moved to secure the scene before the entire borough walked over it, and too, he wished to be seen as doing something, not standing around helpless like them.

Quickly, Hallon determined there would be no physical evidence to be had, though he suggested to Patterson that the doorway area itself bore further scrutiny. He could only hope the body would produce information of value, and against hope, that the killing was unrelated to that of Jamie Hilton. Years of police experience, though little involving this kind of crime, told him after one glance at the boy's jacket that this murder would produce a solution no better or faster than the first one. Yet he was becoming angry that, after so many years of relative quiet, crimes such as these, particularly if unsolved, would sully his record.

While the official dance unfolded itself, Fran Sennett stood by, still in shock. Thoughtful observer that she was, Sennett ultimately reached an unavoidable and frightening conclusion. Over the century of the old armory's existence, neither the building nor the idea had failed, but the people for whom it stood had not yet measured up to the demands of the common good. Most saddening was that fact that in one hundred years, society seemed not to have advanced even one half-step in preventing crimes against its own children.

There were but few such intuitive, objective observers there that January morning; most were those seared with the image of one of their young, dead—the second in recent memory—and left wondering about a next. Within hours, as the ambulance men whispered the evidence of their eyes and the crowd telegraphed the evidence of its emotions, a quiet panic seized the otherwise unruffled mothers and fathers of Foreston.

～

At the Russell home, Strand drove right to the garage. He had the key in his pocket, the local forensic guy having determined it to be free of prints, and after letting himself in, he donned a pair of latex gloves, and set about his task.

On the right side of the car, just where he and Bentsen had first seen it, lay the garden hose. He dragged it to the rear of the Caprice Classic and fed a short length into the tailpipe of the car. As he finished doing so, he noticed something Bentsen had not: a crumpled, grimy rag lying just behind the rear tire. He smiled as he replayed for himself the scene when he and his partner were checking the gas tank. Bentsen had checked under the car from such an angle that seeing the rag would have been impossible. Their luck that day had been bad, indeed!

He retrieved the rag, which appeared soiled with grease and dried bits of rust. Intuitively, he held the rust-crumbed portion of the rag next to the tailpipe in the half-gray, but sufficiently bright morning light. It looked like a match. Strand was willing to bet that the rag he nearly used to gasket the hose to the tailpipe was the same rag used by someone else for the same purpose not more than a month before.

He put the rag aside—science would have to substantiate his guess—and used a plastic trash bag to hold the hose in place. Then he walked the other end of the hose down the spine of the house to where the French doors led out to the patio. It reached with four feet to spare, and it was no problem positioning the hose so that it snaked several feet into the room, not very far from where the Russells sat their last evening. Carefully, he replaced the hose back in the condition and position in which he found it, secured the rag in a plastic evidence bag, and left the scene of a murder. What he was still curious about was this: If there had been less than a half tank of gas, could the engine have run long enough to pump enough CO_2 into the house to kill them? The big question was, of course, *whodunnit?*

He did not return home by the same path, but whistled his way through Riverside, the supermarket just the other side of the foot-bridge crossing Wolf Creek and a short walk from the hotel.

The groceries having been bagged and paid for, Strand was about to exit the store when Jimmy Richards, the bagger, grabbed his arm and said, "Detective Strand, I'm surprised you're here. Haven't you heard what happened at the Community Center?"

∼

Strand could see Fran Sennett placing a sign on the Community Center's front door as he pulled up. "Hey, Fran," he called, stepping out of the car. As the director looked his way, Strand could almost feel the depth of sadness etched on her face. No doubt she felt a lot older than when she got out of bed that morning. As he approached, he could also see a question in her expression.

"Hi, Fletch. I wish I could say it's good to see you, but if you're here about the Paulson boy, you know, Chief Hallon is taking charge."

Strand raised his hand, palm facing his listener. "I'm not here officially, Fran, but I just heard about it at the grocery store, and I had to come over. Professional curiosity and of course, our kids play here, too." He paused, thinking about the best thing to say. "This is going to be tough on you and the Center, Fran, and I just want you to know we'll support you in any way we can."

"Thanks, Fletch, I was hoping you'd feel that way. The town is going to go crazy. That's why I'm taking this step."

Strand looked behind her at the sign she'd taped to the Center's front doors: "Closed Until Further Notice." He nodded, as if in sympathy with the step she'd taken.

"Can you tell me just what did happen? The bagger at the store knew only what he'd heard on the grapevine."

Sennett walked him through the morning's events, identifying the boy, and providing what details she could.

"Did you say this must have happened right around nine o'clock?"

"Yes, why?"

"I was driving by right around then and I just happened to glance down the alley where a mom—a woman in a green coat—was talking to a boy at your side entrance."

"Oh my God, Fletch! You might have seen something." She looked down the street, and turning back to him, said, "Here comes Chief Hallon now—he wanted a list of everyone who might have been here this morning, and I promised it to him before I closed for the day."

Hallon's car pulled up behind the State Vic, and when the Chief pulled himself from the borough ride, he put on his attitude. Before he even reached Strand and Sennett at the top of the front steps, he was saying, "Strand, what the hell are you doing here? This is none of your business." Then he seemed to notice Sennett's presence, too late for his professional lapse.

"Well, maybe it is, Chief. I might be a witness."

"Again? I sure don't like the fact that you're turning up at the scene of every murder."

"You'd better not be implying anything, Hallon."

"N-no, n-no, I'm not. I shouldna said it that way. Now, what do you think you saw?"

Strand ignored the Chief's wording, and relayed exactly what he remembered.

"You sure about that?"

"Yeah, in fact, seeing the woman with the green coat triggered something with me. There was a woman with the same coat walking across the bridge the morning the Hilton kid was murdered."

"Jeez, Strand, a lot of people have green coats."

"Sure," Strand responded with as little sarcasm as he could manage. "You still thinking this is family or drugs?"

Hallon glanced at Sennett, who retreated into the building. "You're a real dumbass, you know that, Strand?"

"You know, Chief, I've had about all I can take of your ignorance. I'll stop by and provide a witness statement—maybe you can get somebody to read it to you—and I'll let Montgomery know what's up, but I think you're going to want my help sooner rather than later.

XXXI

U P IN HIS room, Strand made a note to speak to Montgomery first thing Monday, right after retrieving his partner from Sylvie's clutches. In the meantime, he decided an afternoon nap was in order, and Bo decided it was a good time to jump up on the couch to keep him company.

It wasn't an inner alarm going off at 4:30 p.m. that woke him. It was Bo with his paws on Strand's chest, damp snout inches from his face and sharing breath from the crypt, that jostled him from slumber. The poor dog needed to go out, and that was that.

Strand rose, shivered in the afternoon chill, and quickly ran Bo down the backstairs for a quick in and out near the parking lot. Leaning against the door jamb, he reminded himself of two calls he should make that afternoon. He also vowed to visit Rudy's for their Veal Parm nestled next to a mound of their home-fried potatoes. There, he could get a beer, given the lamentable fact that such libations were not served in the dry Borough of Foreston.

Presently, Bo trotted proudly into the warm stairwell, and vigorously wagged his emotional semaphore in response to praise from his keeper. Then, Strand called Bentsen, who was audibly alarmed by the Paulson boy's death, but elated by Strand's theory about the

Russell fire. "It'll be an interesting week, won't it?" Next, Strand found Pat Curtiss's number and made the connection.

"Pat?"

The response was tentative, like someone not sure whose male voice was at the other end.

"Pat, this is Fletcher Strand, PSP. I need a minute, if that's okay."

"Didn't you and that partner of yours bust my ass enough already?"

"Joe just wanted to make sure we were playing on the same team, that's all, Pat."

"Whatever. So, what do you want now?"

"Hey, relax a minute, and can we have this conversation under Joe's cone of silence?"

"Yeah, I guess so. What's goin' on this fine Saturday afternoon?" The emphasis was on the word "Saturday."

"Right. Sorry to bother you on the weekend, but this is still about the Russell fire on the 23rd. Now, before you get nervous about my asking, let me just say I'm calling you on Saturday, because my inquiry is not official—not yet, anyway."

"And if it gets that way?"

"Your Police Chief will get what I have."

"Fair enough."

"Pat, I'm interested in one little detail about that fire. Please think for a minute. Did you or your men need to use the hose in the garage to wet down the back of the house, assuming the house lines still had pressure? Or did you have enough of your own to do the job?"

"You're right, Fletch. That is one little detail. Let me think for a minute—we've had two house fires since then." The last words trailed off as Curtiss consulted his pyrotechnical memory. "No. No, we didn't," he said finally. "I'll tell you why I'm sure. That end of Capitol is actually short one hydrant sufficiently close to make a difference, so we had to haul our line from one further up, and it took all of our resources that night—it was cold as hell, I remember— to man the lines we had. Even though it may take a little longer to set up, a fire hose is far more effective than the ordinary garden type. There's your answer, but don't quote me on the hydrant thing, Fletch, 'cause I don't need any heat from the citizens right now. I'll get the Borough Council to approve another hydrant in the spring."

Strand smiled to himself as he thanked the Chief and hung up, and added McCreary to his call list for Monday morning. The coroner's assertion about the condition of the bodies, the glass issue, the rag, and the garden hose were all circumstantial, but in his mind, powerful. Would they be enough for the State Fire Marshal to declare the incident arson and murder? *And what will Georgie Hallon say now?*

~

At the dinner hour, almost anyone could be found at Rudy's. Into its Saturday night mix of hunters, bowlers, country club escapees, and other real people, Strand walked—alone. When he called ahead, he remembered to ask for a small table in the back room, relatively unoccupied as it usually was. As he was about to put in his order with John, the harried but efficient waiter, Tony Rettig walked up.

"Detective Strand," he said, smiling, "if you don't mind associating with the locals, Bill Patterson and I are having dinner at the bar—there's a stool next to us if you're interested."

Strand recognized Patterson's name, knew him to be a pretty decent sort, and agreed, with a broad smile, "My pleasure—lead on!"

Drinks and dinner ordered, Strand and the other two law enforcement officers exchanged small talk about one thing or another, all in a way which allowed him to concentrate on other thoughts if he wished, and he did so. Patterson's comment about "the second killing in a week" shifted him out of social autopilot, however. "What's the thinking on that, Bill?"

The young officer proceeded to describe, in general terms, what the department knew about Bradley Paulson's end. His Yuengling untouched, Strand listened carefully. It gave him no great satisfaction that his earlier analysis of the Hilton boy's murder had been prophetic. He asked the men a few questions and then learned Patterson himself was at the scene shortly after the Paulson body's discovery. "Bill, is there any doubt about this being the same killer?"

"Not in my mind, at least from what I saw this morning. But if you're looking for the official version, you'd better ask the Chief. He might have another idea."

"So, how is Hallon handling this?"

"You might say," Patterson offered, laughing a bit, "that he seemed more pissed off than anything. He didn't say much to me or anybody else for that matter."

"Anybody around the Community Center who didn't fit in?"

Patterson considered his answer before speaking. "Don't think so. I was wondering that myself, but no, everyone there looked like they belonged."

"I guess I should tell you what I saw this morning," Strand said, and proceeded to do so. "And by the way, I'll turn in a complete witness statement tomorrow." In fairness, he also let them know about his contact with their boss. His listeners stayed silent.

"Was it clean?" Strand then asked, referring to the crime scene. There was hesitation as the Foreston lawmen glanced at each other. More silence. "Look. You guys asked me to join you. You guys brought up the kid's murder, not me. So, please don't give me Georgie's bullshit if I ask a logical question." There was mild irritation in his voice, not sarcasm. Strand did not want to alienate the two, just straighten them out on the rules.

"Okay," Patterson explained, "sorry. It's just that I work for Hallon and you don't." He paused. "I don't know what all they picked up, but I thought I heard one of the guys mention some hair strands and some kind of powder or makeup or something in the boy's hair. Seriously, Fletch, you ought to get this from McCreary's people, if you're really interested."

"I just might."

"And by the way," Patterson went on, "there's a sense of terror in people's voices—everybody's wondering what we've got on our hands here."

Strand nodded. Dinner came, and Strand wolfed his down.

"Thanks, guys. See you around." On the way into Foreston, he began to replay for himself the fragment of memory from the morning. The woman in the green coat—with long brown hair?—was having a mother-child discussion about something intense. *What could that have been about?*

XXXII

THE NEXT AFTERNOON, after typing a statement on Earl Shannon's machine, Strand presumed upon his old friendship with Coroner McCreary and made a call to his home number. The telephone rang twice before Mrs. McCreary answered it, and he could hear a resigned sigh when he identified himself. Presently, the coroner came on the line.

"Fletch," McCreary answered, "why am I not surprised?" Strand spent a few minutes outlining his observations on the Russell deaths. There were, he reported, at least circumstantial indications someone entered the garage, and after linking the car to the living room with the garden hose, asphyxiated the Russells, or at least rendered them unconscious. Presumably, he said, the individual entered the house itself and set it ablaze. As he was about to finish, McCreary interrupted.

"Nice work, Fletch," he said. "You know I'm interested in the Russell thing, and obviously, we'll have to pursue that one further, but I know you didn't call me on a Sunday for that, so skip the foreplay and get right to it, eh?"

"Bradley Paulson," was all Strand needed to say.

"You know, I was up late with that one, and since you are, indeed, calling me on a Sunday, ours is an entirely unofficial conversation, isn't it?" He didn't wait for an acknowledgement. "My report will state the Paulson boy died sometime around nine o'clock. I place it pretty close to that due to the degree of digestion in which I found the stomach contents—a few facts from the boy's mother confirmed that.

"In response to the only other question I know you'll ask, yes, the killing certainly appears to have been committed with the same weapon as was used in the Hilton murder. All earmarks are the same."

Strand blew an "Oh, shit!" whistle into the phone. "What was Georgie's reaction?"

"I think he already knew what my report would say, and he liked it not one bit. Maybe the consolation is there's only one killer on the loose in his town, not two!"

"Anything else of interest during your examination?"

"Yes, in fact. There were a few strands of long brown hair clinging to the boy's knit cap. Oh, and a smear of makeup."

"The mother's?"

"Don't know about the makeup, but we'll check it out. The hairs, I'm pretty sure, are synthetic."

"You mean a wig?"

"Probably. We'll have to check that out with Mrs. Paulson, too."

"If it's not hers, it could be a male, right?

"Or a female, but not likely," McCreary felt.

"Why do you say that?"

"Women sometimes murder their own children, but rarely others. You'd better find this killer, Fletch, because Georgie Hallon hasn't a clue."

"Thanks, Jack, but you're wrong about one thing."

"What's that?"

"Hallon's got one killer with the boys, and another who killed the Russells."

~

It was around 1 p.m. Eddy listened carefully to the radio broadcast blaring the murder of another Foreston boy, Bradley Paulson, earlier that day. About the Paulson boy's murder there were few facts available, and there was no indication the Foreston Police Chief had connected it to the Jamie Hilton murder. *How dumb can he be!* No arrests had been made and no person of interest identified. The newscaster noted that, according to reports, Foreston residents planned greater vigilance in their activities.

"Hah!" Eddy's loud, triumphant exclamation escaped him. He reveled in the panic and hysteria with which parents everywhere would greet the story. *They'd better love their kids!* Nonetheless, he experienced fear of his own: had someone in another part of the house heard him? It was rare for Eddy to feel anxiety of any kind, and he quickly brushed it off.

In a few minutes, ebullience passed, just as a winter sun might whisk itself behind a snow-laden cloud. Though he believed it unlikely the Foreston Police, or anyone else, could catch him at anything he chose to do, genius like his, he insisted to himself, permitted activities of other kinds.

The blur on the street below presented just such an alternative. It was a bright, new sports car which broke his concentration as it roared up Pine Street at twice the legal speed. All at once, Eddy knew what he wanted. He wanted out, out of a place where someone might hear him if he wanted to scream, out of an apartment not big enough to house his giant intellect.

"Perfect." A car should be easy to steal, and would not attract any attention to him in the same way another murder surely would. Humming in muffled, off-key tones, he again smoothed his hair when the mirror revealed that the morning's grooming had come undone. He found his coat and gloves, put them on, and headed toward the door to the stairs until a second thought caused him pause. It was not at all likely that anyone would break into his apartment and find anything of interest, but this far into the game, he didn't want to take that chance. Into a laundry bag, he quickly stuffed boots, coat, wig, kerchief, and makeup kit, and with alter ego thrown over his shoulder, he exited his apartment in hopes of committing a lesser crime.

As he'd eyed the passing cars from his window seat perch one story up, they'd seemed easy to control. At street level, they were a bit more intimidating. He had never learned to drive—officially, that is—and as he trudged along the street, he seemed more daunted by the prospect of actually driving a car than stealing one. The few times he had been allowed to drive the hospital's old blue Nova around the grounds would have to serve as his training and license, he convinced himself.

Eddy was a full block into his self-described escape from the prison of his apartment when he fully realized what was different. He broke his stride to give himself the proverbial pinch as he accepted the fact he was out of the apartment as a man. Not as a man in a well-executed disguise, he told himself, but as a man. On a bright, sunny afternoon, Eddy was outside and free, as a man. He kept repeating that very obvious and otherwise unimportant fact to himself, and the more he did so, the more he was both pleased and scared. Pleased that for the first time since arriving in Foreston just before Christmas, he did not feel someone was watching for him, masquerade or not. He was scared because the State should still be looking for him as an institutional escapee, and without a disguise, a trooper's task would be all the easier.

Four blocks later, as he crossed the Wolf Creek bridge, Eddy's attention was drawn to the stretch of street just in front of the Post Office. There, he saw a car parked, exhaust quietly chuffing the air, and no driver in sight. At twenty feet away, he came to a dead stop, struck as he was by the made-to-order situation confronting him.

Resuming his pace, he assured himself the driver of the light, silver-blue Reliant was nowhere in sight. Nearing the object of his attention, heart pounding, Eddy's initial reaction was to keep on walking, to look for a car with the keys in it somewhere not so public, where he could more discreetly gauge the likelihood of his success.

His deliberative dawdling took but a second of time, and was broken only by his eye's focus on the reflection of the glass in the front door of the Post Office at it shut itself behind someone. Cannily, Eddy sized up the situation: someone was checking a lobby box for mail and perhaps, was stopping to browse their receipts.

Reserve turned to resolve. He had no time to lose. At best, he had two minutes before the driver reappeared to reclaim his transportation. At worst, he had but a few seconds if the individual merely went inside to drop a letter in the slots.

He moved. In less time than it took to put on a wig, Eddy tossed the laundry bag to the passenger side, jerked the column-mounted shift into drive, and with a heavy, inexperienced foot on the gas pedal, sped quickly away in the traffic-free street. He foolishly went through the stop light at the intersection, terrified as he was that someone was already chasing him. A glance in the rearview mirror told him that was not the case. There was no one. Just him, a car to drive, and freedom for the day. Going up and down a few streets his feet had previously coursed, he chanced on a main thoroughfare, turned right, and recognized the Mercer Road as his highway.

Within a few minutes, the pendulum spell of grandeur and gloom was broken by the solitary car on the road in front of him. Catching up in a few seconds, Eddy's clear pathway was blocked by what appeared to be a codger tootling along at buggy speed. *What's he doing driving a car, anyway?*

Without realizing his actual speed in relation to the other car, and having no idea of the braking time and distance necessary for a car travelling at over sixty miles an hour, Eddy's lack of driving skill and knowledge extended to an acquaintance with brake pedal pressure. Even so, he did the natural thing. He put his foot on the brake, and nearly tumbled the car, end over end.

Yet the Reliant performed as demanded, with inches to spare. Yet for one of the few moments in his adult life, Eddy understood how close he came to serious injury. Shaking, and breathing deeply, he slowed down, and gave the codger space.

A quick, clever learner, Eddy eased his foot down on the gas pedal and the car pulled him effortlessly forward on the smooth, curving road ahead. Eddy noticed a steeple or dome catching the sun not too far distant.

Soon, he was back within a car's length of the slowpoke in front of him. Eddy wanted his car to fly. Why, he could not answer. All he knew was that driving along at his present speed was not the expression of freedom and exhilaration he was looking for. Wherever he was going, he wanted to get there faster. Passing a car might be something else he had never done before, *but how hard can it be?!*

Eddy could not see very far into the curve ahead, but assured himself the car he was driving fast enough for what he needed it to do. People did it on television all the time, *didn't they?* Grasping the wheel firmly, he gave it a one-eighth turn counterclockwise, then back again, at the same time accelerating the car.

Ahead, Eddy saw that the car ahead slowed to make an oblique left hand turn, and for the tenth of a second given him to grasp what was happening, Eddy could not believe what he saw. The car was turning into his path! Nevertheless, he believed himself all-powerful when he jammed his boot down on the brake, but this time, the expected response did not come.

For a split second, Eddy glimpsed the driver's profile, an old man's head capped and scarved for the cold, oblivious to the Reliant bearing down him. His car propelled itself forward and into the driver's side door of the old man's Cutlass. The old man turned his head at the last moment and looked right at him

Eddy laughed as his car struck the other, much like a sparking Dodgem at an amusement park. The Reliant's forward force sheared off the Cutlass's front fender, and Eddy's car caromed, then began a corkscrew-like launch, interrupted only by a metallic screech and thud as the car's roof met the top of a WPA-constructed concrete bridge railing.

The sound of the impact, greatly amplified, was not unlike that of a beer can crushed in the hand of its owner. The roof collapsed, the crumpled steel applying painful pressure on Eddy's head and shoulder. It was the seatbelt which saved Eddy's head from being popped like an overripe melon as the car slammed into the snow-dusted bank of the stream below, and continued its skid for another eighty feet.

In severe agony, Eddy vomited, the acid slime following gravity's direction and penetrating his nose, eyes, and hair. An instant inventory told him he no longer had feeling anywhere in his body except his head. He could see his right arm flailing out of control in futile defense as the windshield shattered inward, allowing waves of snow, glass, and frozen dirt to rush over him and force the breath from his body. Death had finally come for him, he smiled, gasping into unconsciousness.

XXXIII

S TRAND'S PRONE POSITION on the couch remained unchallenged
by anyone claiming space in front of the TV, needing his attention for some important childhood matter, or just wanting to
give him a hug. The late-afternoon nap did little for his disposition,
he knew, and his low state was not altered by the tinny electronic
sound of the hotel phone jarring him awake. It served merely to
heighten the difference between the human caress he longed for, and
the micro-chipped jangle of modern times he had reluctantly come
to embrace.

Swearing under his breath, Strand threw off the afghan and
struggled to his feet. He picked up the phone and heard Joe Bentsen's voice. "C'mon up, 204."

He stood at the open door and promptly saw the imposing figure
of Joe Bentsen lumbering toward him. Though his vascular system
could quickly tune itself to an upright position and mobility, neither
smoking nor the lack of it had changed an essential fact of Fletcher
Strand's nature—the circulation to his courtesy system had never
improved to the point of pleasant civility upon first awakening. For
anyone to have ever suggested otherwise would have been like equat-
ing a soup can to a submarine. "What's your story?"

"Maybe I could come back when you're human," offered Bentsen, obviously having assumed a warmer welcome, but instead, received of a groggy, grudging greeting.

"Then it would be years before we worked together again," returned Strand, with a hint of apology in what passed for a smile. Throwing the door open wide, he gestured his friend inside. Over his shoulder, he said, "C'mon in. I need a drink of water. You thirsty?"

"Yeah, but not for Foreston's water. What do you have that's bottled?"

"Oh. Picky, huh? Well, there's some IC Light or pop."

Looking around, as if to make sure Sylvia hadn't by some chance followed him there, Bentsen said, "I'll take the beer."

"You slumming today, Joe, or you got a good reason to ring my chimes on a Sunday?"

"Friend of mine from County called me late last night—I got my spies, too, Fletch—an' he told me about the Paulson kid. I suppose you heard about it."

"Yeah," he noted, attempting to suppress feelings deep within himself about two murders he did not stop.

The partners spent the next several minutes trading information. At last, Strand thought to ask, in an interested, not unfriendly, manner, "Joe, again, why're you here on a Sunday afternoon? All of this could've kept until coffee tomorrow morning."

"It might have kept. But would you have kept?" He paused, then went on. "When I heard what I heard, I figured it wouldn't be long before you'd do something Montgomery would be yellin' at us about. Actually, I musta had it wrong. I woulda thought you'd be ready about now."

"Ready?"

"Yeah. Ready to do something about these killings because nobody else will. Okay. Never mind. See yuh tomorrow," he said, turning back toward the door.

Strand's eye was on his friend's departing back. "Hey, Joe! Give me a minute." Strand headed inside to change his clothes and wash the sleep out of his eyes.

~

The Mercer Borough police dispatcher answered the call with little enthusiasm. The previous night's three to eleven shift had been zooey, and today, Nellie Nystrom needed a break, she told herself. Snapped into wakefulness, however, when she heard the caller report two probable fatalities less than a half mile from the police station, she radioed one of the two on-duty officers and sent him along, having first sent an ambulance in the right direction. "Probably not within the Mercer Borough limits," she advised the officer, "but we should respond given the circumstances."

At the scene, Officer Mike Hillis, arriving first, ran to the remains of the Olds Cutlass and immediately ascertained the old man was dead. The victim had been half-beheaded by the jagged metal window-trim which had sawn him from his Adam's apple halfway back. That the driver was on another journey having nothing to do with the here and now was the one religious thought Hillis allowed himself.

Swallowing hard, he stood up and began a 180-degree sweep of the landscape in search of the other wrecked vehicle. He spied an older woman standing on her front lawn about thirty yards away. Hugging a purple sweater to herself with one arm, she wagged the other to point him below the road and down the creek bed. It was only the color of her sweater that made his eye catch the semaphore.

Then he saw it. With its smoky-black undercarriage to the sky, there was little to distinguish the mangled metal corpse from its gray-brown surroundings. Hillis trotted toward the wreckage, but as he did so, he told himself there was no need to hurry. From what he could see, even at a distance, it was not likely anyone could have survived the last ride it had taken.

By the time he reached the overturned Reliant, the ambulance's siren had stopped and the volunteer technicians were beginning what, no doubt, would be a brief assessment of the car's driver closest to them.

His thoughts were interrupted, however, by a sound. Stopped in his tracks a few feet from the vehicle, he heard it again. It was a low wailing, a tearful moan, that he couldn't have heard over the siren's decibel level a moment earlier.

Hillis circled the car, feeling foolish as he did so. Given the condition of the vehicle, there was no obvious place to look, or get close to. The policeman again rounded the car one full turn before falling on the ground near what might have been the front passenger's window. Just inside, with no more than five or six inches of an opening remaining in the window's frame, there was a muddied hand moving, feebly, in rhythm with the baleful sound.

Bent down low, Hillis could see a person's head, cut and bloodied. One eye was closed, the other open—only because the eyelid had been torn back. It was a man trying to speak, but unable to talk with the blood and vomit in his mouth. The stench was overpowering. All Hillis could manage was, "Take it easy, buddy. We'll get you outta there."

The officer and ambulance men knew they could not reach the victim. Although the driver's door was not totally crushed, it was beyond use. One of the men reached in and gave a reassuring touch.

∽

Like shattering glass, the ice cracked as Bentsen stepped in a depression near the curb one door away from the Paulson home. Just dusk, the lights were blinking on up and down the street, but not at number 527. Strand and Bentsen knew the family had to be home, however. As homicide investigators, they had to perform a certain duty on many occasions; it was never pleasant and the lights were never on.

The frosty air counted loudly their footfall on the packed snow. Climbing the porch steps, they paused as they heard the sobbing inside. It was not loud, but profound. Strand's heart muscles seemed to tighten as he readied himself for yet another, unsought emotional test.

No doorbell being visible, Bentsen pulled out a hand and

bare-knuckled the glass-paned storm door. He repeated the knell twice before someone came. In the gloom of the unlit front hall stood Don Paulson, Sr. When he stepped forward, the detectives saw that he, too, had been crying. The sadness in his eyes was ever-lasting in grief and guilt.

"Yes?" he said, barely audible through the glass.

Strand spoke. "Mr. Paulson," he said, introducing himself and Bentsen. "Could we speak to you for a few minutes?"

"I don't understand. Chief Hallon left here half an hour ago. Why're you two here?"

Strand and his partner exchanged a second's glance.

"Well, sir," Bentsen began clumsily, "we aren't in a position to provide a reason yet, except that we are two criminal investigators who're interested in this case."

The sad, empty look in Paulson's eyes was quickly replaced with fire and anger. "I can't believe it! Neither the Borough nor the State can figure out who's supposed to be working on my son's 'case' as you call it. Why am I not surprised! As soon as I'm through with you two clowns, I'm going to give Hallon a call, too. That idiot doesn't have any idea what was happening. The way he was talking, you'd think our family all got together and murdered Braddie."

At the mention of his son's name, Paulson's voice broke, because he could sustain the charade of anger for only so long before it gave way to the true state of his emotions. Rage was also the only way to deal with his guilt, the real demon in his soul, Strand knew. At last, he leaned his weight against the doorjamb, hand across his eyes, and wept.

Strand spoke, gently, insistently. "Mr. Paulson. We don't know each other, but we have something in common. I live only a few blocks from here and I have a son, probably about your son's age. It could have been my son. I know it's a wrong time. I know it's hard for you. We've talked to many people—just like this—and it's never easy. You don't have to help us, but if you do, maybe other parents won't have the nights you're going to have." He paused, hoping his words had their effect. They did.

Paulson looked up, focusing not on his sorrow, but on his obligations to others, as little as that seemed to matter right at the moment. "Okay." His voice was hoarse. "We can talk. But I really don't want you to come in. Let me get my coat." In a minute, he returned and they went out to Bentsen's car, still warm inside.

The three men talked for about forty minutes. It did Paulson some good to go over the details again—this time they were clearer. He was less hesitant, his mind and heart less stunned by the impact of the tragedy thirty hours earlier. Thirty hours without his son on earth. "Hallon didn't seem interested in any answers we had," he finished.

After they'd left, Strand and Bentsen scoffed at Hallon's notion the two killings were "family" things.

"And there'll be another one, won't there," Bentsen said. It was not a question.

XXXIV

T HE EIGHT MEN worked for three hours. First, they quickly ascertained the impossibility of freeing the crash victim from the
wrecked Reliant in its present upside-down position. The EMTs
could not determine the man's injuries or overall condition, and dark
was coming fast. Though conscious, the victim was all but unintel-
ligible in his verbal meanderings.

The rescuers determined—with a best guess—that he was pinned
in his position from his neck to his feet. They felt reasonably certain
the man's body could not have been severely punctured. Otherwise,
he probably would have bled to death in the first minutes after the
crash.

Locating the biggest crane truck they could find on a Sunday afternoon, they rigged block and tackle at each end of the vehicle, and
raised it off the ground, duplicating as best they could the exact,
relative position of the vehicle to its previous horizontal axis. With
the vehicle about four feet off the ground, they pried the roof into
its normal position so that medical attention could be paid to the
trapped driver. Next, a pair of men with blowtorches went to work
on the front roof supports, and when that was peeled back, the res-
cue team could clearly see the extent of their difficulty.

The sun had gone down an hour before, and with its retirement, the temperature began its companion descent. Hurrying for fear of losing their patient to the frigid air, the men redoubled their efforts to release him.

Finally, at 7:40 p.m., the dashboard which had perfectly locked Eddy in position was eased away from his abdomen. Within minutes, Eddy was whisked into the ambulance and driven the ten miles to Foreston Medical Center. There was no conversation, as such, but when told where he was being taken, he became noticeably agitated. The technicians made no note of his visible distress for the record, but mentioned it to the nurse on duty when they delivered him to Foreston's ER entrance.

~

The knocking on Strand's hotel room door was insistent. *Who can this be?* He was surprised that no call had come from the switchboard first, but whoever was banging didn't seem to care about courtesy.

For the second time that day, Strand swung open his door to find a fellow police officer. This time, fully awake and with cordiality in full bloom, he was required to greet an obviously angry Foreston Chief of Police. Considering Bentsen's advice on the matter, Strand greeted his visitor with a smile, in vain hope of a return on his investment in the encounter.

"Hullo, Chief," he said, "what can I do for you?"

"Just what're you trying to do to me, you son of a bitch?"

"Beg pardon, Chief? You want to come in, or you going to swear at me out there for the whole Penn Grove Hotel to hear you?"

"Here. Now listen, asshole, and listen good, and listen for the last time. You're screwing around in my territory and I'm goddam fed up with it. I don't ever want to catch you approaching witnesses in a Foreston investigation, hear me?"

"I hear ya, but what the hell are you talking about?"

"I'm talking about your little visit to the Paulson family. Ain't they had enough, Statie? Why you got to go nosing in my case for, anyway?"

"Whoa, Chief! Nobody's nosing in anybody's case. We just wanted to let the family know"—he spoke quickly, hoping that the finesse
would not be too fine for the likes of Georgie Hallon—"there are a
lot of interested law enforcement people behind you and Foreston.
We thought it might make him feel better and help you at the same
time."

Seconds passed while the fuse sparked. "Bullshit!" he finally
shouted. "Did it occur to you jerks that maybe, just maybe, Foreston can handle this without the great State of Pennsylvania messing
it up? Huh?! Did it occur to you that maybe we don't have some killer just passing through, but somebody close to those families? Or
maybe, these killings are unrelated, and Paulson's is the work of a
copycat?" The Chief was nearly hysterical now, bubbles forming at
the corner of his mouth.

The Chief continued his tirade, giving Strand a minute to consider whether to let Hallon know the Russell deaths were not caused by
a short in Christmas lights, but were the result of a careful plan to
murder them. He decided to let discretion overpower his instinct to
ruin the man's day.

While Hallon inhaled for a further blast, Strand got in a word,
quietly. "Chief, the other possibility is, of course, that this killer lives
right here—you're right, he's not passing through—and for some
reason, he's out to get little boys."

If Hallon heard him, Strand couldn't tell. He had only waited for
Strand to finish so he could continue talking. "Look, sport! I'm only
gonna say it once more, to you and to Montgomery, that as long as
I'm Chief, we're gonna operate on my theory, not yours. I don't need
your support, and I don't want you talking to my witnesses. Period."
The Chief turned and walked away.

*Just wait till tomorrow, Georgie! You're going to love what Doc Mc-
Creary has to tell you!* Strand chuckled and closed the door.

~

It was a few minutes before 9 p.m., an hour after visitors were supposed to be gone, when Eddy sensed someone standing over his bed. The sound of leather against leather and the masculine smell told him it was not his nurse. He opened the unpatched eye, took a second to focus, then saw a police officer in front of him.

"I'm Trooper McConnell, PSP, here at the request of the Mercer Police. There's a question or two we need to resolve, and it shouldn't wait."

"Y-yes," Eddy said hoarsely. In the ambulance, he panicked when learning he was on his way to Foreston, but in the four hours he had time to think things through, he concluded there was little to fear.

"Do you mind telling me your name?"

"Eddy. Eddy Snyder, and that's E-d-d-y."

The trooper looked askance. "Not E-d-d-i-e?"

"Well, that's what's on my birth certificate, but I go by Eddy with a 'y.'"

Nodding, the trooper went on. "The people who brought you in here could not locate any identification, no driver's license, not a wallet of any kind. Do you have any?"

"No. Must have lost it."

"Just as a precaution, are you aware of your right to silence or representation?"

"No."

McConnell read him his Miranda rights, then proceeded. "Did you have identification in the car with you at the time of the accident?"

Eddy did not think quickly enough. "No."

"Do you have a license to drive a car, Mr. Snyder?"

"No."

"Is the car in which you were found owned by you?"

"No."

"Who is the owner?"

"I have no idea."

"So, you were in possession of the automobile without the owner's permission?"

"I suppose so."

McConnell jotted some notes. "Mr. Snyder, can you tell me how the accident occurred?"

For the next few minutes, Eddy described what happened, stating repeatedly that it wasn't his fault, as the other driver turned left in front of him.

McConnell repeated his questions concerning his driver's license, or lack thereof. Next, he asked, "Did you see that you were passing on a double-yellow line?"

"A double-yellow line?" Eddy asked in response, having no idea what that meant.

"Yes. Which means that you were responsible for the accident, not the man who died. Did you know he was killed, Mr. Snyder?"

"No. It wasn't my fault."

"Mr. Snyder, we have sworn testimony from the owner it was stolen from its location in front of the Foreston Post Office this morning. Are you admitting that you stole that car?"

Swallowing hard, Eddy concluded the police weren't so dumb after all. *Why make it easy for them?* "I don't want to talk about it."

"Suit yourself. I'm placing you under arrest for auto theft and vehicular homicide. Anything you want to say?"

"No. No big deal," Eddy responded. *Buddy, you'd be surprised what you don't know.*

"Okay, smart mouth. There'll be a guard on the door tonight. Tomorrow, somebody'll be by to fingerprint you—then we'll see who you are, and after you're released from here, it'll be on to county jail."

XXXV

S TRAND PACED THE floor, reflecting on the day's events. It had not been a pleasant Sunday. As his master wore a path in the carpet, Bo kept his spot by the heat vent, his eyes fixed on Strand as a fan watches a tennis match. Strand glanced at his supine companion and forced himself to acknowledge that Bo was indeed old, and that age would soon end their relationship.

There was a time when not a thing could move anywhere in his universe that Bo did not react, comfortable in his ability to discern friend- or foe-like activities, or at least, his perception of them. More recently, of course, Bo could not understand that he could no longer hear or see very well, and he was comfortable in that, too. It was nature's compensation, thought Strand, that when old and in need of rest, a dog's declining senses gave it less to worry about. Strand felt certain just the opposite effect occurred in humans. Strand smiled to himself as he concluded blissful ignorance was just another advantage to a dog's life.

He had allowed his thoughts to meander a bit while he decided whether or not to let another matter come up to the surface where he would have to deal with it. Aurora. For the entire weekend, he could not get her telephone call out of his mind.

Strand knew he had not been very supportive of her in a conversation she must have had difficulty initiating. He had been glad to hear she was dealing with her problems in a positive way, yet he was unhappy that the resolution of them might not come as a result of them working together. Happy for her, for them, for the children—he was that, but at the same time, he wanted them there—with him—despite the possible danger.

He picked up the phone, and after dialing the Columbus number, it rang twice. They talked for more than an hour, like nervous teenagers imitating the courting dance. The most important part of the conversation came at the end, when he heard his wife give a stronger commitment about coming home.

Strand had given her all the patience he had, and it seemed to make a difference. Her father's birthday was on Friday, the 2nd of February, she reminded him, and the day after would be a convenient point at which to make the break from her parents.

That night, he put his head on the pillow with a peace he had not known since their November fight of fights. His sleep was fitful, however, as he tried to script Aurora's return into his feelings for her. As much as he wanted her back, wanted it to work out, he kept on seeing them as on a stage, saying their lines, moving toward an inevitable ending, but not knowing what that might be. And when he saw himself mouthing the words, he could also see himself glancing over Aurora's shoulder, where, in the wings, stood Wendy Russell, patient understudy. The dream became conscious thought when Strand sat up in bed with guilty sweat.

He knew a point of resolution would occur, a time when maturity would have to prevail over juvenile infatuation. *I suppose I have my own devils to counsel.*

～

Over coffee on Monday morning, Bentsen said, "Well, you look better than I left you."

"Aurora and I talked last night. She said she'll be coming home in a few weeks," Strand reported with a broad grin.

"So, the day wasn't a total bust, then!"

"You don't know how bad it got, Joe. Our chat with Paulson must have worked on him, because he apparently called Hallon to give him a piece of his mind."

"Glad somebody in your town does that once in a while."

"Well, Hallon showed up at my door and decided to pass that grief on to me. How come he's always pickin' on me, by the way?! You're the one who got me to go over there—Hallon ought to be visitin' you on Sunday nights, partner!"

"Hah! He'd be too lazy to drive over."

"Anyway, I think I figured out his agenda."

"Which is?"

"Why he's so set on a local killer. Follow this: if Hallon were to decide this was the work of somebody passing through, he could throw up his hands and say, "There's nothing I can do!""

"And isn't that what some small-town cops do, Fletch?"

"Sure, but if he does that, he'd have to turn the case over to us, or worse, the Bureau. No, his ego's bigger than that. If there is a killer, he wants to solve it himself. He wants to be the hero to the Foreston powers-that-be. That's what the son of a bitch is up to. It's purely a turf thing—in the worst possible way."

"Fine, but how does he think he's gonna pin this on somebody local?"

""Cause Hallon's relying on the probability that whoever killed these kids knew them. Some crazed adult. A perv. One of the parents. The woman at the Y. He's hoping to have it fall in his lap. Only it won't."

"In the meantime, Fletch," remarked Bentsen, bringing them both back to reality, "we got a paying job, remember?"

"Knotting."

"Right. Today, we're going to Green Mountain College up in Harrison."

"Actually, I hope Milcher isn't there, and if he is, I hope he has nothing whatsoever to show us."

"Oh," Bentsen said, "and are we going to let Walt know about the Russells?"

"Hell, no. Let's let Doc McCreary be the messenger, and stay out of the line of Hallon's fire."

~

Down the hall, Trooper Nesbitt was going over the report turned in at the end of shift the night before by Jimmy McConnell, and decided at least one phone call was in order, especially if the fatal auto accident the afternoon before was going to fall into PSP's lap.

If Snyder had a criminal background, it was surprising he had no story ready for the police, no phony ID, no nothing. The Foreston PD seemed to know little about him, Officer Patterson said when they talked, only confirming the metallic-blue Reliant had been stolen as reported. Nesbitt scratched his head. That a guy like Eddy Snyder, in his twenties, had no driver's license but had an attitude suggesting he was no stranger to authority made no sense.

Snyder was going to be released from Foreston Medical Center today, Nesbitt finally concluded, and they would just see what the fingerprints told them. He double-checked to make sure he had the National Crime Information Center report in hand. Indeed, a computer name check with the FBI hadn't turned up a hit, so the hard copy prints were on their way to DC and to Harrisburg, he knew, but a complete check would take a week or more, that is, if the Bureau didn't have a backlog.

Nesbitt didn't want to wait a week or more, so he began culling through the lists of institutional escapees and missing persons from Ohio, New York, and Pennsylvania. It took two hours to plow through all of the reports, particularly since he had no identifiers by which to narrow his search.

Finally, he found what he was looking for. "No shit!" Pennsylvania had reported an Eddie Snyder missing from a halfway house in Meadville on December 22. According to the paperwork, Snyder was not considered dangerous, but was living in the Meadville house as an extension of the Corinth Institution. Nesbitt knew then that the fingerprint check would almost certainly prove futile. Even if the State had fingerprinted him, it was unlikely the Bureau had a record of it if no crime had ever been associated with Snyder as an adult.

At the same time, Nesbitt angered. Though Snyder had not been a criminal in the true sense of the word, he obviously had a serious problem of some sort, and to have walked away from custody only to kill an old man with a stolen car was another lesson in social senselessness.

Nesbitt was angry for another reason: in all probability, Snyder would be returned to the State without prosecution, or at most, he'd be convicted of a minor felony with diminished responsibility, if anyone wanted to spend the money. In his view, that meant nothing. Shaking his head in disgust, the policeman picked up the telephone and called the number listed in the notice, and made mental note to let Lieutenant Montgomery know that the vehicular homicide that was almost theirs wouldn't be theirs at all.

XXXVI

THE TRIP TO Harrison—and the Knotting case—took less than twenty-five minutes. After twice knocking on the front door, Strand and Bentsen looked at each other resignedly. Finally, the door opened.

Without preamble, Dr. Milcher said, "My mother told me you might be coming by. I don't mind telling you we're not very interested in cooperating with this investigation."

"Why is that?"

"I was very young when my father died, but he was my idol. He still is. Everything I've read and heard about him suggests that he was a lawyer's lawyer, that he would never give up on a client, even one like Marty Knotting."

Sensing the disposition of his witness, Strand spoke gently, "You and a lot of other people look on your father as having been perfect, but you know, there's always the one possibility that few people consider unless they walk in the right shoes."

"What's that, Detective Strand?"

"What Knotting's defense lawyer is going to say: that your father was also very human. No one is accusing him of throwing the case. On the contrary, he probably did the best he could against some pretty high odds, especially given the circumstances involved. It's just that when he began to appreciate how little time he had left, according to Koenig, perhaps he had other priorities he considered more important."

"It is kind of you to describe it that way, but many would have interpreted that very human reaction, as you describe it, to be a weakness of true character."

"Look, Dr. Milcher," Bentsen intervened, "believe me, we're not interested in dragging down your father's reputation. If it were up to us, Knotting would be rotting in hell, if you'll pardon me, and we wouldn't be bothering you. If there is evidence available, however, it is our duty to secure it for the State before anyone else gets to it. Given those circumstances, you can see why it would be better to turn over your father's papers to us, not to the other side."

"I quite see your point, gentlemen, and I thank you for noting it. Nevertheless, were my father here, I believe he would advise me to require a subpoena before turning anything over to the State. If what everyone seems to suspect is true, at least I will have the pleasure of delaying the inevitable. Thank you." Milcher stepped back into the dimly lit room from which he had emerged, and firmly closed the door.

∾

"Hey, Lieutenant," Strand explained into the phone at Junior's Restaurant, "we're out of luck with Milcher's son, unless you can get to Judge Morrison before Koenig does." Strand brought Montgomery up to date on their activities, weekend included, while Bentsen visited the men's room, then held down a couple of counter seats.

"Yeah, I heard about your weekend forays, Strand. But if we have to get a subpoena for the Milcher papers," Walter Montgomery lamented, "we may as well just hand it right over to Koenig."

"I know, boss, but there's the usual advantage to having it first. So, how 'bout it? If you can get Morrison's signature this afternoon, we can come right back here and nail it down before supper."

"Awright. See you guys around one-thirty. I gotta talk to the both of you about something, anyway."

"I can only guess. See ya later."

Lunch in Harrison was always a treat, and whenever they were in the neighborhood—using that definition loosely—they made a point of visiting Junior's. In the afterthought structure wedged between two buildings, where seating was limited to thirty patrons, Strand and Bentsen had the best cheeseburgers and old-fashioned French fries their money could buy. The fries were made from real potatoes, still had their skins on, and glistened in their hot, thin coating of vegetable oil. With plenty of vinegar, salt, and ketchup, they didn't need anything for company, but Junior's burgers were a standup act, too. Broiled to the point of pinkness and served with a platter of trimmings on the side, just one of them was an all-day sandwich.

Whenever they visited Junior's, and places just like it, Strand wound up confronting himself with the same possibilities, always in the same order. First, the smell of the place and the attack on his taste buds always reminded him of his family's annual mid-July journey to Cedar Point, a wonderful place with an armada of amusements on Lake Erie's southern edge. With that picture in mind, he always enjoyed the first half of his meal, but then, forty-something, sobering views seemed to force their way into his consciousness. Every bite he took put him another pulse closer to a heart attack or one helluva stroke. Images of a fatherless Aarie and Anna complemented the meal, and it was always at that point Strand was glad he and Bentsen weren't in Harrison more often than they were.

⁓

At the Mercer barracks, Montgomery was waiting for them with the one piece of paper that might make some difference for Alice Wagner's case. While Strand and Montgomery chatted briefly, Bentsen telephoned attorney Swanson's office to see if he had, by chance, returned from his Florida vacation. The bright light camping behind the receptionist's desk answered the call. When she learned

Bentsen's identity, she paused, then stated that yes, Mr. Swanson had, indeed, come home early, but was engaged with a client at the moment. She did not invite him to call later or ask for a message.

Concluding his chore, Bentsen found Strand and Montgomery, and declared, "Maybe we're in luck, pard. Swanson's back in town. Let's drop in on him after we get Milcher's papers."

"Hallelujah!" Montgomery exclaimed. "You guys are out of excuses. This case may actually come to an end in my lifetime."

"You'll have to admit," Strand injected soberly, "this is one of those cases we might like to see continued indefinitely—the way it's going."

"True enough. Anyway, get going, you two! Time's awastin'. I'll talk to you later. There's been a development in the Foreston murders."

As they left the office, Strand wondered, *Which ones?*

~

Subpoena in hand, Strand and Bentsen kept their upbeat mood on their way back to Harrison.

Professor Milcher was but mildly surprised at seeing the two detectives twice in one day. "I hope you gentlemen aren't wasting our time. You must have a subpoena, I believe I said."

"Indeed, we do," returned Bentsen with no small measure of satisfaction in his voice as he presented him with the document having Judge Morrison's official blessing.

The younger Milcher nodded solemnly, resignedly, and invited them both inside. "Please wait here," was all he requested, and left the room. In less than a minute, he came back, bearing a manuscript looking to be about three inches thick. Along with it was what appeared to be an old photograph album, crammed full with papers.

"There's little point, I suppose, in playing cat-and-mouse about this whole thing. This," he said, tapping his hand lightly on the pile, "represents the life of a dedicated, professional man. How anyone could say—prove—that he was otherwise is beyond my ken.

Here you are, gentlemen. If there's anything else you need, Attorney Swanson, my father's partner, will have to provide it," he said, and uttered not a word further. He walked to the door, held it open, and inspected the space in front of him while Strand and Bentsen made their exit.

XXXVII

O N THEIR RETURN trip to Mercer, Bentsen drove while Strand sat, papers stacked in his lap. "I wonder what this holds. I mean, what will it say about a good man and his end?"

"Don't know," Bentsen responded quickly, more out of habit than insight or knowledge. "It don't look good, though, and it hasn't right from the very beginning."

"You're right about one thing, Joe. How it looks. The hell of it is this whole case will be decided on how it looks. Evidence might mean very little in the end."

"I'm not sure I follow."

"What I mean is that you can't prove the negative, that Milcher didn't abandon his client. There may be little actual proof that Milcher failed to defend his last client to the utmost. All Knotting has to show is that a doubt exists, and without any witnesses who'll come back for another round of their private nightmare, why would the State bother?"

"I get it. You mean that no matter what we do, you think Knotting'll walk."

"It might not be a lock, I'll grant you that. All we can do is postpone his release and that does not bother my conscience one goddam bit. We might have to feel good society got twenty-two years of him off the street."

"What're we feeling so good about, then? All we did was get another piece of evidence for Knotting."

"Not quite. What we're feelin' good about is doing our job, no matter what, and right after that noble principle is the fact that our luck may be about to change."

Within a short time, they were standing in Swanson's Mercer office. Together, they heard the tanned attorney say with a Cheshire smile, "You missed it, friends. Reinhard Koenig was here less than an hour ago with a legit subpoena for the good doctor's records, and of course, as an officer of the court, I was required to comply."

As Swanson spoke, Bentsen thought of his partner's prediction not one hour old, and looked in his direction.

Strand showed no reaction to the news, and neither did he acknowledge his partner's silent taunt. Never much for patience in dealing with members of the bar, he concentrated briefly on the creature before him. By all rights, he mused, Milcher's surviving partner ought to have defended any records relating to the case with every ounce of legal chicanery available to him, particularly since it was Milcher's reputation which allowed Swanson to survive living. Yet Swanson seemed to have been only too amiable in turning over Dr. Holcomb's medical files.

"So, what about any corporate records for Milcher-Swanson?" Bentsen demanded.

"Well, you can get a subpoena for them, but don't bother. I'm pretty sure Alice has everything that matters already." Swanson smiled through his peeling sunburn as the PSP detectives, nodded, and left.

～

They regrouped in Walter Montgomery's office, where the three men carefully assessed the strengths and weaknesses of Knotting v. The Commonwealth of Pennsylvania. Practically speaking, there wasn't much of the former, at least from their point of view. After twenty years, if a criminal like Knotting could put the State's judgment at risk with a circumstantially attractive appeal, they agreed, the weakness wasn't so much in the case as in the system. The lone alternative was to maintain every piece of evidence from every case and keep tabs on every witness, until the convicted party was dead or otherwise free.

Each in his own way, Bentsen, Strand, and Montgomery decried the seemingly unbalanced scales of the criminal justice system, one in which the State's best efforts represented a mere holding action against an unending, overpowering crime siege.

The watering down of the judicial system had less to do with law than self-interest. When society enacted restraints on behavior, and violations became common, all questions sifted themselves to the one that Montgomery asked: "Was society right when it created the law or when it broke it?"

At some point, they agreed, someone with everything to lose had to stand up and say to the American public: "Enough! If you do the crime, you do the time. Period."

They couldn't say who or when that would be, and so, venting over, Strand, Bentsen, and Montgomery finished their coffee, and resumed custody of the trammeled principles of social order. As they parted, Bentsen asked, "Hey, Lieutenant, wasn't there something else you wanted to talk to us about?"

Montgomery's eyes clouded over. "Oh, yeah! Sit back down here, you two."

Wordlessly, the men sat in front of their chief's desk, and Montgomery continued. "I don't know what you two are doing over in Foreston—maybe you ought to tell me—but I've been hearing from my friend, Hallon, again. Well?"

Strand spoke first, without hesitating. "Couldn't wait, boss. You heard about the other murder, the Paulson kid on Saturday. As far as everyone can see, Georgie's stuck on somebody passing through, a drug thing, or some family thing with Hilton and a copycat with Paulson. He doesn't have a clue."

"So, what does that have to do with you? More specifically, how does the State play a part in this?" It was a rhetorical question, he made clear, by continuing without pause in a low, reserved voice. "Look, boys, I'll save us some time. I think I know how you both feel because I probably agree with you, but unless you've got a hook to get into this case, you'll have to be a whole lot more discreet than you were yesterday with the Paulsons. First thing you know, Georgie'll be using you two interfering with him as the reason he can't find his ass with both hands. Follow?"

Strand was struck by one immediate and obvious fact. Montgomery was not bellowing at them. It was also apparent that Hallon must have given him a pretty hard time, but that he had done his best to protect them, and he had no choice about what he had to say. For the moment, they said nothing. When Montgomery finished, they each nodded, got up, and left.

Comparing notes a minute later, they agreed that Montgomery's words were less important than his message: Find the hook.

XXXVIII

I T WAS NOT any other Monday. Judge Morrison's courtroom was frigid, the building's furnace having been turned down over the weekend for economy reasons. Adding to the chilly atmosphere was a day already shadowed by black clouds in a low, heavy sky. Spectators and reporters showed themselves sullen and apprehensive, as most believed they were there to witness an outcome they did not want to see, but from which they could not stay away.

The Tipstaff said his piece through the silence and heightened the drama to unfold as all stood in reverence to the tradition of justice rather than the hope of it. Judge Morrison entered from the left and climbed the two rubber-treaded steps to the bench, high court that it was in and for the County of Mercer.

Judge Morrison peered across the bench, its hundred-year-old shell gleaming in contrast to the unsmiling jurist commanding it. The entire chamber sat down except for Reinhard Koenig and Alice Wagner, who remained upright in anticipation of coming combat.

After the pro forma announcements, Judge Morrison eyed the opponents directly and asked each, in turn, to attest their readiness to proceed. Both assenting, Morrison spoke. "Ms. Wagner, Mr. Koenig. Let us all understand," he intoned for the benefit of all within hearing, "that this is not a *de novo* trial. It is not a judicial review based on the merits of the case. Rather, it is a hearing to determine, if possible, one and only one narrow, legal question. That is: Whether or not Mr. Knotting received his entitlement to a defense as represented by Mr. James Milcher, now deceased, during the trial which occurred in October 1968. And so, I must caution you," he advised, looking first at Koenig, then at Wagner, "that we will not review trial evidence of any kind nor will there be any attempt to now try this matter using post-Knotting changes to the criminal law, which are unrelated to this issue. I will allow no latitude in this regard." Casting his imperial glance in the direction of the appellant's table he announced, "Mr. Koenig, you may proceed."

With the overhead fans whirring like small helicopters armed for attack, the silence was broken as Koenig glanced at his notes. "Your honor. I submit that Marty Knotting should be free. Almost twenty-two years ago, Mr. Knotting was tried, convicted, and sentenced for a crime he did commit. Of that, there is no doubt." Reinhard Koenig's voice was slow, methodical, and inevitable in its timbre. The attention of the entire chamber was upon him, the moment's champion of society's unworthy.

"What is in contest, as you, your honor, so aptly articulated is whether Mr. Knotting received the representation to which he was entitled, by 1968 standards, given his contributions to the State's case against his co-defendants.

"This is a compelling question, and perhaps we can examine it this way: Would a reasonable person reviewing the trial record conclude that Mr. Knotting had been ably represented throughout his trial by Mr. James Milcher? Or might such an observer conclude that was so until a certain point in the proceedings, when for no discernible reason, the attorney prevailed upon his client to change his plea? The answer to both questions cannot be yes. It must be one way or the other."

Koenig launched his attack. "Your honor, I submit *amici curiae* by four eminent legal scholars who have painstakingly examined the trial record..."

Never shy in courtroom swordplay, Judge Morrison interrupted. "Do I take that to mean," he asked, sarcasm evident, as he proffered his hand, reaching for the briefs, "you've already done the research, and it would be easiest for all concerned if we just accepted their conclusions as final?" The jurist's wry, condescending smile evaporated when, as Koenig spoke, Morrison recognized the fact that the appellant had not yet fired his salvo.

"Not at all, your honor, inasmuch as the subpoenaed notes and records of District Attorney Stevens and presiding Judge Henry Hanscomb must also be considered." Koenig's sparse statement shattered the silence like a chandelier's crystal on the ancient hall's cold, quarried floor that was the State's case.

Alice Wagner thought she had found a comfortable position on the cushioned leather armchair, her elbows the base for a span centered by clasped hands under a confident chin. Although Wagner had arranged herself for twenty minutes of opening arguments, she was unprepared for the immediate and direct hit from her opponent. Shot out of her chair, her voice cut the silence. "Objection, your honor! Under the rules, counsel should have made known his intention to obtain this information."

"Judge," Koenig began, knowing no word could be wasted. "We became aware of this information only late yesterday afternoon. Our subpoena was issued at 6 p.m., and the data itself was obtained after midnight. There was no propitious time to alert my learned friend this morning. For that, we apologize. Nevertheless, it is evidence which must be considered." It was clear that court courtesy required the apologetic stance; Koenig's tone, on the other hand, gave Wagner neither comfort nor quarter.

Judge Morrison sat impassively, glaring at Koenig, ready to explode. Restraining himself, he did not have to wait for the State's reply.

Casting a sideward look of dismissal in Koenig's direction, Wagner quickly rejoindered, "Counsel's position assumes a settled question of relevance and admissibility. Mr. Koenig knows that under ordinary circumstances, trial notes of the judge and the State's representatives are beyond the reach of an appellant. For it to be otherwise, there must be a showing of misconduct by the parties. He is not alleging that here, and for that reason, I am asking the court for a ruling."

"Your honor," countered Koenig quickly, "I must differ. Though my opening remarks mentioned no misconduct, *per se*, Ms. Wagner has raised the question in her objection and I must deal with it. No one has alleged or will allege that James Milcher, respected attorney that he was, evaded his obligation to his client for money or any other disreputable purpose. Nevertheless, we intend to show that James Milcher, due to the extreme seriousness of his disease, found himself so distracted as to decide, deliberately or subconsciously, that he had done enough for his client, and so, failed to pursue a reduced sentence to his utmost. No matter how you or I describe it, your honor, that is misconduct of the most unfortunate kind. Clearly, it proved unfortunate in 1968 for Mr. Milcher's very last client. Mr. Knotting should not have to suffer the same misfortune in 1990."

Wagner, having remained standing, stayed in the fray. Her sarcasm exceeded that of the judge. "On behalf of the people, your honor, I note with some irony and dismay counsel's concern for Mr. Knotting's suffering. Would that his client had shown similar concern for his victims, one of whom suffered the ultimate consequences of misfortune, to put it politely."

"If the State has something to say other than on an emotional level, I am ready to deal with it," said Koenig, speaking words that might have come from the judge.

"Thank you, Mr. Koenig, Ms. Wagner. It seems we have a threshold question here. Mr. Koenig, just how dependent is your case on the notes and marginalia of Mr. Stevens and Judge Hanscomb?"

"The notes are critical, your honor, because of what they do not show: there is no indication James Milcher pursued with any diligence his client's interests in the end stage of the trial. In fact, the notes are devoid of any indication Milcher attempted any serious bargaining with Stevens. They prove by inference the points made by the other evidence I intend to present."

Wagner did not retreat. "Your honor, Mr. Koenig stated he had subpoenaed and received the needed information only last night. Does he mean to assert that without it, his case would have been baseless, his petition for this hearing without merit?"

"That is not a fair summary, your honor. I believe now and did so before last night that Mr. Knotting's petition has much evidence, direct and otherwise, to commend it. The observations and notes from the 1968 trial serve to make the case conclusive. I believe their admission into evidence will speed this action, thus saving the State its valuable resources, not to mention my client's increasingly precious freedom."

The high judicial tones continued, but in seconds, it was over. Judge Morrison announced his decision not to decide any matter of substance that day, but to stay arguments until the matter of admissibility was resolved.

Strand and Bentsen sat, silently listening to the apparently unending litany of rights and benefits for the Knottings of the world, and then had to strain to hear Judge Morrison and the clerk agree, then further announce Monday, February 5th, as the prospective decision date for the pending question. The policemen stood up and made their way out of the courtroom, Bentsen mumbling that the only good thing about the morning was Knotting's continuing view of the world from the other side of Johnston's Jungle walls at Morganville State Prison.

Outside the courthouse, Strand and his lumbering partner walked slowly and spoke little until Bentsen broke the silence. "February 5th is a long time to wait for an opinion."

"He's going skiing out west."

"Hummpf! Do you think he'll walk?" He put his hand up as if to forestall an answer. "Please give me the answer I want to hear, will ya?"

"Don't think I can do that, pal. Of course, I could say that justice—our definition of it—will win the day eventually, but we both know that'd be kidding ourselves."

"That's not what I wanted to hear, but I guess we're both big boys, ain't we?"

Strand smiled in answer. "Guess we better be. I don't know what Morrison's hoping to accomplish, except to drag it out a bit more. Whether the notes are admissible or not, Koenig can make his case in other ways. In fact, I wonder why he hasn't tried a few other tacks. This one was the chanciest."

"You wanna speak English?"

"Joe, all Koenig really needs to show is that Milcher had no income whatsoever from any client activity beyond October 1968—he can do that with Swanson's cooperation. Other witnesses could be found to testify—with complete credibility—that Milcher did no work subsequent to that timeframe. Holcomb's records with the date he informed Milcher of his prognosis would seal the deal, I think. One would have to conclude Milcher knew his fate, it hit him hard enough to cease practicing law, and that Knotting received short shrift in the end."

"Whoa, Mr. Koenig," Bentsen mocked Strand, "there's a long legal leap from the mere knowledge that he would soon die, to the position that he abandoned his best efforts on behalf of his client. You're right, proving one thing ought to be easy, but I don't agree that the other conclusion naturally follows. Defending Knotting back then was an impossibility. I think Koenig has a row to hoe yet."

Strand eyed his partner with respect. Bentsen had defined the point precisely. "Let's hope, partner, that Morrison somehow has the advantage of your great legal mind. Want to submit a brief?"

They laughed, picked up their pace, and found the Vic. It, like the crime files in their assignment folder, waited patiently for them.

XXXIX

THAT NIGHT, AURORA called. Strand had been expecting it, and once again, he found himself waiting with anticipation for the sound of her voice, or at least Ma Bell's rendition of it. As he listened to and hung on her words, he put out of his mind the actual distance her voice traveled, the thousands of miles to and from a microwave satellite, instead of the mere 150 miles which parted them. He was glad she was that close.

"Fletch, are you with me?"

"Yes...that is, no. I mean, yes I am, but you wouldn't believe I wasn't thinking about work and you wouldn't believe what I was thinking about."

"Oh, try me. Let's see how quick you are."

"I don't have to be quick to come up with something," he said, and they both laughed. He noticed—they both noticed—they were laughing with each other. Strand confessed the whereabouts of his mind while she was talking, and Aurora positively giggled.

"Oh, Fletcher, I can't believe you—do you really miss me?"

"As if you really were thousands of miles away—sure you can't come back sooner?"

"Don't think so, hon. Let's stick to our plan for the third. My heart and my head tell me it'll be better that way. Will you wait for me?"

"You bet I will," he said, his voice thick with emotion.

"Fletch...? Do I have your attention now?" she solicited with the sweetness of a new bride.

"Yes?"

"Fletch, I love you."

"I love you," he echoed, and let the exchange play itself back over and over as he savored not merely the words, but the warmth behind them.

"Honey," she said, after a few seconds, "I need to tell you something about my family."

"What brings this up?"

"On the six o'clock news here, there was a small piece of video about the Knotting case back home. I thought I caught a glimpse of you and Joe amongst the spectators."

Strand chuckled. "You're kidding. Well, Joe and I had that one tossed in our laps, and it's been driving us crazy. What does that have to do with your family?" A thousand possibilities raced through his mind.

"To be honest," she said, "my counselor told me that this might be one of the things that's stood between us. So, sit down, Fletch, because it's a bit of a story."

"Phew! I'm sure it's nothing we can't handle."

"I'm glad you think so. The short of it is that Marty Knotting is my older brother."

"WHAT? I didn't know you had a brother. How can this be?" *Was this the secret?*

"I didn't know, either, until a few weeks ago, and I've been wrestling with it ever since. Didn't you ever wonder why my folks left Foreston and moved to Columbus?"

"Yeah, sure. I guessed it was because they were tired of all the bigotry and just wanted to leave it behind."

"That's part of it, but it's much more than that. I always thought there was a missing piece about my childhood, but I never knew what it was. I assumed my parents had just decided to have one child and I came later in their marriage. I just didn't know.

Strand could hear her take a deep breath. "What I know now explains a lot. My grandparents, Giovanni Tomaselli and Maria Russo, came to the U.S. and then to Foreston just before World War I—if you want their dates, you'll find them in the Hallville Cemetery."

"I don't understand," Strand said, knowing the cemetery was in an area outside of town, where the Italians were forced to live until the 1920s. Some families still buried their dead there.

"They married and had four children, all born 1923 or earlier—my father, Leonardo, was the last. The oldest, Francesco, died of the Spanish Flu on Halloween night in 1918. There was a brother, Lorenzo, a Marine KIA in World War II, and a sister who died of breast cancer. I barely remember her as a little girl—she died when I was seven."

"Good Lord, Aurora, how are you keeping this all straight?"

"I have notes—it took me hours to drag all of this out of my folks. So, my parents, Leo and Gina, had a little boy not long after the war, in 1949. His name was Martin."

"What happened to him?" Strand felt his muscles tense.

"When he was born, my mother told me they had no money, as their people were dead and there was no one to help. My father lost his job because vets coming back from the war wanted to work and even in the mines, they were given preference."

"The church couldn't help?"

"Father Patricio did all he could, my mother said, but in the end, they gave him up to a family named Knotting."

"Oh, my God, Aurora. This is unbelievable! And your parents never thought to tell you any of this?" He could feel anger rising in his voice.

"I don't blame you for being upset, Fletch. They said they were going to tell me before I met you, but somehow, they didn't." Her voice trailed off.

"Jesus H. Christ! It wouldn't have made any difference with me, but it might have with the PSP. When we were married, that case was only ten years old or so."

"So, you can see why they moved away."

"But they left you with it, didn't they?"

"I thought of that—this whole story is what I've been thinking about these past few weeks. For days after I heard it, I couldn't sort it out, and I had to deal with it."

"Now I'm beginning to understand." He paused. "So, you've never met or seen this guy, Knotting?"

"Never, and of course, there wouldn't be any pictures of him around my parents' house."

"That's one helluva story, isn't it?" As he said it, he thought back to the few hours he'd spent with Knotting, wondering if he'd missed any signs of resemblance.

"There's more," Aurora said, piercing his concentration.

"God, how could there be?"

"The grandfather I told you about? Giovanni? He was murdered in May 1924—he's in Hallville, too, right next to Francesco. If you go there, you know, they used to cement porcelain black-and-white photos of the deceased to the gravestone. They're still there, as if they were taken yesterday."

"Wow! But he was murdered?"

"This part I knew, but never wanted to tell you—not that it means anything. He worked in the Number 5 mine with a lot of the other guys, but he also had other jobs, as did my grandmother, and over time they saved quite a bit of money. A cousin wanted to open a grocery and borrowed $2,000 from Giovanni, and that simple act cost him his life."

"How so?"

"Fletch, all of these people were from Naples—home of what they called the Black Hand. I guess even here, they had a hold on the people. Italians were supposed to borrow money only from them, my father explained, as his mother explained to him, so that it was the Black Hand collecting the interest, not my grandfather."

"So, what happened?"

"It was Decoration Day weekend, and my father and his friend, Angelo Sanderi, were walking home from Mine Number 5. A man came up from behind and slit my grandfather's throat. Later, the authorities believed that Sanderi must have been involved somehow but they could never prove it."

"What a way to go. Did they catch the guy?"

"Sure. My father has the newspaper clippings. His name was Bruno Cliotti and, unbelievably, they found him on a train in West Virginia a few weeks later. He was executed, but he never said a word about Sanderi."

By then, Stand had fallen back on the bed and was staring at the ceiling while Aurora's story unfolded. "God, please don't tell me there's more."

"I'm sure there is, honey, but I don't have any more to tell you."

∼

When they finally hung up, Strand turned on a pot of water for a cup of instant coffee. Maybe it was for something to do while he processed the most amazing story he'd ever heard. Of course, he'd have to tell Montgomery even though it was highly unlikely anyone would ever make the connection between him and his newfound brother-in-law, the despicable Marty Knotting. *The past is always with us, indeed!*

While the hotplate did its work, what Aurora told him made him realize why there had always been a distance there, and breathed a sigh of relief. At the same time, he assured himself that the only reason he was tempted by someone like Wendy Russell was because she wanted him to be, and because in a moment of foolishness, he thought he needed someone when Aurora left him. *Good thing nothing ever happened there!* Now, he could put Russell out of his mind— at least in that respect.

The water bubbling and spitting pulled him from his reverie. Strand enjoyed his cup of coffee, watched television without seeing it, and, despite the caffeine, slept soundly.

XL

THE NEXT MORNING, Strand snagged a few minutes with Montgomery and told him what he'd learned from Aurora about Marty Knotting. Montgomery stared at him wide-eyed, and whistled. Then he nodded. "Okay, I'll make a memo for the file to cover your ass, but knowing you, I'm guessing you'll still shoot him if he tries to escape even if he is your brother-in-law."

"Oh, you bet. Sure you don't want to reassign this one?"

"Naw. Why make a big deal out of this? It's almost over, anyway."

Days passed. Strand and Bentsen immersed themselves in the routines of new cases. Foreston began its return to normalcy, whatever that was for a small town with unresolved murders. Subconsciously or otherwise, Strand supposed that many people thought Chief Hallon was right. If the murders of the two boys weren't a drug or family thing, then maybe they were the work of some crazy passing through.

Much like Strand's Polish ancestors in the low Carpathian Mountain villages who could only hope Cossack marauders would not soon return, Foreston residents, hoped, too, that a killer was loose, just not in their backyard. About the Russells, people knew nothing because Hallon hadn't told them, and reporters at the *Herald* must have been asleep.

Toward the end of the week, Bentsen raised the issue. "Yuh know, Fletch, I hate to bring it up, but we haven't done anything on the Russell case or the kid killings at all. Not that I'm lookin' for work or anything..."

"Yeah, I know. Did we ever get anything back from Harrisburg on the stuff we sent to the lab from the Russell case?"

"Not that I know of, but you know, Fletch, I can't figure you sometimes. For a few days there, you were Crusader Rabbit about those cases—we even took time from the Knotting thing just so you could satisfy your curiosity. For the last four or five days, though, it's like those two cases never existed. Not that it's any of my business, but what's been going on with you, anyway?"

Strand sipped his coffee, acknowledging to himself that the tar-like liquid in his cup might easily meet the requirements for road patch, and considered what he should tell his friend. He decided to be candid. "Joe," he began, "you know these have been a tough few months for me. I haven't said too much to you because...well, for a lot of reasons.

"Anyway, Aurora and I talked again on Monday night, and things are looking much brighter for us. In fact, she's planning to come home a week from tomorrow." As he finished the sentence, he didn't know whether to laugh or cry. He did neither, but Bentsen almost did.

"Fletch, that's great," he almost shouted, extending his arms in a broad, embracing papal gesture. "You have no idea how happy I am for you—and Sylvia! Hah! Wait till I tell her. Now she can quit worryin' about you."

"Worrying about me?"

"Yeah, you," Bentsen said, excitedly, pointing an animated finger at his partner. "She takes all the cop-divorce-depression-suicide stuff real seriously. So, what's the date?"

"Probably on the third. Not all of the details have been worked out yet, but her father's birthday is on the second. She wants to stay for that. Only a week more."

"So, everything's okay, then."

"Not exactly okay, Joe. We have a lot of rebuilding to do. What'll come of that, I don't know."

"Well, Fletch, needless to say, I'm happy for you," Bentsen declared with an air of elder wisdom. "I'm not sure I understand one thing, though. What does all this have to do with those cases gathering dust?"

Strand looked up at his partner wondering how much more he should say. As much as he regarded him, discretion with Joe was a much better plan. "Joe, I've been thinking about exactly that. The Knotting case, the Russell thing, and the kid killings filled a void for me. They were my life for those few weeks..." His voice trailed off.

"Fletch, what do you mean, 'were'?" Bentsen asked, trying to hide growing chagrin.

"Sorry. Did I say 'were'? I guess I did." Strand tried to catch his partner's eye, to ask without words his friend's professional tolerance, but Bentsen continued his downward gaze at his own black whirlpool of a well-stirred, as yet unsipped cup of coffee. "Okay, Joe," he said when the quiet had sufficiently filled the vacuum, "I'll return to earth."

Stopping in at the barracks was their mistake—there had to be a cause-and-effect relationship between checking in at the office and plans going awry! While they were scanning the phone messages on their desk and checking on some paperwork, Montgomery appeared.

Smiling with satisfaction at their presence, he handed Strand another of the yellow phone notes. Minutes before, the barracks had received a call from the Hermitage area, and troopers had already been dispatched. "Here you go, Fletch! This one's right up your alley—child's play, if you ask me."

"Mind telling me what alley?"

"Could be a domestic. You can go see Mrs. Jarvis at 4930 Farnsworth Rd., Hermitage. She said her husband, Orville, fell down the stairs, then mumbled something about a gun going off. Have fun." When Montgomery's audience made no effort to move, he added, "Now would be a good time!"

~

Strand and Bentsen didn't get back to anything resembling a plan that afternoon, or indeed, for several. As always, in their particular professional lives, duties materialized which took precedence over all other pursuits, especially those which had never been official-ly assigned to them. There was no choice, really. Never were there enough hours to check out every incident the instant it became known to them—and have a private life.

Typical of most in their profession, Strand and Bentsen had spouses, children, and all of the family obligations belonging to the accountant or store manager. True, they knew, there were many eve-nings and weekends spent not with the family, but with a corpse and baggies of grisly evidence. Television cops were one thing. Life was another.

XLI

I T WAS A moonless night, the countryside covered with a blanket
of winter darkness. Into the pitch, Eddy studied the view out of
the meshed window over the scrubby, brown front lawn of the
Corinth Institution. His picture presented little more than the few
feet illuminated by the single-bulb light fixture swinging in the wind
over the driveway. The distant sound of a truck engine reminded
him how far he was from the main road. *No way I can go now! How
far would I get?*

The night's forbidding loneliness also brought to mind the hundreds of nights without the touch of another hand, without the story
at bedtime, without the caress of a mother's lips on his forehead. Except for his sister, no one ever made sure he ate or bathed properly,
brushed his teeth, or had clean clothes to wear. She had been everything to him. *Or was she?*

Her love for him, once close, was rapidly becoming a distant memory. They spent their early years together in a succession of foster
homes. Like orphans bundled from one place to another, they were
nomads permitted a brief rest in strange and impersonal waysta-
tions. In most places, their so-called parents were interested only in
supplementing meager family incomes. Few warm memories found

their way to Eddy, whether his sister looked out for him or not.

Sometimes, Eddy wondered why she never seemed to have it so bad. At all the houses where they stayed before being moved on, Eddy seemed to face the brutality of deprivation alone. She did not. *Why did she always get things like clothes and warm food? She always had a birthday cake. Why not me?*

With the Nicholsons, nothing bad ever seemed to happen to her. *Why wasn't she forced to sit in the closet with the spiders? Why didn't she have to sit in her own piss and endure the hunger and the headaches?* Though he didn't understand it, he never held it against her. *Should I?*

All he knew was that every one of those people, parents and other children alike, were jealous of him. They didn't like him because he was so smart. His cleverness made people angry and maybe that's why he was singled out. It was unfair, but it was the price of brilliance.

Eddy contented himself with the lot of genius, but resented those who spurned his talents, who denied him love. As he reviewed his life, mostly a string of personal rejections, he acknowledged the growing but uncompleted peace within himself for having begun to satisfy the debts owed him. *If I could find the Nicholsons they'd find out what the Russells did.*

The Russells were the first. They never once punished him, and in fact, they were the only people who ever seemed to care for him. But, he reminded himself, the Russells deserved to die because they turned him away. Oh, they cried at the court hearing, but it was over that stupid Natalie, not him. That's all they ever did. Never once did they say they wanted to keep him.

Eddy was glad he killed the Russells. After all, they tried to kill him, didn't they? When they let the court send him go to Corinth, wasn't that just like killing him? They had killed his one last hope for recognition of his remarkable intellect. It may as well have been murder.

So, he showed them. Eddy smiled into the darkness, the light from the driveway catching the glint in his eye and reflecting into his soul. He was thinking about the night he burned the Russells into a hell on earth as they sat, unconscious.

It had been easy, so simple. After walking away from that piece-of-shit house in Meadville—*Halfway to what?* Eddy snorted to himself—he could have gone anywhere he wanted. The addresses of the many places where he had lived were no longer in his memory, if indeed, he ever actually knew or wished to remember those places. While he had vivid, tortured memories of and dreams about the families and their children, he had no real idea where they lived. What would he tell whoever picked him up along the road? Where would he say he was going? He was comforted by his foresight. Before he left the Meadville house, he had thought it all out.

Foreston was an easy place to get to from Meadville, and he knew the Russells' address. It was the last real place on earth he lived—how could he forget it? If he couldn't find anyone else with whom he could settle accounts, he knew he could find the Russells. For what he needed, they would do. Wendy's recent visit revealed to him her weekday work schedule, and so he knew the best time to pay them a visit.

Wendy wouldn't be there most nights, and no one would see him. All he had to do was watch through the window. Hah! The old farts were so predictable. Just as he had hoped, they fell asleep in their over-heated living room, the one where he was rarely allowed to go when he lived there. And they died right in front of the lighted Christmas tree. Eddy laughed out loud as he remembered how every little detail had fallen into place. Once again, he congratulated himself for his insight and brilliance. He had formulated his plan on the spot. *And the cops still haven't figured it out!*

True, it had taken almost two hours before he felt sure they were sufficiently unconscious that they wouldn't wake up and escape their appointment with him. It had been a long cold walk to the Russell house, and he nearly froze, until he snuck into the kitchen, closed the door, and waited it out. So, while they were getting gassed up—a hilarious play on words, he thought—Eddy used the time profitably to fix himself something to eat. In the kitchen, he warmed himself as he sat on the chrome chair with the plastic, tufted seat and back, and ate his sandwich. In the background, he could hear the low drone of the car's engine as it pumped the carbon monoxide into the next room.

After pulling the hose back to the garage and generally cleaning up after himself, the last thing to do was light the fire. In the garage, he found the old man's gas can, the one Russell used for his lawn-mower, and finding it partially full, Eddy took it into the living room and doused the carpet near the Christmas tree. He did so, retracing his steps out of the house, and stood for a few moments outside the French doors at the back of the living room.

As the room lit itself anew, Eddy stood and watched the fire quickly reaching the Russells' feet. They didn't move. When the flames engulfed their bodies and the chairs in which they were sitting, Eddy smiled to himself and walked quietly away into the night. His only regret was that they could not have been awake to know what was happening to them. Maybe they would then have had some idea of all the pain and misery he had endured.

In that still Corinth night, Eddy smiled as he savored the memory. He was still alive, but alive only in the mechanical sense. Grim satisfaction was the only gift he could give himself.

XLII

S TRAND'S INNER CLOCK told him it should have been dawn, but
daybreak it wasn't, judging from the lack of light fall in the un-
shaded window. Just then, the air-raid buzz of the clock radio
startled him awake, and Sunny FM filled the chilled air with details
of local news and weather.

With his head still on the pillow, Strand's one opened eye could
see the winter sky, blackened not by night, but by sullen, heavy cloud
cover. He groaned, knowing that Aurora and the kids would be leaving Columbus right after breakfast. Jackie Morrone's morning radio
voice soothed the air with sometimes useful information, and Strand
tuned in, hoping for good weather news.

"It's 6:45 a.m. and time for the Foreston and area weather for you
Saturday morning early birds," announced Morrone, knowing that
many borough old-timers were listening attentively, especially those
at the Penn Grove Hotel and other golden-ager warehouses. Strand
could imagine their ears perked for any potential topic of conversation, and weather always topped the list.

Strand let Morrone drone on as his thoughts turned to Aurora
and the kids, hoping there'd be no problems with the Olds. Would
his father-in-law check the car for her? Probably. Nevertheless, he

did not tuck the worry in the back of his mind, but kept it in front of him, where he could play with it and consider the many what-ifs.

As the light crept slowly into his consciousness, it occurred to him he had done little to get the place up to a standard higher than his own. He'd said goodbye to the great Earl Shannon and his hotel a few days before, and when possible, had spent every free minute after work dusting and cleaning—in a fashion all his own. There was much left to do.

Strand realized he had but three or four hours to finish the job and lay in a few groceries. He sprang out of bed—a rare feat—and took to his work with a vengeance. The bathrooms and kitchen were his focus—largely because Aurora would inspect them closely, he knew.

The final touch was a quick vacuum all around, a one-hour endeavor with much aerobic potential—if one remembered to alternate push-pull arms. Whether Aurora would be pleased, he did not know. Nevertheless, Strand excused his efforts by telling himself there had to be enough of a difference for her to believe she was needed. After all, he rationalized, would her ego be satisfied to walk into the house and not make some rearrangement or find something which needed her immediate attention?

In the excitement to complete household chores—as if the act of completion would bring his family home that much sooner—Strand did not acknowledge his question. Later, as he stood in the kitchen compiling a grocery list—veal parmesan, egg noodles, and salad for dinner—he paused. He caught himself, again, staring at nothing as he stirred the courage to answer his own question: he truly hoped he—no one or nothing else—would be the object of her immediate attention. Yet he also reminded himself not to expect romance as a principal ingredient in the homecoming tableau.

House cleaned, groceries fetched, attitude positively charged, the latter a constant battle, Strand was ready. He donned his heavy parka, wrestled the Hambone to a conscious state, and began a long, conspicuous walk up and down Pine Street. Though man and dog could always use the exercise, neither needed the marrow-chilling cold a February day could muster. They wished only to glimpse the Olds and its passengers as they made their way home.

Few people stopped to chat. Neighbors had become used to Strand without his family and no one asked. Perhaps it was his imagination, but people seemed more hurried, and not because of the frigid air. True, some days had passed since the Paulson boy's death, and true, Georgie Hallon had found no one to arrest. While the absence of a brutal act might be comfort to some, others felt the absence of a solution meant that like a wolf in the forest in search of prey, a murderer was amongst them, looking for another little boy to kill.

How totally self-centered can I be? I've let Aurora bring our kids back into this setting where two boys have been killed within blocks of our home! I'll have to tell her.

Snow began to flurry and a westerly breeze joined in to lower the practical temperature. Strand knew that he and his dog would soon have their resolution embrittled by their rapidly numbing extremities, but then the old dog, sniffer still intact, demonstrated his prowess in identifying familiar sounds. They were a block away from the house, and Bo whimpered, jerking his head back with such force that Strand turned around. Across the bridge one block away was the Olds' familiar shape, headlights on in the already-darkening day.

Aurora must have spied them as well—headlights brightened, then dimmed several times in repetition, reflecting the overwhelming gladness he himself felt. In a moment, Aurora pulled the car in the drive. Aarie and Anna practically broke their arms waving at Strand and Bo, and though the dog could barely see or hear, his tail wagged the fullness of his heart.

Strand's eyes moistened as he moved closer to the car. Aurora got out and came toward him, quickly at first, then more hesitantly as she came close. Perhaps she wanted to gauge Strand's welcome. Perhaps she wished to check her own enthusiasm, lest she be greeted with less than that for which she had hoped. Whatever the purpose, Strand, for once, did not attempt to divine it. He paused, ever so slightly, possibly listening to a voice whispering of an uncertain future for them. Instantly, he dismissed the devils of doubt. Aurora's response was immediate.

Closing the distance between themselves, their arms outstretched and inviting, they embraced. Aurora looked into her husband's eyes, and with conviction strengthened by separation, said, "Oh, God! How much I need you!"

"I love you so much," he said, adding nothing—it was the sum of his emotional state.

Aurora playfully grasped his coat with both hands, pulling him even closer to her. "You'd better," she intimated, "because I plan to give you every opportunity!"

XLIII

MORNING CAME AND Strand arose before the sun. The pull-shades were down, but his biological alarm told him Bentsen would be idling the State car in the driveway for more minutes than he cared to if Strand did not move quickly to his morning tasks. Aurora pulled the covers over her head at the sound of the electronic jangle her husband failed to disarm. Soon enough, she would be jarred awake by kid noise, he knew. Sitting on the edge of the bed, he looked back at his wife and smiled. It had been a wonderful reunion, not without its tentative moments, each of them weighing words and gestures in an effort to build emotional structures within which they could live together. Even so, it couldn't have been better. Aarie and Anna were at their best, and their emotions ran full.

As Strand dressed, he savored the small sounds of life he heard in the house: his wife's deep, contented breathing; Aarie and Anna moving about, readying themselves for a return to Foreston schools. He warmed himself with replays of their loving, tender moments of reunion and commitment. Smiling as he knotted his tie, the low rumble of a car's engine announced Bentsen's presence in the back driveway.

Strand kissed Aurora goodbye, and tiptoed out of the room. In the hallway, he heard Anna's whisper, "Daddy, where's my hug?"

Strand picked up his daughter, and gave her the biggest morning smile he could manage when he whispered, "I'm sure glad you're home with me!"

"And me?" asked Aarie, with the hopeful innocence of all boys his age, as he snuck up and gave his father a hug from behind.

"Yes! What would I do without my two very best friends?"

Aarie and Anna returned his smile with wide grins. Children, Strand reminded himself as he thought of other, not-so-fortunate youngsters, give so much in return for even the least bit of tenderness.

The sobering thought reminded him of his profession and his waiting partner. Hurrying down the stairs, Strand couldn't get the troublesome question out of his mind, and wondered why so many offered so little to those who need it so much.

In the unending cycle, he told himself, children are always the easiest, most defenseless victims of those who can find no other outlet for their distemper. Each generation repeats the same crime, condemned as they are to endure and render the same pain over and over again. Strand did not regularly begin his workdays with philosophic insight, but he could not help but guess how that most important of life's lessons applied to the murders of little boys, boys like Aarie.

The frigid air snapped at him as he walked out to the warm, waiting car, and the reality of his work. As he settled himself in the passenger seat, he noticed Bentsen quietly taking note of the two cars in the driveway. Bentsen looked his way, arching an eyebrow, half-smiling. Strand returned the smile with one of his own. "They all said you were sharp!" he teased. "They're home. 'God's in His heaven and all's right with the world.'"

"No it's not," Bentsen corrected, injecting the routine unpleasantness of the day's agenda. "Don't you remember? Today, we hear more about the byways of justice in the Knotting case."

"Oh, yeah," Strand acknowledged, focusing.

"It starts at ten," said Bentsen, not bothering to explain. "Let's go to the office, see Walt—or maybe, not see Walt, if we're lucky—take care of a few chores, then mosey over to the courthouse."

"Sounds like a great master plan to me."

~

A few minutes before 10 a.m., the short walk from the barracks behind them, the partners planted themselves in the back row of courtroom A, having obtained seats nearest the door. Two minutes after the hour, the Tipstaff loudly issued his formal invitation for all to draw near and be heard.

Looking gray from whatever flu bug had tagged him, Judge Morrison shuffled into the chamber and up to the bench, glancing briefly at the spectator seats as he did so. Strand could see him adjust his robes in a routine enjoyed by all courthouse regulars, and once done, he looked up, signaling his readiness to proceed.

Had there been a look of relief in the jurist's eye when he saw so many empty seats? Strand thought so, and leaning over to Bentsen, whispered his bet: Morrison would rule the Hanscomb-Stevens notes admissible. His partner responded with an arched eyebrow of his own, surprised as he was at Strand's prediction.

The clerk read the court's purpose and looked in the judge's direction, cuing him. Morrison cleared his throat, gaveled the room to silence, and took command of his stage. "Mr. Koenig. Ms. Wagner," he said flatly. "Please approach." When they did so, he asked them, quietly, "Are you in a position to settle this matter?"

"No, your honor," responded Wagner. "The State believes there is nothing on which to settle."

Morrison glared at Wagner, but made no comment. Swiveling his head in a smooth, level motion, he smiled invitingly at appellant's counsel.

"Mr. Knotting cannot surrender a case for his freedom, your honor. We elect to proceed on the motion."

Waving them back to their positions, Morrison returned to the script. "Do either of you wish to address this court further before a decision on the matter before us?"

"No, your honor," Wagner responded, speaking first, with Koenig echoing her.

Judge Morrison sat up straight in his chair, pulled papers to him, and donned his reading glasses. He began: "I have carefully reviewed your written briefs and have taken into careful consideration your oral presentations. Mindful of community sensitivity surrounding this case, I have also made special efforts to research all available material well beyond what each of you has conscientiously supplied.

"The threshold issue, concisely put, appears thusly: whether or not peripheral evidence irrelevant to the question of guilt or innocence, ought to be considered in determining the competency of representation. The answer to that question," Judge Morrison underlined, "is a resounding 'Yes,' when framed in that context.

"I said 'appears' because one could too easily misconstrue one issue for another. The question in this case, in my opinion, is subordinate to the larger one, and in that different factual setting, a determination becomes less clear. The issue for us, then, is whether or not certain pieces of peripheral evidence, not ordinarily relevant or available under any circumstances at trial, are admissible on appeal.

"There are, lamentably, few cases from which one can fairly discern and objectively apply relevant principles to the instant case. That is so, no doubt, because proven representational or judicial misconduct is relatively rare. In point of fact, the particular question raised in the instant case is nearly non-existent in the available literature.

"Though exhaustive research leaves us with a nearly unplowed field, there is, nevertheless, one case which provides us limited guidance on this question: *Stewart v. Commonwealth of Pennsylvania, 1947.* In that case, State Supreme Court Justice Brendan Thomas spoke for the majority in reference to a similar issue arising out of Stewart's earlier trial in 1939, in which the defendant had been convicted of armed robbery. In 1946, his attorney appealed after confirming a story heard, quite by chance, which indicated that Judge Torrance had continued with his client's trial after having suffered a heart attack."

Bentsen whispered, "I don't get it."

"Just get your money ready! He's laying the groundwork for a ruling favorable to Knotting. Just watch."

Strand noticed the coughing and throat-clearing had stopped as the other spectators became keenly interested in what the judge had to say. He, too, leaned forward and fixed his concentration on the figure at the bar.

"Justice Thomas had to consider whether or not the trial judge's physical condition rendered him unable to sit, or in the narrower sense, whether the judge could have made objective judgments in Stewart's or, for that matter, any case. Judge Torrance had, in fact, experienced two chest seizures, as calendar notes and an autopsy later confirmed. Both seizures occurred in the middle of the trial. Whether out of devotion to duty, or due to motives unknown, he neither sought treatment nor did he confide any potential medical impairment to anyone. Judge Torrance died only a few hours after sentencing Stewart to a fifteen-year prison term.

"The similarity between *Stewart* and *Knotting* is striking," Judge Morrison intoned. "The salient point for the purpose of this motion is that although the appellate court denied a motion to consider Judge Torrance's physical condition, Pennsylvania's Supreme Court ruled in appellant's favor on this point—not because of the judge's heart condition, but because he failed to inform counsel about it. Therefore, Ms. Wagner, Mr. Koenig, it is the ruling of this court that the trial notes of both Judge Hanscomb and District Attorney Stevens are admissible. Appellant's motion is granted."

All at once, the listeners collectively and audibly exhaled. A smug but not happy Strand held out his hand, palm up, waiting for it to be warmed with cold cash. He did not seriously expect to be paid, and only smiled when his partner suggested a physically impossible act.

Out in the courthouse lobby, the pair ran into several of the regulars who wanted to chat and within thirty minutes, the hearing's remaining spectators poured out when Judge Morrison gaveled for lunch. Strand signaled to the prosecutor and she ambled over, none too happy.

At the Mercer Inn, as Wagner, Strand, and Bentsen inhaled

sandwiches and opinions, the Assistant District Attorney spoke about what Judge Morrison did not say. "The Stewart case is relevant only because Jim Milcher should have informed Judge Hanscomb and DA Stevens—not to mention Knotting—if only to give Knotting an opportunity to obtain new counsel."

"I still don't get it," Bentsen said.

"What it boils down to, Joe, is that while Stewart said there was no problem for a judge to have such a condition, assuming no harm to the defendant could be shown, there's the implication such harm would be assumed if defendant's counsel were viewed as impaired in any way."

Strand exhaled. "I guess that does it, then."

XLIV

O
N THEIR WAY back to the office, Strand and Bentsen quickly
moved on from further discussion about the Knotting case.
They knew the hearing would drag on for at least another day,
with Knotting and his erstwhile friend, Frederick Cathcart, making
possible witness chair appearances before it was all over.

"Knotting may win the battle, but will he win the war?"

"Speaking of our Morganville friend," Bentsen said, "you'll never
guess who I ran into on the way to the restroom."

"I don't want to guess," bid Strand.

"Well," Bentsen began, Cheshire-like, "sitting there on one of the
stools at the blind stand, I heard Jimmy chatting with one of his
other customers," Bentsen reported, referring to one of the human
fixtures of the courthouse.

"You know, it's funny," he continued, "but when Jimmy talks
about 'seeing' somebody, it seems so odd because he can't see anybody at all. It's all in his hearing."

"And...?" interjected Strand, hoping to get his profound partner
to his point.

"Well, what caught my ear from around the corner was Jimmy
saying to this woman, 'I haven't seen you around here before—an'

you don't sound too happy to be here!' She said she didn't know whether she should be happy or not.

"Anyway, I turned around just as Jimmy was asking her name. All she said was, 'Viki Mae.'"

"That Viki Mae—Knotting's girlfriend?"

"Has to be. She's telling Jimmy about how her boyfriend's hearing is going on, and how he really got screwed by his lawyer, and on and on. I listened for a while, not so much because she had anything of interest to say, but because I couldn't help thinking I knew her."

"Knew her? From where?"

"Hell, I don't know! Underneath the fried red hair and the layered makeup, she reminded me of somebody."

Just then, they reached the barracks and checked their desks for notes. Important was the absence of an assignment from Walter Montgomery to pick up and deliver Knotting and Cathcart for the current courtroom production.

There were a number of other items, however, and they began to sift and sort, deciding their priority order. In their job, everything might be considered "First on the List," or so it would have seemed to an outsider. For homicide detectives, like emergency room doctors, decisions had to be made borne of experience, judgment, and the laws of probability as artfully practiced as they could be.

Strand and Bentsen took about an hour organizing their week, or at least making a rough plan they both knew would be changed many times over. There were no fresh homicides or other serious crimes occurring in their district—a respite of several days was not unusual for the time of year. Their priorities, therefore, were unfinished business. Phone calls and evidence checks helped in the decision process, but there was plenty of time to devote to an unofficial assignment—the Foreston killings. The trail was getting colder and Hallon was doing nothing to produce any results.

∾

Dr. Michael Harkansen's office at the Corinth Institution was like the interior of many ancient buildings renovated with public monies. For Capitol officeholders, the re-dos could be luxurious; for worker bees, not so much. Often, a Victorian pile like the one in which his office was located had institution-like drop ceilings poorly installed. Yellowed with age, cigarette smoke, and leaks from above, the 2x4 tiles topped a box sided with ill-fitting brown paneling which crowded the large, badly painted window mouldings.

The arms of the padded chairs were slit by the fingernails of many a tense patient uneasily grilled by well-meaning head doctors. In one of the chairs, its orange vinyl the victim of many attacks, Eddy sat waiting for an official conversationalist to arrive. He took in what details of the room he had missed on prior occasions, then examined the distant view through the window's defining frame. His eyes' focusing mechanism was able to blur what cheap curtains could not disguise: heavy steel mesh guarding the glass from direct, inside attack.

Eddy's thoughts took him well outside the old building in which he had been stored. Despite the icy edge to the winter's day, his vision took him to the warmth of waiting arms and the loving caresses of a featureless parent he could not recall—because in his life there'd been no one like that. Into this peaceful state, thinly masking a seething quest for revenge, walked Dr. Harkansen.

Long accustomed to attempting the very best possible on little money, Harkansen knew the state's citizens gave people like him just enough to cover up what no one wished to see. The citizenry was conditioned to expect the best and felt cheated with less. As a result, when one of them fell beneath the standard of civilized behavior, they found their way into the State's unloving, institutional hands, or they were consigned to places like the Corinth Institution, imprecisely named so that the worst of the misfits—of whatever age—could be warehoused under its roof.

One of misfits was Eddy Snyder.

The young man's back was to the door as Harkansen walked in and said, "Hello" in as warm a tone as he could manage. It was not a meeting which he relished. Eddy Snyder had run away from the halfway house in Meadville, and among other things, stole a car and caused someone's death. Despite earlier indications of social reintegration, Eddy had continued to show he had not learned to control his behavior or deal with his status in life.

"Hi," Eddy responded with an emotionally traceless voice. "I'm doin' great, huh!"

"Yes, you are, Eddy, if you're talking about your recovery from the accident. If you're talking about how you're coming along overall, I'm not sure 'great' would be the right word," he concluded firmly, hiding any sarcasm he felt.

Surprise showed on Eddy's face as he made his case. "Hey, how was I supposed to know that old fart was goin' ta turn when he did? If it hadn' a been for him, I just woulda been out for a little drivin' practice, an' you'd a never known it." Eddy's air was one of superiority, as if the shrink in front of him possessed an intelligence far beneath his own.

"I think you missed the point, Eddy. Our whole approach with you has been based on your demonstrated understanding of the rules—rules here at Corinth, at the halfway house in Meadville, and on the outside. We thought you were ready for the next steps on the way to being more on your own."

"I am ready. I've been ready for a long time!" His fingers dug into chair arms, clawing at the disintegrating yellow foam underneath.

"Two months ago, I would have agreed with you. I don't know if you understand this, Eddy, but the State can still press charges against you for car theft, not to mention a man's wrongful death. The fact that you are considered socially impaired..."

"Socially impaired!? What kinda bullshit is that? I'm no more impaired than anybody else. In fact, I'm a whole lot better than a lot of other people out there—people who don't deserve what they have."

"What people are you talking about?" asked Harkansen, accepting the distraction.

"Never mind."

"Eddy, if there's something you want to talk about, let's do it. We have time."

"When am I getting out of here? When am I going back to

Meadville?"

"Not for a while." Harkansen saw the anger in Eddy's face, and hastened to add, "Eddy, there are people out there who are very upset by the accident you caused. There were people who knew and liked Art Wilhelm..."

"Who the hellz he?" interrupted Eddy sullenly.

"The man who was killed in the accident. Eddy," Harkansen continued, pleadingly, "don't you understand? You—YOU—are responsible for his death. YOU have to take responsibility for that. YOU have to accept responsibility for your acts before we can let you be on the outside." The psychiatrist leaned forward. "Do you understand what I'm trying to tell you?"

Eddy did not answer right away. He was ready for anything, but the answer in his head wasn't the answer the shrink wanted. If the whitecoat wanted to hear magic words, then that's what he would hear—anything to further his goal of greater freedom. "Yes," he said meekly.

Harkansen's smile held no satisfaction. He knew from experience with Eddy and people like him that an honest answer was not to be had easily, that self-serving, manipulative behavior was more the norm. The acknowledgement Eddy offered was superficial, but it was a mandatory step. The state had not decided whether to prosecute, given Eddy's social development and sense of responsibility—or nearly complete lack thereof. Echoing one of his thoughts, he offered, "That's a good first step, Eddy. With continued progress, we'll reconsider your future."

"When?"

"In time—when you get out of here is really up to you."

"Yeah, doc. You're right. It is up to me."

XLV

A S IF IT had been waiting offstage for a grand entrance, luck joined Strand and Bentsen as they pulled the Vic up to the Simpson house on Woodfield Drive just before 1:45 p.m. on the 6th of February. It was not Mrs. Simpson who answered the front door, but Wendy Russell.

After a minute's chatter, she agreed to meet them at the hospital, where they could speak privately, but for only ten or fifteen minutes before her shift began.

The cafeteria's mauve carpet underpinned the nondescript oak and vanilla furniture greeting all who entered. At precisely 2:10 p.m., a uniformed Wendy Russell appeared, a cup of caffeinated ambition in hand.

"You two look like two down-and-outers in some eternal waiting room. I wasn't that long, was I?"

"Not at all," Strand responded with a wan smile. "Can you tell us more about the people your parents knew or were acquainted with over the years? Was there ever anyone with whom they had a serious quarrel, for example?"

"Many people knew them very well, and they were well-respected in the area, but surely, you must know all that. Furthermore, I'd be extremely surprised if anyone would ever or could ever hold a grudge against them—not enough to do something like, like that, to them."

"I remember Doc McCreary mentioning something in passing about their ages at the time of death—how old were they again?" Strand asked, wanting to clear up a point of interest.

"My father was seventy-six and my mother, seventy-four."

"And you're...?" he asked, gesturing to her.

"Twenty-six. Why?"

"Of course," Strand cleared his throat, "it's not that unusual, but that means your mother was forty-six when you were born. And you're an only child, is that right?"

Smiling, Wendy responded with the quiet glee of someone with a secret about to be revealed. "You've made a couple of assumptions, Fletch."

Strand caught the use of his first name, and forced himself to respond to her comment, not by speaking, but by lifting an eyebrow, as if to say, "Such as?"

"That I was the Russells' natural child. I'm not. They adopted me. In fact, I was one of a number of children the Russells fostered—they never had any of their own. I was never placed, so they adopted me several years ago."

"Isn't that unusual? I mean, for the State to allow older people to adopt?" The question came from the childless Bentsen.

"Maybe. But don't forget the Russells had had a lot of experience with other people's children. By adopting me, they were merely legitimizing what they and the State were coming to accept as fact—no one was going to take me. Though they weren't my biological parents, they had come to be 'real' to me."

Bentsen maintained his interest, mostly professional, idly personal. "Were there a lot of children in the house over the years, then?"

"Oh, yes, very much so," Russell answered, "but none after they adopted me."

Strand interjected. "Were there ever any problems with any of them?"

"No. None that I can recall—from what Mom and Dad told me and from what I saw, every one of the kids—except me—was eventually placed. Not a one of them would have anything but gratitude for the Russells. In fact, I received a number of sympathy cards from their former wards, most I didn't even know. I guess they made quite an impression, huh!" she remarked with a brave pride.

Just then, a younger woman passed near them, carrying a tray with some difficulty. Strand could see Russell watching her.

Bentsen turned, asking curiously, "Is she a nurse?"

"No," answered Russell, flushed. "She's an aide."

"Born that way?" Bentsen continued.

Strand became a little irritated at the distraction, but he could also see that Russell seemed nervous about something.

"There's something I need to explain. A little bit ago, you asked me if there had ever been any trouble at our house. My answer wasn't exactly correct."

The detectives remained silent.

"There was trouble—once. It's so silly even to bring it up, but seeing Natalie—the person you asked about, Joe—reminded me about it. When I was placed with the Russells, my little brother came along, too. Eddie couldn't seem to adjust well, bothered as he was by the nightmares from other placements."

As she talked, Strand noticed Russell seemed to look more and more inward, as if it took great concentration to bring back the details about which she was speaking. Bentsen didn't move a muscle.

"Why he couldn't seem to make things work in the best home we had been in, I don't know. Oh, he got along with the Russells, alright, but they weren't the problem. One day at school, Eddie's temper got the best of him. Natalie is the result."

"What do you mean, the result?" quizzed Strand.

"I wasn't there, but from what I heard, Eddie went crazy on the playground and for whatever reason, he grabbed little Natalie around the neck and hit her head against a wall—either a brick wall or the bleachers—more than once."

Strand could see that the details from memory didn't require the concentration so much as Russell's attempt to deal with it.

"Apparently, Natalie had been a normal child—she was only eight when it happened. Eddie was ten, I think. The trauma to her head was enough to cause permanent damage—Natalie has almost full faculties, but what you saw there is as good as she'll ever be."

"Wendy," Strand prodded gently, "what happened to Eddie?"

"I guess that had been the last of a number of problems at school. I don't mean to minimize what happened to Natalie by calling it 'a problem,' but for Eddie it was the end of the world. There was a hearing. My mom and dad—the Russells—stood up for him, but the judge wouldn't hear it. They took him away after that."

"The State?" Bentsen asked. "What exactly happened, do you remember?"

"Well, I was about thirteen at the time, so some of the details did not stick with me—some of it Mom and Dad probably didn't tell me. All I know is the court decided to send him to Corinth."

"Committed?"

"Yes. Mom and dad told me the court considered Eddie disturbed in some way, enough, anyway, not to release him. From my nursing studies—at least from the courses dealing with emotional health— I've always guessed Eddie to have sociopathic tendencies."

"What else?" Bentsen prompted.

"Hey, don't hold me to any of this. I don't have the degree, but from what I recall my Mom and Dad saying, Eddie didn't seem to make much of a distinction between right and wrong—he didn't ap-prehend what he had done to Natalie—and he didn't seem concerned about the consequences. When I've seen him on visits, though, he seems normal enough. That's the scary part—he acts normal, but he's not."

"You see him? At Corinth?" Strand wondered aloud.

"Oh, yes. Sometime after Natalie, I think they placed him with somebody else, but then he was back—I don't know those details. Ever since I got out of nursing school, I've visited him about every six weeks or so, but he's not there now. Last fall, they moved him closer—to a halfway house in Meadville—I saw him there the week before Christmas."

"Is that when you saw him last? Or talked to him?"

"Yes, but I don't know what's going on with him now. They called me from the halfway house, and I guess he just walked away from there."

Strand could feel his pulse quicken. "When was that?"

"Well, they called me right after Christmas, and I haven't heard back. I guess they don't know where he is."

Strand took a deep breath. "How long did you say he lived with the Russells?"

"About two years or so, actually. I guess I haven't been in a hurry to tell him about the fire because I wasn't sure what his reaction would be."

"Why is that?" helped Bentsen again.

"Well, somehow Eddie had the impression that the Russells didn't want him, just like all the others. I've always tried to explain to him there wasn't anything the Russells could have done for him, but he doesn't accept that. He still thinks they could have kept him somehow."

"Could they have, Wendy?" queried Strand.

"I don't know. Probably not. I think they were a little scared of him. They were older, and he did have a pretty bad temper at times. They once told me the social worker said that keeping Eddie meant they couldn't have other children around—including me. The psychiatrists said Eddie harbored deep resentments. It was very hard for Mom and Dad Russell. They didn't want to let him go, yet they knew they couldn't keep him. Anyway, I still don't know how Eddie's going to take the news."

Strand risked an incomplete thought, half under his breath, "Maybe he already knows."

Bentsen asked for and wrote down the name of the psychiatrist they should see.

Russell had been looking at her watch and seemed surprised at its signal. "Oh, my God!" she interjected, "it's quarter to three. I'll miss Report."

"Wait—just one more thing," Strand said, and didn't wait to continue. "You obviously took the Russell name. But Eddie? What's his name?

"Oh, Eddie Snyder. I have to go."

Thanking her, they left with the quickened heartbeats of homicide men possessed with a vision suddenly made clearer.

XLVI

"**O**KAY,**"** B**ENTSEN** **SAID** as he keyed the Vic's ignition, "Corinth it is. Let's stop at Country Fair, get coffee, and call ahead to make sure this Dr. Harkansen doesn't head home early."

"Right," Strand responded, "but we'll do more."

Ten minutes later, coffees in hand, they headed toward the I-79 interchange and north.

Strand reported what he'd heard. "The Meadville halfway house still hasn't retrieved their escapee, but yes, Dr. Harkansen was expecting my call and he'll wait for us."

"No APB on Eddie Snyder?"

"Apparently, halfway house walkaways are a low priority, Joe. What a news story this could make."

Bentsen drove and hummed. Strand thought about the options. Of course, Snyder could be completely innocent of anything, but as he'd learned at the police academy, good cops don't believe in coincidences. If Snyder escaped just before Christmas and the Russells were murdered shortly thereafter by someone with a grudge, the likelihood of the two events being connected were quite high. In any event, it was the only untrodden path in the case so far, and it wouldn't take much time, they felt, to rule the possibility in or out.

The ride north was quick, especially given their animated rehash on their caseload. "Hey, are we sure about Mrs. Jarvis—the Hermitage case?"

"Oh, yeah! Her story about him falling down the stairs will never wash—she's lucky he lived, even though he's in a coma." Confirmation of preliminary findings was virtually certain, Strand added, and lab reports were due from Harrisburg momentarily.

Strand and Bentsen agreed Mrs. Jarvis had been entirely too nervous when they questioned her, and her spirited, defiant air just under the surface convinced them she had much more to say. With Mrs. Jarvis, it was only a matter of time, good forensic evidence, and an above average interrogation technique. That the case would come together in the next few days in a particular way seemed, for them, a foregone conclusion.

"You know what, Fletch? Since we're heading up there and Meadville's on the way, why don't we make a quick stop there before heading to Corinth?"

"Good idea. Harkansen said he'd wait."

Wendy Russell's description of the halfway house at 2426 McPherson Avenue was reasonably accurate. Nestled in a neighborhood of forty-year-old ranch style homes, the large house looked much like any other except for the flotilla of cars in the expanded driveway area to the side of the two-car garage. They parked the Vic on the street.

As they walked toward the house, sun streaks splashed the patched green grass, and they could hear running water as melting ice in the gutters made its way to earth. Ice sheets on the street shattered as the asphalt warmed and expanded.

Having heard a doorbell ring somewhere inside the house, he and Bentsen waited quietly, IDs ready. The door jerked open suddenly, and the men reflexively started for their firearms, their hands just above their hearts, as if ready to say "the Pledge Allegiance," when they took in the unarmed older woman standing in front of them.

Standing there, blocking the doorway, was a formidable woman, both in size and presence. Her raspy voice was as intimidating as any sergeant reading Miranda rights to an arrestee as she set the tone of the interview. "So, who did what now?"

Bentsen chuckled.

No stranger to police officers of whatever variety standing at her threshold, she went on. "Let me guess," she whined, "you two stiffs are here with a million dollars from Ed McMahon!"

It was Strand's turn to smile.

Unable to resist temptation, Bentsen countered, "Why yes, my dear lady, I have the check right here in my pocket." With that, he maneuvered his credentials, checkbook fashion, and slid the case open for her. "Is it what you expected?" he queried, adding his own bit of irony, as she glanced first at the bright brass shield, then at his official mugshot under the lamination.

"Okay, so again, who did what now?"

"We'd like to see Eddie Snyder," ventured Strand.

"You can't," she responded with relief and satisfaction.

"Not here?"

"That's right, and I don't think I should give you any more information without a warrant."

"You're under State contract," Bentsen affirmed, "and if Eddie isn't here, he's a fugitive, no? So, no warrant, no problem. And who are you?"

"Pauline Buchanan—I run the show here."

"This time, we just want some information, Mom."

"If it's Eddie Snyder you're lookin' for, I'll offer no opinion unless he's dead and I'm lookin' at the body. I'm glad he's gone, and in fact, I told that Dr. Harkansen to keep him away from my house. I have to be careful. You guys know that." She opened the door, just a bit.

"So, what can you tell us, Pauline?"

"What I can tell you is that he's not here, but at Corinth."

"So, what happened?"

"I told you guys, I can't talk about a resident's activities—an invasion of their privacy or some crap like that."

"This is police business," Bentsen intervened, "and we're not asking you for a statement, only some facts about Snyder's residence here."

"It's a fine line you're askin' me to walk!"

"We all walk it, Pauline. How 'bout it? Take a step or two."

"Look, I haven't seen Snyder since a few days before Christmas—the crazy bastard just left. No big deal. Now he's been back at Corinth. May even come back here after a while, God forbid."

Strand knew she had more to say.

"Why're you makin' a federal case outta this? These people walk away from here alla time. I didn't keep track, an' he didn't come back here. They took him back to Corinth."

"Yeah, you said that," Bentsen said. "Who's they?"

"They. They, meaning some cop outfit."

"Hey, hey! What'd we do to you?"

"Nothin'. Except you guys are always around askin' questions—never tell people what it's all about."

"We can't say anything at this point, Pauline," Strand observed in a conciliatory tone. "We're just checking something out, that's all. Are you telling us he was gone from what, the 22nd? 23rd?"

"Twenty-third, I think. Wait—maybe it was a day or two earlier than that."

"Till when? Do you know?"

More cooperative now, she looked heavenward for a calendar. "Well, he went back to Corinth about a week ago, I heard, so, yeah, I was right," she said, pleased with herself, "he was on the loose about a month. So? What's so important about those dates, anyway?"

All the while that she meandered through her logic processes—out loud—Bentsen riffled the pages of his worn black leather notebook, easily molded to the palm of his hand, looking for dates. Glancing at his partner, he nodded, almost imperceptibly.

"Like we said, just checking to see what fits and what doesn't. By the way, what was he like, Pauline?"

"Now you're making me take a step off that narrow path," she laughed nervously, "and besides, that's what Dr. Harkansen gets paid for."

"Oh, Pauline," tried Bentsen on another tack, "when he left here before Christmas, did he take anything with him? Suitcase or anything like that?"

Once again, she reached back in memory, though not with great concentration inasmuch as the men were almost out of her day. Finally, she said, "You know, they don't have too much. A few clothes and things like that. Most of 'em, when they walk, they don't take much—almost as if they know they won't be gone long."

"Was that what he did?"

"He was different," she said, offering a shade of opinion for the first time in their meeting. "I guess I can't forget what he took. You know, all the while he was at Corinth, he was involved in the theater group—for therapy reasons, I guess. Well, when he left here, he took all his acting stuff—you know, makeup and things like that—acting getups. Like I said, he was different. When he dressed as a female, he called himself Eddy, with a 'y.'"

"Interesting. Why do you suppose he took that stuff? If he was like the others, and coming back here, why would he bother taking it with him?"

"Oh, well, Eddie was always good at putting on another face, so to speak. Maybe he needed that stuff with him like kids need their teddy bears. Hey, look! That's all I'm tellin' ya. See the doc!"

XLVII

EDDY—WHO'D COME TO think of himself as Eddy, not Eddie— perched himself on the edge of the day room's ruby-colored vinyl couch, and rubbed his aching right arm. On the knobless television, CNN's financial analyst seemed bent on trumpeting an economic downturn, mentioning the word recession with theatrical hesitancy and emotional commitment. Eddy, smirking, knew little about the commentator's subject, and cared less. He continued to massage his arm, each stroke reminding him of years-old pain requiring requital. It reminded him of the McGruders.

When he about twelve, someone decided he needed another chance, and that was when the McGruders came into his life. Eddie thought they had everything—that he was going to have everything, everything he'd been denied. In the evening of his first day with them, Hannah McGruder, his new "mother," was settling Eddie in his room. Having observed the look of wonderment in his eyes, and enjoying the pleasure she had seen there, she couldn't help but ask him what he was thinking.

"I guess I can't believe it". "Why?" he asked, curiously and suspiciously. This was the first placement without Wendy.

"'Why,' what?" Mrs. McGruder asked.

"I mean, why would rich people like you want to take me in? Do you need the money, or something?"

She laughed with him at his innocence. "We aren't exactly rich, Eddie, but perhaps, we're more...let's say, comfortable, than you've been. We've been blessed with a great deal, and maybe that's the reason you're here." That was all she could think to say, apparently.

Eddie laughed. "I'm just glad you did it. Are you people really going to adopt me, or what?" Eddie saw the woman's eyes shift to look at something, not at him.

"Well, I don't know, Eddie," she admitted. "Right now, we're just making a home for you. There's a lot of things that have to be worked out, and well, we'll just have to see..."

"Oh. I guess you're gonna check me out first. Is that it?"

"If you put it that way," she quickly responded, laughing lightly, so as not to betray her nervousness, "I guess that's what we're both going to do. Isn't it?"

Eddie knew then, right at that second, he remembered, that it wasn't going to work out at all. Having already passed through at least four foster homes he could recall, he had become adept at recognizing the first tiny signs of rejection. Enjoy it while it lasts, he told himself. For however long that turned out to be, he wouldn't be hungry, cold, or left out, or so he had hoped.

At first, life with the McGruders was almost like being hip-deep in presents around a Christmas tree, just as Eddie had dreamed it would. The bright and large farmhouse, remodeled many times, and long since a residence for escaping urbanites, was well-established amidst the tall pines, and gave the McGruders a great deal of privacy.

Mr. McGruder, a busy, ambitious banker, who travelled much of the time, had little contact with Eddie, except on the weekends. For the most part, Eddie was Hannah McGruder's charge. Months went by, and for the first time in his young life, Eddie had begun to look forward to the days and weeks ahead of him.

One thing he noticed was that Carolyn, the McGruder's only child, was constantly with her father, and though she and Eddie were about the same age, she stayed away from him. They developed no real acquaintanceship and like casual friends passing daily in the street, they spoke politely to each other, but with as little personal interest as possible. Carolyn's deliberate distancing made him wonder: Why did Mrs. McGruder want him around? Why did Mr. McGruder—and to some degree, Carolyn—make him feel like he was in the way?

It was on a shiny Saturday afternoon in late June that Eddie's fragile world spun too quickly on its axis, learning as he did more about life and the McGruders than he could want to know at his age. As it happened, Mrs. McGruder, at the Mill Creek Mall for the day, had left Carolyn and her father home alone. Eddie was there, too, of course, but the McGruders, father and daughter, he knew, considered him nearly invisible, and apparently, had forgotten all about him.

About three o'clock, after playing in the barn, Eddie made his way to the house, where he made and quickly finished his favorite afternoon snack of peanut butter and butter on a folded pocket of whole wheat bread, chased by a glass of chocolate milk. Leaving the kitchen and heading up the stairs, he thought he heard muffled, pleading cries as he neared the top. They sounded like protests of sorts, feeble ones, belonging to Carolyn's tiny voice. In a half-crying, half-plaintive voice, he heard her say, "Daddy, we shouldn't be doing this!" He heard no response.

Eddie stopped to listen to the one-sided conversation, not because he wanted to eavesdrop, but because it made little sense to his ears. He took another step. Over the years, in one household after another, he had been told to mind his own business, to shut his ears to the intimate noises of familyhood. He had been shut out of other lives, and learned to have no interest in the lives of others. Having learned the rules well, he told himself that Carolyn was simply whining to her father about something. He repeated caution's tale to himself, but the tiny spark of care left in him made him pause.

Seconds later, amidst his turmoil, he heard Carolyn say, pleadingly, "Oh, Daddy, why are you doing that to me?" The tone wasn't one so much in pain as it was surprise, shock, distaste. When he heard her inhale, as if startled, caution and fear vanished. He crossed the few steps to her door, knocked, and without waiting for an answer, went in. What he saw was odd and bewildering, but one thing was certain—it was not right.

There, in the middle of her spacious bedroom, some ten feet from him, on the edge of her bed, sat Carolyn. Actually, he recalled as he replayed the scene for himself, she was reclining, pale green and rose-colored dress pulled up to her middle. Kneeling on the floor in front of her was the proper, upright banker, her father, Martin Mc-Gruder. For a full five seconds, neither father nor daughter saw him standing there.

All at once, Carolyn loudly inhaled again, managing to nearly shout in surprise and embarrassment, "Eddie!"

Martin McGruder's face turned an angry red. "What! What are you doing here, you little shit?" he screamed. Then, preoccupied with the full realization of what the boy must have seen, he asked, quietly, "Why did you open that door?"

Speechless, Eddie could utter nothing other than, "I...ah..." Much as he tried, his mind could not help him respond to a meaningless question, at least, not until it sorted out what it had helped him see but not comprehend. As he had done so many times in his life, present but without an answer the adult was willing to accept, he ceased trying to answer, but waited for the reaction. It came.

All but ridiculous in his underwear, McGruder nevertheless managed to gain his height and make a lunge at him. Stepping back, the hapless twelve-year-old bumped into the doorjamb. Had Eddie been just a bit faster and moved a little to his right, McGruder's grasp would have been empty. As it was, McGruder's right hand easily clasped itself onto Eddie's T-shirt. With his left hand, McGruder clumsily swung, intending to slap Eddie's face. Instead, he hit the bony part of the boy's head, just above his ear.

Eddie could not duck quickly enough. Hardened though he was from years of abuse, the tears came quickly. He was crying not because of a misplaced smack to his head, but out of fear for what he had seen. Although he had seen one or more of his many parents in various stages of undress and physical activity, those scenes had seemed somehow natural, somehow okay. What he had just seen with McGruder and his daughter was not at all okay. The way the father had behaved, Eddie began to understand he had caught him at something, and he wished he hadn't.

McGruder dragged his foster son down the hall and pushed him into the catch-all closet. The man was screaming—did he sound afraid?—shouting hoarsely that he would deal with him later.

The key turned, clicking the lock in place. He began to slide down the wall, reaching for the floor in the utter darkness of the tiny room. The line of light at the bottom of the door helped guide him to the dismal certainty of the floor. It was then he felt the blood on the back of his head. He pushed a hand up there to feel—it felt strange trying to find himself in the dark, like some of his parts didn't belong to him. He must have grazed his head against one of the hooks there in a row, now above his head. There wasn't much blood, just enough to leave his hands sticky and wet as he rubbed them together. Drying them further on his pantlegs, he didn't think Mrs. McGruder would be mad at him about it. Mr. McGruder wouldn't be mad, either, he hoped, when he saw how unfair he was being.

In the darkness, he listened for noises, anything. He thought he heard Mr. McGruder shouting at Carolyn, but he wasn't sure. He touched the walls, ran his fingers through the carpet fibers, and re-membered one of his school lessons, where they made you pretend you were blind. There was no way to tell how long he had been in the closet, much like an upright casket, Eddie thought. Then the click in the lock, the turning knob, and the opening door, all in one motion, caught him by surprise. He hadn't had time to form the beginning of a smile he hoped would appease the man in front of him.

"You son of a bitch!" McGruder shouted. "Look what you've done, you little shit!" There was blood on the walls and the car-pet. "Goddammit," he yelled, stringing his profanity together like Christmas lights, "go get a washcloth and soap and scrub this clean! Then I'll deal with you!"

Eddie scurried under the big man's legs, got to his feet, and ran to the bathroom. He told himself to do what Mr. McGruder wanted. Then he would be nice to him. All the while he worked, his "father" stood over him, screaming orders every other minute. Carolyn was nowhere to be seen.

When he was finished, he was told to follow. "Where are we going?" asked Eddie, half-asking, half-demanding.

"To the barn, that's where."

Immediately concluding he would get a whipping, he begged, "Why? I didn't do anything!" When he heard no answer, he asked several more times, "Why? What did I do?"

Once, he stopped and shouted in defiance, "No! I'm not going with you. It isn't fair."

McGruder turned to look at him. "Who the hell do you think you're talking to?" He slapped Eddie, this time with his right hand, and he didn't miss. "You do as I say." Then, McGruder gripped Eddie's left arm like a pair of pliers, and at a quick pace, marched the boy out of the house, and to the barn some yards away.

When they got inside, McGruder closed the doors, and turned on him. The screaming inside the house was nothing like it sounded in a big, open old barn. McGruder's voice roared in Eddie's ears. "What the hell did you think you were doing?" he started. "We give a nasty little shit like you a home, and you poke your nose into our lives? Everything was great before you came—you screwed everything up." He didn't stop. "What did you think you saw?"

"Nothing!" shouted Eddie, abject fear edging his voice.

"You're right! You saw nothing. Understand me?"

"Yessir!"

"What did you say?"

"Yessir," he repeated in a monotone.

McGruder was angry, and frightened, he could see. He stood in front of the boy, staring, intent on a plan. In an instant, without forewarning, he grabbed Eddie by the arm, and twisting it outward and sideways, slammed it against the hard wooden edge of the horse stall.

Eddie heard his arm crack, then saw the bone protrude from the skin, jagged edge looking just like a dry, barkless branch, bleached by the sun. Only this branch had blood on it, a lot of it. He screamed.

"Quiet, you little bastard. It won't do you any good—none at all. I've got you all taken care of." McGruder exhaled a small, satisfying chuckle.

Eddie was on the ground, unable to cry or make a sound. In wrenching pain, he squeezed his elbow as tightly as he could, as much to distract himself from the sight of his arm as to lessen its piercing ache. As he struggled to maintain consciousness, he wondered what had happened to him, why his arm had been broken, and why McGruder treated him that way.

XLVIII

WHEN EDDIE WOKE up in the hospital emergency room, the staff worked on him, but something wasn't right. They did their jobs, but showed little interest in him or concern for what had happened to him. He was more confused than ever.

A few hours later, Mrs. Hawkins, his social worker, came in to talk to him. She was very business-like. "Well, Eddie, I guess you'll be coming back with us—that is, if the judge lets us have you."

"The judge?"

"Of course, Eddie, we don't know if this will go to court or not, or what will happen to you."

"Happen to me? What about Mr. McGruder?"

"What about him? He was just defending his daughter. No one will blame him much for what happened to you."

Tears welled up. "What are you talking about?"

"Oh, come on, Eddie. You know very well what I'm talking about, and if not, I'm sure the authorities will explain it to you."

"I'm sorry, Mrs. Hawkins," he protested. "Really, I don't know what you're talking about. Really! This isn't right. It isn't fair."

"I'm afraid that's what all twelve-year-old boys say when they lie."

He remembered that day well. *Someday, I'll find Mr. McGruder—and that Mrs. Hawkins, too.*

In the present, Eddy continued to stroke his arm, sore from the break so many years before. The man on the TV screen was parroting the latest NFL scores—something Eddy could care less about—and two others from the institution were with him, mesmerized by the electronic image or one within their own minds.

Eddy resisted replaying his mental tapes of the McGruder episode—they were too painful for him, yet he was drawn to the happenings of that year because they made him feel good about his twenty-third.

Although it had taken him some minutes to realize it when Mrs. Hawkins was talking to him, Martin McGruder had arranged it so that Eddie turned out to be the bad guy. He felt the anger rise up in him, much like the bitter tears salting the eyes of his youth, the more he grasped what McGruder had managed to accomplish with the sweet lies of influence.

McGruder's plan had worked well, indeed. Eddy reflected on the irony of McGruder's words to him in the barn that day: "I've got you all taken care of." The white-shirt-and-tie banker, proper church-goer and civic leader, managed to convince everyone that he had come upon Eddie forcing himself on the innocent Carolyn. His beautiful daughter, McGruder swore, had had her clothes pulled from her, and was made to endure the juvenile groping and fondling of a disturbed foster child. When Eddie heard Mrs. Hawkins finally recite the story, he hastened to volunteer that it was substantially correct, with one exception—it was McGruder in his underwear doing those things to his own daughter. He could see the shock on Mrs. Hawkins' face. Instead, she said, "After what you did to Natalie Hobson, and now this, I'm just so glad not every foster boy is like you. I doubt you'll get any more chances, Eddie," she said, and left the room.

McGruder also claimed that what he had seen so enraged him that logic and reason escaped him. Without thinking it through, he testified, he reacted as any father would when he tried to drag the boy off. The boy fought ferociously, and it was just an accident the boy stumbled down the stairs and broke his arm. Eddy remembered scenes in the hearing rooms when the whole incident was replayed—everyone believed McGruder, totally ignoring the physical evidence, or lack thereof. Given Eddie's history, State officials did not care to contest the charges, and the outcome was foregone. Carolyn didn't testify—McGruder simply told the judge what Carolyn's testimony was going to be and they all accepted it.

No one, not the social worker, the police, or the judge, weighed McGruder's story against Eddie's. It was clear from the way everyone behaved that no one wanted to disbelieve Martin McGruder. It was all too easy to look with disgust at the pitiable, troubled boy who had been turned away from so many homes—and had a history of bad behavior. So, in the end it was Eddie, just as McGruder had planned, who was made to bear the guilt of wrongdoing. For what? For daring to go where he was not wanted.

∾

When Strand maneuvered their official chariot into the visitor's lot, he and Bentsen sat for a minute and took in Corinth's most imposing building, gloomily framed by the oncoming twilight. It wasn't just a hospital, they knew. It was an asylum, holding pen, warehouse, and also, a prison for some, but there were no high walls or barbed wire.

They'd arrived much later than they'd imagined they'd be. As they got out of the car, Bentsen looked at his watch. "Just past 5:30. Hope this Harkansen isn't a clock-watcher."

"We'll see how our luck is. So far, today, I'd say it's a toss-up." They took a few steps in the half-empty parking lot. "You need to call Sylvia—tell her we're running late?"

"Nah! This is her card-club night. She'll be glad I'm not around."

The lobby had once been bright, open, and airy, qualities yet discernible in the architecture and the window arrangements. Once meant to display a cheerful face to those who visited and needed encouragement, it had become a room jury-rigged with ancient, tattered furniture, an empty receptionist's alcove, and a less-than-imposing guard station. With its dingy and peeling institutional paint exposing patches of stark plaster like open, unhealing wounds, the entrance to the State's purgatory deceived no one.

The uniformed guard, an elderly black man, doubled as receptionist, it appeared. He motioned to the hallway behind him as the direction for Dr. Harkansen's office.

Bentsen found his utility room and disappeared. Strand continued on to an open door marked "Staff" and walked in. In a suite of adjoining offices, he found one with the light on, the sound of keyboard clicks punctuating the silence of the steam-heated building. Strand followed the sound, and found Dr. Harkansen's office.

His steps apparently unheard on the institutional carpet, Strand found himself facing the psychiatrist's back as the doctor worked the keys to fill the blue screen in front of him. The detective had time to take in the grubby look of the outdated office, the diplomas on the wall, the cheap art. He waited for a few seconds, then realizing the writer to be absorbed in his work, cleared his throat softly.

"Yes?" Michael Harkansen turned calmly. He stood up, bringing his six-foot frame to its full height. "How can I help you?"

Strand approached the physician with care. He and Bentsen were there on what they called a "swag"—otherwise known as a scientific wild ass guess. With no warrant in hand, he knew any conversation with the psychiatrist would wander a line somewhere between a professional sharing of information and an outright invasion of privacy.

"Dr. Harkansen? Fletcher Strand. This," he continued affably, gesturing to his partner, who had scooted in behind him, "is Joe Bentsen. State Police. Can we talk for a few minutes?"

In a second or two, Harkansen said, "When people come in and say they're from the police, there's usually a way to tell. Uniforms. Badges. Credentials? Do you guys have any of those?" he inquired without sarcasm.

Strand smiled to himself. Making the doctor ask for the credentials was what he wanted to do. It told the men this was someone used to dealing with police, not easily intimidated, not easily finessed. It set the rules of the game. He and Bentsen fished in their breast pockets for the leather and, without any officious bearing, made their presentation jointly.

Harkansen inspected what he was offered, and nodded.

"Doctor, I appreciate your willingness to talk with us. It's late in the day, and you're absolutely right: we're here on a matter most would not consider routine." He smiled.

Michael Harkansen leaned back in his chair, listening.

Strand proceeded to tell the story, starting with the unattributed Russell fire on the night of the 23rd, the murders of Jamie Hilton and Bradley Paulson, and the death of an elderly motorist.

Strand had no evidence whatsoever linking Snyder to the boys' murders, but the timing of him being in Foreston, and his interest in dressing as a woman at times were coincidences he didn't want to ignore.

Harkansen asked few questions as the tale unfolded. Strand fixed his own focus on the details of his case as well as the eyes of his listener. The latter was most important, Strand knew, because it would tell him what a witness might know. Harkansen was good, and except for an occasional, inward flash of concentration, the doctor betrayed little.

When Strand finished his factual presentation, Harkansen commented, "I must be missing something. How does any of this apply to anyone here?"

"Oh, didn't I mention it? I believe our killer is here—right now."

"I'm sorry to disappoint you, Detective Strand, but I don't see how that would be possible. Just who are you talking about?"

"About Eddie Snyder."

Harkansen maintained his professional demeanor, masking shock—not surprise. "You know I can't give you much of anything without a court order. So, unless you have the paper...?" He did not rise from his chair.

Strand did not speak for a moment. He knew the psychiatrist had to say what he did out of simple professional and ethical responsibility. At the same time, his own trooper's instinct told him Dr. Harkansen had not fully closed the door to further cooperation.

"Doctor, let's try it this way. It's a game of twenty questions that shouldn't get you into trouble, but might help us with factual information we need."

"We can try. Believe me, gentlemen," he said, acknowledging Bentsen, "I understand your predicament, and I'll help all I can. Go ahead."

"Okay. We'll stick to purely factual data, but if you care to offer any insight whatsoever, we'd like to hear it." He considered his first question. The oldest investigative technique in the world had to do with the order in which questions were asked. Newcomers to the business, as well as old-time amateurs, never grasped the premise that generally, there was psychological value in making the first questions easy ones, the kind both helpful and hostile people might answer.

"Joe," Strand looked at his partner, "check your notes, will ya? Was it the 23rd of December the Russells' house burned?"

"Yeah," Joe answered, without needing to check.

"And the Paulson boy. What was the date of his murder?"

This time, Joe double-checked. "It was January 12th, nine in the morning."

"Doctor," he inquired, fixing his gaze on the psychiatrist, "can you tell me the date Eddie left the halfway house, and the date he returned?" It was the easiest question he could formulate, given his promise to deal only in factual data, and by implication, only that having occurred outside the confines of Corinth. He was surprised by the response.

"Did we establish that he ever left?"

"Doctor," suggested Bentsen, his voice not overly heavy with irony, "do we need to establish that? If we were all certain Eddie never left the State's custody, we wouldn't be here and you wouldn't have spent your valuable time listening to my partner's tale of woe. The fact that you're still sitting here establishes an awful lot in my mind."

Harkansen's glare failed to hide his disdain for those who did not enjoy the cat-and-mouse of official interrogation. "Alright, gentlemen. I'll get the file, but let's be certain we stick to the facts—this won't take long."

XLIX

EDDY STOOD, SEETHING. Little did the McGruders know, he smiled to himself, how lucky they were. Finding them not at home—it looked like they were gone for the holidays—he had settled for the Russells.

The Russells got theirs, he muttered, jaw clenched with rage, and it was time someone else got it, too. *If not the McGruders, then the Nicholsons.*

Why am I staying here at Corinth, obeying their silly rules? In control of himself, and far too smart to let himself be screwed again by people who never cared one bit about him—"just protecting society," they always said.

Eddy walked to his room, as orderlies turned to watch him, but knew not to get in his way. Once upstairs, he put on his oversized winter coat, one the staff had seen him wear many times. Next, he stuffed it with as many warm clothes as he could without looking like a human snowman.

The thought of a female disguise reminded him to stop in the theater room and see what he could scavenge for his most important performance to date. The staff would think he was someone's mother or aunt, wouldn't they? He had little to lose. Collecting the other things he would need, and preparing himself carefully, he simply walked out a side door not used much. *Funny. They have the mesh in all the wrong places!*

In the nearly darkened parking lot, he climbed in the bed of a pickup truck equipped with a camper top. Flattening himself, he waited for visiting hours to end—not more than thirty minutes of shivering, he promised himself, and he would go wherever the driver took him.

At one point, a state car pulled up—easy to spot—dark-blue Crown Vic, blackwalls, plain. Two men got out. Eddy caught nothing more than a glimpse as he raised his head just high enough to peer through the nearly opaque plexiglass at the rear of the camper top. State employees didn't show up at the hospital late in the afternoon. *They're cops!*

A few minutes later, an older man hopped in the cab, and without so much as a backward glance, drove off.

~

Harkansen returned and sat down again, swiveling to put the thick file on the desk, and began flipping through it. He seemed to find the right place, but then began going forward and backward in the file to be sure of what he had found. At last, he stopped, and looked up at the detectives, waiting to be asked again. "The dates?" Bentsen queried, not impatiently.

"Oh, yes," Harkansen stated, then looked through the file once again. "Eddie left the halfway house in Meadville on December 22nd. He was returned here two weeks ago."

"Two weeks ago, you say?"

"Yes, on the 21st, to be exact."

"How had he been picked up?" Bentsen was quick to ask.

Again, Harkansen paused, careful to weigh each particle of information revealed. Facts were one thing. A psychiatric opinion was another. "He came back to us via Foreston Medical Center."

Strand smiled. His heart's pace quickened palpably. "What was he doing in the hospital, Doctor?"

The professional medical man looked at his guests plaintively, resignedly. "I guess I won't be telling you anything not at your disposal otherwise." Again, he glanced back through the folder, collating the dates. "According to this," he recounted, hoping by his tone that the official record could grant him an unofficial reprieve, "Eddie was involved in an accident on Saturday, January 12th, just outside Mercer. He suffered mild to moderate injuries, was hospitalized for a day, and finally, was returned here." The doctor's recitation was flat. "Hmmm!"

"Something the matter?" Bentsen asked.

Harkansen chuckled. "You know, guys, you should have all this. The accident was handled by the Mercer Borough PD, but turned over to the PSP since it was in your jurisdiction."

Strand and Bentsen exchanged looks. "The hell you say," Bentsen said.

"Sorry about that, doc. We'll get the whole file back at the barracks, but as long as we're here, what kind of accident was it, did you say?"

"I didn't, but it was an automobile accident." Dr. Harkansen turned to the factual account in the record, keeping his eye focused on the page. "Eddie was extricated from an overturned car after it had collided with that driven by an elderly man. The other driver was killed instantly. Before you ask, I should tell you that Eddie was driving a stolen vehicle at the time and apparently, crossed the yellow line to pass when a Mr. Wilhelm was making a legitimate left turn."

"Does the report say where the car had been stolen?"

Dr. Harkansen riffled through a few pages, then said, "It appears the car was taken from in front of the Foreston Post Office—on Pine Street, it says here—earlier that morning."

"That makes five," Strand said, quietly, his voice betraying more conviction than he would have preferred.

"I beg your pardon?"

"Mr. and Mrs. Russell, Jamie Hilton, Bradley Paulson, Wilhelm. Five," Strand repeated, with bitterness edging out the reason in his speech. "Five people," he observed, once again, "have had their lives obliterated, and Doctor, I think your resident, Eddie Snyder, is responsible for all five." He could feel his face flush.

"I think you've reached that conclusion quite prematurely," Harkansen noted, attempting to sound dispatched and objective.

"No reach, Doctor! I'll make this brief—mostly because I don't want to think about this any more than I have to. Your boy leaves here on the 22nd of December. Just by coincidence," he continued, "his former foster parents are burned to death the very next evening—two people against whom he held a grudge, we understand. The Russells were in their living room, and we think they were asphyxiated, then burned. To me, there's no question but that Eddie had the opportunity and the motive. No other explanation makes sense, and I believe the actual proof of murder is on its way from our lab right now.

"Now, let's go to the end of our story—there's no doubt, according to your record, that Eddie was responsible for the death of the other driver—what was his name again?"

"Wilhelm. Arthur Wilhelm." Harkansen winced as he repeated the name.

Bentsen scribbled in his notebook.

"The Russells. Wilhelm. Now let's go to the kids. What we have is this. Two boys, eleven years old, stabbed to death in January. Given that Eddie was probably in Foreston from about December 22nd until January 14th, he had the opportunity to commit all the killings. None of his activities are accounted for during that period." Strand did not stop.

"Both boys are normal, happy kids. Eddie was not. Moreover, his freedom was taken from him when the Russells decided they couldn't keep him—after he assaulted a girl in school. Eddie was about ten years old at the time. We have no eyewitnesses to either killing—except, possibly, me."

At that, both Bentsen and Harkansen broke their concentrated listening and stared at him, each with the same question on his lips.

"On the morning Jamie Hilton was killed, I happened to be

walking across the Pine Street Bridge when I saw a woman across the way—put that in quotes—wearing a long, green coat. She was carrying a package, and I assumed she was coming from the Post Office. I'm quite certain Jamie Hilton was killed a few feet from where I was standing, and not more than a few minutes before I arrived.

"The Saturday morning Bradley Paulson was killed, I was driving by the Community Center, and out of the corner of my eye, I saw a woman—I thought it was a mother—giving a boy a hard time. Same color of hair, same long, green coat. I'm reasonably certain the so-called mother was the same so-called woman I saw on the bridge."

"A woman, you say? How is all this relevant, Mr. Strand?"

"Joe, haven't we heard about Eddie's flair for the theatrical?"

Bentsen nodded. He knew his partner couldn't be more specific without giving away the source of information.

"Doctor," Strand continued his case, "is it possible that Eddie might have been dressed as a woman, might have stabbed those two boys just because they were happy, just because they had everything he never had?"

"Now you're way over the line." Harkansen stood up. "You've gone from the factual data available to the purely speculative. Yes, it may be true you saw the same person near two crime-scenes, but stretching that possibility into the suggestion that one of our patients was dressed as a woman to carry off two murders is something I won't bother to discuss. I'll volley back, Mr. Strand: Why in the world would Eddie dress as a woman?"

"Good question. Simple answer. Actually, two answers, now that I think about it. One, he couldn't take the chance of running into his sister, except to observe her in disguise, perhaps. She lives and works in the same town. Two, it's far easier to approach a young boy as a woman, a mother figure. Most kids know to stay away from strange men, but in their minds, if you ask them, strange men are dangerous, not women. That's why, Doctor."

As Harkansen listened, he seemed to be putting the pieces together in his own mind. "Detective Strand, I think you're at a dead end, and I'm not in a position to plow a new path for you. You've got some facts, and I'll grant you, a number of interesting coincidences, but what am I—what is anyone—supposed to do about that?"

"Look, Doctor," Strand declared, feeling his temper about to escape its containment, "what we're supposed to do is attempt to demonstrate it one way or another—guilty or not guilty—just so that parents in this part of the state don't have to wonder if their little boy will have his heart sliced in half by some mindless son of a bitch. That's what we have to do—and please don't stand behind some screwy ethical barrier or give me any BS about poor little Eddie's right to privacy." He paused to collect himself.

"I think that bastard killed five people, and given the so-called security of this place," Strand continued, mockingly, "we have to do more than just prove something—we have to ensure that if he's guilty, he can't do it again. What I want is your help—before we lose any more time going through the hoopla of getting a subpoena."

"Just a minute, Strand..."

"No, let me finish. Joe and I aren't assigned this case, Doctor. Yes, that's right. What's more interesting is that right at this instant, there isn't any law enforcement authority that thinks there is a case!" Strand was almost shouting. "Doctor, do you understand what I'm saying? Nobody, but nobody has put this thing together. If the three of us don't do anything—nothing will stop him. Doctor, I'm not here as some officious cop—I'm here as a citizen and father. Let me put it this way. If we're on the wrong track, what can happen to him?"

"Listen, my friend, you have no monopoly on securing the public good. You come in here on a hunch and want to settle a case in our own little kangaroo court, and I won't have it! Just because somebody like Eddie Snyder, someone with a problem, was out in the community, that doesn't mean he's guilty of everything that happened there. But before you ask me to help you crucify him, you need to hear another story—or rather, the story of this Eddie and all the other Eddies around us—because he won't be the last one we deal with."

Strand cooled, nodding. Bentsen sat, stone-faced."

"When Eddie was born in 1967, in that year alone in this country, there were over three-quarters of a million people—just like Eddie—having episodes of schizophrenia requiring treatment. Think of it—over 750,000! You know, we used to treat people like him by taking them out of their home setting, getting them up to a level of functionality, then putting them back where we found them."

"I thought they changed all that," Bentsen contributed.

"You're right, Mr. Bentsen," Harkansen nodded, and continued. "In the decade or two before Eddie was born, we learned that not treating the whole family at the same time we treated the dysfunctional person was an exercise doomed to failure. We became immensely more successful in treating many kinds of mental illness."

"Then what happened in his case?"

L

"I N EDDIE'S CASE, there was no family to treat—that's the short of it," Harkansen explained, but "a number of other factors contributed to the Eddie who lives here with us, and to the millions like him who exist year after year as idling engines of violence. By 1968, we had reached not only the height of the Vietnam War, but also the beginning of the end of what people had hoped would be The Great Society. Remember all that?" the doctor asked rhetorically.

"Remember the demonstrations, the violence, the national instability because we couldn't have guns and butter both? Because of the war and for other reasons, people began to tire of throwing billions of dollars at social problems with no discernible—and immediate—results. There was hope with *Wyatt v. Stickney* in 1971, when the court held that a person could not be committed without adequate treatment. Nice words, great principle, but, without money? How does this apply to Eddie, you ask? It is a truism, gentlemen, that a fair number of children with psychosis can be treated successfully if they're detected before the age of five."

"Five?" asked Strand, astonished. He had never thought of kids, anybody's kids being mentally ill.

"Five. That's right."

"You said 'a fair number.' Meaning what?"

"I have to tell you it's only about 20 to 30 percent who achieve a fair to good recovery, Detective."

"Good God!" Bentsen muttered.

Strand looked at his watch. "Back to Eddie?" he pleaded.

"When Eddie was five—that would have been 1972—the war was about to end, and so did a lot of sympathy for funding programs and treatment he would have needed. Anyway, it wouldn't have made any difference, I suppose."

"Meaning?" Bentsen queried.

"I didn't mention that Eddie was given up right after birth. He was a ward of the State almost immediately. That's what I meant earlier when I said he had no family. The State," Harkansen said, looking at both guests, fellow civil servants like him, "was never meant to take the place of mom and pop..."

"Yeah," Bentsen completed the thought, "but a lot of people think government can do everything."

Harkansen nodded. "Worse, Joe. A lot of people think the government *should* do everything. Anyway, I don't know what kind of love and attention baby Eddie was given. What I do know is that there were a lot of mothers and very few fathers in his early life, nobody to notice much about him, and certainly not in time to do anything about it."

"And?" Bentsen prompted.

"Without giving you chapter and verse, Eddie undoubtedly suffered—suffers—from what we call deprivational syndrome—from the time he was a small child, there was impaired physical growth, emotional dysfunction along with intensified personality development disorders."

"That's not plain English," Bentsen grumbled. "Are you telling us this Eddie Snyder was bad news, right from the start?"

"No, I'm not telling you that. You've got to understand, Joe, that Eddie was not all that special a case—that's my point—he's just one of thousands. We see a lot just like him here every year—rejects by family, by society. It's just that some, some like Eddie, do not have that inner something to cope, to adjust, to bridge the split between perception and reality. In his case, we thought he was getting better, when maybe he wasn't.

"So, now we have this young boy who, after a few years in a State home, is shunted from place to place, from one incident of family rejection to another, over and over again. To make a long story short, no one really noticed anything at all clinical about Eddie until the incident you mentioned, Detective—the one where he hurt a girl in school. Yes, he was about ten years old then—I can remember that without looking at his file."

"I don't get it, Doc. So, the kid was moved around, so some people didn't like him. So what? Hey, I'm sorry. That's a sad story, but lotsa kids go through that and turn out okay. Why should I feel sorry for this kid?" Bentsen demanded.

Harkansen blinked, and responded carefully. "I don't mean to sound like I'm a bleeding heart, men, but I just gave you the '"For General Audiences'" version of things. So, you think his story is no big deal, Joe? Fletch? Well, let me see if I can make it a bigger deal for you." Sarcasm tinged his tone. "This was a kid who was thrown out of the house to freeze, barefoot, one winter, because he tracked snow on the kitchen floor. This was a kid with little round scars on his back—cigarette burns. I'll bet he did something really bad, like spilling his milk, to deserve that. This was a kid whose arm was broken by a foster parent in an apparent attempt, we suspect, to cover up sexual abuse of his daughter. Eddie was only twelve. That particular case remains open, by the way."

"This was a kid," Harkansen continued, his voice becoming more intense, "who never had a birthday party, who never had clothes of his own, who never had a mother's love or a father's concern, who for whatever reason, was pushed away, rejected, discarded like so much garbage by nearly everyone who had ever known him.

"This is their story—all the Eddies—it's just like thousands of other stories—except in this Eddie's case, maybe he didn't turn out okay. He is not a number, you know, not a one-of-a-kind who just happened to be here with us. The Eddies aren't a case of the flu that just goes away. Right here in this country, right now, there is an epidemic of Eddies, nearly all a result of years of systemic neglect or just plain, personal meanness in a society too busy with its own greed to care for those born alone. If you're right about him," Harkansen added, resignedly, "I'm sorry he got loose."

"Doctor, answer me one more, if you would. Do you think he was born with his problem, or did we make him the way he is?"

"It's not that simple, Detective. I wish it were. Maybe the question should be: No matter what he was born with, did we do what we could for him? I'll say this, there's a lot of research to support the notion that some mental illnesses are familial—Eddie's may be one of them." He reflected a moment, then continued.

"Had anyone truly cared for him, noticed him, or just gave him a bit of personal attention when he needed it—giving him good emotional care year in and year out—maybe, just maybe, we wouldn't have the Eddie you're looking for today." Harkansen stopped, then looked directly at his guests. "You know, Dr. Karl Menninger once said something like, 'What we do to our children is what we do to our future.' I don't need to spell that one out, do I." It was not a question.

Neither detective spoke.

An urgent knock rattled the door.

"Yes?"

"Doc, sorry to bother ya, but Eddie Snyder is gone again," Murchison, an orderly, informed the group. "Around 5:00 p.m., we think."

Immediately rising from his chair, Harkansen wore a look of controlled terror. His voice shook. "How in God's name could that happen?

"We're not sure, Doc. We think he left in one of his theatrical get-ups. Whatever—he's missing—we checked everywhere."

"You checked everywhere? All of the places they like to hide?"

"Yessir. He's nowhere. Should I alert the PSP?

"No need. They're here!"

Strand looked at his watch. "Six seventeen," he announced to the room. "Five o'clock, you said?" Strand asked, looking at Murchison, but continuing without a response. "That means he could be well past Meadville by now, if he got lucky with a ride! Son of a bitch, Doc! Don't you keep an eye on people like him?"

"Yes, we do!" insisted Harkansen. "This is not exactly a prison, Strand. That's your line of work, remember?"

Strand stared back at him. "Let me use your phone. Joe, get on the other line, will you? Call Meadville with a description. I'll alert the barracks."

Harkansen and Murchison headed to the lobby. In a minute or two Strand and Bentsen appeared, grim and ready.

"Will you be able to catch him?" Harkansen asked.

"Maybe. We're getting closer to him."

"You still have no proof, remember."

"Doctor," Strand agreed, halting in mid-stride, "I'll be sure about the Russells when I see the lab reports, but we know about Wilhelm. As for the boys, right now it's circumstantial, coincidental to be sure, but we'll get it if it's there to get."

"By the way," Harkansen said, "get me that court order!"

LI

SNOW WAS ON the way. Eddy sensed it in his first deep breath of chilled air as he extricated himself from the coccoon of hay bales which kept him warm throughout the night. By the following morning, Eddy was standing on the berm of I-79 South, waiting for any fool to take him closer to Foreston, closer to where he had to be. *I'm coming for you, Mom Jody!*

A day of petty theft and begging sharpened his senses, filled his stomach, and kept him going. His smile, smug with the certainty of completing his mission, seemed like one of friendliness and innocence to the interstate driver who stopped to give him a ride.

During the long intervals of silence, Eddy quietly fed his obsession. With a shock, he recognized that getting back to Foreston had so consumed every hour's thought at Corinth that he had never formed a clear plan for what he wanted to do once he got there! For someone unused to second thoughts about anything he did, it caused him more than a moment's uncertainty. His out-loud chuckle unnerved the already quirky driver, and Eddy explained it as a private joke.

Aside from the driver's crude and unpracticed physical advances on him once they reached the city, the trip was uneventful. Bob, as the driver introduced himself, made his awkward approach upon stopping the car, a tactical error of which Eddy took quick advantage. Deftly, he pushed away Bob's reaching hand with his left arm, and with his right hand, managed to shove open the car door. With a smirk and a wave of thanks, he turned and trotted off. At Corinth, he had seen and heard of men who liked other men, but otherwise, had no interest in sex—with anybody. All of his urges, he confidently reassured himself, were directed at righting wrongs, not in meaningless couplings.

Back in Foreston, Eddy trudged through the six inches of new snow to Mrs. McKittrick's fourplex, his home and hideout. The key was above the lintel where he left it. Breathing easily in the comfort and safety of the only home he had ever known, Eddy was stimulated to greater concentration on a master plan. Pacing back and forth, whispering to himself, Eddy played back the many scenes and events in his life that gave it meaning, that brought him to the present time. Killing the Russells helped even the score as it deprived them of the same bright days he had once hoped to enjoy. While he had no intention of killing the old man on the road to Mercer, it, too, gave him vicarious pleasure.

From the back of his mind, the bottom of his cold heart, he began to focus on the one person who'd betrayed him more than anyone else. All along, it was she who seemed to benefit in every situation, someone who always wound up doing well, no matter what the circumstances. She, he convinced himself, could have saved him from all that was rotten in his life. *Did Wendy ever really do anything for me?*

~

Strand and Bentsen sat in Walter Montgomery's office as the sun highlighted the dirt, dust, and bird crap plastered to the office window behind their chief. As Montgomery droned on about the weekend's sports, the sun's intrusion reminded Strand of the wonderful weekend he had spent with Aurora and the kids.

Bentsen interrupted both Montgomery's live sportscast and

Strand's inner pleasure when he reminded them both of "what we're here to talk about."

"For cryin' out loud, Joe, what's the hurry!"

"They told me the file from Corinth—the one on Eddie Snyder—got sidetracked somehow, and it's not here yet. I thought he had the subpoena there in time to get it here by this morning, but who knows."

"So, what's the problem?"

"If we don't have the file to look at, there's a lot of other things to do—and they ain't gonna get done here!"

Montgomery laughed. "Sounds like my line, Joe. Okay, but first, bring me up to date a little."

"You said you wanted a hook on the murders of the Foreston boys. Maybe we got one." Bentsen's unraveling of the tale brought Strand's concentration back to the present, and he, too, joined in its telling. When, at last, they found their way to the prior evening with Dr. Harkansen, Strand brought up the issue of jurisdiction.

"It occurs to me, boss, that this case is ours now, no matter what Georgie says—to you or anyone else. Eddie Snyder's escaped from Corinth's custody pending disposition of the vehicular homicide in Mercer, and that puts it in the State's backyard, don't you think?"

"Yep. No matter what Georgie says, you boys have done an excellent job of running it to ground..."

"Excuse me, boss, but we haven't run anything to ground yet. That's really our other purpose for being here—we need you to officially assign this thing to us."

"Yeah," Montgomery chuckled, "I probably oughta do that! So, go ahead and open case files on the Russells, the Hilton and Paulson killings, and, of course, on Wilhelm. I knew him, by the way. He was active in our church. Nice guy!" He paused. "So, what're your plans?"

"Well, first, informing Hallon seems to be at your pay grade, boss. Right?" Strand looked at Bentsen, then said, "Today, we were going to go over the file—assuming it gets here—hoping for a lead as to his exact whereabouts in Foreston, but I was thinking over the weekend,

Joe, it wouldn't hurt to go back over whatever we have from the accident. Nobody had reason to check the car or the scene over more carefully than they did, but now we do. Maybe, there'll be nothing there. But maybe... ."

"Okay, boys. Consider yourself assigned. We'll call about the Corinth file and see if we can't get it expedited for you. Of course, the file on Wilhelm should be in this building somewhere. In the meantime, pursue whatever leads you can. I don't need to tell you that this crazy bastard will probably do something soon."

"Of course," observed Strand, "we're betting he found his way back to Foreston, and that's where his activity will be, but boss, you might want to put something out to the local PDs."

"Yeah," Montgomery agreed thoughtfully. "You know, though, this is kinda touchy, since you guys don't have this guy pinned yet— if we were near-certain about him, we could alert the media."

"Let's do it anyway. If something happens, how would we explain that we didn't? Hallon can fight about jurisdiction all he wants."

"You're right—the kids," Bentsen agreed. "There's been no activity for what, three weeks now, and if he does do anything, it'll catch everybody by surprise."

"C'mon, Joe, let's see if we can't tighten the screws on this one a bit. I don't think it's a question of if—it's a question of when he's going to strike. We'd better get lucky—and soon."

"Yuh know, Fletch, something is botherin' me. If Snyder was in Foreston Hospital for a week, wouldn't Wendy Russell have known it?"

"Not necessarily. It's a hundred-bed place and Snyder would have been kept in isolation, I suppose."

"Okay, but the question is on my list."

LII

A FEW HOURS LATER, having located the records for the weekend of the 12th, according to Bentsen's notes, they were carefully reviewing the jacket for accident citation 900038, the 38th for the new year. On the phone to Mercer Borough, they learned the officer at the scene, Mike Hillis, worked second turn, and was believed to be at home. Bentsen reached him there and asked him to meet the two State men at the accident scene.

Just before lunch, Strand, Bentsen, and Hillis strode across the frozen ground together, following the path plowed there less than a month before by the overturned, out-of-control vehicular missile piloted by Eddie Snyder. Not knowing the reason for their curiosity, Hillis recited the details of the incident in near-perfect harmony with the official record. Strand listened carefully, particularly when Hillis brought up the post-accident investigation.

"We're interested in his personal effects. Did Snyder have anything on him or with him?"

"Like what?"

"Like a wallet, for instance?" quizzed Bentsen, trying not to show impatience with one of the locals.

Hillis chirped officiously, "I believe that if you check the report, sir, you'll find he had no personal identification whatsoever. We found him and the clothes he had on him. The car was totaled, you know, and we had no reason to tear it apart looking for anything else. Just what were you looking for?"

"Not sure," responded Strand. "This guy likes to play 'dress-up' and we thought he might have had some of his stuff with him?" Hillis's look of complete incomprehension prompted Strand to add a pleasant, "No problem. We're just fishing, that's all."

"I'll tell you what we do need, though, is the name of the owner of the stolen vehicle. Any help for us?"

"Yeah. As I recall, they were local people, the Pearsons. They live halfway to Foreston from here. I happened to know their neighbors, and they told me Madge and Jim haven't been out much since then—that car was their only link to the world. They're old, live alone, and have nobody around..."

"Excuse me," Strand interrupted, "do you know where that car is, exactly? Was it towed somewhere here, to the Pearsons, or where?"

"You got me!" Hillis answered. "But why don't you ask the Pearsons? They can help you."

Within fifteen minutes, the detectives were driving up to what had long ago been the center of a large, working farm. Now it was divided, not by the gravel track of days gone by, but by a fast-paced highway. The farmstead's barn and outbuildings were across the road from the house, and it wasn't difficult to determine that many years had elapsed since a baler or any other implement droned its engines on the nearby acreage.

"You from the insurance people?" Behind the storm door stood a sinewy, white-haired old man. Apparently, he had seen their car pull up the long drive, and waited in anticipation.

"Nosir," said Strand politely, and with understanding. "We're from the State Police, Mr. Pearson. It is Mr. Pearson, isn't it?" The old man nodded, equally polite, but disappointed. He reached forward to open the door in invitation.

Comfortable in the warmth of the living room, Bentsen explained plainly. "Mr. Pearson, we're here about the accident a few weeks ago.

Can you tell us, sir, where the car is?"

"The car?" Pearson repeated. "Why, it's right next door. Jack Justin's boy works on cars, and when we found out what happened, we had it towed there. No harm to it. They told us it couldn't be driven again, anyway, so we figured the Justin could use the parts."

"Mighty nice of you," Strand complimented him, speaking louder than Bentsen had. "Mind if I ask you a question? Did you folks get all of your things out of the car—after the accident, I mean?"

"I suppose you could say that."

"Suppose?" hinted Bentsen.

Wordlessly, Pearson got up and ambled toward the kitchen, calling, "Madge!" on the way. In a minute, they both came out, Mrs. Pearson carrying a cardboard box. They bent forward slightly, dropping it in front of the hassock where Bentsen sat.

The sodden pile in the box wouldn't have been worth a second glance but for the ashen brown wig which sat atop it. Mrs. Pearson explained. "Not that we ever expected to keep this stuff, anyhow, so I'm surprised somebody would come by to pick it up, but for what, I don't know. Property of that boy who stole the car, I guess, 'cause it sure ain't ours."

"You sure, Mrs. Pearson?"

"Sure? Just how do you fellas think I'd look in that wig? And look at this makeup—I've never worn that kind of thing in my life. Why, I wouldn't know what to do with eyeliner. Men!"

All three men laughed, Strand and Bentsen the hardest. They laughed as men lost in the desert only to discover an oasis when they least and last expect it. Except to take the items out of a sack and let them air-dry in the house, a book, wig, makeup kit, and sundry other items in the pile had not been disturbed by the Pearsons, or anyone else. The detectives took a custodial statement for evidentiary purposes, carefully secured the box, thanked their benefactors, and left. Taking no chances, they immediately drove to the Justin residence, interviewed the would-be mechanic son, and once again assured of a good chain of evidence, gleefully drove back to Mercer, speeding all the way.

At the courthouse, they breezed into Coroner McCreary's office, signed for the Paulson case/evidence file, and exited hastily. Lucky they were that McCreary himself was absent for the day inasmuch as no time had been lost answering what would have been his interminable questions. The rest of their trip to the barracks the officers made in seconds.

Rather than trust the courier system, they immediately collared a young officer, marched into Montgomery's office, and explained their find. They needed someone to make the five-hour drive to the state labs in Harrisburg as quickly as possible, to compare the contents of the bag against the evidence samples from the Bradley Paulson case. They also wanted an expert fingerprint analysis and comparison made, assuming there were latent prints on the book surfaces. Stressing the urgency of their request, and knowing that Harrisburg would need at least a day to make and confirm their findings, they pressed Montgomery to spare the officer.

Strand said, "And as I recall from an officer at the scene of the Paulson killing, McCreary found strands of synthetic hair, he thought, along with a makeup smear from the boy's knit cap. They need to be compared to what we have here, and the sooner, the better."

With further discussion, Montgomery agreed. Over ninety minutes was spent locating and securing the proper evidence samples from the Paulson case, as well as the local copy of the fingerprints taken at Foreston hospital. It was late in the afternoon before Strand and Bentsen could call it a day, highly satisfied with the turn of luck, if luck it was, but at the same time, scared to think how close Eddy Snyder might be to identifying another victim.

LIII

AARIE AND ANNA Strand were the only kids to get off the #17 school bus at East Pine and Monroe Streets. Their mother liked the idea of the bus coming at precisely 2:40 p.m. every school day, and as soon as she saw or heard it pass in front of the house, she knew her children were less than a block away. Of course, today, the kids had half-day sessions and would be home earlier, but what time exactly, she didn't know.

Aurora Strand wanted to be careful. Her husband had told her about the murders of the two boys several weeks earlier, and even though the local hysteria had died down, she paid close attention to the kids' whereabouts, especially Aarie's.

Anna ran ahead, while Aarie half knelt to tie a straggling shoelace on his left high-top. His full concentration was on keeping his knees from touching the dirty, wet sidewalk so that he could avoid his mother's tongue-lashing if he got his good pants dirty again. So involved was he undoing the sodden knot, he didn't notice the other pair of feet a short distance from his own. He looked up, squinting, to see a lady in front of him.

"Can I help you?" Eddy asked, speaking in a soft, soothing voice.

"I can get it," Aarie responded, full of an eleven-year-old's confidence. Aarie also didn't know the woman, and was hoping she would just go away. Besides, he didn't want a "girl" to help him unknot a shoelace, of all things.

"Here, I'd better help you," Eddy insisted, bending down to the boy's level. He began to work the knot. "If I don't, you'll be here till heaven knows when," he added, smiling to himself over the reference to another world. A few seconds later, shoelace properly tied, they both stood to full height. "Can I walk with you?" he asked, keeping his voice as light as possible.

"Well, I'm not going very far, but okay."

"Alright, I'll just go with you a ways. What's your name?"

"Aarie. Actually, it's Aaron Strand, and I live right down there," he said, pointing to the white brick house, which they could see. As Aarie spoke, he noticed for the first time the lady was wearing a wig. He began to speak, but quickly stopped himself when he remembered his mom telling him that often, when people have been treated for cancer, they wear wigs. He felt so bad for the lady, and wanted to like her.

"You were going to say something?" Eddy prompted.

"No," Aarie put forth too quickly. Then, feeling guilty, he spoke the first words that came into his head. "I mean, yes. Well, actually, all I was going to do was ask you if you liked hockey? Do you ever watch the Pens?"

"Oh, yes," Eddy said, answering both questions. At the same time, he shoved his hand down in his coat pocket. "You're about eleven, aren't you?

"Good guess, lady. Oh, what's your name?"

"Edie. Edie Snyder, that's it." Eddy smiled. "I guess I'd better go—and you, too. Your mother will be waiting for you. Bye," he said pleasantly, turning to go.

"Sure," Aarie said, hoping to meet his new friend again.

~

At nine o'clock Tuesday morning, Judge Morrison's courtroom was nearly deserted, the few observers, retirees, and gadflies there mostly because they were able to walk to the courthouse. The surprise eight-inch overnight snowfall had all but closed the county seat and the surrounding boroughs, including Foreston, and under the circumstances, nothing was running on time. Schools, businesses, and public buildings and activities gave themselves generous tardy slips for the morning as people dug out and made it to their destinations with good-natured spirits evident.

Not so Judge Morrison, but his bailiff convinced him to be patient. Morrison instructed his man to have those present remain in place.

At precisely 9:25 a.m., Reinhard Koenig hustled into the courtroom, returned Wagner's "so nice you could make it" smile, then caught his client's look, one of sarcastic appreciation.

In a minute, the bailiff reappeared and approached both counsel tables. "Judge Morrison wishes to see you both," he said, glancing left and right, "in chambers." He stretched out his hand in a gesture to lead the way.

Alice Wagner, looking puzzled, went first, followed by Reinhard Koenig, who grinned the grin of one who always did well in conference.

"Ms. Wagner, let me ask you a question, and please do us all the honor of a candid answer," the judge began.

"Of course, Judge Morrison."

"You have no one on your witness list save Mrs. Milcher and two others who knew Mr. Milcher well during his last months. Is that correct?"

Wagner so averred.

"Will any of those witnesses, number one, testify to other than we should expect, and number two, will any of them have a factual basis for their statements, as opposed to a mere expression of opinion?"

"If, your honor, you're asking me if their testimony will bring any greater weight than as character references, then, my answer would have to be, 'No.'"

"Thank you. If just a few of you were as honest in discussions of this sort, the courts would save much time and money, and most of all justice would have greater meaning. Now, to the point." He continued, "I have reviewed the record in its entirety. As I see it, there are three options. I could let this case proceed and be decided on the merits. If for the State, I'm sure there would be an appeal, the results of which might or might not be favorable to Knotting, and he would remain in jail. If for Knotting, the State might appeal, but either way, Knotting could be released immediately. You both know this case could run indefinitely, if we let it.

"My third option is to let you both win. Inasmuch as you two could not get there on your own, I'm suggesting you consider something along the lines of shock parole as an agreed upon settlement of this matter. That way, Knotting gets his chance at freedom, albeit earlier than he might otherwise, and secondly, the State is able to walk away from what is, presently, a likely untenable position."

There ensued a spirited discussion of case points, each side hammering away at its strongest. Judge Morrison participated but slightly, the jurist having already engaged in the matter's intellectual battles. Neither party appeared to move from its position.

Wagner directed her gaze at the judge. "Your honor, did you say, 'untenable'?"

"Yes, Ms. Wagner. In my considered opinion, the State cannot win this case outright, only delay the inevitable, given the live, unchallenged witness for the appellant and the record itself. Is that clearer?" he submitted, not unkindly.

Wagner was silent, knowing as she did that the case, like so many others she worked, hinged not on good sense, but on technical points, some obscure, some not. In the instant case, however, no matter the high feeling in Foreston, Knotting had served twenty-two years of hard time, more than he might have had there been more aggressive plea bargaining. Moreover, there was nothing in or out of the prison record to suggest a probable recurrence.

Finally, Wagner agreed. Koenig, of course, was overjoyed.

The in-chambers discussion turned to what some would have considered the anti-climactic, administrative details necessary to conclude the case. Neither attorney's attention wavered, however, as

each knew that many an otherwise favorable decision had been for-
feited in the fine points. Minutiae passed, the bargainers agreed on
Thursday, February 15th as a date for shock release on parole. The
order would be transmitted to Morganville in due course.

The parties removed themselves to the courtroom where, all in
place for the judicial tableau, Judge Morrison announced a settlement by the parties. In his remarks, Morrison stressed that neither
side won or lost in this matter. By their agreement, he stated, appellant withdrew his charges against the State and James Milcher, and
the State committed itself to the view that Knotting's twenty-two
years in prison was sufficient official vengeance for his crime.

"The court," Judge Morrison declared finally, without irony, "ac-
cepts this settlement in the interest of justice."

LIV

I N THE MORNING, the wind was still howling as it whipped and swirled ice crystals through the air and made them cling to any surface. It was 6 a.m. when the clock-radio buzzed, and Strand's arm reached in automatic motion to still its noise. When he next permitted one eye to open to see the time, he also saw the big red envelope leaning against the lamp on his nightstand. Smiling, he sat up and listened to the wind, then leaning on one elbow watched his wife sleep. Good thing he thought to have picked up a card and flowers the day before.

The snooze alarm went off a few minutes later. Aurora awoke, saw him watching, and with a warm, sensuous smile, asked huskily, "Want something?"

Strand made no answer except his own smile in return, then let himself fall into an embrace. They kissed like new lovers with no concern for morning mouth or other unappealing traits that come with familiarity and marriage. Embrace led to caress, caress to arousal, arousal to slow, gentle, and finally urgent love.

It was a heartful morning for both, further cementing the tentative, uncertain steps they'd carefully taken in their recent days together. Aarie and Anna, always the pair, knocked and entered the room sometime later, reminding their parents it was time for school, but clearly delighted to see their mom and dad smiling together as they cuddled under the blankets.

Grinning sheepishly, parents and children eyed each other, and at nearly the same instant, all four asked, "What are you looking at?" They all laughed, wished each other a "Happy Valentine's Day," and began their morning.

Down in the kitchen, Aarie was excited about the weather. "Dad, it looks like the pond will freeze over, if it isn't already, and we can go skating."

"We'll see what the weather brings, young fella," his father said, and gave his shoulder a squeeze. They were talking about the pond behind the Penn Grove and an offshoot from Wolf Creek flowing by. It was a favorite winter mecca for the kids when the ice had thickened.

Coffee and bagel behind him, Strand felt his inner tension rise as he considered the possibilities in what he began to think of as the "The Orphan's Revenge." In his soul, he knew what Eddie Snyder was all about, why he was killing, why he had to be stopped. He believed Snyder was getting even for all that had been done to him. It didn't matter that he was getting even with the wrong people for the wrong reasons—murdering four people for revenge was a rampage that would not stop on its own.

Underlying Strand's intensity was the emotional residue of Tuesday's late afternoon radio report that Marty Knotting would be set free in two days' time. Feeling the emotional pressure building in him, he knew his best tack was to get dressed, smile at Aurora as much as possible, and get out of the house. His bitter experience taught him that even letting it appear the job had control of him would reawaken her anger and frustration.

On his way out the door, she threw her arms around him, saying, "You're pretty darn nice to wake up to, you know that?"

Strand smiled his best in return, "And you're pretty good to go to bed with!"

Aurora shushed him. "The kids, Fletch!"

"I think they're even happier than we are. Gotta go, hon."

"Fletch, I know something's on your mind. Is it about those little boys?"

"Yeah, and I think we're getting close. Now would be a good time to remind Aarie—and Anna, too—about talking to strangers. I'm sorry, hon."

"Oh, I understand—a lot more than I used to." She gently patted his cheek, not in condescension but in tender support, and whispered lovingly, "Be careful!"

Outside, the results of the night's frolic greeted Strand with bright, white snow, the airborne crystals stinging his face. Bentsen and the warmed-up car were waiting. Strand climbed in, and in a wink, they were off to begin what neither hoped would be an exciting day.

LV

WARDEN JOHNSTON CALLED for a Hurry Search at 7:15 a.m., and at once, Morganville's correctional staff sprang into action. For them, it was an old routine. They caught the residents just before breakfast, always a good time, they believed, because few of the 812 were fully awake or witted for the day. In one cell block after another, the officers scrambled to conduct the random searches the warden required, and in Johnston's jungle, results mattered.

By the time the searches were done, and the men herded to the mess hall, three pieces of contraband had been found amongst the seventy-five quick-searched cells. What got the men talking, however, was what happened in cell 603, the long-term home of Varnie Lynn Davis.

Davis had nothing to hide. But, resenting the constant attention given him by the guards, he was experiencing what his mother would call a distempered mood. Four guards subdued him with truncheons after he talked back to them. Bloodied and beaten raw about the head and hands, he was being hustled to the infirmary when he was seen by many of his friends in line for food.

It was 7:47 a.m., a most vulnerable timespan for the staff. The mess hall nearly full of convicts and lines streaming in and out, it was the period of the workday when the ratio of staff to prisoners was at its lowest.

"Awright! Knock off the crap, an' stay in line!" one of the correctional officers barked.

Fred "Matchie" McHugh gruffed, "Yeah, move the wrong way, an' you get to meet Varnie's friend," as he held his baton in one hand and tapped the cupped palm of his other, chortling all the while.

In a flash, three convicts jumped McHugh from the rear, disarming him in an instant. One of the men took the baton and began thrashing the downed man about the head. Blood poured.

McHugh's offhand and unthinking comment, otherwise unremarkable, proved the ignition point for all of Morganville. Within seconds, hundreds of convicts in every area of the facility traded smoldering hatred for breathtaking violence.

By 8:30 a.m., Johnston's Jungle was in the hands of its inhabitants, and it stayed there. Morning hours disappeared into the cold, noon sun as law enforcement and media units converged, as cued, on the Columbiana County scene. CNN cut into its broadcast for live updates. Amongst those interviewed were Warden Johnston, who professed to be stunned at the carnage in his "model facility."

Dozens of inmate and guard relatives began to descend on the scene, much like loved ones of coal miners standing hushed in the gloom over a cave-in. The vigil continued on into the afternoon, observers and reporters moving sluggishly in the cold, bone-chilling air. News was meager. There were deaths, they heard, inmates and guards alike. There were hostages. There were demands.

Reinhard Koenig made an appearance for Knotting—and for the cameras, of course—making sure to mention his client was an inmate due to be soon released. His attempt at contact with Warden Johnston was summarily rebuffed.

Inside the prison, there was mayhem and miscalculation. Because there had, indeed, been no well-organized plan, no leaders, no servants to good order, the goings-on were randomly brutal, the simple result of festering anger unleashed on the nearest victim. Every homemade tool and weapon never discovered on a Hurry Search was brought out for a grisly show and tell. Cell blocks were trashed, food and factory facilities destroyed. Well before the first thirty minutes of the riot had elapsed, all who would die that day were already dead. Of the staff, Matchie McHugh had, in fact, become the intimate acquaintance of Varnie's friend, while Cheris Cortland, a beefy, ignorant sadist, was sodomized, then strangled with his own Sam Browne belt.

Eight inmates also died, none in peace. A few were killed by early guard reaction, some were shot through open windows by police snipers, and a few died at the hands of fellow residents, who considered a riot excellent cover for other score-settling.

Fred Cathcart fell in the latter category, his crime against the confined brotherhood having been to curry favor with the zookeepers much too frequently and publicly. When the avengers rushed into Cathcart's cell, they uttered not one word or accusation or judgment before throwing him on his back and stretching his neck over the steel footboard of the bunk. They yanked his head downward to expose his Adam's apple and the blue, pounding carotid arteries, then slashed his throat, literally from ear to ear, and watched as Cathcart's blood spurted nearly three feet in the air, marking the accountant's departure for what they hoped would be another hell.

Marty Knotting watched as his friend, former lover, and evidence-giver left his place on the planet, while he, scheduled for release within twenty-four hours, sat silent, staring, coated in warm, sticky blood. Knotting's thoughts as he felt urine dripping down his pantleg were two: for the first time in over twenty years, he grasped what he had done to Ronnie Lassiter in May 1968, and second, he wondered if Freddie had AIDS, or did it make any difference?

With the heat turned off and windows broken everywhere, the late-afternoon sky outlined the wispy smoke from small fires lit to keep the insurrectionists warm. Just after sundown, with the temperature dropping ten degrees in a few minutes, negotiations began and became more and more productive. First, a few hostages were released, then a small amount of food was sent in—enough to fight over—and within an hour, came complete surrender.

In the victory's evening darkness, Warden Johnston calmly explained to Reinhard Koenig that the State Bureau of Corrections had no intention of ignoring or otherwise disobeying a decision of the court. Neither would he, Johnston insisted, permit Koenig's relatively minor matter to interfere with or delay the massive investigative and recovery responsibilities which lay ahead of him.

"Simply put, Mr. Koenig, and you know I don't mean to be rude, the fact is that Marty Knotting will not be released from this facility tonight or even tomorrow. What will happen in the next few hours is very important to us, and you can rest assured we will carefully determine Knotting's role in this affair before we release him under any circumstances. Is that clear?"

"Okay, Warden. What next?" To Reinhard Koenig, who had no doubt but that his client had nothing to do with the riot, it came as a shock that Knotting had to suffer because of the acts of others. His fundamental assumption rested on the innocence of his client—at least, insofar as the events of February 14th were concerned.

"Look, Koenig, we don't know how many men are left in there, and we don't know exactly what we're going to do with them. In all likelihood, we will transport as many of these men to the nearest State or County facilities that can handle them. Once identity has been established and assuming there's no culpability for today," Johnston said, inclining his head toward the shell of Morganville, "I'm sure you can get him released. In his case, we'll probably take him to Williamsport—it's less than two hours from here. That'll work out best, I'm sure."

～

Strand and Bentsen might well have taken the day off. By mid-morning, they'd heard about the Morganville riot, and heard substantially the same radio announcements hour after hour. The tenor of the news became uglier as the day drained away, and both wondered about the fate of Marty Knotting and several other familiar inmates.

Nothing was in from the labs in Harrisburg, and hope began to wane that they'd have an answer anytime soon. Toward the end of the day, a call to Corinth revealed, unsurprisingly, that Eddie Snyder had taken wigs, makeup, and clothes from the institution's theatrical kits. Now, they learned, Eddie could be a brunette, possibly wearing tan slacks and sweater under a winter coat of some sort.

LVI

O N THURSDAY, THE weather was colder still. Frost ferns webbed the windows, and the thin ice sheeting the sidewalks shattered with a clattering finality as Strand and Bentsen hurried across the parking lot to another cup of cophouse coffee. The briskness with which they made their morning way lifted them from the frustrating lack of movement in the Snyder case over the previous three days. Yet the supercharged air was not just from the chilled, crisp current of the weather, but from another kind of electricity, the kind men felt before a battle's last shot, like that in a third-movement crescendo, or perhaps, in the precise instant before hounds brought a fox to ground.

As they walked through the front door, the dispatcher caught Strand's eye, and gesturing, finger pointed upward, called out through the small metal-screened circle in the bulletproof glass, "Detectives. Hey, Detectives! Montgomery wants to see you. First thing."

"Thanks," said Strand, and with Bentsen, they moved quickly down the hall.

"Be with you in a minute," mumbled Bentsen, hurrying to the sanctuary of necessity. When Bentsen finished his business and found his way to Montgomery's office, he could see one of them was annoyed.

"Could this be a screw-up?" Strand was on the attack.

"Settle down, boys. Let's think about this," Montgomery said as soon as Bentsen found a place of repose. "I'll check with the lab in Harrisburg, but I'm sure there's a reason."

"What? Somebody didn't get their Bunsen burner?"

"What's the problem?" Bentsen asked, both to get up to speed and stop Strand before he went too far.

"The problem is we still don't know whether the makeup and the hair samples link Eddie Snyder to the murders of the Foreston boys. And," Strand added, emphatically, "we still don't have a result on the stuff we sent in on the Russell case. Nothin.' Nada." He caught his breath. "So, what do we do now?"

"Like I said," Montgomery jumped back in, "you like this Snyder for the Russell murders, and there's no doubt about the vehicular homicide, is there? So, one way or the other, we've gotta find this guy."

"Right," Strand said. "He's the only one with motive and opportunity—and I'm sure the lab will confirm it—we know the means."

"Still doesn't prove its him," Montgomery insisted. "And now there's still a question about a tie between him and the dead boys."

"I know," Strand admitted. "That's why we're here, O' Great One. Got any ideas from on high? Because if we're right and we wait on Harrisburg, some other boy will not make it home."

"Well, we've got to find this guy. You've already got an 'all points' out on Snyder, right? Can you add to it?"

"Yes, we can," responded Strand without hesitation. "Now we can add descriptions for him—with and without his getup—and a file pic as well."

"Of course, you know us getting a call on him is one in a thousand!"

"Oh, I know, Chief, but at least we can get the word out. Both times he's struck, it's been in the mornings and in the environs of kid activities. Hallon's got to get the lead out in Foreston—odds are Snyder went back there."

"I know all about odds, but with crazies like him, he could be anywhere."

"Sure. Anywhere," Strand repeated. "But he's been to Foreston and knows the area. And now we know his sister is there. To him, anywhere is Foreston."

"I get it," Montgomery quickened. "You want me to call Hallon again, right?"

Strand and Bentsen smiled at their boss in unison, and watched as Montgomery picked up the phone and dialed the number for the Foreston PD. It took a minute for the dispatcher to locate her chief. "Probably in the can," chuckled Montgomery, on hold. In a moment, Montgomery grinned through the phone and began his official waltz with a recalcitrant borough police chief. The conversation lasted only a few minutes, the tension lines in Montgomery's face becoming more and more visible. "Alright, Chief. You do that!"

"Do what?" Bentsen inquired.

"Nothing. And I mean nothing. The dumb bastard still doesn't get it. You heard me tell him we got a make on this guy, that we think he's the prime suspect for the killings there. But two and two don't make four for him, I guess."

"You mean he's really going to do nothing?" asked Strand incredulously.

"Not exactly nothing, but close to it, if you ask me," Montgomery responded. "He said he'll put another man on the street in daylight, but overtime's tight in the Borough, and he doesn't want to piss off the Council by spending too much money on somebody else's case. Somebody else's case! Kin you beat that?"

"I'd like to beat his brains out, but there'd be nothing to work on. My kids live there—so do a lot of other people's. That asshole didn't spend a dime of regular or overtime money when he thought it was his case." The trio fell into silence.

"Hey, boss," Bentsen said, finally. "You mind if me and Strand spend the next several mornings in Foreston?" He raised a conspiratorial eyebrow with his question. "That is," he added, "if nothing else requires our attention."

"You'll probably find out more in Foreston than around here! Beat it."

∾

Strand and Bentsen divided the phone calls, faxing and carefully detailing Eddie Snyder's dual descriptions to each department. On their way out, they alerted the dispatcher to the latest identifiers, but it was their turn to be updated. According to the message, Montgomery had decided to buzz the local media. "He said, 'Listen to the radio.'"

The two men smiled at one another. "That Montgomery can be a real peach at times," Bentsen chuckled.

"Yeah. Guess he felt Hallon would be just too busy to think of that little detail."

In the car, Strand reminded his partner it was time to bring Wendy Russell up to date as well.

"Agreed. You want to call or stop."

"Let's take a chance. Doesn't she work afternoon shift? Let's go to the house."

"And avoid Mr. and Mrs. Simpson, if at all possible," Bentsen snorted.

"I don't have time to talk," Wendy Russell said when she came to the door. "I saw you pull in, but the hospital called me. It's *Frazzle Rock* there, and somebody called off."

"It won't be a good time any later," Strand maintained, an official tone creeping into his voice. His view of her had changed, and in his detached, professional mode, he eyed her as he would any other person surrounding a crime.

Strand's tone and manner held her attention. "Just a moment." She returned and said, "Okay. Five minutes. Step in the front hall."

Within three minutes, Strand and Bentsen recounted what information she ought to know, their suspicions about the murdered boys, and about the auto wreck and her brother's escape from Corinth. "He's probably back in town," Strand said.

"There's a question you need to answer, Ms. Russell," Bentsen said. "After the wreck, he was in Foreston hospital for at least a day or two, we're told. And you didn't know he was there?"

Wendy reeled as if slapped. "My God! You mean he was that close to me?" She shuddered. "I did not know!" she said, emphatically.

"That doesn't sound like sisterly concern to me," Bentsen countered.

Breathing hard, she remained silent for a moment, apparently processing all they had told her. "You just don't understand," she said, finally. "I know what you're saying is true, but I just don't want to accept it." There were no tears—only a few more seconds of complete stillness. "He always had that part of him that torment wouldn't reach."

"Beg your pardon?" queried Bentsen.

"Most kids take punishment pretty well, you know—they're resilient, or at least, that's what adults like to believe in justifying the hurt they hand them. But not Eddie—it all got to him, but nothing destroyed the instinct for revenge. He kept it, nursed it, and made it part of him. I thought they were managing that at Corinth and at the halfway house, but I guess not. The business about him dressing up as female—that's how he hides himself."

"So, only he knows when he's Eddie with an 'e,' or with a 'y.' Is that what you mean?"

"Yes, that must be it."

"And I guess," Bentsen chimed in, "he also didn't want to be recognized by you."

"I never thought of that," she said. "What do you think that means?"

Strand nodded. "It might mean he has something against you."

The lonely look in her eye was not directed at anything in the room, or her visitors. It was as if she was thinking of lost childhoods, of lost parents, of lost lives. She returned to the present. Very quietly, she asked, "He's here in town, you say? He's been here?"

"Yes, to the last part. And yes—I believe—to the first," answered Strand, nearly in a whisper. "A lot of people will be looking for him—it'll be on the radio, maybe TV."

"Yes, of course. Do I need to worry?" Her hands shook.

"We don't know, Wendy," Bentsen responded, "but at this point, we don't know what's in his mind. You ought to watch out for yourself, just in case..."

"Can you catch him without hurting him?"

"We'll do what we can—the next few days will be the most important," Strand surmised. "Whatever he's planning to do, he'll do soon. If we don't catch him, we'll know exactly where he's been."

Wendy looked at him questioningly.

Without taking his eyes from her, Strand drew it out. "He's going to kill again." He rose. "We'll try not to hurt him, but I have to tell you, his welfare won't be our first priority."

LVII

THE GLAZE OF ice on Pine Street sidewalks annoyed Eddy as he staged himself for the meeting. The last thing he wanted to do was slip, fall, and attract attention from the row of residences on either side of him. He picked his way carefully in front of the blue frame house near the street corner, pacing himself so as not to get there beforehand.

In a minute, the muffled roar of the school bus engine whined its way toward him from behind. He heard it stop, gear up, make speed, and begin to brake for its drop a few feet in front of him.

A young girl—Aarie's sister, he remembered—got off first and immediately turned and ran for home, as if chased. Seconds later, the boy exited with a quick jump from the last step. Spying his new friend, Aarie spoke first.

"Hi. You haven't been around."

"I've had a cold—stayed in, but here I am," Eddy added, brightly, brushing hair away from his face.

"I wasn't sure I'd see you again. You want to walk with me?"

Eddy smiled. "Sure. I can go a little ways."

"I can't invite you inside," Aarie said, pointing to his house, "I don't think my mother would like it."

"Oh?"

"You know. Moms are strange about strangers. Anyway, Edie, you can meet her on Saturday if you want. There'll be a ton of kids, and it'll be a lot of fun. You can come and watch us skate."

"Watch you? Where would that be?" inquired Eddy.

"At the park," Aarie responded in an "of course" kind of way. "We skate there and play as well—don't you know about the park? Right behind the Penn Grove Hotel."

"Sure. I know the place, right next to Wolf Creek. I always enjoy it when kids your age have fun. I'll be there. In fact," Eddy said, "I'll make a point of it."

~

Strand exhaled. It was the Friday morning of a long week, maybe the end of a long case, and he, like his partner, was looking for the pieces to begin fitting together. Bentsen got up from his chair and walked down the hall.

A quick call to a friend, Tommie Guffey at the State Police Laboratory in Harrisburg, soon answered the question dogging him and Bentsen. Receipt records indicated the small glass shards taken from the Russell residence had been processed on the 24th of January, about a week after the envelope had been sent from Mercer. Results were sent on the 25th and should have been received at the Mercer Barracks within a few days. They were long overdue. Strand asked Guffey to fax him the two pages of lab analysis. Unfortunately, Tommie knew nothing about hair and makeup analyses. *Dammit!*

While waiting for the fax, Strand checked around the Barracks, asking if anyone had seen what he was looking for. Within a few minutes he held in his hand the original of what was coming over the wire via facsimile machine. It had simply been misrouted, and there being no record of a "Russell" case assigned in the West Central District, the recipient merely waited for an interested party to make inquiries. Strand swore again.

Bentsen shambled his way back toward their island, and said,

"Well?"

"As always, Joe. Good news, bad news. No clear fingerprints could be lifted from the glass; the good news was that the pie-shaped wedge of glass had been formed, not by the shock to the door or by heat from the fire, but by the microscopically rough edges of a hardware store glass cutter—the kind of item found on home workbenches everywhere, in basements and in garages. That rag you picked up? The rust on it came from the tail pipe."

"Well, we haven't got a picture of Eddie standing at the door," Strand speculated, "but we have the high probability of him being in Foreston on the night of the fire, a motive for revenge on the Russells, familiarity with the scene, and physical evidence indicative of death by carbon monoxide poisoning or suffocation via the French door window, along with McCreary's post-mortem."

Bentsen rocked back and forth in his state-issue gray metal desk chair. "This is a bit belated, Fletch, but maybe we ought to have the rest of that house checked for Eddie's fingerprints. Now that we know two murders were committed, we can get a warrant, and have the right work done. Wendy Russell hasn't really touched the house, so if he'd spent any time inside or if he took anything of value, traces of his activity might still be present. You think?"

"Damn, Joe! I didn't think of that. He wasn't supposed to have been there in years, so a set of prints in the right place might nail it. Let's poke our heads in Montgomery's office and let him know we're drummin' up some more business for him—another one he can call Hallon about!" They both laughed.

LVIII

A T WILLIAMSPORT STATE Penitentiary, conditions for the 1,472 prisoners were already overcrowded. It was difficult for the correctional staff to keep track of all that happened there, in good times and in bad. Nevertheless, the institution was administered in a tough, but fair-minded fashion, and so what proved incendiary in Johnston's Jungle was but a minor irritant in a more contented population.

Notchie Falerno, in fact, had achieved prominence as a work crew chief for non-critical, internal construction. It was a fancy, official term for construction work which could be performed totally by resident sweat, and which did not in any way compromise the physical security of the plant. Falerno was responsible for the daily activities of twenty-four men, all of whom had learned one or more aspects of the construction business.

A February day did not usually provide the very best conditions for their latest project involving outdoor cement work, but with modern equipment and materials available, even behind bars, some concrete work could easily be accomplished. Falerno and his crew worked hard to set the forms for the foundation of the new sports equipment station, nicknamed the "Sportstop," near the ballfield.

They had their own self-imposed deadlines to meet, and given their plans for the spring sports season, the station had to be completed by April 1. That meant the concrete had to be poured, and the blocks laid on schedule so that the many remaining steps in the construction process could be completed in order, and on time.

Despite the crowded conditions at Williamsport and the increased tension amongst the population because of the riot and the killing at the Morganville Jungle the day before, work on the Sportstop continued. Falerno concentrated on his work and paid no attention to the vastly increased numbers of men in the yard.

Because of the size of the building and the sandy soil, the footers were designed to be twenty-four inches wide and eighteen inches deep. Falerno's attention was broken only by the sound of a familiar voice, long unheard, in the milling men around him. It was a snippet of conversation, just a phrase or two, but enough to jostle him free of thought for his work.

Marty Knotting and the dozens of Morganville refugees found themselves amazed at the difference in freedom and attitude amongst the prisoners of a maximum-security facility. It galled them that in what had been their moderate-security institution, they had been subjected to humiliations and demeaning treatment not apparent at Williamsport. Standing at the edge of the construction site for the Sportstop, the visitors chuckled at the "Pardon the Inconvenience" sign erected there.

Knotting's voice carried over the din, anxious as he was about an impending departure. He was never again to reside in Williamsport, Morganville, or any other prison, he told one and all. His speech came to a sudden halt, however, his voice gagged in mid-syllable by the sight of the face in front of him.

The man's eyes shone like hot coals in a furnace, like caged hate with subhuman impulses. They were the same eyes which had looked on him in drunken conspiracy over twenty-two years earlier, when each of their trio had pledged to the other loyalty and companionship forevermore.

Knotting swallowed hard, summoned from within him a

courtroom bravado strangely out of place in his present circumstances, and greeted the apparition. "Hey, Notchie! I'd forgotten about you being here. What a break!"

With a wan smile, Falerno managed to say, "Yeah, a break." He walked over to Knotting and put his arm around him. Looking directly at him, he continued, "Getting out?"

"H-how did you know?"

"Word gets around. All the shithouse lawyers been talkin' about your case. Way to go, Marty! You beat 'em all."

"Yeah. Yeah, I guess it worked out fine," he said, nervously. Mentally, he dissected every nuance of Falerno's greeting. What had he read there? Every man for himself? Friendship despite betrayal?

Yard time came to an end. Set to return to the relative warmth of the inner walls, most residents preferred it to the ice-cold freedom of a winter's day on the breeze-swept, treeless yard. They moved as a receding tide, leaving the lifeless gravel as lonely testimony to their having been there. Knotting made his move to go with them. "Better git. See ya later."

"Later?" Falerno queried, his voice ice cold.

"Well, I mean, whenever," Knotting giggled, nerves strung taut.

"I'm gonna help you escape this place, Marty," Falerno muttered.

"Did you say, 'escape'? Why, Notch," Knotting responded, attempting to back away, "I don't need to escape—I got my ticket out." A shrill quality crept into Knotting's tone.

As the exchange continued, Falerno's crew gathered around, sensing as they did, a score about to be settled. Accustomed as everyone was to crew meetings—guards included—their crowding around the work leader posed no unusual circumstance for unnecessary observation.

The code of equity required Falerno to offer justification to his crew for an act of violence of which they would all be guilty. He made a simple statement: "This is the guy I told you about," he declared, his arm once again gripping Knotting's shoulders, "the guy who made sure I would never get out of here."

Terror in his eyes, Knotting looked around for support. There was none. He opened his mouth to scream, but no sound came, his windpipe crushed by the powerful, lateral clamp of a twenty-pound steel pry bar pulled against him from behind. Literally speechless, Knotting was walked upright by controlling hands to the trenches awaiting new footers. Someone shoved a rag into his mouth. He was made to lie on his back, hands bound behind him, between the wooden foundation forms.

Knotting identified the last clear sound he heard as the heavy, grinding whine of the cement mixer churning the gravel, sand, and lime into its proper consistency for pouring. Someone in waders stood on his legs while another man kept a booted foot on his forehead. Falerno stood by, leaning on a shovel while the remainder of his crew went about their work.

The thick, gray mass of concrete began to surround his legs and arms, the dense flood of construction sauce sliding ever higher on his body, holding him in its grasp. He tried to shout, but gagged as his eyes searched wildly for pity, for hope. They found Falerno's gaze of satisfying revenge a few feet above him.

"Want your lawyer?" Falerno taunted.

Soon, his struggle was stilled by slow entombment as the gritty substance found its way over his face and into his nostrils and eyes. He choked, convulsed, as his body began the short, violent spasms of system shutdown. Blackness and utter silence commanded his last flash of conscious existence. Images of the boy he saw buried in a grave behind an abandoned gas station flooded his memory. The irony struck him...silent.

Falerno watched the swirling concrete smother and still its prisoner. He grasped the handle of the shovel he'd been leaning on and rammed its glinting steel blade deep into the thickening encasement below him. Finding his mark, Falerno pulled at the handle and yanked the blade upward, bringing with it the scarlet sign of a found target. The big man quickly swirled the shovel round and round, dissipating the color as best he could. When the concrete had reached its depth, one of his men used the float to finish off the work, the job having a slightly pink cast to it in one particular place.

Falerno sealed the moment in memory for his men with a wise-crack: "I knew he'd support our project!" They laughed uproari-ously, catching the attention of two men in the guard tower some distance away. The staff paid no notice to men who clearly enjoyed their work.

LIX

ANOTHER SATURDAY MORNING came, and Strand hauled himself out of bed shortly after seven o'clock, then shambled down to the kitchen in search of coffee. He fed Bo, let him out for his morning duty, and then let him in for one of the hundreds of man to dog monologues they'd enjoyed together. Strand rambled about the vicissitudes of life while the aging canine listened with patience and understanding.

The dog's damp coat made Strand get up and check the weather more closely. It was snowing lightly, just enough to powder all the horizontal surfaces. With coffee and a toasted bagel in the making, he wondered aloud about the family's plans for the day.

"Who were you talking to?" Aurora asked when she entered the room some minutes later.

"My other best friend," he responded, scratching the dog's ear vigorously.

"Other?" she asked in mock seriousness.

In kind, he smiled, "I do reserve the top spot for you, you know." It was his offer of conciliation after a bit of Friday-night tension, at one point loud enough to disturb the prevailing quiet.

"We certainly do talk to each other, don't we!" she said, kidding the two of them alike.

"And we make sure the other one hears what we're saying, don't we?" Strand countered as he rose and walked up behind her, putting his large hands on her shoulders. Her once lustrous black hair now gave off a sparkle of silver in the morning light. He leaned forward. She smelled awfully good, he thought.

"Harrumph!" she charged.

"Yourself!" he countered with the unspoken ditto to her gambit. He turned her around and kissed her squarely, tenderly on the lips.

She responded in kind, but added, "We've got a busy day," and gently shoved him aside.

Falling in step with the script, he asked, gamely, "Okay, just what great state events are on the calendar today?"

"Anna is being picked up by a friend before noon, so you'll be responsible for her before then. And Aarie is supposed to be going skating at the park at ten."

"Glad it's just a short walk away. Will there be plenty of adult supervision?"

"Huh?" she responded, already preoccupied. "Oh, sure. Several of the moms will be there. I think one of the firemen checked the ice. It's pretty thick in most places, and before you ask, yes, the unsafe spot near the creek is marked."

"Okay. That sounds pretty good."

"I'm going there about 10:30 to help with the cider and donuts when they take a break, but they won't be finished until just before noon. Everything sound okay to you?"

"Sure," he answered, not unwillingly, but without any demonstrable enthusiasm. He would have wanted some time alone with her to further patch their marital boat without the kids just around the corner.

His ruminations became punctuated by the radio announcer as he hissed the day's events through the static until Strand adjusted the tuning knob. The reproduction cathedral radio sitting in a corner of the kitchen counter must have been sold on its looks, rather than its performance. Finally, the sound from the local station filled the room with weather and obituaries, followed by the network feed of national news and, finally, regional news. Jackie Morrone's voice soon returned with the local headlines.

"Area residents will be interested in events at Williamsport State Penitentiary," he intoned, "where prison officials are being forced to admit they've lost a prisoner or that he's escaped, but they're not sure which. It seems that Marty Knotting, recently ordered paroled by the court after more than twenty years in prison, was believed to have been transferred to Williamsport from Morganville Prison after the Valentine's Day uprising there, but he has disappeared."

"Records show that Knotting, aged fifty, actually arrived at Williamsport, but when his attorney, Reinhard Koenig of Pittsburgh, attempted to arrange Knotting's release, he was declared missing. Prison personnel have scoured the physical plant to no avail. Knotting's attorney and Warden Lonnie Kuparich both agree on one thing: Knotting did not escape."

Seeing her husband's concentrated gaze, she asked, "Fletch, what's the matter?"

"It's about your brother. I just can't believe it. They can't find Knotting! What the hell is going on down there?"

"My brother? Hmmm. You may as well be talking about the man in the moon. I have no feelings for him, Fletch, except idle curiosity. And for Pete's sake, I don't want the kids to know about my relationship to that guy. Can you put that stuff out of your mind, at least for a Saturday morning?"

"Sorry. It follows me around, and as you say, the past is always with us. And just remember, hon, the kid killer we're looking for around here is still on the loose. He will have to strike again—he'll do it because it's beyond his control. Only now we know more about him. He does it in drag."

She interrupted with a nervous giggle. "What...in drag!? Sick."

"He...or she...or it," said Strand, pausing for emphasis, "will probably look like a brunette, wear a teal-colored winter coat, and maybe, tan slacks." As he finished, Jackie Morrone was making a similar announcement over the air. "Thanks, Walt," he prayed to the ceiling. "Anyway, hon, please tell the kids to be careful, especially over the next week."

"Okay, dear," she said, preoccupied with breakfast chores, "but don't worry about them. They take after you," she tried to joke, "and they're too ornery for anything to happen to them."

He chuckled. "I sure hope so. Anyway, after Anna gets picked up, I need to check in over this Knotting thing. I think they're overlooking something."

"Overlooking what? Can't they make it without you, dear?"

"Of course," he responded, with a trace of defensiveness in his voice, "but not too many people have read Knotting's file of late, and I think there's something in it—something that might help." Strand leaned down, elbows on the counter, chin in his hands, eyes focused on the snow in the backyard. "Only I don't know what the hell it is!"

LX

ARIE BOUNDED DOWN the stairs heading for the kitchen's aroma of pancakes and sausages. His mom and dad were drinking coffee while each worked on their part of the day's first meal. His mom flipped a trio of cakes in the pan while his dad turned the sausage to keep it from crisping over. "They're picture-perfect," Aarie said, and each parent smiled. When Anna joined them a few minutes later, the pair efficiently set the table and poured orange juice for everyone.

Table talk centered around Aarie's need to do his homework before dinner Sunday night. Anna sat, smug, while her brother received the kind of motherly scrutiny most children wished to avoid.

"What time are you being picked up for the skating party?"

"About a quarter to," Aarie responded to his Dad. "Remember? Josh's mom is taking us."

"Oh, yeah," Strand remembered. "Just how many boys'll be there?"

"Prolly fifteen or twenty."

"Girls?" volleyed Strand with a teasing grin on his face.

"Dad, quit it!" Aarie responded quickly, a shy smile forming on his downturned face.

"I see you've got your hair nicely slicked down—couldn't imagine you doing that for a bunch of boys," Strand observed.

"Dad, there will be girls there," Anna giggled.

"Shuddup, Anna!"

Aurora couldn't help herself, having been silent for more than a minute. "See, Fletch, look what you started!"

Strand laughed and said, "Okay, guys," addressing himself to the children. "We don't need to make a big deal about this. Just be careful on the ice, Aarie," he added, looking directly at his son.

"C'mon, Dad, there'll be plenty of big people there," Aarie chimed in, knowing as he did there would be at least one more than anyone thought.

"I know, son, but skating on a pond can be tricky, and I understand there's some thin ice out there."

"Remember, I'll be going by there around ten-thirty or so with hot chocolate, so don't worry yourself, Fletch. Nothing'll happen."

Not much later, Aarie came down the stairs for the second time dressed for a cold day at the park in the sweatshirt and jacket hood his mother made him wear to protect his ears. His yellow, black, and red poly-filled coat inflated him to a much larger version of the son they all knew. Strand chuckled while Aurora arranged the protective layers to her liking, Aarie's young eyes searching heavenward for patience while she did so.

Strand watched his son leave the house alive with the anticipation of fun. He smiled with both satisfaction and the envy parents feel when their children are about to have a wonderful time, innocent of worldly cares, little heads and hearts empty of life's sometimes nasty nuances.

"Daddy, are you going to keep your promise to me, or not?" challenged Anna plaintively.

"What was that, sweetheart?"

"You were going to walk me up to the bookstore, remember? You said it was your chance to read the paper and drink coffee in peace—and I would be on my own to look at the kids' books. Remember?" she encouraged, her voice holding the assumption of disappointment.

"Oh, honey, I haven't forgotten. I'm all yours until your friend comes for you later. I'll be ready to go in a few minutes. Make sure you go to the bathroom, then get your coat on—wear your gloves!—and we can go. How's that?" He needn't have asked—when the first few positive syllables left his mouth, a bright, wide smile formed on Anna's face.

Within a few minutes, they were out the door. "See you around lunchtime, honey," Strand said to Aurora, kissing her on the lips as he spoke.

"Okay. Fletch, please keep an eye on her in the store," requested the ever-worried mother.

"You got it—don't worry, she won't be able to come down the stairs from the kids' section without me seeing her from the cafe. She'll be fine."

When Strand and his beloved daughter reached the bookstore, he grabbed the *Herald* and headed for a table where he could see the whole place. Anna followed so she could deposit her coat with him and proceed upstairs. "Hey, honey, you can go on up, but how 'bout coming down in about ten minutes and checking in with me," he said, without the tone of a request in his fatherly voice.

"Oh, Dad!"

"'Oh, Dad,' nothin! You're barely eight years old, not eighteen. So, please check in," he added with mock severity.

"Okay, Dad," she smiled, and disappeared up the stairs.

～

Eddy awakened later than planned, and that surprised him. There were no clocks in the apartment, but then, he had never needed any. Getting up early had been a forced habit at the Nicholsons, who depended upon his free labor for early farm chores each day. The punishments for oversleeping were painfully memorable, so much so he wished he could be reunited with the Nicholsons just one more time. *I will make it quick, Mom Jody!*

A few minutes later, the old-fashioned tabletop AM-FM radio

across the room came alive when the tubes warmed in readiness for the local newscrier. It was time for the 8 a.m. weather and news, the announcer chirped.

Eddy half-listened to the report about a missing inmate at the Williamsport State Prison. Whatever happened to a guy named Knotting had nothing to do with him. His concentration heightened, however, when the announcer transmitted a warning from the State Police to be alert for a person wearing clothes like his. He hadn't heard the entire news item, just enough of it to recognize his celebrity. They were truly afraid of him.

Realizing the time, Eddy quickly washed his face and brushed his hair straight back to finish the job. Next, he found some saltine crackers and jelly to eat, and drank a large glass of milk behind it. He didn't bother to clean up his mess.

With quiet ceremony, Eddy proceeded to become his other self—Edie. He laid the pieces of her on the rumpled daybed. Each from their place and each in their turn, they became the outer testament to his metamorphosis. First, he wiggled into a pair of pantyhose, tucking his T-shirt in at the waist as he did so. Next, he slipped on a bra, each cup stuffed with toilet paper. It looked like his breasts had sprung out of his chest at the collar bones, but after a few frustrating minutes, he had the fake anatomy arranged to look as natural as he could make it. Careful was he to appear relatively flat-chested, thus making less likely the unwanted visual attention of either men or women.

As the navy-blue turtleneck sweater presented itself to him, he pulled it over his head, meticulously folding the layered collar underneath at the neck so that he could apply the makeup easily. His fair and smooth skin, along with his light hair, made it easier for him to make a successful transformation. The creams, powders, and eyeliners did not have to be overbearing to be believable on his face, but they enhanced the femininity of the soft features he already possessed, and at the same time, hid the hardness behind his eyes.

The chestnut slacks, a heavy wool, slid on easily over the hose, and then, his winter boots, a woman's size 8. The penultimate touch was the medium-quality wig he carefully fitted to his head. He was most proud of the wig, purloined as it was from Corinth the day after he arrived the most recent time. Lastly, he laid on a light coat of lipstick, more to enliven his lips in contrast to the makeup than to paint them. Finished, he looked in the mirror, delighted with the image he saw reflected there, exactly how Edie should look.

In truth, he told himself, he had no conflicts about his own sex. He considered himself a male, but hated so much about himself, despite his incredible brilliance, that being a female once in a while allowed him to escape his real self. And today, he needed to be "Edie," as he told his new little friend. *His name is Aarie, isn't it? And I can't wait to see him. But first, Wendy.*

LXI

S NOW FLURRIED IN the breezy arctic air, as Eddy trudged the six
long blocks or so to Foreston Medical Center. His quick steps
were made with the deep satisfaction of knowing his plan for the
morning was as perfectly fashioned for success as any could be. The
only question left to be answered was: *Just how rewarding is today
going to be?*

If he could easily find his sister at the hospital, and have a suitably
private moment with her, a quickly settled score would constitute a
high achievement, indeed. It was chancy at best, but it would give
him a tremendous sense of accomplishment to stand near her, to
breathe the same air, to catch her scent, and watch her reaction when
she realized who he was.

In the hospital's lobby, bright from the glaze on a red tiled floor,
Eddy walked up to the information counter and asked for Wendy
Russell's floor.

"Is she a patient here?" asked the volunteer.

"No. She works here—a nurse, I think," he answered in a throaty
voice to the woman in the peach-colored duster.

Martha Silvestri, as her name tag said, seemed dubious, but after a minute of paper rustling, enhanced by an arthritic index finger

wagging its way through a telephone listing, an answer was had.

Eddy made his way to the elevator, and once inside, pressed the button marked "3." For reasons he could not explain, he had been nervous in his lobby encounter. The palms of his hands were damp, and his heart pounded his chest wall. Taking two or three deep breaths calmed him outwardly, but in his core, Eddy felt the tremors of uncertainty and hesitation. *After all, it's not everyday somebody kills his sister.*

As he stepped from the elevator, he found himself directly in front of the nurse's station, less than twenty feet away. He scanned the floor layout, as anyone might do when looking for a room number. No Wendy, anywhere in sight. He stepped up to the desk and asked for her.

The ward clerk dropped her brownie, startled. "Oh, you want Wendy Russell? Not until this afternoon, ma'am. Did you want to leave a message for her?"

"Uh, no—no, thank you." Flummoxed, he turned to leave. *Damn! I knew that!*

"Uh, could you tell me," he asked, turning back to the desk, "how I might reach her at home?"

Looking up again, the clerk seemed hesitant. "Ma'am, I'm sure you know we can't give out personal information like that. If you need to see her, come back this afternoon." Without waiting for a response, she turned her attention to the paperwork in front of her—and the brownie.

Eddy could hardly believe his plan was going awry, and that made him increasingly nervous, sweaty, and most surprising of all, unsure. Quickly, he retreated to the elevator, head down. When it chimed, he stepped in, and was everlastingly grateful when the doors closed him in, alone. At the lobby level, he glanced at the clock on the wall. It was a few minutes after 10 a.m.

I guess it's to the park then—and Aarie.

∿

After a fifteen-minute walk, slowed only a little by the snow idling down, Eddy could see one of Wolf Creek's many serpentine turns as he passed through the borough park's entrance. Not more than fifty yards away from him, in a snow-laden glade surrounded by evergreens and barren bushes, lay a good-sized pond fed from the sluggish waters of the creek running nearby. The frigid weather had done its work, and now the pond seemed solid, except for the narrow neck of water where the pond met the creek, and the spot staked with a warning sign.

At the nearest edge, closest to the parking lot behind the Penn Grove, a group of people clustered around a lit barbecue grill, warming themselves in their company and good cheer. There were a few adults, all women, attempting to supervise about two dozen boys and girls, whose constant motion created a blur on the ice.

After surveying the entire scene for some minutes, Eddy strode between the parked cars, approaching carefully so as not to draw attention to himself from any of the party. He and Aarie had only to make eye contact, so that the boy would greet him as someone he knew. Otherwise, he would be presumed a stranger and noticed quickly.

In a moment, he saw his new little friend, and waved. The boy seemed delighted as he waved and skated over to the edge, some twenty or thirty feet from the adults.

"Hey! You made it—I'm surprised."

"Surprised?" asked Edie in a husky, feminine voice.

"Well, I don't mean surprised," answered Aarie with some embarrassment. "Sorry," he added politely, "I'm just glad you came. C'mon, have some hot chocolate."

"No thanks. Diet, you know. Actually, I'd rather skate, but I forgot to bring mine."

"Gee, that's too bad. Wait a minute, there's an extra pair or two over there. I'll go ask."

In a minute, he returned with two pair to try. "Go ahead. Put these on, and you can come out on the ice with us. None of the other mothers are—it'll be cool."

"Why, thank you, Aarie. One of these will fit, I'm sure. Just a minute and I'll be right with you." Planning ahead, he tied the laces of his walking shoes together, and draped them around his neck.

"Edie, why're you doing that?" Aarie asked, referring to the shoes. "Nobody'll steal 'em, you know. This is Foreston," he added with a laugh for having stated the obvious.

"You're right, Aaron, but it's been a while since I've been on skates, and I just might need my shoes if I have to leave early." Gingerly, he rose to his new height atop the white figure skates, and found his balance. Smiling in tentative triumph, he said, "Okay, young man, now you've got a skating partner. Let's beat the others!"

Nearby, the group of moms, including Aarie's own, huddled as they served seconds of steaming chocolate to the skaters.

Edie and Aaron pushed off, and soon, they were approaching the area where the "Thin Ice" sign waved them off.

"Aarie!" someone called with the mildly exasperated tone of all mothers whose sons never bother to tell them they're leaving.

"What?" Aarie called back to his mother with the impatience of all sons whose mothers never seem to perceive the obvious.

"Where are you going?"

"Just skating with Edie—we'll be right back. She needs my help."

Before she could respond, nine-year-old Erin MacKenzie tugged at her sleeve, and asked, sweetly, "Can I have some more? With extra marshmallows, please?"

Edie and Aarie held hands as they ventured about. "Hold on tight, Aaron. Remember, I haven't done this in a while. Let's do some circles."

LXII

S TRAND LOOKED AT his watch. It was 10:15 a.m. *Where's Anna?* Just then, she reappeared, excited to tell him about the books she had seen upstairs. Strand enjoyed her recitation for several minutes, knowing full well her animated voice caught delighted ears at nearby tables. Although their reaction appeared benign, it prompted him to have a talk with her about strangers.

"Anna," he said in a quiet voice. "Sit down here for a minute, please," he said, when she finished. He bent his head low, toward her, and said, "Your mother and I have told you this before, I know, but we want you to be very careful about strangers. It's very important that you understand, and do as we ask."

"Daddy," she responded with what adult manner she could muster, "what's the big deal? Why would you tell me this right in the middle of the bookstore?"

"Well, it's just because I don't remember if I said it at breakfast, and I didn't want to forget it again, that's all," he said, pecking her on the forehead. Seeing the look of acceptance in her eyes, Strand returned his concentration to the newspaper in front of him.

"Do you mean men-strangers or lady-strangers?"

Surprised by the question, Strand hesitated. "Both, actually.

Both, honey."

Suddenly, Anna's enthusiasm spilled over into her words. "You'll have to be sure to remind Aarie about this, Dad." And with an air of tattling for the common good, she continued, "He's been talking to a lady stranger."

The remark did not immediately register with Strand, embedded in his head as it was that men were more dangerous than women toward children, but when it occurred to him what Anna's perception might be, he turned to her. "Oh?" he prompted. "And what do you know about it, young lady?"

"Well," she continued, "when we got off the bus one day this week, Aarie stopped to talk to this lady—I don't know her name."

"What was so special about her?"

"Nothing. I didn't stay and talk with her. Aarie did."

Strand glanced back at the page-six story he had been reading.

"We saw her again—yesterday, I think. No, maybe it was Thursday."

"Anna, I'm trying to read. Was the lady nice?"

"I guess so. Anyway, I think she was wearing a wig."

Swallowing hard, Strand asked, "Honey, what else do you remember?"

"Nothing, except that Aarie told me she might be at the skating party this morning."

"What did you say?" Strand asked, his voice reduced to a husky whisper.

"The lady was going to go to the park this morning," reiterated Anna with the smiling impatience of a child attempting to communicate with a dim-witted adult.

Strand looked at his watch. It was nearly 10:25 a.m. In a controlled panic, he looked around for anyone he knew. He saw Barb and Karen, two friends of Aurora's, having coffee a few tables away. At their table before he knew it, he leaned down, ready to speak.

"Fletch. You're white as a sheet. You okay?" Barb Harkness asked.

"Fine," he responded, tersely. "Look, I know I'm interrupting your morning, but I need you to take charge of Anna for a bit—it's an emergency. She's got to stay with you." His pleading voice must have been unmistakable.

"S-sure, Fletch. Whatever you say—she can sit with us, and I'll take her home later. Is everything okay?"

"Tell you later. Anna!" he called, turning his head. When she ran over, he knelt down, put his hands on her shoulders and quickly explained that she must stay at the bookstore with the neighbors. She nodded seriously.

Strand ran out of the store, where the snow was laying a new, white carpet before him. Turning right, he caromed off the "Keep Foreston Clean" container at the curb, but dashed across the street, slipping perilously, and ran as fast as he could. It was two city blocks. *Can I make it?*

Across traffic, busy on a Saturday morning, he ran through the Riverside parking lot and to the bridge across Wolf Creek. He could see the back of the Penn Grove looming over the far creek bank and down another block.

On the bridge, he slipped on the fresh snow hiding the wet wood planks beneath his feet. Crashing his knee into the metal stanchion, he cried out, but ignored the oncoming pain and forced himself up. Once steady, Strand made himself go as fast as he dared across the remaining span and stumbled down the stairs on the other side. Now he could make out the adults around a fire. Then he saw Aurora, but not Aarie. Through the falling snow, it was hard to see everything clearly, but he moved as fast as his screaming knee would carry him.

"Aurora! Aurora!"

The collection of parents chatting and dishing out hot chocolate turned when they heard, then saw him running toward them.

"Fletch, where's Anna?"

"Never mind, she's safe! Where's Aarie?"

Aurora turned toward the crowd of skaters, "Somewhere out there, why?"

"Is he with anyone?" Tension laced his words.

"Yeah, she's with some woman—Aarie's helping her learn some moves," she said, wanting to smile, but becoming afraid.

"My God!" Strand looked across the ice and thought he saw a woman in a green coat, but not Aarie. Then, he caught sight of his bright, tri-colored coat.

"Hey! Aarie!"

~

"I hear my dad calling," Aarie said to his skating companion. "I wonder what he wants." Eddy held tight to Aarie's hand. "He's probably worried about you, Edie, 'cause I'm not supposed ta be with strangers."

"That's a good father, for you. He's worried because we're close to the warning sign. The ice must be thinner out here."

"Yeah, that's prolly it."

"You're lucky to have someone who cares about you, Aarie. What does your father do?"

"Oh, he's a detective with the PSP," he said, pride in every word.

"A detective, you say?"

"Yeah! He catches murderers!"

The Russells. "Then, you can introduce me," Edie said, wondering how he could avoid exactly that.

"Aarie!" His father's voice was closer now. "Run, Aarie!"

"Why is he saying that, Edie?"

"Oh, my. He must think something is wrong."

At the same moment, a woman in a long, green coat skated nearby in and out of the swirling snow, but at the sound of the man's shouts, she skated away.

~

Without another thought, Strand stepped out onto the ice, determined to reach his son, who, it seemed to him, was about thirty yards away. Through the snow, he stumbled, limped, ran, forgetting what pain throbbed in his knee. He covered the distance in seconds, the skaters parting as he charged through them toward the two figures near the warning sign.

"Aarie! Run! Get away from that woman!"

Strand saw Aarie drop the woman's hand, unsure about what to do or why. His eyes connected with the woman's. His voice, too. "Police. Stay where you are!"

She turned and began to skate away, but Strand launched himself into a flying tackle. They went down hard on the ice, which gave a loud crack as their combined weight made its impact. Aarie slid from the solid ice, careening into his father and Edie, driving them forward, toward the thin ice.

Strand could feel the frigid water enveloping them as the large shards of ice dipped and parted. He reached for Aarie and grabbed hold of his collar. The pond wasn't deep at this point, only a few feet from the creek flowing under its icy mantle beyond, but he couldn't find a footing.

The woman's wig flew off in the moment Strand and Eddie Snyder faced each other in mortal embrace, and Snyder's struggling legs prevented Strand from slowing their drift. He could feel them being sucked down. He grabbed fast to Snyder's coat lapel—*It's not green?*

Strand could see Snyder's eyes wide with fear, as if wondering why this was happening to him.

Neither man could let go, and Strand could feel them being pulled into the creek's current and under the ice, summoned to eternity. Strand knew their chances for survival depended on what happened in the very few seconds left to him. If he allowed himself to be submerged, it would be impossible to surface again.

All but Snyder's head was under, and weighing on Strand and his son. Strand's feet were being tugged by the swift undercurrent like tree limbs in a gale. He had to keep his head and arms above the surface no matter what, and he clung to his son with all the hope a father can have for a future.

With all his strength, he tried once again to find the bottom in hopes of righting and saving them both, but the pull was too powerful. Then, as if surrendering to fate, Snyder let go, and Strand could see his face as he slid down and under the creek ice—too thin to walk on, too far to reach.

Strand leaned back and at last, one foot caught a rock near the edge of the eddy, and he made himself crawl halfway onto the bank. Though almost completely numb, Strand could feel a flailing, coughing, spitting Aarie, still attached to him, half drowned but alive.

The sounds of screaming children and their elders broke the fuzzy silence. Tears of joy, relief, sorrow, and utter, everlasting frustration filled the detective's eyes as conscious thought merged with an underworld of dreams, hopes, and other nightmares. He whispered, "Thank God" to the One who mattered, then smiled, seeing Aurora in tears and on her knees, hugging Aarie for dear life.

Into his delirium, he whispered, "Where was the green coat?"

LXIII

THE DAYS AND nights were mixed with tense comings and goings, uncomfortable attachments and insertions in all parts of his body, but most of all, with words of hope and love whispered in his ear. In his unconscious mental meanderings, Fletcher Strand knew from his last moments of wakefulness his family was safe, and that Eddie Snyder was probably dead, but he wasn't sure if he himself had survived. *Am I still here? Where's here?* After all, if he was alive, why couldn't he wake up and tell himself so. If he was dead, would he know it? What did he believe? Was God with him?

With a sudden, deep spasm, he awoke to Aurora's hand in his, and her life-giving warmth and smile. While one moment's gladness could never erase the challenges they had together, nothing or no one could have improved upon it.

"How long has it been?"

"Two days—it's Monday afternoon."

Strand tried to put his hand to his forehead but couldn't, harnessed as he was to the plant of modern medical engines by his bedside. "Oh, God! That long? What happened?"

"I don't know everything," she responded, "but I'm sure glad my husband is the detective he is, or we'd be crying over Aarie right now."

"Is he okay? No one else hurt?"

"Everybody's okay, dear, that is, except you!"

"What exactly happened to me...I mean, I didn't think I was hurt. When do I get out of here?"

"Soon, honey, I'm sure, but they don't know yet. You just woke up. Just be patient. All I know is you have a hairline skull fracture—probably from hitting the ice, and they found a chipped bone in your knee—that was fixed with a bit of manipulation, but you'll have to wear a brace for a week or so. That and the hypothermia—your body was defending itself by knocking you out."

"That doesn't sound very medical to me," he laughed, "but I guess I'm lucky to be here, after all."

"You know, Joe Bentsen came to the hospital as soon as he heard, and he's spent a lot of time with you this weekend. When I couldn't be here, he was. By the way, he's got a lot to fill you in on. Oh," she exclaimed, "I'd better let them know you're awake!"

~

Later in the afternoon, after all the excitement, tests, and unending pinpricks, when Strand was alone, dozing, he heard someone in the room. It wasn't just the little noises people make in hospitals that made him take notice. It was a familiar sense, a presence, a scent. Strand opened his eyes and saw Wendy Russell standing at the foot of the bed. Her body language was cool, her expression tentative. *What is she doing here?* Strand gave her the best smile he could.

"I had to see you, but now that I'm here, I'm not sure what I should say?"

"I know. I'm sorry about your brother." He stopped, afraid to say more.

"Maybe. Maybe not. I'm sorry, too, that I didn't think about him and the Russells. Had I done so, or mentioned Eddie to you, maybe some things might not have happened. Is what they're saying true? That Eddie killed the Russells, the man in the car, the two boys?"

Strand didn't answer immediately, but gathered his strength and his words carefully. "If you're asking me whether there were eye-witnesses to anything, no one saw him at the scene of any crime. There's a lot of physical evidence—circumstantial—all pointing to Eddie," he said.

"Pointing to—not proving?"

"Yes. Anyone looking at the known facts would probably close any further investigation into either of the boys' deaths, or those of your parents."

She exhaled deeply. "Thank you."

Relief? What am I seeing, hearing?

"Thanks for coming in—am I your patient?" he asked, after a moment.

"No. I would have come to see you, anyway. I'd better go. You need a lot of rest, and," she added, glancing at her watch, "your wife will probably be back soon."

Strand nodded, almost imperceptibly.

"I met her. Nice woman."

Again, he nodded. "I think so, too, thanks."

"Bye," she said, her voice not quite a whisper, then she turned, and left.

Strand felt exhausted. It seemed like Wendy had been there for hours, so powerful was her presence, but Strand knew without checking a clock, it had been only minutes. Exhausted, he let himself fall back into a chasm of unconsciousness. In that nether world of illogical thought, something about Aarie and Eddie did not quite fit together.

He felt like a contestant on a surreal television gameshow in which he had to choose a prize behind the curtain. Would it be Eddie behind one curtain, or who behind the other? He couldn't make a choice because he didn't know what the choice was. *Where's the green coat?*

Why he awakened when he did, Strand did not know, but he found himself wet with perspiration, his head shaking back and forth in a violent negative to the suggestions of another plane. He couldn't seem to protect himself from seeing behind the curtains, his arms pinned to his sides as if he were straitjacketed there. *Which curtain?*

~

Later, with dusk shadowing the room, Strand found himself propped up in bed, eyes closed, tenuously sipping a liquid supper, and waiting for Aurora to come with Aarie and Anna. Looking up, he saw Bentsen slouching against the doorjamb.

In mock displeasure, Strand exclaimed in a hoarse whisper, "Huh! Some partner I have! Where is he when I need him?"

Bentsen flung a folded newspaper at his friend, deliberately missing him. With an equally unsympathetic tone in his voice, he countered. "Montgomery told me to tell you there was no authorized overtime for Saturday, so whatever you did was on your own—after all, you were just helping out your family—but the State of Pennsylvania thanks you!"

Strand eyed his partner with appreciation and mirth, as he pretended to lift the bowl of soup and hurl it at him in return. Rather than continue the banter, tired as he was, he said, seriously, "Aurora says you've been wasting a lot of time here. Thanks."

"No problem. Actually," he continued with false officiousness, "we wanted to be sure you weren't malingering in here. After all, there are reports to be filled out, and you're the one to do it! And you thought you could get away from the paperwork—just by being unconscious!

Strand actually laughed.

"Look, I know you're tired, so I won't stay long... ."

"Stay. Aurora won't be back for a bit yet. Let's talk."

"Okay, but just for a bit," he nodded, and sat in the lone visitor's chair.

"You know, Joe, something's bugging me."

"What's that—not enough ice cream here for ya?"

"Seriously, Joe, what's bugging me is that Eddie wasn't wearing a green coat."

"What? You sure you're not delirious? Listen, Fletch, leave that alone for now. He's dead."

Strand exhaled. "Okay, let's switch killers. Did we ever find out what happened to Knotting?"

Bentsen chuckled. "Oh, yeah! You know what a stink Reinhard Koenig made when Williamsport couldn't find him? That made no difference at all, but what did get the warden moving was the girl-friend—remember her? Viki Mae?"

Strand's face lit up in anticipation.

"Well, she raised such hell, they took another look around, and of course, somebody talked. In the case file, do you recall one of the other perps, Notchie Falerno? He's at Williamsport, too, and the head of the construction gang there. Seems as if ol' Notchie helped Marty Knotting fall into a footer where they were pouring cement." Bentsen laughed. "I guess Notchie finally got his revenge,"

"Wow! What justice!"

Aurora and the kids appeared at the door. "There's more, Fletch, but nothing to be discussed now. I'll check in with you again—maybe Montgomery and I can stop by the house—if Aurora can come up with some of her cannoli—and we'll bring you up to speed."

"The two of you?"

"Yep. There's a lot more to talk about, but not now!" Bentsen pecked Aurora on the cheek as she came into the room, said hi to the kids, and made his exit.

More?

LXIV

A DAY LATER, STRAND was released from Foreston Medical Center, but assigned couch duty by his doctor for a few more days. At home, he took it easy, indeed, mostly resting or taking slow walks with his other best friend while the kids were in school. It was pleasant, for sure, but he couldn't get Eddie Snyder out of his mind.

A rap on the front door from the heavy brass knocker yanked Strand out of his musings, and he remembered Bentsen saying he and Montgomery wanted to come by. *Why both of them?* Inviting the two men inside, he pointed to a pair of French doors into the family room, in actuality a converted porch, and a perfect room in which to have a private conversation.

Montgomery, he could see, carried with him a pair of thick files. When all three sat down, and after Aurora had supplied coffee and a trio of chocolate cream cannoli's, Montgomery cleared his throat, and began.

"I guess you never filled Bentsen in on your in-law connection to Marty Knotting?"

His words hit Strand like a ton of bricks, and immediately, he was embarrassed. "No, I hadn't, and I'm sorry, Joe, but when I found out, Knotting was going to be out of our hands, and it didn't seem to make any difference." Strand turned to Mongtomery, "I can't believe this has to come up now, boss."

"I understand why you didn't tell me, Fletch, so, no problem."

"Thanks, Joe. So, Walt, what's going on?"

"There's more, and we're gonna have to deal with it."

"More?"

"This is a bit complicated, so stick with me on this." He cleared his throat and began again. "It seems that Marty Knotting had someone else in his life other than this Viki Mae person that Bentsen goes on about. At some point, he hooked up with a Francie Lynn Snyder, and together they produced two children, Wendy and Eddie. You know them, of course, as Wendy Russell—after she was adopted—and Eddie Snyder."

"Jesus H. Christ!" Strand couldn't breathe as he began to process what that meant.

"That means Wendy and Eddie are your niece and nephew, Fletch," Montgomery said, "and..."

"And that I killed my own nephew," said Strand, finishing it for him. "Oh, my God."

"Now you know why I didn't want to pursue this at the hospital, Fletch," Bentsen said. "I'm sorry I couldn't tell you, but it wouldn't have been fair."

Ever in charge, Montgomery continued. "But it gets worse."

"My God, how can it?"

"You know the report about hair and makeup samples that never showed?" he asked, but didn't wait for Strand's answer. "Turns out it was another act of genius by some Harrisburg clerk. The Requestor's page had fallen off and the idiot sent it to New Castle Barracks. If it hadn't been for my good friend Bill Keely—one of the best troopers ever—it'd still be there."

"Yeah, I know Bill Keely. Good man. What about it?"

"The wig hair and makeup samples *aren't* a match, and neither is the footprint off the bridge near the Hilton killing a match for any footgear in Eddie Snyder's possession. The good news is that prints in the Russell kitchen are a match for Eddie Snyder's."

"Thank God, we can put him at the scene." Then, Strand leaned back, his eyes closed, weary of his world. "But, I had a hand in my nephew's death—and he wasn't about to murder my son as I'd thought?"

"What we all thought, Fletch, but be careful what you say here. If you knew he didn't do it, there'll be questions about his death…"

"Look, it was all about the green coat."

"What's with you and a green coat, for cryin' out loud?" erupted Bentsen.

"I told Hallon I'd seen a woman wearing a long, green coat near to where we found the Hilton boy. Days later, I saw a woman in a long, green coat talking to the Paulson kid. I didn't put it together until later, and when we heard about Snyder and his thing for wigs, makeup, and dressing like a woman, I thought we were talking about the same guy. God, how could we have been so wrong?!"

"Not to mention," Bentsen chimed in, "all the stuff Harkansen told us, the timing, his mental state, the history of abuse, his need for revenge—and, you know, the familial thing."

Strand looked at him, as if processing the words—*the familial thing?*—but a more immediate question struck him. "Then why, for God's sake, was he dressed as a woman and with my son?"

"Don't know, my friend," Montgomery said, but I'm sure glad you identified yourself and ordered Snyder to stop when you did. After all, we had enough to go after him for the Russells and the vehicular homicide. And he attempted to get away."

"Good Christ! If he didn't do it, the killer is still loose. To kill again," Strand added, despair in his voice. He turned his focus inward, on the facts of his relationship to at least two killers in his wife's family. "I'll have to tell Aurora about her brother—and her nephew," he said, and his voice trailed off.

Silence enveloped the room.

Montgomery cleared his throat. "Before I forget it, boys, something came in this morning I hope you two can hop on bright and early Monday morning, that is if you," he said looking at Strand, "are through laying around here."

Strand and Bentsen sat, holding their breath.

"Don't give me that look, Bentsen," Montgomery said. "If you guys read the Snyder file from Corinth, you'll remember the Mc-Gruder case—where Eddie Snyder was accused of molesting the daughter?—well, the old man was found dead late last night. Likely not an accident, not suicide. I'm betting it's either the wife or the daughter—you guys figure it out."

"What goes around, comes around, right?" Bentsen commented. "We'll get on it, Chief."

His breathing less strained, Strand looked straight at Montgomery and said, "If we're satisfying curiosity, boss, why would you be the one to add all those clippings to the Knotting case file?"

Montgomery eyed him closely, then smiled. "Frank Duffy—the other boy with Ronnie Lassiter?—he was the one who was killed in Vietnam. Frank was my sister's boy, and I was proud of him—he was a Marine, too—never got the chance to tell those bastards he served his country."

After a moment, Montgomery said, "Joe, give us a few. You mind?"

Bentsen nodded. "Maybe there's another cannoli Aurora can find for me," he said, and left the room.

"What's up, boss?"

"You never had any reason to check the other file I brought along, did you?" he asked, and tapped the ancient, deteriorating folder giving off a faint musty smell.

Strand remained silent, knowing something more was coming that he probably didn't want to hear.

"I don't know if Aurora told you—if she ever knew—about how her grandfather died."

"In fact, she did tell me the story—just recently."

"Did she talk about the guy who was in on it, but never convicted?"

"She mentioned that, too, but nothing else. Why?"

"Only in small towns can this crazy stuff happen, Fletch. Here's the rest of the story. Snyder wasn't Eddie or Wendy's true surname. It was Sanderi—the same Sanderi who murdered your wife's grandfather."

"You've gotta be kiddin' me!"

"I'm not. Sanderi and his wife had one child, Francie Lynn, and right afterward, it appears the Sanderis decided they no longer wanted to be Italian, so they changed their name to Snyder. It was Francie Lynn who gave birth to both of Marty Knotting's children—Eddie and Wendy." Montgomery paused and let that sink in. "Marty never married Francie Lynn and so the kids went by Snyder."

"What happened to her?"

"Suicide. She couldn't take the fact that Marty threw her over for Viki Mae Nardonne."

LXV

THAT NIGHT, FLETCH and Aurora broke out a bottle of Merlot and sat together after the kids went down. It took two full glasses of the middle shelf brand before he could broach the topic of her brother and his children, but eventually, he did.

And as if he'd flipped a switch, Aurora broke down, and through her tears, went on about all the things she never knew, for her parents, and what she could never have had—the rest of her family. As he held her, Dr. Harkansen's words could not leave his mind, no matter how much wine dimmed their meaning. Some of these illnesses, he had said, are familial. *Marty? At least one of his children?*

He didn't ask Aurora if she wanted to meet her niece. And he didn't mention the connection between her family and the family involved in her grandfather's murder. *She's right—the past is always with us—but this time, we'll leave it there.*

~

The next morning, Strand decided to visit Hallville Cemetery—just to see something for himself. Near the end of a patchy road at the north end of Foreston, he brought his car to a stop at the rusting gates of the only Catholic cemetery in town. Aurora had said it wasn't used much anymore, but she'd described the location of her family's plot, and after a few minutes trudging through the crusty snow past dozens of markers, some over a century old, he came to the Tomasellis. Just as Aurora had said, her grandparents lay at rest closest to Francesco, the little boy who died of the Spanish Flu.

Strand said a prayer or two, as Aurora had taught him, and just as he turned to leave, he noted the recent work done to his right—work he knew something about. Near the Sanderis corroding stones were two mounds of fresh dirt blanketing Marty Knotting and his son, Eddie Snyder. Only a dusting of snow softened the harsh finality of death.

~

Of course, the question lingered, nagged. Strand was sure who murdered the boys, but he didn't know why. He headed to the one place where he knew the answer would be.

On the short drive over, he remembered Harkansen's reference to familial things, then stopped talking for a moment. *Had another possibility crossed his mind?* Strand felt certain of it.

In his mind's eye, he could see only her stone, cold eyes. And what was the look on her face when he said, mistakenly, that all the deaths could be put down to Eddie—who was dead and unable to answer? *Could it have been relief? Would a loving sister be relieved to know her brother was a serial killer? Or was she relieved for another reason?*

As he pulled into the Simpsons' driveway, and exited the old Explorer, he was startled that the front door opened, and out walked a young woman in a long, green coat. In her wig, Strand didn't recognize her immediately. The look on her face was one of surprise mixed with hate.

"Stay right there, Wendy," he said, "I'm arresting you for the murders of Jamie Hilton and Bradley Paulson," and recited the Miranda warning. Sensing this arrest might not end well, he eased the Glock from under his coat.

Russell froze, glaring at and through him. "So, you figured it out," she said, "and now what?"

"But why? Why murder those boys?"

"Don't you get it, Fletch? They were happy boys and I resented them. Oh, how I hated the lives they had! And I had to live with crazy Eddie! He could never be happy—he just didn't have it in him. Why should those boys get to live a good life? Or you?!" On the last syllable, she raised the long-bladed knife she'd been hiding at her side and lunged for him.

He fired a single shot. The nine-millimeter round blew through her stone-cold heart.

For one full second, she kept her focus on him, then fell to the ground.

His heart pounded.

As he caught his breath, he knew he'd have to arrange still one more burial in the Sanderi plot.

ABOUT THE AUTHOR

PHILIP WARREN is a retired national security executive who reads extensively in historical, espionage, and crime fiction and various non-fiction genres, but prefers writing historical fiction as well as political and crime thrillers. He lives with his wife in western Pennsylvania's Amish country.

Email: philipwarrenwriter@gmail.com
Website: www.philipwarrenwriter.com

As John P. Warren, the author invites readers to enjoy *Turnover* and its sequel, *TurnAround,* political thrillers about national election fraud published in 2013 and 2014, respectively. What was true then about political ambition and the lengths to which someone might go to achieve the presidency remains true today. Stories like these never get old.

Made in the USA
Middletown, DE
25 June 2022